HEAVENLY BODIES

HEAVENLY BODIES

IMANI ERRIU

Random House Canada

PUBLISHED BY RANDOM HOUSE CANADA

Copyright © 2022 Imani Erriu

www.penguinrandomhouse.ca

LIBRARY AND ARCHIVES CANADA CATALOGUING IN PUBLICATION

Title: Heavenly bodies / Imani Erriu.
Names: Erriu, Imani, author.
Description: Series statement: Heavenly bodies ;
book 1 | Previously self-published in 2022.
Identifiers: Canadiana (print) 20240419332 | Canadiana (ebook) 20240419367 |
ISBN 9781039012592 (softcover) | ISBN 9781039012608 (EPUB)
Subjects: LCGFT: Fantasy fiction. | LCGFT: Romance fiction.
Classification: LCC PR6105.R75 H43 2024 | DDC 823/.92—dc233

Cover design: Charlotte Daniels at Penguin Random House UK
Cover photographs: © Getty Images, © Shutterstock
Typeseting: Jouve (UK), Milton Keynes
Map and zodiac illustrations: Lucy Melrose

Printed in Canada

2 4 6 8 9 7 5 3 1

Penguin
Random House
RANDOM HOUSE CANADA

To Marco, without whom none of this would be possible

AQUARIA

PISCEA

ARIETE

TORRA

GEM &ELI

CANCIA

CAPRI

SAGITTON

SCORPIUS

LIAS

VERRA

LEXON

THE STARS

Ariete (Ah-ree-ett) – Patron Star of **Perses**.
The King of Stars. God of wrath, war and blood.
Also known as '*the Tyrant*'.

Torra (Tor-a) – Patron Star of **Aphrodea**.
Goddess of lust and pleasure.
Also known as '*the Seductress*'.

Gem and Eli (Jem and Ee-lie) – Patron Stars of **Castor**.
Goddess of spite and trickery; god of riddles, cunning and knowledge.
Also known as '*the Trickster*' and '*the Silvertongue*'.

Cancia (Can-see-a) – Patron Star of **Altalune**.
Goddess of pain, sadness, rivers and lakes.
Also known as '*the Weeping Goddess*'.

Leyon (Ley-on) – Patron Star of **Helios**.
God of pride, arts, prophecy and the Light.
Also known as '*the revered Lord Light*'.

Verra (Veh-ra) – Patron Star of **Verde**.
Goddess of earth and decay.
Also known as '*the Virgin*'.

Lias (Lie-as) – Patron Star of **Concordia**.
God of love, justice and lies.
Also known as '*the Beautiful Liar*'.

Scorpius (Scorp-ee-us) – Patron Star of **Neptuna**.
God of envy, oceans and poisons.
Also known as '*the Merciless One*'.

Sagitton (Saj-i-ton) – Patron Star of **Kaos**.
God of wine, madness and ecstasy.
Also known as '*the Reveller*'.

Capri *(Cap-ree)* – Patron Star of **The Sinner's Sands**.
God of greed, money and success.
Also known as '*the Merchant*'.

Aquaria *(Ah-quer-ee-a)* – Patron Star of **Sveta**.
Goddess of misfortune, air and ice.
Also known as '*our Unblessed Lady*'.

Piscea *(Pie-see-a)* – Patron Star of **Asteria**.
Goddess of fate, fear and the Dark.
Also known as '*the Slumbering Goddess*'.

CHAPTER ONE

Elara Bellereve had been able to walk through dreams for as long as she could remember. Some were Stygian black and jagged nightmares; others were sherbet-painted and cloud-filled, the daydreams of the innocent. Then came the brown, flat dreams of the day-to-day and the incense-perfumed prophetic dreams, those that the seers throughout Celestia dreamed.

She had fallen into the dreamscape of a Helion. She knew that much. Yet, as she crept around the red sand dunes of his dreams, something struck her as familiar about them. Had she walked here before? The colours were vivid and bright, the air dry and hot, so unlike the cool and dark dreams she was familiar with. She saw the back of a male figure, strong and lithe as he wielded a golden sword, battling against something. But as she crept closer, she saw shadows surrounding him, attacking him, the figure gasping for help as they slowly began to suffocate him.

She woke with a start, her surroundings filtering through the remnants of her dreams. A panicked blink showed her only darkness. A coarse fabric itched her cheek – a sack by the feel of it.

She had been running down the cobbles of the Dreamer's Quarter, dress damp with blood, and then—

She racked her brain. There'd been the scent of dread-poppies pressed to her nose, arms around her waist and . . . nothing.

She swallowed, raising her rope-tied wrists to try and remove the sack, but a sharp yank on them stopped her. She hissed, lowering them and forced herself to sit up as much as she could. She was moving, the *clop-clop* of hooves and hard wooden slats digging into her back suggesting she was in a wagon. 'If it's money you want, I can give you money,' she said, blinking away the fog.

There was a faint laugh, and a man with a slightly lilting accent spoke. 'We have enough of that.'

'Then what?' Elara asked, forcing her voice steady. 'Are you in league with the Star?'

Silence.

She slumped back, her last memories before the darkness flittering around the edges of her mind.

One moment she had been dancing with Lukas at her birthday ball and the next . . .

Red starlight, blood – so much blood – seeping over marble, and a scream to run.

Her breath began to race away from her and she forced herself to drink it back in – once, twice, as she squeezed her eyes shut.

Into the box, into the box, into the box.

She chanted it until her emotions had been rammed down inside of her, a veneer of calm replacing them.

She took stock of her position. It seemed she'd been kidnapped. Fucking kidnapped. Aquaria, the Star of misfortune, must have been laughing over her shoulder.

Elara blinked, forcing herself to remain present, to gauge

as much as she could of her surroundings. The memories of the last few hours rattled, desperate to be let out, but she gritted her teeth as she ignored them. She couldn't stay with those memories right now, couldn't think of home – or she might unravel entirely.

Think.

How could she escape these people? She checked in with her well of magick. It was awake all right, writhing in the pit of her stomach, ready to be siphoned into her Three.

She didn't even bother to try and summon the shadows she was born with. If they hadn't appeared in eighteen years, then they wouldn't now.

And her dreamwalking was useless in this instance, which left her last gift. One she could actually use.

'Where are you taking me?' Elara demanded, in a tone as bold as she could muster. She looked down – light was visible through a tiny sliver at the bottom of the sack covering her head. Shifting herself carefully, slightly increasing the size of the sliver, she could make out her shoes, and a pair of heavy boots to her right, all drenched in Asterian light.

'You'll see soon enough.'

She kept her eye fixed on the soft violet light – the only indication that she was still in Asteria – as she tried to form a plan. All she had to do was wait for the cart to stop, which it inevitably would have to. And as these brigands – whoever they were – attempted to haul her to whichever terrible fate awaited her, she would make her break for freedom. She could do it. She had to. The cart rumbled on, as Elara bided her time, turning over her plan of escape as she softened her body, feigning sleep.

Hours must have passed from the way the light began to turn indigo, when a voice broke the silence.

'I'm hungry.'

Elara tensed at the different voice, this one with a similar lilting accent.

The first voice, the one that had spoken hours ago, replied in a low tone: 'You can eat when we cross the border. Though if you spent as much time worrying about your king's orders as you do what you're going to shove down your gullet, you'd have been promoted by now. It's your own fault you're not in the King's Guard.'

There was a muttered response as Elara picked through the conversation. King? Border?

Dread crept up her spine. They were taking her to Helios.

It took every ounce of control within Elara's body not to struggle then and there, as she realized she was being led into enemy territory. Not just by some bored Asterian thugs, but by Helions. Soldiers, by the sounds of it.

The force who had plagued her kingdom with raids and blockades for years. Who had encouraged the rest of the world to shun her people. All thanks to the man at the helm of it all, the one who had waged the War on Darkness against her father, two decades ago. King Idris D'Oro.

'You know, for one of the King's Guard, you're not the most adept at espionage,' she said. 'Shouldn't you be, I don't know . . . guarding your king?'

There was a beat, before the first voice – the leader, she assumed – replied, 'What makes you think we're the King's Guard?'

'You don't exactly use inside voices,' she replied.

There were muttered curses, enough so that Elara counted between five or six other people within the cart, before the leader spoke again with a note of finality. 'No more questions.'

'You may as well save us the journey, and drag me outside to kill me now,' she said. It would be death, or a fate far worse if she set foot in the Palace of Light, so if there was any chance of escape near the border, she'd take it.

'We're not going to hurt you,' he replied.

Elara tried subtly to work her wrists against their binding again. As she shifted, she felt her dagger press into her thigh. It was relief that washed over her first – the soldiers hadn't discovered it. Shortly followed by a string of mental curses as she realized how far it was away from her incapacitated hands.

Finally, the cart ground to a stop followed by a sharp rap to her left.

'State your business,' came a voice heavy with the accent of the Asterian Borderlands.

Elara took a deep breath, ready to scream, but a solid hand clamped down on her lips, gifting her a mouthful of sack. She coughed against it, but the hand held firm, another pushing down upon her shoulder when she tried to struggle.

There was an inaudible murmur from the driver up front, and the sound of coins clinking.

There was another rap on the cart, and it trundled on, until finally the hand released her. She spluttered and spat the burlap out of her mouth, as she blinked down once more at the slice of light. To her horror, it had shifted from her familiar lilac-blue to fierce orange. She was across the border.

The sack was yanked off her head, and Elara winced at the horrid burnished glare of Helion light that flooded her sight. It was so much more garish than the comforting tones of home, casting the cart in a bright gold. When she blinked it away, a man was looking at her, a very handsome man, a slight frown on his face. His eyes were warm brown, skin brown too, and he had the closely shorn haircut of the militia, though with an intricate pattern shaved more closely on one side of his head, which stretched into straight lines of the Light's rays. Oh, he was Helion all right.

'Who are you?' she demanded, before taking quick account of the rest of the group, draped in golden armour.

'Leonardo Acardi,' said the brown-eyed man.

Her stomach plummeted. 'You're the general of the Helion army. The King's Thunderbolt.'

He shrugged, something like a twinkle in his eye. 'Is that what they call me?'

She forced her gaze off him, if only to look desperately back to her home as they rolled further into Helios, the border growing further and further away. She caught sight of the Temple of Piscea, Asteria's patron Star, which signified the entrance into Asteria. A familiar resentment clung to her chest as she glanced at the glossy black obsidian pillars – perfect and out of place within the soft twilight hues of her kingdom. Piscea's prayer stood out in glittering silverstone, a fairly new one that had only been coined a few decades before.

So worship her. So fear her.

Apt, for the goddess of terror, of fate and darkness. Though she slumbered now, thank the Stars. Elara raised her eyes to the sky, and the split torn through it, the patch of gold and orange growing larger as her sapphire sky diminished.

'The palace horses are waiting on the outskirts of Sol,' Leonardo said. 'We'll leave this cart there,' he said to a comrade.

Elara reached back to her geography lessons. It was just as she'd thought – she was being taken to the capital of Helios, where the Palace of Light waited. She remained silent as she settled back, and waited, spiralling into her magick. As she moved, the dampness of blood on her dress pinched at her, and nausea roiled through her, along with unwanted memories.

The blood.

The starlight.

'Run!'

She squeezed her eyes shut again until the images had disappeared once more. When she looked out from the cart, she saw dusty streets rather than the lush, dark vegetation that lined every road in Asteria. Though the sounds were muffled through the wood it sounded louder than her home too, and gods, it was sweltering. Her thick woollen dress felt cloistering, her corset beneath digging into her chest and waist uncomfortably as sweat began to gather at the base of her spine. But she cared not, when she didn't plan on staying in the Stars-forsaken city for a minute longer than she had to.

When the wagon stopped, and the doors were flung open, Elara was ready.

As she was pulled up by Leonardo, and led off the cart, she struck.

Her magick danced out of her, threads rapidly weaving a cocoon of sweet invisibility around her. Leonardo cursed, as the other soldiers shouted, but Elara had already slipped from his grasp.

She pelted away from the cart and into the streets of Sol.

CHAPTER TWO

Light, sound and heat assaulted her. The hustle and bustle of drivers going to market, the sound of children's laughter and gossiping washerwomen swamped her senses as she worked to maintain her illusion. She was one with the air, the ground, she was—

'Shit!' she yelled, grinding to a halt before she was nearly trampled by a moving spice cart. She sprinted across the road once it had cleared and heard shouts. But her magick had slipped. She had no idea where she was going, only that she had to lose the guards. The scent of exotic flowers, fragrant spices and freshly washed laundry wafted her way as she twisted and turned. It was too much, too overwhelming for a woman who hadn't set foot outside her own realm before. Finally, as she hurtled down yet another alley, she was met with quiet, and shade. The shouts of her pursuers faded.

A sharp pain in her head told her that she'd used her magick too strong and too fast, her well depleting. She looked around desperately, and it was only when she was assured that she was completely alone that she leaned against a cool, terracotta wall, gulping in lungfuls of arid air. She only allowed herself three before she hitched her dress up, awkwardly angling herself so that she could pull her dagger from its hilt around her thigh. She placed the hilt in her mouth as she sawed her bindings upon the dagger, its blade glittering as deep and blue as the starlit sky of home. When the last threads finally snapped, she breathed a sigh of relief, rubbing the obsidian and sapphire crystals embedded in its hilt out of habit, before sheathing it once more.

Her thick, powder-blue dress was heavy in the heat, not to mention covered in drying blood. She couldn't have looked more conspicuous if she tried. From the few glimpses she'd seen as she'd ran past, Helion fashion certainly wasn't modest, and Elara cursed, before tearing the dress off, corset too, leaving her in her thin, white undergown, saved from blood by the thick wool of her overdress.

She dumped the sullied dress in the alley and began to walk. She passed various piazzas, ones decorated with extravagant fountains and surrounded by white, dazzling houses. Some were filled with people, others quiet. She ventured into one that she saw was empty, turning in a circle. All she had to do was find out the direction of the border, and keep walking. Whether her feet bled or her body gave out, she had to get back home.

It was as her thoughts wrapped around home, of the scene she had left behind, her mother's scream, her father's roar – the starlight, the laughter – that she realized too late who was approaching.

There were shouts, the draw of steel, and as Elara made to run, more guards entered the small square.

She turned to another alleyway. Soldiers in golden armour marched out of that one too. She realized she was completely entrapped.

'Looks like a little birdy's trying to fly home,' grinned one soldier.

Some of the others whistled and twittered. Her hand longed for her dagger, but it was strapped to her thigh, too far from reach as another man with a nasty scar upon his cheek advanced. 'I say we clip her wings,' he said, displaying yellow teeth with his smile. She didn't recognize him from the cart. He had to be a city guard.

'They weren't General Leonardo's orders,' piped up a younger soldier.

'Well, General Leonardo isn't here, is he?'

Elara began to back up a step, but felt a blade at her spine. Her head was still pounding, but she dragged up the last available droplets of her illusioning power, as the scarred man advanced, tossing his sword between his hands.

'Hold her, lads.'

Though every instinct inside her wanted to scream and cry, to beg, she forced herself to be calm.

She said nothing as rough hands grabbed her shoulders, excited guffaws from the small group ringing in her ears.

'Don't you think this is all a little cliché?' she sighed.

The soldier frowned.

'Big, bad scar? Dark alleyway? Little man given a dram of power, decides to accost a woman with it?' Sofia would have been proud of the unruffled tone.

'Who the fuck do you think you're talking to?'

Elara tilted her head as though considering. 'Well, from the smell of yesterday's beer on your breath, I'd guess an alcoholic waste of a city guard, who's never made it up the ranks past being the general's lapdog.'

The scarred man's face contorted in rage. 'Oh, I'll make you pay for that,' he snarled. 'Drag her down there,' he ordered a soldier, nodding to the dark alley she'd come from. She was hauled along to jeers and taunts, though she did not struggle, keeping her eyes on the scarred soldier.

One cannot see clearly through stormy waters, she reminded herself. One of her many, many tutors had tried to drum the sentence through her skull during Elara's various outbursts. When she was pushed against the wall, she spoke.

'I'm going to give you one more chance to be a gentleman and let me go.'

A different soldier, this one stocky and short, gripped her hands behind her back.

The scarred soldier's laugh was empty. 'Shut the fuck up, you entitled little bitch,' he barked. His dirty hands tugged at the fabric of her white gown, ripping the neckline. His lips came close to her neck.

You control your emotions, they do not control you.

Yet another lesson from another tutor.

He drew his slimy tongue across her throat, and she forced herself to remain still as her magick swirled and snapped until it poured out of her – the final drop in her well.

Into an illusion. This time, a nightmare.

She felt her magick rear behind her, blocking out the Light above them, as the guards all around her stiffened. The hands at her back fell away, whimpers sounding. Before the inevitable screams.

Elara's illusions were a magick of will. And what she willed was to show the soldiers their worst fear.

'I wonder what you see,' she said softly, to the scarred guard now backing away. 'Is it a wraith? A soulless monster?' She advanced, as more screams sounded, like music. 'Is it your own reflection?'

A tear trickled down the guard's face. 'Please.'

'Is that the sound you wanted me to make?' she whispered.

'Do you enjoy preying on women? Defenceless? Innocent? I wonder if what you see is a man doing what you just tried to do to me, to your daughter.'

He sank to his knees, eyes wide with fear. She vaguely noticed some of the other guards on the ground, wailing and crawling, or curled up in a ball. All so easy to terrify.

She gritted her teeth as she forced one final bout of power into the alley. She willed her nightmares to haunt these men's sleep for the rest of their miserable lives. And smiled, at the faint scent of ammonia as a wet patch spread across the scarred man's crotch.

A bloodcurdling scream rose from the man's gaping lips, and she clamped her hand firmly over his mouth. Tears streamed down his face as he shook against her, muttering hysterically.

'This is for every woman you've preyed upon, every girl you have accosted and taken from without asking permission. I know I'm not the first.' She leaned in. 'But I will be your last. If you or your men ever try this again, you will pray for these nightmares. Because they will be *nothing* compared to what I will do to you.'

Footsteps pounded and she turned to see Leonardo arrive in the alleyway, a look of shock on his face, and two guards in tow. He surveyed the various soldiers slumped on the floor, or wailing, or praying.

His eyes widened, and she tried to force her nightmares upon him, enough so that she could run. But that piercing pain scorched through her head, as the last of her magick sputtered out. She swayed, and Leonardo launched forwards, catching her. She felt rope – soaked in shadowsbane – bind her wrists. She almost laughed. The dampening venom made no difference when she couldn't even wield the most common, and powerful, of Asterian magick.

However, she didn't have any energy or any other magick left to fight back as she was marched out of the alley.

An elderly woman hiding in her doorway blanched when Elara walked past her.

'Who are you?' she breathed, fear sharp in her eyes.

Before the last of Elara's bravado left her, she winked. 'Just an entitled little bitch.'

CHAPTER THREE

The heat did nothing to soothe the pounding in Elara's head as she was pushed to the foot of the Palace of Light's promenade. Reality had begun to set in, her veneer of cool confidence shattering as she tried not to tremble, as she tried so desperately to keep a leash upon her emotions. And yet, even through the pain, and the anger, and the Stars-damned ropes biting at her wrists, Elara couldn't help but look at the structure before her in awe. Spires reached into clouds, casting shadows that seemed to shimmer upon the cobbles below. A waterfall, its waters streaked with molten gold and bronze, rushed down behind the palace, framing the home of the D'Oros. She was pushed up the incline towards the palace entrance, the cobbles making way for smooth ground stone that sparkled in the Light, neat flowerbeds filled with apricot-coloured flowers lining the wide path. She tried to ignore the trickling of sweat down her back, or the fact she was in only her ripped undergown, about to enter the home of her sworn enemies.

'Enjoying the view?' Leonardo asked from beside her and she scowled.

'For a city so beautiful, it's a shame your monarch is such a conceited prick.'

Leonardo pulled her tighter to him. 'You will watch your tongue,' he said, voice low. 'And keep your traitorous spew to yourself.'

She bit back a retort as they arrived through a pair of gilded gates to the palace entrance.

Flanking either side of the towering doors sat two winged lions, carved from the pure gold that seemed to pour from the city, evidence of the riches of Helios. The mythas were said to have flown through Helion skies once upon a time. The sentinels stood mid-roar, wicked fangs gleaming in the Light. As she was pushed through the doors – carved with reliefs of the infamous Descent of Leyon, the patron Star of Helios – she couldn't help but feel she was stepping right into the lion's maw.

The cool marble corridors passed in a blur, the art – so much art, all hanging from intricate frames – seemed to morph and shimmer in the airy space as she was led onwards. More doors swung open, these inlaid with twirling flowers and vines, and she was shoved unceremoniously through by Leonardo.

Elara took two staggering steps in and stopped. The throne room was cavernous. Painted frescoes adorned the ceiling, walls and even the windows, depicting images of the history and myths of Helios. She saw the infamous battle between the ancient winged lions of Helios and the angels of Sveta. Her eyes narrowed as she saw a mural dedicated to the War on Darkness, King Idris painted as a grand saviour as he lay siege to Asteria's walls, wearing a crown of light.

The arms at her back propelled her forwards, and she gritted her teeth, praying that her magick would replenish by the time she arrived by the thrones she could see waiting at the other end of the massive room. She passed a small pool lined with peach-coloured flowers, noticing the scent that wafted from them. Frangipani, exotic and sweet. Small alcoves were hewn into the walls, gauze curtains drawn across them. Before she had time to check her magick again, to even pause, she was shoved in front of the larger throne.

She didn't look at the king, instead looking up to the frescoed ceiling, knowing the dismissal would infuriate him.

'Apologies for our tardiness, Your Majesty,' Leonardo said behind her. 'This one gave us more trouble than we expected.'

Elara made a small sound of dry amusement – of course the general hadn't wondered *why* Elara had exercised her power upon the guards – her gaze finally sliding to the king.

Idris D'Oro's skin was olive; his nostrils flared in a permanent sneer. His frame was one of an ageing man; she could see where muscles had once been, gained from the infamous battles she had heard the stories of, but they had been replaced with a paunch of gluttony. His black hair was slicked back, revealing slanting eyebrows, but it was his eyes that made her shiver. They were golden, but like shards of glass. Empty.

'Princess Elara.' Oil slid over his words, as she inclined her head.

'It's Queen now, technically.'

It was then that her attention was taken by the figure in the throne beside the king, who had leaned forwards as she spoke, his chin now resting indolently on his hand. She felt a dull thump as she locked eyes with him. He was so handsome that for a moment, her mind froze. His skin was darker than the king's – a golden shade of brown. His jaw cut into his face, and the hard planes of it were accentuated with black brows and black curls that fell across his forehead. A small hoop in his ear glowed in the Helion rays casting through the stained-glass windows. But it was his eyes that made her pause. They were gold also, but the liquid gold of the waterfalls outside. They glinted like the crown he wore tipped on his head, and they looked at her like she was prey, glancing down her figure, taking in her torn nightgown.

Elara realized with a start who she was staring at. He gave a slow, hungry grin as he saw the understanding dawn in her eyes. Prince Lorenzo. The Lion of Helios.

'I believe there needs to be a coronation to officially become queen,' Idris sneered.

Elara's attention was still fixed on the prince. 'I suppose I was a little busy getting kidnapped to attend mine.'

With a blink she tore her eyes from him, the stories and whispers she had heard of him roiling below the surface of her consciousness. She willed calm into her veins and forced her focus back on to King Idris, trying to ignore the prince's piercing gaze.

'Which brings me to my next point,' Idris said. 'We were sorry to hear about the late king and queen's passing, princess.'

The truth spoken aloud nearly made Elara crumple to the floor. But she kept her back straight, even as her hand twitched by her side. All she wanted was to retaliate against Idris's disrespect, but no magick reared up, her source empty.

'You mean their murder.'

'It's a good thing my guards found you when they did, or perhaps *your* death would have been next.' Idris inclined his head. 'Or perhaps not, if the story of how you escaped the wrath of a Star is true.'

The dry heat had dissipated from the room, Elara's entire being growing cold and stiff.

'How do you kn—?'

'Come, now. You believe that every king and queen across Celestia doesn't know? As servants to the Stars, of course we heard the news. Star Leyon called us to his temple the moment he heard of the events that took place last night. And also told me of your little prophecy that started it all. That summoned Ariete in the first place.'

Elara fought against the images that once more bubbled up – her mother and father in tears as she had returned from the fair only the night before, and demanded to know if the prophecy that the Concordian priestess had spoken there was true.

'Then you risk much by dragging me here, now that you know the King of Stars will do anything to find me. He killed an entire throne room of people for concealing me from him. Think what he would do to you.' The smile that crept upon her face was tight.

The crown prince was still silent beside Idris, though his eyes had narrowed.

'It is for this exact reason, that you were brought here.'

'Elaborate.'

Idris's nostrils flared at the order. He looked back to his son, who only raised an eyebrow, still silent, before he stood. There was a gleam in his lined, pale eyes.

'I want to kill a Star. And you're going to help me.'

CHAPTER FOUR

Elara took a step backwards, bumping right into Leonardo.

She must have misheard.

'You want to kill a god?' she asked hoarsely.

Elara was a royal. She knew the flaws of the Stars who the subjects of Celestia worshipped so blindly. Though her lands had been untouched by Stars – their patron goddess slumbering – when she was only eight she had heard her parents whisper to each other of what the Stars were capable of when they descended from their home in the Heavens. Capri had turned more than one subject in his land to solid gold for beating him at a game of cards. Aquaria, so Sofia had once told her, flew into such fits of rage that she could cast misfortune and curses upon an entire family line. And Ariete . . . well . . . any royal could recount the rivers of blood he had spilled in his time. She had questioned for years why they should pray to such cruel and capricious beings. And yet . . . to even speak the words aloud? It was utter sacrilege.

Idris twirled the yellow topaz ring on his little finger. 'Not just any god. Ariete. The King of Stars.' He rose from the throne and began to pace.

The emotions Elara had been trying so desperately to swallow now ignited in a pit of fire as she thought of the god who had cost her everything.

'Why?' was all she managed to say.

'If the King of Stars falls, so will the others. For centuries, Elara, the monarchs of Celestia have had to kneel at the feet of these gods. Lick their boots, be nothing more than servants. I had thought that the Stars were invincible, impossible to kill. Until now. Until you.'

She turned. 'Find someone else. I have no interest in being smitten by *divinitas* when the Stars inevitably discover your plan.'

It was the worst way to die, by *divinitas*. The Stars' deathly starlight would blind you, then flay your skin, before quite literally obliterating your existence. Leaving not even a body to bury – and with that, no way to get to the Hallowlands, or the Graveyard at the very least, which sat somewhere between the paradise of the Hallowlands and the damnation of the Deadlands. She thought of the look in her parents' eyes as red starlight had thrashed them, and squeezed her own shut.

'Do you think you have a choice?'

As she opened her eyes again, horrible light seeped from the king's fingertips as he sat back on his throne. He could wield that light, inflict pain on her with it. She forced herself not to even blink.

'You can't very well return to Asteria. Not as the god of wrath and blood himself hunts for you. Where else would you go?'

It hit Elara then. She had been trying so desperately to get back home. But how could she when the god who had murdered her parents would be waiting with open arms?

Nowhere. Elara had nowhere to go, no one to turn to.

She had the years locked away in her silver tower to thank for that.

'You will stay,' Idris said. 'I will put you in the finest quarters. You will want for nothing. So long as you allow us to train you. To make you the weapon you were always destined to be – one to bring down the very skies.'

This, or death. Elara weighed the options in her mind. To be a slave to Idris, or to spend her life running from Ariete's clutches.

'How will you train me?'

'I know you possess the Three, princess. All of your kingdom's powers, rather than just one. Rare, indeed.'

'How could you know?' she demanded. It was impossible. No one but her family's innermost circle and trusted tutors had known.

'I have my sources,' Idris replied. His son's lips twitched then. 'You will be trained rigorously, and ruthlessly. The D'Oro way.'

'And how will you hide me from Ariete?' she demanded. If her pale skin didn't give her away, then her silver eyes did – Elara was Asterian through and through.

He clicked his fingers, and the presence at Elara's back disappeared, before she heard the doors swing open once more. She turned, seeing a beautiful woman glide into the room. She looked different from the other Helions that Elara had laid eyes on. Her golden hair glowed, her green eyes sparkling – so enticing that Elara found it hard to look away.

'Merissa will see to it that you're well disguised. We've already taken care of the details of your stay.'

'Such a lovely euphemism for imprisonment,' she said. Leonardo shifted behind her. 'Let the record show that I will not agree to stay here, in the kingdom of my enemy.'

'Then you'll be dragged to your new chambers. It would be easier if you went willingly.'

Elara clenched her jaw. Toyed with the idea of struggling. But her bones were so weary, her mind more so. And so she straightened her spine, and spun on her heel, giving a look dripping with derision to Leonardo. 'And I suppose it's you who will be overseeing my training?'

There was a cold laugh behind her. 'No,' Idris said. 'That would be my son.'

Her eyes flew to the prince's as his glare bore into her.

She scoffed, making sure her only visible reaction was one of ridicule, before tossing her hair over her shoulder as Leonardo escorted her out, feeling the prince's glare scorching her back.

CHAPTER FIVE

She was deposited, in silence, in front of an ornate door by Leonardo, who nodded at Merissa and left.

Merissa looked furtively at Elara, then away, before removing a key from the pocket of her gauzy, pink skirt and twisting it in the lock. As the door opened, the sight that greeted Elara was so enticing it irked her. She tried to master the awe on her face as she walked inside. Her rooms in Asteria had been grand, but she had never dreamed that such a place as these rooms existed. Two marble pillars flanked a huge four-poster bed and large doors, which stood ajar, allowing a warm breeze to waft gently from a balcony. As she trailed closer, wondering just how high the jump from the balcony would be, she saw it was spacious, enough for a divan, with an assortment of throws and cushions scattered around it, with ornate oil lamps floating by some magick through the air. She could see matching balconies and rooms across the way, a neatly manicured lawn between her side and the opposite. A fountain trickled in the centre.

She walked back inside and craned her neck up to inspect the ceiling, noticing the same frescoes that decorated the other rooms that she had seen earlier. Hues of blush, peach and yellow blended together. At home, the fashion and decorations were mostly tinted blues, lavender and black in honour of their twilit sky. She rubbed her eyes irritably at the Light, beaming through the room. It was really going to take some getting used to this glare.

Merissa wrung her hands in between fussing with the pillows and curtains of the bed, and Elara crossed her arms, staring at the woman until she finished her activity and turned to her slowly.

'I-I've tried to make your stay here in Sol as comfortable as possible,' she said, eyes averted, her voice barely a whisper.

The anger and indignation that had filled Elara deflated, and she relaxed her shoulders, trying to soften her face.

It wasn't this woman's fault that Elara had been dragged into her enemy's lair, then basically forced to aid their cause. And she certainly didn't want the poor woman to be scared of her.

'I appreciate it,' she said softly.

Merissa's hands stopped fidgeting quite so much. 'I—' She started again. 'His Majesty has requested my skills to help disguise you while you're amongst our court.' She walked through to an adjoining chamber, which only served to grudgingly impress Elara more.

Sunken into the floor at the centre of the chamber was a bath the size of a small pool, full of crystal-clear water and soapy bubbles. Painted tiles lined it and were warm to the touch. The room smelled of jasmine oil, a smell that caused a sharp pang of longing in her. It reminded her too much of the night-jasmine trees that had grown outside her window, soothing her when she could not sleep with the fear of the nightmares she might fall into.

'And what skills would those be?' Elara asked, blinking away the memories.

Merissa's lip quirked slightly. 'You'll see. For now, let's get you clean.'

Elara was suddenly aware once more of the state of her dress, the sweat that had dried sticky on her skin.

Merissa began to undo the laces of Elara's undergown, not that Elara minded. She'd grown up dressing and undressing in front of handmaids. When the torn and dusty white undergown slithered to the floor, Merissa picked it up gingerly.

'Would you like this cleaned, Your Highness?'

'Elara will do,' she replied. 'And no, I don't want to keep that thing.' It still bore the memories of the day that had changed her life irrevocably.

'Thank the Stars. I'll burn it then,' Merissa muttered.

When Elara turned, the maid looked mortified that she'd uttered the words aloud. 'I-I'm sorry, I—'

'Incineration sounds fine.' Elara's lips twitched as she undid the thigh sheath that held her dagger, and Merissa smiled shyly back.

She placed it carefully by the water's edge before gingerly stepping into the bath. Deliciously cool water lapped at her, a balm to her heated skin.

Merissa reached for the holster and knife. Elara stopped her. 'I'd rather it remained close,' she said.

Merissa gave a nod, and a reassuring smile. 'Of course. A wise choice.'

It was a damned shame. If she had been in any other circumstances, perhaps she could have become friends with this woman.

She pushed the thought aside as Merissa crouched down next to the bath. 'Soaps are laid here for you, Your Highness.'

'Elara,' she corrected again.

Merissa's cheeks grew pink, and Elara tried to force another somewhat friendly smile as she turned her back to reach for the soaps.

'That's beautiful,' she heard Merissa breathe behind her.

Elara turned, craning her neck to look at Merissa, and realized what the woman had to be looking at. An elegant rendering of a dragun was tattooed down her spine, snaking down in black, its scales and wings laced with shards of silver.

'Ah, my dragun. The sigil of our family,' she replied.

Merissa nodded. 'I know the tales.'

Elara turned her attention back to the soap. 'My best friend has one of a nightwolf.' It wasn't the sigil of Sofia's house, but Elara had always been told that she herself had a dragun spirit and Sofia had wanted a tattoo to match her own spirit – ferocious, protective and loyal.

'Nightwolves. The ending of "The Nightwolf and the Silver" always made me cry as a child,' Merissa replied. 'I hated the Nightwolf.'

Elara paused her washing, frowning. 'The Nightwolf was the hero of the story. He was slain by the maiden.'

'Yes,' Merissa said slowly. 'But he was slain because he had befriended the Lightmaiden, then betrayed her with his bite. She was left no choice. And she died too, with his venom in her veins.'

Elara put down her sponge. 'Then you and I know very different tales.'

Merissa shrugged, blushing again. 'Perhaps I spoke out of turn.'

Elara resumed her scrubbing. 'No. It sounds just like Helios to vilify the Dark and glorify the murderer who was stupid enough to try and tame a wild beast.'

Merissa said nothing more, nodding meekly as she tidied around the bathroom.

An ache had settled deep in Elara's stomach the moment she had brought up Sofia.

'I'll let you relax,' Merissa said. 'Call if you need me, I'll be in the bedroom.'

'Thank you,' Elara replied, her mind elsewhere. As soon as the door closed, she submerged herself under the water, allowing it to fill her ears, to wash over her thoughts. Being near water normally calmed her but try as she might, she couldn't erase the unwanted and terrible thoughts beginning to creep in. The ones that asked what had happened to Sofia, to the rest of her court – to the kingdom she so loved, even if she'd only ever seen it mostly through the panes of window glass.

A buzzing started in her ears, her hands beginning to tingle as familiar panic gripped her. She tried to breathe and choked in a mouthful of cool water.

She came up spluttering and coughing, her sopping hair blinding her.

'Elara? Is everything all right?' she heard Merissa call.

'Fine,' Elara got out.

She gripped the warm tiles of the pool's lip, trying to ground herself as her thrumming heart slowed.

'You will not survive a night here if you allow your emotions to drown you like this,' she hissed to herself. She brought to mind her box – the one that Sofia had taught her years ago to create. It was obsidian black, its glossy surface reflecting Elara's haunted face. There was so much already sealed within there, but as she opened it, she didn't look at a single memory or emotion. Instead she imagined each feeling and image, all her panic and pain, being laid into the black box. Then she resolutely locked it, and shoved it down within her.

When she walked back into the bedroom, wrapped in a fluffy towel, the water on her skin already drying in the heat, Merissa was stood by a dressing table, an enormous oval mirror in the centre of it.

Elara took the hint, and sat gingerly on the stool.

'The king stressed to me that you had to blend into the kingdom as much as possible,' Merissa said, as she set about combing Elara's hair. 'To those who have already seen you before, my magick won't work. But to most of the kingdom, who have never set eyes on the Queen of Asteria—'

Elara jerked, facing Merissa. 'What did you just call me?'

'The – the Queen,' she stammered back.

Elara swallowed. 'Thank you.'

She turned around, Merissa resuming her brushing. 'To most of the kingdom, the magick will hold. They will see a Helion citizen, if you are ever glimpsed around the palace.'

A rosy glow stretched from her fingertips, heating Elara's scalp. The blue tint of midnight hair, so long it skimmed her hips, warmed as rich golden hues began to streak through it. She looked in shock to Merissa.

'You're a glamourer?'

Merissa nodded, and Elara looked at her features once more.

'You're not from Helios.'

She shook her head. 'I'm Aphrodean.'

It set Elara more at ease, as the glamourer continued to cast the rose-coloured charm over Elara's features. In the mirror, her eyes deepened to a dark brown, her skin began to glow a little in the way all Helions – the worshippers of the Light – did. There was a brilliance about her, that hadn't been there before. She looked almost unrecognizable.

'This is what others will see,' Merissa said. 'But this—' She clicked her fingers, and the mirror rippled, to reveal Elara exactly as she had been – her silver eyes shining back at her, hair blue-black, skin dulling a little in pallor. 'This is what you and I, and those who have already seen you, will see.'

Elara nodded, grateful that at least she recognized her own reflection.

Merissa gave an encouraging smile, before walking towards a large wardrobe. Sheer garments were pulled out and held in front of Elara. 'You'll be wearing Helion attire, of course.'

Elara's eyes widened. In Asteria, with its chilled climate, the fashion had always been somewhat modest, with little skin exposed, if ever. Yet here, due to the Light's bounty, the clothes were barely more than a suggestion. Merissa had selected a loose silk skirt that pooled to the ground, and Elara's eyes bulged as Merissa brought a top into view. Off the shoulders, the blouse bunched, with short cuffs to leave her arms bare. The blouse was white to match the skirt, embroidered with small gold flowers all over it. But what alarmed Elara as Merissa forced it over her was its length. It was cropped, leaving her midriff exposed.

'This is barely going to cover my breasts,' she said in horror.

Elara could have sworn the corners of Merissa's lips lifted. 'Isn't that the whole point? Helions believe that their Star Leyon created the Light, in part, to display the beauty of his kingdom proudly.'

'Skies,' Elara muttered, taking the clothes from Merissa. 'I'll dress myself,' she added hurriedly.

Merissa ushered Elara behind a screen, waiting as Elara attempted to wrangle the flimsy cloth over her chest in a way that wouldn't show her nipples.

'Clothes here are designed for comfort as well as style,' Merissa called over. 'We don't restrict ourselves, and you'll find corsets are only used for formal occasions – balls and such. You'll get used to it before you know it.'

Elara dressed hurriedly, making her way out from behind the screen.

Merissa raised her eyebrows. 'You're going to blend in perfectly.'

'Wonderful,' Elara said flatly.

'I just have a few finishing touches.' Merissa twined some small white starflowers through Elara's hair. The fragrance of them calmed Elara as she breathed it in deeply. 'There. Now you're ready for a royal dinner.'

Elara turned to herself in the full-length wardrobe mirror and stilled. The outfit, although still too revealing for Elara's liking, fit her like a second skin. The silk seemed to drip off her frame. Then she took in her face in the reflection, and felt a twinge of sadness. Merissa had made her up beautifully, but no makeup or glamouring could hide the haunted look that Elara saw in her own silver eyes.

Merissa clicked her fingers, and her reflection evaporated, replaced with the dark-eyed, golden-lit Elara once more.

She tugged a strand of silky hair through her fingers and forced a smile.

'Thank you, Merissa. I appreciate the kindness you've shown me today.'

She meant it. In this place, she would grasp on to any kindness that she could.

Merissa's eyes filled with warmth, and she gave a little curtsy. 'It's best I escort you to dinner now.' She squinted at an ornate clock mounted on the bedroom wall. 'It will be served soon, and it will be a good test for my glamouring. Especially as you meet the court.'

Elara looked once more to the room – her new prison – then begrudgingly followed the glamourer out of the room to where the hungry predators waited.

CHAPTER SIX

The banquet hall opened on to a terrace, half of it exposed to the balmy evening air. It was surrounded by a cream-coloured veranda, the sound of birds trilling through the night. Long tables graced the length of the space, with a raised table made of oak for the more distinguished members of the court, looking out over a lush garden blooming with exotic flowers.

Although, as Elara was coming to realize, the sky never fully darkened to the blue-black she was accustomed to back home. Here, late into the evening, the sky was painted a deep red, streaked with vivid orange.

She noticed other guests, dressed in the finer clothes of Helion courtiers, sat around lower tables, chatting and laughing. King Idris was seated at the head of the raised table, his crown gleaming in the flickering lantern light. Further down that same table, she saw Leonardo. He'd swapped his golden armour for umber-brown linens, though she didn't miss the knives lined upon a strap slung across his chest. His face lit up as he spoke to the woman next to him. She was stunning, with tan skin and chestnut curls. There was something odd about how high she seemed to be sitting, and as Elara neared the raucous tables, she saw why. She was perched in someone's lap, and as Elara saw the jewelled hand teasing up and down her waist, she saw that the owner of that lap and hand was Prince Lorenzo.

All three were laughing, the pretty woman tipping her head back and flushing girlishly at something the prince was whispering in her ear as she leaned in. Elara looked away quickly.

Merissa yanked her arm as they stuck to the outer edges of the room, and Elara saw that she had reached the high table by the king. The raucous laughter and upbeat music mercifully didn't halt, though the king noticed her presence immediately.

He looked over her appraisingly. 'Helios suits you,' he said with a serpent's grin, his stare greasy. His eyes flicked to Merissa. 'Good work, glamourer.'

Merissa curtsied, and Elara tried not to curl her lip at the king's words, instead raising her chin. *You are a queen now*, she reminded herself.

She heard a yelp and turned. Prince Lorenzo had pushed the brunette off his lap, and his gaze was piercing Elara's.

She matched his stare, making sure to look down her nose at him. His eyes dragged over her body, pausing on her exposed midriff. She clenched her hands by her sides to stop herself from covering the bare skin with her arms. Tilting her head, she stared back defiantly. King Idris followed her gaze as the brunette girl who'd been on Lorenzo's lap sidled away, her cheeks flushed.

'Ah yes, you will sit by my son,' he said, raising his voice over the music that had jumped into a boisterous, loud tune. Elara's stomach dropped as she saw the seat next to Lorenzo was vacant. Merissa left a moment later, and Elara debated calling after her. Glowering, she made her way to the table, slotting in to her appointed seat. She stared straight ahead as she waited for her food to be served, unwilling to acknowledge the prince who sat next to her.

'I think we've met before,' a low voice rumbled, and she turned finally. She smiled coldly, ignoring how up close, the prince was somehow even more handsome than when she'd seen him in the throne room.

'Elara,' she said quietly with a tight nod. 'Although you already know that, don't you?'

'Elara.' He rolled her name off his tongue, under his breath, the word sounding lyrical with his accent. 'I'm sure you already know who I am.'

'Your reputation precedes you,' she said in a bored tone, looking away.

'Does it now? All good things, I hope.'

'Quite the opposite.' She turned back to him, and her smile was razor sharp. 'Unless you count the stories of you burning, whoring and killing your way through my kingdom as "good things". Your reputation is that of a wicked rake. Nothing more.'

He turned in his seat so he was fully facing her, elbow on the table, leaning his fist against his temple as though he had all the time in the world to look at her. She bristled at his arrogance. Already she could see the entitlement etched into every line of his face. But still, she did not break from his gaze.

'I'm flattered that you already know so much about me when I hardly know a thing about you,' he said. A grin slowly formed, along with a dangerous light in his golden eyes. Elara's attention caught on them, noticing that they were flecked with bronze.

'If you ever want to pay homage to the man who you're

clearly so fascinated by,' he continued, 'my room is across the garden from yours.'

'What did you just say?' She was unable to keep the bite out of her voice.

He shrugged. 'I can show you just how "wicked and rakish" I can be.'

She summoned every drop of disgust on to her face as she looked down her nose at him. Then, with a small smirk that she knew drove men mad with anger, she flicked her hair over her shoulder and ignored him.

She felt him shift in his seat.

'You scrub up well, you know?' he persisted. She exhaled loudly. He leaned back, taking a sip of peach wine. 'Bedraggled, in that tattered undergown, you couldn't have looked further from a princess.' He chuckled low as her temper flared. 'But now, I can see that you are royalty.' His eyes remained on the starflowers of her hair.

'My title is "Queen", actually,' she said yet again. 'And do you always charm strangers with such compliments?' His easy smile faltered. 'Probably the same way you charm poor maidens by shoving them off your lap. I'd rather let a winged lion maul me to death than ever set foot in your bedroom.'

She heard a splutter and peered to see Leonardo coughing into his wine, his shoulders shaking.

'I'm sorry,' he said, when the two looked at him. 'It's just, I've never heard anyone talk to Enzo like that.'

'Maybe if someone had already, he wouldn't be such an egotistical bastard.'

Leonardo gaped as Lorenzo bent forwards, blocking the general from view.

'Watch your tongue, darkwitch.'

'Or what? You'll burn me on a pyre? I thought you needed me for your father's go at world domination.'

A nerve ticked in Lorenzo's jaw, and Elara took it as a victory, settling back into her chair. She took a sip of wine, her nerves jangling. The honeyed sweetness of the wine dissolved on her tongue, as she waited for the prince's fury to explode. But instead he said, in a voice lethally quiet, 'Unfortunately, he does need you. Which means that I, by some terrible fate, am charged with training you. If you insult me again, our training together won't be pleasant.'

'I wasn't under any illusion that it would be anyway,' she replied to him. 'And what could *you* possibly teach *me*?'

He laughed then out of the side of his mouth, as a server started to lay plates filled with food before them. He waited until she had left, before replying. 'I possess the Three, ignorant woman.'

Elara's eyes flew to his.

'Yes,' he continued on, smiling with clear delight. 'What are the chances? I am sure you know how rare it is to possess all three of your kingdom's gifts. So it turns out, *princess*, that I'll be able to help you quite a bit.'

It was said that when each Star had fallen to Celestia, they had gifted a drop of their magick to their patron kingdoms – enough to create three powers in each one.

She didn't reply for a moment, instead yanking a platter of rice jewelled with pomegranates that had just been set down, to her. No wonder the prince had been able to dole out so much destruction to her kingdom. The thought of what he, his father and their entire sorry kingdom had done to Asteria reignited the fury within her.

'What exactly are the Three in Helios?' she asked tightly, vowing there and then that she would learn everything she could about this man, and then destroy him.

'I can wield the Light,' he replied, and the finger he had

wrapped around his goblet began to glow. Elara winced, and Lorenzo's eyes narrowed.

'I abhor the Light,' she snapped. 'The Stars-damned entirety of Celestia revels in the Light and curses the Dark, thanks to you and your family.'

'Good,' he replied. 'Then you probably won't like my next power much either.'

He lifted his hand and, as his fingers danced, a small flame fluttered between them. This time, Elara didn't wince. The flames, she did not fear. They weren't what had shoved down her throat, cutting off her scream when—

She slammed the memory back into its box, irritated that it had escaped. Her cool demeanour gave nothing away as she slid her gaze over his hands. 'Wielding fire. A little inelegant. But I'd expect nothing less from a Helion brute.'

The flames reflected in Lorenzo's eyes as he leaned in. It took every ounce of her years of etiquette coaching for her not to lean back. But her mother had taught her well – queens did not make space. The people around them did. So she sat, her chin raised, her back straight.

'I have one more gift,' he said quietly. 'You know of the seers of Helios, don't you?'

A drumming picked up in Elara's chest.

'At your naming ceremony, your future was foretold by a seer,' her mother had wept, mere days before. *'We did what we had to. We tried to keep you safe. We tried to rewrite fate, but—'*

The darkness stole the memories away and she took a deep inhale.

'In Asteria, we call you flaky quacks,' she drawled back. 'Speaking in riddles, able to see mere glimpses of the future. An impressive "gift" indeed.'

He laughed, cold and low. 'Then how is this for impressive? My gift is a special kind of seering. Nothing hides from my light. I can see when someone is lying. I can see through glamours and tricks. I can see just what someone's soul is made up of, whether they are good or bad at their core. And what I see when I try to look at you, is a shroud of shadows that reek of night-jasmine. I don't yet know what it is you're hiding behind them, princess. But I promise, I'll find out.'

Elara blinked, and she pushed her chair back. But still, he leaned forwards until it felt like his body was blocking out the whole room.

'My father may want you here for his plans. He may truly believe you can help us. Maybe you will. But if I discover that you pose a threat to my kingdom, I will kill you without a thought.' He spoke the words so calmly that she almost wondered if she had imagined them. He reclined, taking a slow sip of wine. But the steely stare remained. She pushed down the fear as her lips curled into a sneer, fingers itching to hold her dagger, pressed in its home against her thigh.

'Then I should warn you,' she murmured, her hair brushing his cheek as she bent close, 'that I don't take kindly to threats. And if you make another, it might just be your last.' She snatched the cup from his hands and took a sip of the wine. 'I'd sleep with all your lanterns lit if I were you. Who knows what might come alive in the night.'

She set the cup between them, before leaning back in her chair, conjuring once more the image of regality. With poise, she speared a slice of meat from another platter laid before her, ignoring the dangerous smile that had crept upon the prince's lips.

Though her heart pounded at his warning, she'd be damned if she would give Lorenzo the satisfaction of seeing any reaction. She turned her attention to the food. It was delicious, everything richly spiced. Steamed rice, mint-stewed lamb and hunks of crusted rosemary bread were all savoured until the plate was wiped clean. She ate in silence, her mind turning the prince's words over and over, as she ignored his oppressive presence beside her.

She lounged back when she was done with a satisfied sigh, relieved to see that Lorenzo had turned away and was in deep conversation with his general. Her attention fell to the room as a drowsiness took over her, observing the Helion court as tea was served. She asked for honey – anything to sweeten the bitterness that swirled through her – and spooned two teaspoons into the fresh mint before taking a sip. As she looked around, she saw a few people who she guessed were from the kingdom of Aphrodea, based off the similar features they seemed to share with Merissa. Everything she had learned about them, about the different kingdoms, had been through books. It made her ache, to see the world she had been deprived of, the people. All because Asteria had been forced to shut themselves off from the world. All because of the D'Oros and their War on Darkness.

A loud laugh broke her reverie. She saw the chestnut-haired girl from before back by Lorenzo's side, draped over him like a curtain. The girl jostled Elara, and Elara rolled her eyes. She watched as he whispered something in the girl's ear, and her gaze snagged on his hand, which was making its way down the girl's back. She thought of the flames that had danced between his fingers and drew her eyes back to his face. Her breath caught as she saw his eyes on hers, and he smiled lazily. Unable to stand the stare she knew was trying to find a way past her shadows, she stood.

Merissa was nowhere to be found, and so she stepped in front of the general, who had played escort once before.

'Leonardo, I'd like to go to my rooms, please.'

He nodded, rose to his feet and stood at her back, waiting.

'*Enzo*,' she said mockingly, and the prince's eyes narrowed. 'It's been . . . well, *pleasure* is a strong word.'

The chestnut-haired girl gawped at Elara's insolence. Elara shot her a withering glance before turning away, Leonardo at her side. As she began to walk, a hand grabbed her wrist, the skin hot. She whirled in indignation.

'We start training tomorrow,' Enzo said, his voice low. Elara's eyes flew to his hand as it gripped her tightly. 'Meet me by the grand staircase. Leave your attitude at the door.'

She smiled sweetly, snatching her hand away from him. 'I will if you do.'

CHAPTER SEVEN

Elara sank into her feathered pillows and dreamed deeply that night. She knew when she was walking because the quality of the dream changed. Images became sharper and clearer, until they became a reality that moulded itself around her. In this dreamscape, she felt fire. So much of it, hot and close.

She was standing in a bedroom. The darkened room was carved from white marble, inlaid with glittering goldstone. A bed was sunk into the stones, covered in silk sheets, and lying upon it was a woman's figure. Naked curves glimmered in the waning candlelight, and long black hair spilled to the woman's waist. The silken sheets rode down to the soft curve of her hips and Elara felt desire pulsing through the dreamscape as an almost visceral thing. She looked around for the dreamer but could only see the outline of a figure in the shadows.

'I've been waiting for you,' the woman before her said silkily, and as she slowly turned on the bed, Elara found that she was staring into her own silver eyes.

She woke in cold sweat, gasping. Quickly, she jumped out

of bed, flung open the wide doors and paced to the balcony, flooded with the deep crimson of the Helion night, the feel of cool tiles beneath her feet steadily grounding her. In all her years walking, she had never seen herself.

She continued pacing, worrying her tangled hair, then stalked back into the room and snatched the soft blanket folded neatly on the armchair beside her bed. Trailing it back on to the balcony, she peered over the side once again. It was too high a drop – low enough to be enticing, high enough that she'd break her ankles with the leap on to the manicured shrubbery beneath her. She walked back and forth, trying to get rid of the itching desire to run from the palace. She knew that Idris had stationed guards outside her door, that there were sentries at every exit. And where would she go should she find a way past them anyway? She cursed, before looking to the divan and slumping on to it in defeat.

Her eyes were drawn to a neat pile of books on the low-slung table. Her fingers trembled as she picked up an edition of *The Mythas of Celestia*, intricately illustrated with swirls of gold leaf. For the first time since she had been taken from her kingdom, she smiled a real smile.

That trove of tales had kept her company on so many lonely days and nights in her room. Before she'd dared ever sneak past the palace walls, this book had been the only way to travel beyond them. To Elara, a reader was an alchemist. They turned the mundane into something extraordinary, transforming words on a page into entire worlds. To steal away from reality, to feel real emotions for things that didn't exist? Elara knew she possessed the Three, but reading was a special kind of magick.

She settled down with the book, the strange red hue of the Helion night illuminating the pages. 'The Mermaids of Neptuna' was the first tale, and she smiled as she read of the vicious merfolk who, legend said, had fought for dominion over the seas against the sirens of Altalune. She didn't know if she truly believed in the fanciful tales; either way, if the mythas had ever existed, they were long gone now. But she allowed herself to walk down the familiar passages of her book, before her eyelids finally closed.

The argument had happened again. She'd demanded to know why she couldn't go outside the palace. Her parents had replied, as usual, that she shouldn't ask questions. It had escalated from there, until she'd been sent away in tears to her room. Moments after she arrived there, however, Sofia appeared at the door with a plate of food in hand, and sat and listened as Elara cried.

'You have me,' she said gently. 'Even if you don't have anyone else, I will always be here.'

The shadows around the room had grown darker.

'Do you think Lukas is listening?' Elara sniffed, looking into the darkness.

Sofia shrugged. 'If he is,' she said, pitching her voice into a shout, 'then the little sneak needs a new hobby!'

'Don't, Sof,' Elara said. 'It's so hard when you don't get along.'

Sofia rolled her eyes. 'I don't trust him. You shouldn't either.'

More tears threatened to spill, and Sofia softened in response. 'What would make you feel better right now?'

'Seeing something other than these four walls,' Elara said sullenly.

Sofia smiled. 'I may have a plan.'

The night that followed was the first time Elara ever set foot outside the palace grounds. Thanks to Sofia's encouragement, she used her illusions for the first time to rebel – managing to sneak herself and Sofia beyond the sentried doors – and saw a glimpse of her kingdom. They pinched cinnamon sugared buns from a night stall, and burned their mouths after gulping them down too fast as they waltzed through the Dreamer's Quarter, hidden under Elara's illusions. It was the best night of Elara's life.

The sound of pots clinking woke Elara. She blinked, rubbing the remnants of the dream that had been more of a memory out of her eyes, and saw Merissa's honeyed head bobbing as she hurried around the room. The woman smiled at Elara, bringing a tray out to the balcony.

'I tried to let you sleep as much as possible. But the prince requires that you meet him immediately.' She poured some mint tea, and pushed a plate of fresh berries to Elara.

'Ah, I'm sure he was in a pleasant mood when he *demanded* my presence.' She popped a raspberry into her mouth.

Merissa tried to school away a smile. 'He was . . . a little irritable.'

Elara snorted. 'Good. Hopefully I got under his skin last night.'

Merissa bit her lip. 'I was watching you from across the hall. I'm not sure what you said to him, but I think you made quite the impression.'

'He threatened to kill me, so I threatened him right back.'

Merissa's eyebrows shot up as Elara stuffed a blueberry into her mouth, shrugging. 'What did you expect? Him and his father are holding me hostage. I'll train with him, but I won't make it easy.'

And with that, Elara sauntered into the bedroom and prepared for her lesson.

The soft linen of her new clothes caressed her limbs loosely as she strolled down the grand staircase. Elara craved the dense protection her Asterian wools would afford her, but Merissa had promised her these were appropriate training clothes, breathable and cool for the heat, and Elara had trusted her word. She had also topped up Elara's glamour, explaining that her magick only lasted a day and a night without being replenished.

She slowed when Lorenzo came into view, pacing in olive green linens, a shining gold sword slung at his waist.

From his thunderous face, he was in a black mood.

'*Enzo*,' she said lightly.

'You're late,' he spat. 'And it's "Your Highness".'

Elara laughed. 'I'll call you Your Highness when you call me Your *Majesty*.'

'Then I suppose we're at an impasse, Elara.'

She flicked her plait over her shoulder as she breezed past, the prince practically bristling with rage. 'Training is going to be fun.'

The heat was bearing down on her, and Elara found herself cursing Enzo under her breath for the fiftieth time that day. Great company he was not. He'd marched in front of her, not uttering a word as she'd followed him out of the palace and through the outskirts of the city to a forest trail. The ground was dry and cracked, the trees sparse. There was little to cover her from the burning Light, and it made her antsy. After an hour of climbing in silence, she called after him in exasperation.

'You know, if you were planning to take me somewhere secluded to kill me, you could've stopped at that boulder a few metres back and saved me the trek.' Wiping a bead of sweat from her brow she collapsed to the ground.

He stopped, tensing, and turned. 'Believe me, princess, if I had plans to kill you, you'd already be ashes in the wind.' He looked pointedly at her, sparking fire at his fingertips. 'Now get up.'

'I need to rest.' And she needed to eat. She eyed the bush of berries beside her.

'Get up, *now*,' he hissed.

She feigned a sigh, lying back on the hot earth as she reached out and pulled a handful of berries off the bush beside her.

'Mmm.' She savoured the sweet tang of gildberries, chewing torturously slowly. 'Only if you say please.'

He cast her a venomous look. 'I hope they're poisonous.'

'Me too. It will be preferable to suffering through another conversation with you.'

'Insolent child,' Enzo said under his breath, striding further ahead without her.

She saw him disappearing into a shaded grove and thanked the Stars for the respite from heat she saw within it as she dragged herself up the hill, the cool of the forest wrapping around her.

The grove was peaceful. White trunks, pale as starlight, twisted up into shades of red, orange and gold, the leaves gilded. It was quiet, the only sign of life from the song of the dawnbirds. The sole thing ruining the moment was the great hulking figure of the prince currently storming through the grove as if it were the last place he wanted to be. She rolled her eyes, following him.

At long last they reached a flat clearing. Fragrant flowers grew in patches, blush-coloured and beautiful. The trees formed a circle, shelter from the sight of any wanderers. She heard the trickle of babbling water and spied a small brook, clear and ice cold, running alongside them. With a desperate look, she bent over, cupping water in her hands and splashing her face before drinking deeply. She sighed when she'd taken her fill, wiping her mouth with the back of her hand and looked up. Enzo was looking at her with a disgusted expression.

'It's comforting to see that my view on Asterians was correct all along. Were you dragged up?'

She had taken his cruelty all morning and her temper flared faster than she was able to push it down. With only a thought, she willed her illusions to grow behind her, into nightmares once more that were fuelled by pure hatred.

It satisfied her to see his face blanch as he looked above her, to whatever she had conjured – whatever fear of his her magick had drawn upon.

And just as quickly as he had stumbled, light flew from his hands, whizzing past her.

She winced, avoiding the light, and she felt the illusion disperse. Flames erupted in Enzo's eyes, and he cracked his neck. Elara didn't know if it was just her imagination, or if his golden skin had paled a little.

'Don't you dare fucking do that again, darkwitch,' he growled, his tone deadly.

She threw him a look of disdain. 'Do you kiss your mother with that mouth?'

Faster than lightning, lustrous rays spilled from his

fingertips, whipping out in streams towards her. She threw her hands up in defence but it was useless. What illusions, what nightmares, could stop them? His light gripped her like it was a tangible thing, slamming her against the trunk of a tree. Her teeth rattled in her skull as her head flew back. The air left her as Enzo's magick wrapped around her throat, suspending her a foot above the ground. Flames wrapped around her wrists and ankles, their heat strong, though not enough to burn her. But the light, the terrible light, blazed on, blinding her, drowning her as it spread until it had surrounded her. She struggled, begged for her shadows to help her. But they swirled inside her, doing nothing to come to her aid.

Tears streamed down her face and she could only make Enzo out in a blur, stalking towards her. He walked through the wall of light, and she shook.

'My mother is dead. But you already knew that, didn't you?'

Elara's mouth worked. 'I didn't, I—'

'Don't *lie*. You want to know why I hate you? Your family? Why I'm *glad* your parents are dead?' Each word dripped with venom as he stepped closer. 'Because it was your parents who killed my mother. When she travelled to your Starsforsaken kingdom. *They* are the reason your kingdom was cut off from the world. *They* are the reason my father started the War on Darkness, why even now you're all trapped in your dark fucking wastelands.'

Fury spewed out of Elara faster than she could chase it. 'You filthy bastard *liar!*' she screamed.

His eyes searched hers, and he let out a dead laugh. 'Oh, they didn't tell you. You ignorant, sheltered princess. Did you think Mummy and Daddy were good people? Fair and just?'

'They wouldn't have—'

'They did. And I hope their souls never reach the Hallowlands.'

Elara spat at him. The lowest, most degrading thing she could think to do. Spittle landed on his cheek, and he only tilted his head, his light still blaring around her. 'You thought yourself so powerful, with your tricks and your dreams. But what good is your magick now? You're weak. Useless. My father was wrong about you. You are no one's saviour. You can't even save yourself.'

Elara was rendered immobile. But something within her had begun to wail and tear, something so furious, so writhing, that it spilled out of her. At first she thought it was her shadows – that they had at last come to save her. But as Enzo's light dimmed, as the form behind her grew, blotting out the light, she realized what it was. She only saw the shadow of her illusion, stretching across the grass towards Enzo. It was a nightmare more visceral than anything she had ever been able to conjure. A monster.

Enzo walked back, drawing his sword. The thing roared, and Elara closed her eyes, still trembling as she felt it pound the earth. She could feel it as a part of her; when she wanted it to move, it did. When she told it to swing, she heard Enzo grunt.

'Elara!' he shouted. But she wouldn't open her eyes. She didn't want to see what she had created – what dwelled within her. She shook with anger as she let the monster attack. She wanted him to die. Truly, in that moment she wanted to kill him, for him to feel the terror and helplessness he had made her feel.

There was a cry of pain. 'Elara, stop!'

Her eyes fluttered open at the request, and she saw a mass of something silver and hulking bear down upon Enzo. She blinked, and just as fast as it had appeared, it evaporated into the hazy air.

The prince lay panting, as she stood, still against the tree, her hands white-knuckled and balled into fists.

'I warned you,' she said quietly. 'Perhaps next time you'll listen.'

Blood poured from a gash in his arm, and inwardly she reeled. Her nightmares had never been able to touch someone before. Her illusions had always been just that – illusions.

'We're done here,' he hissed. 'My father can throw you back to Ariete for all I care.'

He turned away and strode off back down the hill, without so much as a glance back to see if she'd still follow.

CHAPTER EIGHT

That night, Elara asked to take dinner in her room, giving a tight nod to Leonardo, who seemed to have taken up residency outside her door. If she had been in a different mood, she may have taunted him about his apparent demotion to guard duty, but her hands were still shaking as she twisted the knob and closed the door firmly shut. It was only then, with a door between her and the rest of the world, that she dissolved into desperate sobs.

The light, the memories, the feeling of helplessness, the prince's *words*, it all crashed upon her. She hated him. She had never hated a person more. The pain in her chest was almost cracking her in two when she heard soft, slippered footsteps approach.

Elara looked up, desperately trying to wipe her tears as Merissa stood there, concern plastered over her face.

'Elara,' she breathed. She set down the heavily laden tray of food she was carrying, and then disappeared into the bathroom with quick steps, returning with a clean hand towel that she passed to Elara. The gesture – the small kindness in such an evil fucking kingdom – set off another fresh wave of tears.

A cool hand rested upon her chest. 'Breathe,' Merissa soothed.

Elara tried to, another big, shuddering wail leaving her.

'Once more,' Merissa said.

Elara tried again, this time able to take a full breath. Merissa kept her hand on Elara's heart until her whimpers had subsided.

'My brother used to do that for me when I was little,' she said quietly, her eyes crinkling. 'Better?'

Elara nodded, sniffing.

Merissa opened her mouth, then closed it. Elara watched as she wetted her lips before speaking. 'I know this is hard,' she began hesitantly. 'I know this kingdom isn't one you want to be in. I know that life has taken so much from you in the space of a few days. But remember this. You are a queen. It is in your blood. Try as they might, no one can take that from you.' She lowered her voice. 'Not Prince Lorenzo, or King Idris.' She paused, and Elara waited. 'I-I hope I'm not speaking out of turn. But if . . . if you ever need a friendly face, you're allowed to roam freely through the palace. I'm usually in the kitchen during the day. So if there's anything you need after your training, or if you just want a break from His Highness, you can find me there.'

Elara squeezed Merissa's hand. Perhaps she shouldn't have. Perhaps she should have seen her as an enemy too. But so little kindness had been shown to her, and here Merissa was, offering it on a silver platter.

'Thank you,' she replied hoarsely.

The next day, Elara was woken in the same manner, by Merissa with a tray bursting with treats. This time she'd included some pastries, and Elara made the glamourer share one with her. As she ate, she wondered whether King Idris would do exactly what Enzo wanted and hand her over to Ariete. But to her reluctant relief, she was dressed in clean linens, glamoured and led once more down the great staircase.

This time, Enzo wasn't waiting for her, and Merissa took her towards the throne room. As they reached the doors, she heard shouting beyond them.

'I cannot, Father! Her illusions, her tricks – this magick is beneath me. It's humiliating. Moreover, she is weak – uncontrolled. She tried to kill me, for Stars' sake! I refuse.'

'Refuse?' Idris's voice replied coldly. 'You will do well to remember that I am your king. To disobey my order is to commit treason. You know the punishment for that, don't you?'

There was a pause. 'Yes, Father.'

Merissa tried to usher Elara away, but she shook her head, pressing her ear against the door. 'Her attempt on your life belies *your* weakness, Lorenzo. *That* is the embarrassment. Now get out of my sight. If she tries to kill you again, good. If she succeeds, so be it. It means she has power. The kind of power that might rise against a Star.'

More silence. A resigned sigh.

'Yes, Father.'

She heard footsteps, and hastily walked back over to the bottom of the stairs. Merissa gave her a reassuring look, before disappearing down a corridor. Elara nervously patted the braid Merissa had tied in her hair, strewn with little carnelian gems to match her linens.

When Enzo appeared, he didn't even look at her. 'Come

along,' he said tightly, hitching a brown rucksack upon his
shoulder.

This time there were no forest paths. Instead, they took a
right past the palace gates, and around the back of the east-
ern side of the massive building. A small, dusty side path
wound them away from the palace, up a steep incline. She
found herself needing to drink in deep lungfuls of the clean
air the higher they climbed.

'Can you seriously not find anywhere flat to train?' she
asked him, his tall figure storming paces ahead.

'How about you save that breath for climbing? You're
going to need it,' he retorted.

She raised her hands in exasperation as she continued in
the blistering heat.

As they finally reached even ground, her mouth fell open
in astonishment. All worries and hatred from the day before
vanished in a moment. Because there, stretched before them,
was a plain of sands, deep red and shifting as though a tide
was pulling it. But what had really caught her attention were
the two statues stretching over fifty feet high. Two winged
figures, their hands shielding their eyes, gilded and shimmering. A cooling breeze tickled her hair as it rolled in from the
sea of sand.

'Welcome to the Angel's Graveyard,' Enzo said to her over
his shoulder.

'Cheerful place,' she muttered under her breath.

'Legend says,' he said as he walked up the steps hewn into
warmed brown stone, on to a stone dais, 'that the angels of
Sveta died here in a mighty battle against the winged lions of

Helios. Their leader Celine took the last stand against the mighty Nemeus and was vanquished.'

'They were burned to ash, their blood mingling with the earth, creating the Sea of Sands,' she finished. Enzo finally looked at her, frowning.

'That's from—'

'*The Mythas of Celestia*. Shocking, I know, that Asterians are taught how to read,' she said sardonically.

Enzo scoffed.

'I thought you refused to train me,' she said.

He paced the circle, across stone that Elara now noticed was etched with small, indistinct symbols. 'I do as my father commands. He implored I continue. Apparently he sees something in you that I don't.'

'He has my deepest gratitude,' she replied drily.

Enzo sighed, grudgingly turning to look at her. 'I suppose we had better start. You need to tell me about your magick, so I can gauge what you need to be taught. It's not just a king we are planning to attack, it's a god.'

She slumped on to the hot stone dais, rooting through the pack Enzo had laid down until she found a canteen. She took a drink of water before answering. 'What do you want to know?'

'Well, I know that you possess the Three, and that you can't be killed by a Star.'

She fiddled with the lid of the canteen as she tried not to think about the day that Ariete had tried and failed to kill her.

'So, what are your Three?' he continued. 'I know that one is illusioning. And what was that other one – from yesterday?' Was that real fear his eyes were betraying?

'That's part of illusioning,' she said. 'It's not real. But I've found a way to tap into someone's fears. For my illusion to become their nightmare. I can never see what it is though,' she added, when his jaw set.

'It's not real? But . . .' He paused. 'Yesterday, I felt it. The moment it came into contact with my light, it was as though it became real.' He glanced down to the bandage wrapped around his arm.

'I don't know what that was,' she said, not meeting his eyes. 'That's never happened before.'

He searched her face, as though trying to find the lie with those seer powers of his. A moment later, his professional formality returned. 'We'll revisit it later,' he said, 'and see if it's something that can be honed.'

She fidgeted with her braid. 'The next gift I have is dream-walking. I can visit dreams and nightmares. I can speak to people within them. I can help them, or damn them.'

He stiffened. 'And that's a common Asterian gift?'

She shook her head. 'It's the rarest. Most Asterians are shadowmancers, the rest illusionists. There aren't many dreamwalkers in my kingdom.'

Fire flickered frantically between his hands, but when Elara noticed it, it extinguished.

'The last is shadowmancing then?' he demanded.

Elara tried to swallow, but her mouth was too dry, so she just nodded.

'Then where are your shadows? I've met many a shadow-mancer in my time who has tried to kill my light with their darkness. Where was yours yesterday, when I had you pinned to a tree?'

The cool amusement in his face made her stomach writhe.

She didn't want to say it – she wouldn't say it. But skies, she could feel a magick settling over her, something that probed and pushed. It was invisible, but it felt as foreign as the Light, urging her to be truthful. It wrapped around her, trying to push past the shadows stuck within her, and Elara desperately tried to push her box deeper within the shadows, somewhere that Enzo could never find it, could never know that she was hiding terrible secrets from him. But to her horror, a ray of light shone a gap through the shadows, beaming right over the obsidian chest. His light tried to prize it open, but it remained firmly locked.

'Well, well,' Enzo said. 'It didn't take long for your wall to break down for me.'

Elara stood quickly, pulling out the dagger that until now she had kept hidden on her thigh. 'Get out of my gods-damned head,' she spat.

Enzo looked at the weapon, cruel amusement in his eyes. 'Not until you can be honest. What are you hiding in that little box, Elara?'

'I will gut you where you stand if you don't get your filthy light out of me.' She was heaving breaths, his element so wrong within her. Enzo chuckled, but she slowly felt her shadows wrap around the box inside her again, his light dissipating.

'Something happened to your shadows.'

'I can't wield them, if that's what you are so desperate to know,' she said, voice hardening.

'What do you mean, you *can't*?'

'I mean that I can't conjure a single one,' she snapped.

'Why?'

'I don't know,' she lied.

Enzo's magick crept in tendrils over her once more, trying to coax the truth out of her, trying to scour her soul for the lies upon it. But Elara gritted her teeth, making sure the shadows trapped within her wrapped more tightly around her truths, until he brought his seer magick back to him.

'The shadows are still within you,' he said.

'I know,' she replied.

'So I suppose our work is going to be to release them.'

'And how exactly are you going to do that?'

'I am the most accomplished magi Helios has seen in generations,' he replied calmly.

'Are you the most modest magi too?' she asked, smiling sweetly.

His eyes flattened. 'You're going to have to at least try to work with me.'

She hesitated. She didn't want to help him, or his father. But if he could help her access her shadows again, if she could feel them between her fingertips once more, then perhaps she really could kill Ariete, and reclaim her throne.

'Fine,' she gritted out.

'Believe me,' he added, stretching out his shoulder muscles. 'I'm as happy about this arrangement as you are.'

'Well, that makes me smile.'

He stood. 'Come on then. Let's try and loosen these blocks.' He turned, lifting his shirt up over his head. Elara's breath hitched.

His back was a masterpiece of carved rippling muscle, appearing burnished in the heat. But it was his tattoo that had stopped her. Between his shoulders, a snarling lion in mid-roar was etched in gold, its teeth glinting. Wings stretched out over each of his shoulder blades, drawn in such breathtaking detail, Elara couldn't look away. As he rolled his neck, the taut muscles straining, the lion's wings rippled as though it was about to take flight. It was beautiful. Vicious.

'What are you doing?' she managed to breathe. He turned, mirth playing on his lips.

'Does a little skin make you feel uncomfortable, Princess Elara?' His torso gleamed with sweat in the unforgiving brightness, shining on the hard muscles carved into his stomach, and deep lines that disappeared into his loose-fitting trousers. He stretched his arms out, and she averted her eyes.

'I just didn't think a prince would need to flex his glamour muscles for an ego boost. Nice tattoo by the way, *Lion of Helios*. Subtle.'

He smirked as he paced, infuriating her more. 'Where do you think people got the nickname?'

For once, she didn't have a reply ready and cursed herself, her traitorous eyes drawn back to those muscles.

He drew his sword, tossing her another from his belt.

She caught it, looking to it warily. 'I don't fight with swords.'

'Then today you'll learn. You're too in your mind. You need to be in your body. As a boy, it was when I would reach the point of mental exhaustion that my light would pour out of me. Right now you don't need to worry about control. Only release. We'll start there.'

He raised his sword, and Elara copied the motion, the weapon too heavy in her hand. Elara had been taught combat growing up, but always with a dagger or knives. Cunning and illusions were what had helped her during her training in Asteria.

'No magick,' he warned. 'Only weapons.'

Enzo struck, and Elara's sword immediately flew from her hand.

In another clean move, Enzo had Elara on her back, the point of his sword pressed to her neck.

She wheezed, the wind knocked out of her. 'Up,' he said.

She hauled herself to her feet, and picked her sword up once again.

'Change your stance,' he said. 'Put more weight on your back foot, so that it can anchor you when defending, or propel you when you attack.'

She blew a strand of hair out of her face, obliging. This time, when Enzo struck, she gritted her teeth, keeping her sword up. She felt the impact jar through her entire hand and shoulder, and cursed, but it held. Until Enzo struck again, and she was disarmed once more.

'Again,' he said.

Strike, parry, disarm.

Strike, parry, disarm.

Again, and again, Enzo moved, until her shoulder ached and her breath heaved from bending to pick her sword up every minute.

Something in her began to fray every time Enzo laughed as he beat her, as he mocked her. This was meant to be hand-to-hand combat. But the thread on Elara's temper grew too thin, and she was tired of following the rules he had set. There was a shimmer as she weaved an illusion, a serpent slithering across the ground, its scales shining emerald in the Light.

Enzo saw it and stumbled to the left, out of its way. Right into Elara's trap. She had dashed behind him, and now kicked his legs out while he tried to right himself.

Enzo grunted as he was knocked to the ground, sand billowing up in clouds. His sword fell, and Elara kicked it out of his grasp as she pounced upon him, thighs locked around his waist as her sword grazed his neck. She could do it. In one swipe, she could slit his throat.

Enzo's eyes flashed.

'Do it then,' he hissed, pushing his neck closer against the blade. A bead of blood formed, and she gritted her teeth, willing herself to end him.

But Enzo's furious gaze didn't once show fear, he didn't once plead or beg, or back down. Those eyes just continued to simmer. She shifted upon him, her mouth drying, her plait grazing his bare stomach. And maybe it was the stubbornness he displayed that convinced Elara he truly could help her. Or his stupid courage, which had him staring death in the face with utter wrath. Either way, her hand trembled with adrenaline as she lowered her weapon and lightly jumped off him.

She chuckled quietly to herself, the euphoria of triumph coursing through her veins. Then there was a loud pop, and she turned to see him back on his feet again, flames sparking from his hands, a look of thunder on his face.

'You illusioned.'

She shrugged. 'It doesn't matter what I did. I had the Lion of Helios's throat under my blade.'

'It was fucking darkcraft.'

She expertly twirled the dagger in her hand, before sheathing it, raising the sword in her other hand.

'Ah,' she exclaimed theatrically, 'but the question is, who was at whose mercy?'

'There would have been no honour in that kill,' he seethed. 'You tricked me.'

'And you're so honourable are you, *Lion*?'

His face shifted, and she saw the familiar arrogance place a veneer over his fury. 'Oh, honourable is about the last thing a woman would call me.'

Elara ignored his attempt to rile her up.

Instead, she slumped to the ground, taking a long swig of water. 'Your plan didn't work. I'm exhausted, mentally *and* physically, yet not a wisp of shadow has appeared.'

'I know,' he said shortly, sitting down next to her. 'And my magick isn't helping. I can't get far enough past your shadows to see what might unblock them.'

He looked at Elara hopefully, but she stayed mute.

He let out a frustrated sigh. 'I'm going to have to take you to Isra.'

'Who is Isra?'

'A friend. And one you sorely need if we're to stand a chance of honing your gifts into any kind of fighting shape.' He stood, and so did Elara.

'Really? I thought I was doing so well,' Elara replied drily.

He gave her an irritated look as he reached for his shirt. 'Tonight, practise your illusions,' he ordered. 'See if there's a way to deliberately bring weight to them – like you did in the forest yesterday, but deliberately. And dreamwalk tonight. I don't care where, but it's important you keep training the two magicks you *can* use, until we figure out a way to access your shadows. Which we will, though no thanks to you.'

'You make it sound so easy.'

'Do you think it was easy for me to become who I am today? It was never easy. I just never gave up.'

She studied him for a moment, a familiar anger settling in her bones.

'Yes, you don't give up. Even when innocent Asterians are begging you to,' she said. 'I've heard many stories about how you became who you are today. And now I know you, I think I believe every single one.'

Enzo rose, a dry, hollow laugh echoing from him as he stepped towards her.

'And what exactly is it that you've heard, princess?' he murmured. He made his way closer. 'That I'm an incredible lover?' He stretched one arm with the other. She ignored the ripple of his biceps. 'That I'm a feared warrior?'

'That you're dangerous and merciless. We were warned about you. The Lion of Helios, who razes anything to the ground which stands in his way.'

'Aren't you afraid?' He was inches from her now, his towering figure blocking the Light above. He brought his hand to a strand of hair blown across her face by the hot, arid wind. Her eyes flashed, and she raised her chin.

'I fear nothing.'

'Lying fool,' he replied. 'Everybody is scared of something.' He reached out, grasping the errant strand of hair as he wound it around a finger.

She jolted at his touch, her shadows rearing within her. 'Perhaps,' she got out. 'But you certainly don't scare me.'

'Oh really?' he asked softly, and tucked the hair behind her ear, grazing her neck. 'Because your pulse tells me otherwise.'

He pulled away, a smug smile on his face as he strolled across the flat sands, back towards the path they'd climbed. She took a deep gulp of air before snatching up her flask. Swearing under her breath, she made her way down the winding sand path, wishing fervently she'd just driven the damn blade through his neck.

CHAPTER NINE

When she arrived back at the palace, light-soaked and dust-drenched, she didn't go to her rooms, but instead sought out the kitchens. As she walked, she twirled the wildflowers she'd picked on her descent from the Angel's Graveyard. Forget-me-nots, Elara's favourite flower, starred through the bunch, along with apolliums, a stunning golden bloom, a little lavender and some godslily – said to have begun growing when the Stars first walked the earth.

She followed the smell of food, the bustling activity of maids who looked at her a little strangely, but not too much – after all, Merissa's glamour was doing its job – and finally found the kitchen door, which swung open as more servants poured out with trays and trolleys of food.

She slipped in, searching past the marbled countertops, the stoves with sauces simmering and bubbling upon them, the racks of herbs, until she found a blonde figure in the corner, and approached.

'Merissa?'

Merissa turned, flour dusted on her nose. 'Elara!'

'Sorry to disturb you, I didn't realize it would be so busy—'

'Nonsense, this is just for the king's afternoon tea. In five minutes, quiet will ensue once more.'

'I just, I wanted to thank you for last night.' She pushed the flowers forwards. 'For you to show me kindness . . . it meant a lot.'

Even covered in flour and pink-cheeked, Merissa dazzled, her smile radiant. 'Oh, Elara, they're lovely. You didn't have to.'

'I wanted to,' she said.

True to Merissa's word, the kitchen had begun to quiet as it emptied, now that serving time had arrived.

'I'm going for my break, Merissa!' someone shouted.

'No problem, Mauricio!' Merissa replied. 'Here,' she said to Elara, 'sit down. I have some cakes just about ready, and you can try them for me. See if they're any good for His Majesty.'

Elara did, allowing the warmth and smells of the kitchen to soothe her. 'So,' Merissa said. 'Did your training go any better today?'

Elara cricked her neck. 'Well, I disarmed the prince and had my sword to his throat, so I'd say better.'

Merissa tried to master her shock. 'Stars,' she whispered. 'Don't say that too loudly.'

Elara sighed. 'I'm having problems with my shadows though, and maybe he can help, but most of the time he's acting so superior I can barely stand to be around him.'

'Try to trust him,' Merissa replied, as she pulled some small sponge cakes from the oven, releasing a gorgeous scent of blueberry and lemon. 'I know,' she said, when she saw Elara's look. 'But . . . if there is one thing I've come to know about the prince, it's that he always keeps his word.'

She began to whip up cream and vanilla essence into a bowl. 'If he has promised his father that he will help you, and if he has promised *you* that he will find a way to aid your shadow-work, then believe him.'

Elara tried to find the lie on Merissa's face, any tell-tale that the glamourer was being dishonest as she began to decorate the cakes. But she found nothing.

'I'll try,' she sighed. 'I suppose it's in my best interest to.' She stood, and winced. 'I'd better go and practise. But skies, I'm sore.'

Merissa finished icing the cakes, and handed one to Elara. 'Eat that, and follow me.'

The bath house that Merissa led Elara to was a piece of art just like everything in Helios. Palm trees arched over the door that they walked through. Elara stepped on to mosaicked tiles and passed into a sheltered, rock-hewn room. Flamed sconces lined the dim space, and the only sounds were the quiet crackle of the torches and the gentle lap of water.

'These are the palace baths,' Merissa explained. 'We have saunas, cold plunge pools and heated pools, ones infused with oils and minerals. It's exactly where you need to be after training.'

As Elara ventured further into the baths, she saw the saunas, little open wooden nooks functioning with the fire magick that the Helions were known for. They let off fumes of eucalyptus wood, clearing her tangled thoughts.

Cabinets were filled with potions, dried flowers and oils of every kind, mingling and permeating the air with fragrance. Pillars descended into the depths of the water, and she gasped as she finally reached the main, vast pool. Petals and flowers in a range of colours from bright yellow to lightdown orange floated on the cerulean water like an offering. Other smaller pools led off it, and lanterns drifted through the air.

The ceiling of the bathing house was painted a deep indigo – the first time she had seen the hue in Helios. Constellations were painted in minute detail – Leyon's lion, Verra's maiden, even Piscea's coffin.

Merissa squeezed her hand. 'I'll leave you to relax. It's usually quiet at this time of day.'

'Thank you for showing me this place.'

Merissa beamed, before leaving her alone.

With an indulgent sigh, Elara shrugged off her sand-ridden clothes, gritty against her grimy skin, and descended the steps into the water. She tugged at her plait, undoing the knotted strands until her hair fell loose. She groaned as her screaming muscles felt the lap of warm water and waded out until her feet could no longer touch the bottom. Then she began to swim, stretching out all the aches in her arms and legs. She flipped on to her back, allowing herself to float as she looked at the painted sky above her.

The stars looked back, and so she closed her eyes, the water soothing her as it always did. The last time she'd floated like this had been in the Still Sea, on the eve before her birthday.

The water had been like glass, reflecting the entire sky of stars. Elara had slunk out of the palace with Sofia in tow and a cloak of illusions firmly in place. Sofia had been laughing with her as they took a dip and planned her birthday. They were going to venture further than they'd ever gone: to the travelling fair that had arrived in Asteria on the other side of the city of Phantome.

'I want to eat pumpkin cake and marshmallow cream until I'm sick,' Elara had giggled. 'I hope they have the acrobats from Sveta. I want to see how they fly! And ooh, do you think the strongman from Perses will come? I've heard he can lift an entire snowhorse with one hand.'

'Perhaps,' Sofia had replied, with her usual unruffled calm. 'They say there are those from all walks of life at the fair. And we can't miss it — not when it's the only time of year that anyone visits Asteria.'

It always upset Elara, how many were deprived of the chance to experience the umbral allure of her kingdom. How they all believed the lies that King Idris spun.

'You know what I think we should get?' Sofia added, before gamely

springing on to her hands in the shallows. Her legs waggled in the air yet she still somehow looked elegant all the while. 'Our palms read.'

Elara frowned. 'I'm not going anywhere near a Helion seer,' she said angrily.

'No, not a Helion,' Sofia had said, mollifying her. 'The last time I went, there was a Concordian priestess there who did love readings.'

Elara tutted. 'What do I need to know about love? I'm betrothed to Lukas.'

Sofia had gone sullen at the mention of him, her easy smile diminishing, which made Elara's chest tighten. 'You don't want to know what your future has in store?' Sofia had said. 'There's a whole world out there, Lara.'

Elara had floated further out, looking up at the stars. 'Maybe,' she said quietly. 'Maybe I do want to see what's beyond Asteria.'

Elara dunked her head under the water, trying to rid herself of the memories. But when they wouldn't go – when the thoughts of Sofia, Lukas and her parents threatened to drag her under the surface – she gave up, leaving the pool, and her memories with it.

As she lounged on her balcony in the warm night air, Elara attempted to shadowmance. The hour was late, candles flickering from the windows, the Light transitioning from a deep orange to a burgundy red.

She willed herself to focus, breathing deeply in as she plunged into her shadow power, trying desperately to drag it out of her. She saw it within her, the black wraiths twisting and turning, cool as they brushed her insides. She could feel them travel along her arms, but the moment they reached her fingertips, and she tried to will them out of her, there was that flash of torturous light in her mind, and then . . . nothing.

She had tried everything over the years with her tutors – meditation, night bathing, breathwork. Tough love – threatening and cursing her shadows. She'd tried using muscle memory to work her hands as though shadows really drifted from them, to jolt her body into action. She'd practised with Lukas, and Sofia – both talented shadowmancers. And both of them had eventually given up, sighing in frustration.

She looked at her hands in exasperation, still outstretched. 'Just fucking *do* something!' she shouted.

She jumped as she heard voices in the gardens below her.

Leonardo was laughing as he swaggered on to the lawn, Enzo loping after him. Gods, they were so tall, Enzo perhaps an inch taller than the general. Both built of hard, toned muscle. They were half-naked, swords in hand, and Elara had to roll her eyes, even as her cheeks heated. Did anyone in this realm ever wear a shirt?

There was a clang of steel on steel as the men engaged in combat. Elara had never seen fighting like it – and she could grudgingly admit that it looked far more sophisticated than anything she had done with Enzo that day. Both men were a blur of muscle and metal, attacking and then defending. Feinting, jabbing, stealth gracing every move. But the more she watched, the clearer it was who had the upper hand. There was a muffled command, and then she gasped as light and flame erupted. Enzo wielded his flames as Leo channelled his light. It began to warp and twist, crackling until lightning wreathed Leo's hands. *The King's Thunderbolt.* Elara suddenly understood why the general had been given the title. She should have flinched at Leo's magick, but her attention kept being pulled towards Enzo, who was forming his own magick into a shield, pushing Leo back across the lawn.

Sweat glistened off them as they fought, grunts and yells resounding as they danced quick-footed around the garden. Light flew as Leo channelled it into his sword, but Enzo was too quick. He had deflected before Elara had even blinked. The power, the precision with which Enzo fought, whether he made use of his powers or not, was mesmerizing. The light could be defeated. Enzo was showing her how, with his own flames. Leo faded into the background as her entire attention zoned in on him. She reached over the balcony to see closer. As Enzo ruthlessly advanced, barely out of breath, she saw him smile that lion's grin. And with brutal efficiency, he struck out a line of fire.

Elara gasped out loud, the roar of fire and clash of swords muffling the noise easily. Her heart beat furiously as she saw Leonardo, struck to the ground. The way the light dimmed, the way Enzo had complete dominance over the element.

Trust him, Merissa had said.

Leonardo laughed, Enzo grinning as he raised a hand to pull him up. She blinked. Enzo's fire hadn't even singed the general's clothes.

Complete, lethal control.

And Elara understood in that moment, that she should listen to Merissa. She should try to trust Enzo. At least, in helping her to master her magick.

The two men clapped each other's backs, sweat streaming down their bodies. She saw a nod from Leo, a wry grin, and a bow of defeat. Then he exited the grounds, leaving Enzo on the lawn.

The bleeding sky framed the prince, and Elara could have sworn the very Light was contained within his skin, the way it shone. Without any eyes to watch her, she let herself take her fill.

He truly was devastating. She loathed to admit it. His

muscles were like carved marble, viciously toned to deliver death swiftly. His back rippled as his figure turned away from her, the lion embellished on his skin glowing. His curls were tousled as he raked them back, chugging from the water canteen beside him. One curl fell forwards into his eyes, and if she was an artist, she'd have tried to capture the way he looked against the lightdown – despite how much she hated him, despite how much he drove her mad.

He stilled, bringing the canteen from his lips. Then with a predatory slowness, he turned in her direction.

Elara shot down below the edge of her balcony, crouching. *Shit, shit, shit.* He couldn't have seen her. There was no way. She didn't move, until a lone ray of light shone through the bars of the balcony.

Her breath quickened as it moved from left to right, as though searching.

She watched that small chink, her hand shaking as she reached out towards it. She didn't know why – didn't understand the pull she felt. But with the tip of her finger, she touched the ray. It stilled, and warmed her skin with a feathery tingling sensation. She breathed through her terror, forcing her finger to stay for a few more moments. It dimmed, disappearing, and she held her breath, staying tightly crouched; she didn't know how long for. Only that the sky darkened further, and cramp found its way into her leg.

Her finger smarted, and she rubbed it as she debated whether to crawl to the doors of her room. Cursing herself, instead she slowly straightened, seeing to her relief that the lawn was empty. As she left the balcony, there was a movement. To anyone else, it could have been a flicker from the lamplight that drenched the terrace. But Elara knew better. There, right where the light had been, the tiniest wisp of shadow floated through the air.

CHAPTER TEN

Elara dreamwalked again that night. As she began to fall asleep, she held herself in limbo, the crucial moment between sleeping and waking, and secured her tether to the waking world. A dreamwalker's tether was their most important item. She always visualized it as a cord, growing from just below her navel, flowing into the ground and anchoring her to the earth.

Her tutors had told her horror stories growing up, of dreamwalkers who had become untethered, their soul lost to the Dreamlands – or, even worse, the Deadlands right beside them – if they had wandered too far, their body cursed to remain in the waking world, sleeping, until it withered and died.

Confident that her tether was secure, seeing the shining, midnight blue rope with its familiar silver patterning, she rose. It always felt a little like falling upwards, her stomach shooting up as her dream-body became weightless.

She looked at the differently coloured and perfumed clouds around her. Each one belonged to a dreamer, and she flitted between them.

There was one that smelled like light-baked earth and sandalwood, another that smelled like amber. A few others smelled sweeter, more inviting. But tonight, she was drawn more to the darkness than ever.

She settled on the deep golden cloud that smelled of sandalwood, and drifted through the perfumed mist and into the dream.

A young boy with shorn hair and torn clothes was climbing up a dew-rose trellis to a balcony in the Palace of Light, a knife between his teeth.

He couldn't have been older than ten, and yet the way he scaled the balcony with agility and precision made him seem far more mature.

She followed, the surroundings morphing into a grand bedroom, gauze curtains fluttering. The little boy stole through them, taking the knife from his mouth and creeping towards a sleeping figure in the bed.

Elara's pulse pounded as she watched the boy press his knife to the sleeping figure's neck.

'Give me all the gold you have,' he demanded.

And when the other boy opened his eyes, she gasped.

To her surprise, the little Enzo in the bed did not scream. He laughed, emptily. A laugh too jaded for someone so young. And a blast of light burst from him.

The boy with the knife cried out as he flew backwards, crashing into Enzo's armoire.

Enzo leapt up, no weapon but his hands as flame flared in one, another ray of light in the other.

'Who sent you?' he hissed, as the boy flared up his own light – this one crackling and writhing. When Enzo launched a fireball at the boy, lightning writhed, deflecting it, and Enzo's eyes widened. The boy gave a grunt of pain, throwing a fork of it at Enzo, and it sizzled against his arm as it passed.

'Give me your money before I kill you, prince,' the little boy snapped.

'You think I'm scared of a street rat?' Enzo mocked, and this time his powers extinguished as he launched himself at the boy. He pummelled him, so angry, so ruthless with his movements. But the boy held up, going against him blow for blow.

When one of the boy's punches made contact with Enzo's nose, the prince stumbled, and his eyes flared with light.

The boy scrambled back. 'What are you doing?' he stuttered, as something Elara couldn't see began to happen between the two.

'I'm *seeing* who you are,' Enzo snapped. 'Leonardo Acardi. From the Apollo Row slums. Poor. Destitute. And wants my money to—'

'Stop!' the boy shouted.

'To pay for a healer for his dying mother.'

The light extinguished, casting the two boys into darkness.

Leonardo sat panting, wiping blood from his mouth, as Enzo held his nose.

'She . . . she got a fever, a few weeks ago. I thought it would break but it's only getting worse. And as "street rats from Apollo's Row", we can't afford a healer.'

Enzo looked at him, and Elara guessed he was using his gift again, to see if the boy was lying or not.

'Can your mother work, when she's better?' Enzo finally asked.

Leo frowned, before nodding. 'She's the best gardener I know.'

'Bring her to the palace.'

'She didn't ask me to do this,' Leonardo stammered, all bravado gone. 'This is nothing to do with her. If you're going to punish anyone, punish me alone.'

74

Enzo cocked his head. 'You're the only boy I've met that can come close to matching me in a fight. All these lords' sons are prissy wimps.' He held a hand out, and Leonardo took it hesitantly, before Enzo pulled him up. 'Your mother can take board here. We have the best healers in Helios. And you can make yourself useful by training with me.'

Tears filled Leonardo's eyes. 'Are you – thank you. Thank you, Your Highn—'

'Don't cry,' Enzo snapped. 'Don't let anyone see you cry, least of all me.'

'I'm sorry—'

'Don't apologize either.'

Leonardo stood up straighter, sniffing as he nodded. 'Thank you,' he said.

'Go back home now and bring her by morning. I'll speak to my father.'

Leonardo nodded, bowing before hurrying back to the balcony.

'And it goes without saying,' Enzo called after him. 'Don't mention to anyone you had a knife to my throat. Unless you want to burn for treason.'

Leonardo's face blanched a little, before he nodded once more. 'Thank you, prince,' he said hoarsely as he swung a leg around the balcony.

The prince's lips quirked. 'Call me Enzo.'

A streak of magick shot past Elara out of nowhere and she cursed, ducking to avoid it. The dream had changed around her – now instead of the palace gates, she stood in a forest filled with dappled light. When she turned, Leonardo stood, no longer a boy but fully grown, lightning writhing between his hands. It crackled, and she stumbled back. But when he recognized her, the lightning vanished.

'Elara?'

'This is your dreamscape,' she said hoarsely.

He frowned at the word. 'I'm dreaming?'

'Yes,' she said hurriedly. 'Yes, you are. I'm sorry, I didn't know this was your dream, I should go.'

'You saw it?' he asked. His brow was furrowed, eyes pleading – strangely vulnerable for a general.

She nodded. 'I didn't realize you grew up in the palace with Enzo.'

Leonardo sighed. 'If it wasn't for him, I'd likely be dead. I owe him my life. And so much more.'

She didn't know what to say, so she said nothing at all.

Turning, suddenly anxious, she tried to feel for her tether. She shouldn't be here, especially in the dreams of a man who had helped Enzo and his father with their raids of the Asterian–Helion border, and had carried out attacks like the Borderland Fires. She shouldn't be anywhere near him.

Leonardo walked closer, but there was something softer about him in the dream. As though the mask he wore as a battle-weary general had slipped a fraction.

'Please don't tell anyone what you saw,' he said quietly.

Elara frowned. 'I wouldn't. But why?'

'It took me blood, sweat and tears to become the general of the Helion army. To captain the King's Guard here. If they found out I tried to kill the prince of Helios . . . I'd be put to death. Whether Enzo came to my defence or not.'

'I won't breathe a word,' Elara said. And she meant it. She didn't like the man, but some kind of honour lay within him. An honour that contradicted all she knew of him, and for that, she would keep his secret.

Leonardo's face softened. 'Thank you, Elara. You may be the enemy of the kingdom I swore to protect. But I see that what you are doing is to help us. The Stars have ruled above us with their arrogance and cruelty for too long.'

76

'I think you overestimate my magick greatly.'

He shook his head. 'I have an eye for these things. As a general I have to. And what you are doing helps Enzo. Which is all that is important to me.'

'I'll never see the goodness in him that you seem to,' she said tightly.

'Perhaps not,' Leonardo said. 'But I know that for the people he loves, Enzo would set the world on fire, if we asked.'

Elara finally grasped her tether. 'I have to go,' she said. She latched on to the midnight-blue rope, and in a swirl of magick, the forest disappeared as she dreamwalked back to the waking world.

CHAPTER ELEVEN

The next morning, Elara felt like she'd barely slept after her night walking through Leonardo's dreams. When a smart rap came on her door, she pulled herself blindly out of bed to open it, wishing Merissa would just let herself in.

To her surprise, it was Leonardo who stood there in his general's armour. It shone golden, the D'Oro crest upon the breastplate.

'Your Majesty,' he said.

She stilled at the title. His lips quirked a fraction. 'I'll escort you today.'

'Oh, you really don't have to. If this is about last night, I promise I won't—'

'It is,' he interrupted. 'But I wanted to thank you.'

He produced a paper bag, and gave it to Elara. 'I brought you breakfast.'

She looked into the bag. Two round peaches were nestled in there.

'They're from the palace gardens. My mother grows them.'

Elara took one out and inhaled the sweet scent.

'They're not poisoned,' he said, the small boyish smile she recognized from the dream bursting through his serious demeanour. 'Here.'

He took the other one and bit into it. Elara did the same with her own peach.

'Mmm!' she exclaimed. It may have been the best peach she'd ever tasted, bursting with juicy sweetness as though honey had been drizzled through it.

'I'll wait until you're dressed to take you to Enzo. You're going to see Isra today.'

'The infamous Isra,' Elara said. 'Who *is* she?'

'You'll find out soon enough.'

Elara went to ask more, but Merissa appeared holding a tray with pastries and pear juice upon it. Her eyes widened as she looked between Leonardo and Elara in the doorway. 'G-General Acardi,' she stuttered. 'I wasn't expecting you.'

'You know what to call me, Merissa.' His grin displayed dazzling teeth, and Elara couldn't help but smirk as Merissa's cheeks grew pink.

'What brings you here, Leo?' she asked, her eyes on the ground.

'I'm escorting Elara to his Highness today.'

Merissa raised her brows. 'Right, well we'd better get you dressed then,' she muttered, pushing herself into the room.

'Be right back, General Acardi,' Elara said with a mocking bow, and pushed the door to as she heard Leonardo snicker.

Merissa dressed her in fresh linens, picking out a skirt with a slit up the leg for movement and a matching cropped blouse. She carefully pinned Elara's hair off her face with a few pearl clips while she glamoured her. Then, with a levelling sigh, Elara returned to Leonardo at the door, following him out towards another day of misery.

She found Enzo waiting by the palace gate, leaning with his arms crossed against the warm stone. His blue sleeveless tunic and trousers accentuated his eyes, which tightened when he saw Leonardo escorting her. He pressed his lips together as the general nodded at Enzo. 'See you for training later?' Leonardo asked.

'Don't worry,' smirked Enzo, 'even after a day of combat, I'll thrash you just like I did last night.'

Leonardo laughed. 'I was going easy on you.'

'We'll see,' Enzo crooned.

'Elara.' The general bowed, and Elara inclined her head, turning to watch him walk away.

'What is that?' Enzo said roughly from behind her.

She twisted her head, registering that his eyes were burning into her nearly bare back. She had Merissa to thank for the blouse she'd donned, just a thin tie across her back leaving her feeling cool and comfortable.

'What? You think you're the only royal with your sigil upon your skin?' She smirked, sweeping her hair around her shoulder.

'And why is that mythas the Bellereves' sigil?'

She swallowed the lump in her throat. She was the only Bellereve left now.

'Because the dragun keeps to itself. It may be shunned by the other mythas. But when called, it will raze a battlefield. With no mercy, and no regret.'

Enzo snorted. 'And I suppose you believe you share similarities with the dragun?'

Elara tilted her head. 'I *am* the dragun.' Then she raised a brow. 'Are you done gawping?'

The mocking smile had slid off Enzo's face. 'We're still training after we visit Isra. How are you going to learn to fight if you can't even dress appropriately?'

Elara smoothed her hands up her skirt. 'Oh this?' she asked. The fabric bunched around her thigh as she slipped her dagger from its place there. She cocked it towards him. 'Why can't I look pretty as I stab you?'

'Put that away,' Enzo hissed, but Elara didn't miss the way his eyes burned into the bare flesh of her thigh, before she re-sheathed her knife and dropped the hem. 'Your skirts are impractical.'

She smiled. 'Lest you forget, I am a queen. Which means I'll be wearing gowns a lot. So I should practise fighting in one.'

'And those ridiculous flowers and jewels you always have strewn through your hair? What's your excuse for those?'

Elara's smile widened. 'You know, there's no harm in enjoying beautiful things.'

'That's true,' he said, and the dangerous lilt to his voice set Elara's nerves alight. When she stole a glance, his furrowed brow had cleared, an arrogant smile playing on his lips. 'You can attest to that last night, can't you? Did you enjoy drooling over my *glamour muscles*, princess?'

It was as though a bucket of ice had been dropped over Elara's head. 'I don't know what you're talking about.'

'Ah,' he said as they walked. 'So you weren't watching Leo and I fight?'

'Oh no, I was,' she said coolly. 'There was just no drooling involved. Unless you count me looking at *Leo's* rippling pectorals.'

Enzo's arrogance vanished as he scowled, and Elara swanned ahead.

His hand gripped her wrist and she whirled, the warmth of his touch stirring the shadows within her.

'You're to stay by me. Keep close and do as I say.'

Elara rolled her eyes. 'As much as I love the idea of following your every order, can you at least deign to tell me why?'

'Because although Merissa's glamour holds, we do not know who could be lurking. One of Ariete's spies, or someone poor enough to want to kill an Asterian heir for him, should they see through your glamour.'

'Who can?' she asked.

'Only a handful of seers – Isra included. Though most seers' gifts lie with prophecies. We should be fine.' He handed her a cloak from his satchel. 'But just in case, put this on.' Enzo settled his own over his shoulders, pulling up the hood, and once she had donned hers, Elara followed his lead.

The path narrowed as Elara was plunged into the centre of Sol.

A horse and cart zoomed by, nearly mowing her down, before Enzo plucked her back. Her shadows swirled inside her stomach. 'See?' He looked both ways before pulling her into a warren of cobbled streets. 'I love Sol, but it's mayhem. Watch out!'

Elara yelped as a man heaving a tray of oranges shouldered past.

They turned a corner and bright carnelian orange and saffron yellow flooded her vision, rows of market stalls lining the way ahead. Street hawkers noisily sold their wares, shoving hands in her face, tempting her to come to their storefront.

Exotic aromas washed over her as she walked past barrels spilling with spices. Frying onions and paprika, then the scent of fresh mint, rosemary and the enticing smell of baking bread. Her stomach growled, and she slowed.

With a sigh, Enzo followed her to the stall she'd halted at.

'What do you want?' he asked.

She peered at some delicious-looking herbed bread, with some cured meat upon it.

Enzo spoke to the woman, slipping her some coins, and handed Elara a square of it.

'Thank you.' Elara smiled to him, surprised.

'If I knew that to get you to be agreeable all I had to do was buy you food, I would force-feed you all day.'

She chuckled against her will as she bit into the still-warm bread. It melted on her tongue, and she sighed as they walked, the salt dancing on her taste buds.

'This place is like nowhere I've seen in Asteria,' she said, as they passed a shop filled with blown glass in every colour of the Light.

'Do you not have bazaars?'

'We have markets, but nothing like this, no.'

They turned a corner, and the bazaar stretched on, stalls overflowing with jewels and silks.

'So what's Isra going to do?' she asked, as they passed a stall of flowers. She absent-mindedly brushed a bunch of forget-me-nots.

'She's an oracle. She should be able to read exactly why you can't access your shadows. Once we release them, the rest will be easy.'

Elara froze.

'Get your silk!' yelled a voice from nearby. 'Finest silk in Celestia! Cerulean, magenta. You, pretty lady! Come and try my wares.'

'Not interested,' Enzo said flatly, walking onwards. He almost vanished into the crowd ahead until he glanced back and realized she'd stopped in her tracks.

'Past, present and future readings for five argents a pop!' yelled another voice. 'Come to Madame Artemis's now!'

Enzo strode back to her, frowning. 'What are you doing?'

'No,' she said quietly.

Enzo looked exasperated. 'What do you mean, no?'

'I mean, no. I am not going to have a stranger look within me. And I'm sure as shit not going to have another prophecy told. *No.*'

'Elara,' he snapped, moving in front of her as a man carrying a sizzling plate of meat ran by. 'Each day is another day Ariete gets closer to finding you. Each day is another day you are not sat upon your throne. And each day is another day the Stars continue to rule above us. You are our only weapon. And you need to be ready for Ariete.'

'Can you just stop?' she cried in exasperation. 'I am sick of hearing it. I know that I am a weapon. I know that Ariete cannot kill me.' She squeezed her eyes shut.

'I won't come,' she said. 'You'll have to drag me kicking and screaming.'

Enzo folded his arms. 'Challenge accepted.'

In one fell swoop, Elara had been lifted in the air, and thrown over Enzo's back. She screamed, wrestling against him, but the man was made out of fucking marble. He didn't so much as flinch when she tried to bite him.

'For a princess, you sure do behave like a wild animal.'

She clawed at his back in response, and he only hitched her up. She shrieked as she lurched, her hair swinging as the ground bobbed closer to her. She finally went limp, seeing that her efforts were utterly in vain, and instead contented herself with plotting all the ways she would hurt him when he put her down.

The sky was buttered yellow as the Light began its climb to its midday peak. The deeper they entered the city on the dusty streets, the more gold and white adorned every building in sight. They seemed to glow from within the same way that Enzo did, the smooth cool stone rendered with elaborate mosaics. The grander buildings that they passed—museums, fountains and other monuments – were all carved with detailed figures. Some were the Patron Star of the land, Leyon, his tall, burnished figure wearing the pelt of a winged lion. Others were beautiful women, saints and martyrs, mythical creatures. Even in Asteria, a land known for its dark beauty, they didn't possess this kind of art.

Though, in all fairness, Elara was viewing it all upside down.

She cursed again, drumming her fists on Enzo's back, but he only laughed.

'Sweet, really, your attempt to hurt me.'

'What's wrong with her?' a passer-by asked, nodding as she walked past.

'Escaped one of the Kaosian madhouses,' Enzo said, shaking his head. 'I'm taking her back now.'

Elara cursed him, and Enzo only chuckled as he continued to weave her through the streets.

They reached the end of the bazaar, the streets widening again, the scent of spices and herbs in the air shifting to blooming summer flowers and hot stone. She breathed in the dry air, trying to banish her unease.

Enzo finally halted them before a cobalt blue door with an eye carved in its centre, in azure, white and black. It stared back at Elara, and she fought off a shiver. A small boy with tight curls was throwing a ball against the wall beside it, and she saw Enzo nod.

'Hello, Rico,' he said to the boy. 'She in?'

The boy gave a gappy smile and nodded. 'Hello, prince,' he said, and frowned at Elara. 'Who's she?'

Enzo plonked Elara unceremoniously on the ground. She bit back a foul word as she dusted herself down.

'Oh, this one? She's trouble, is what she is.'

Rico giggled, as Elara rolled her eyes.

'Password the same as last time?' he asked the boy.

Rico nodded again, and Enzo walked towards the eye at the door. 'Three of Swords,' he said.

The eye blinked, much to Elara's horror, before the blue door swung open.

An empty, dark corridor greeted her, leading deeper into the building. Enzo pulled her through.

The moment her eyes adjusted to the dim space, she was hit with the cloying smell of incense. It wafted heavily around her, sultry and smelling of magick. They followed the thin corridor into a faintly lit room, the candlelight filtering purple into the shadowy space. A figure sat cross-legged in a chair, face turned down as she studied a splay of cards in front of her. Elara peered over Enzo's shoulder at the cards. She recognized them as the infamous Stella deck – a group of cards with depictions of the Stars, their weapons, their kingdoms. It could be used for playing games like Bard, or even to try and scry. But what it was most known for, was for summoning a Star, if blood was spilled upon the relevant card.

Elara's stomach lurched sharply, and she willed her attention to anything else. She could hear the sound of a pot bubbling, and it was only when it began to whistle that the mysterious woman looked up.

'Hi, Iz.' Enzo kissed the woman's cheek. An easy smile came to his face, and Elara's lip curled in disdain. He turned his charm on so easily with others.

'Hello, darling,' Isra replied.

The woman's accent was more clipped and guttural than Enzo's lyrical voice. Her hair was knotted in war braids, a Svetan style of intricate patterns swirling around her scalp, the black braids falling well past her waist, crystals of topaz and tourmaline threaded through them. The seer still hadn't bothered to look at Elara yet, and she felt her royal indignation begin to rise. Just as she was about to step in front of Enzo and introduce herself, Isra's gaze flicked to her, holding her still. Her eyes were a captivating hazel, lighter than most Helions', against her rich brown skin. She was stunning.

'I've been expecting you,' she said to Elara. Elara moved forwards warily.

'Isra, this is Elara. The girl I want you to help.' A charged look passed between them. Elara caught it, raising an eyebrow.

'Girl? You mean queen.'

Warmth suffused her hazel eyes, now a swirl of greens and browns like a summer field. 'Enzo never had many manners. I had to drill them into him.'

A sound of amusement emerged from Elara against her will. 'He certainly hasn't shown me many.'

Isra tutted, pushing her cards away into a neat pile, before bringing various pots to her upon the table. She idly added herbs from them to a stone bowl. Her fingers danced around, knowing each plant without looking. 'Enzo,' she admonished. 'You're usually far more charming with beautiful women.'

'Beautiful? I hadn't noticed,' he muttered.

'Yes, Enzo seems to think scales grow beneath my gown, and horns grow from my forehead, all because I'm Asterian.'

Isra tipped back her head and laughed. 'Oh, I like *you*.' She slid her cool gaze to Enzo. 'Now I see why you tried to keep her from me.'

Enzo only rolled his eyes as he propped a leg against the wall and leaned back. Isra winked at Elara.

'Sit, Your Majesty.' She gestured to the wooden chair as she stood, making her way through a small arch to where the kettle whistled. 'Can I offer you a tea?'

'Yes, please,' Elara replied, parched from the city walk.

'Mint okay?'

'Fine, thank you,' Elara called.

'How do you take it, Elara?'

'With honey,' Enzo's voice sounded roughly behind her. 'Two spoons of it.'

Elara stilled. She turned in her seat, but Enzo was scowling as always, studying a painting of snow-capped mountains above Elara's head.

'How do you kn—'

'So, Elara,' Isra interrupted from the kitchen, cutting Elara's question short. The sound of teacups and spoons clinking drifted through. 'Why is it you need my help?'

Heat rose to Elara's cheeks, and she focused on the worn wooden table as she spoke. 'It's my shadows. I can't access them.'

Dread was beginning to drip like poison into her gut.

Enzo spoke. 'I've tried to find out how we can unblock them. But I can't get a read on her. Too many damn shadows.'

Elara glared at him. Isra reappeared with a mug for Elara, handing it to her.

'And why do you want to unblock your shadows?' she asked.

'What do you mean?' said Enzo. 'You know of my father's plans. It's so that she can kill Ariete.'

Isra cast a withering look at Enzo. 'Not you, fool. I'm asking Elara.'

She turned back to her, as Enzo sputtered in indignation. 'Why do *you* want to wield your shadows?' she asked tenderly.

Elara fought past the panic that had begun to rise. 'Because they're a part of me, and walking around without being able to use them feels like having phantom limbs.' She took a sip of tea to try and stop the croak in her throat. 'Because I don't ever want to feel helpless again.'

Isra regarded her coolly. 'Hmm. There's a deep wound within you, Elara.'

Elara averted her eyes. 'I don't want to do this.'

Isra looked at Enzo. 'Maybe you should bring her back when she's ready.'

'Over my dead body,' Enzo snapped. 'If we don't find out the cause of her blockage, then we cannot find the cure. My father will not allow more time. You will read her now, and that's a royal order.'

Ice froze in Isra's eyes as she glared at Enzo, a tight set to her lips.

'If it is *a royal order*, I suppose I must, Your Highness,' she bit out. When she turned back to Elara, her expression softened. 'Elara, you have nothing to fear. And I give you my word that anything I see won't be used against you. I'm sorry that I have to do this when you aren't ready.' And she sounded earnest. 'But Enzo is my prince. As well as a pain in my arse.'

'And what if I refuse?' Elara said, forcing her voice to remain even.

Enzo's eyes found hers, arresting her in her seat. 'Then you won't stand a chance against Ariete.'

She turned back to Isra, her entire body rigid.

'Will you use the Light on me?' Elara asked.

'No,' Isra replied. 'I don't possess the Light. From my father's side, I received the gifts of an oracle. To seek answers, to see glimpses of the soul, of the past, present and future. But I'm also half-Svetan. From my mother . . . I received a darker kind of sight. One that can commune with the dead. As well as a magick, cold and powerful . . .' She trailed off, waving a hand through the air.

Icicles formed before her, crystal clear and viciously sharp, the temperature in the room dipping.

Then with a tap, Isra finished crushing her herbs, as Elara fought back a shiver.

'If you so please,' she gestured to Enzo, who pushed himself off the wall. He gave a flick of his wrist and the herbs ignited into flames, their earthy smell pungent as they burned. The smoke curled around Isra as she breathed it in.

Isra held her arms out, palms up, and Elara held them, trying not to display a tremor. Isra's touch was frosty. The moment she touched Elara, Isra sucked in a breath. Her eyes clouded over, turning milky white. Elara shivered but continued to grip on to her as Isra muttered in a language she didn't recognize. It had the same guttural tone of Svetan, but the language sounded archaic, powerful. The candles around her flickered, casting intermittent darkness.

She felt Isra's magick settle over her gently, like a blanket of snow. Light, pure and clean. When she closed her eyes, she sensed it searching tentatively, hoar frost creeping through her soul, trying to clear the shadows.

Hide the box. Hide the box.

Elara's breath began to come in shallow gasps as panic took over. She squeezed her eyes steadfastly shut.

Isra fell suddenly silent and Elara could feel as the frost searching her mind suddenly found the box, as the temperature in the room around her dropped sharply.

The magick from Isra didn't stop, and now she could feel a strange pressure in her head as the ice tried to find a way inside the box.

'No,' Elara rasped. But Isra persevered.

The shadows that had been wrapped around the box tried to fight the ice, but they were useless – stuck inside Elara – and the ice continued to work until the box cracked open an inch.

A truth drifted out of it, the very one that Elara had tried so hard to bury.

Isra's magick paused, as the oracle viewed the memory. Tears were streaming down Elara's face – she could feel them; she was both inside and outside her body. And then, a cool layer of ice was placed carefully over the memory, before it was put gently back into the box. When it closed, Elara breathed again. But just as Isra's magick began to retreat, as she saw it wind a path out of her, silver light flared within her, and sank its teeth into Isra's magick.

'Elara?!' she heard Enzo say.

She opened her eyes, to find a frigid breeze filling the room. Isra's eyes were still full white, and frost was rapidly coating her entire body. She shook as the temperature plummeted.

'What the fuck was that?' she said, voice high with panic.

'What?' Enzo demanded. 'What's happening?'

But Isra groaned, and gripped Elara more tightly.

'Enzo!' Elara gave a strangled cry. The candles spluttered out, plunging them into darkness.

'Shit.' She heard Enzo move. A ray of light flared behind her as he lit the room, and for the first time in Elara's life, she did not fear it.

Isra moaned, plumes of arctic mist billowing from her mouth. Elara shook as a strong hand rested on her shoulder, and she felt Enzo's light suffuse her being. It was soft and warm as it melted the frost creeping up her limbs. Her shadows spun rapidly within her, bubbling up, up, and in another breath, two small streams of darkness whispered out of her hands, swirling around her and Isra's clasped hands.

'Stars,' Enzo whispered.

'Don't move,' Elara strangled out. She didn't take her eyes off her shadows, twin wisps, only a little bigger than the one she had seen on her balcony the night before.

'I won't,' he murmured, squeezing lightly. Isra groaned, a low keening sound that fast became a wail of agony. Elara's gaze flew back to her, her hands clenched painfully in Isra's grip. The oracle was rocking backwards and forwards, speaking in tongues faster than before, her head shaking from side to side, eyes still milky and translucent.

Elara tried to tug away, but Isra clutched her more tightly, reeling her in. Her wisps of shadow dissipated in the air, and Elara gave a cry of frustration. Ice was gathering on the table, burning as it bloomed upon Elara's wrists. The gale howled around them, Elara's hair swirling wildly in the tempest. With a loud shriek, glass shattered. Elara screamed in terror as sharp, glinting fragments of it scattered.

'Elara!' Enzo roared. She felt Enzo's body move in front of her, a wall of flame thrown up against the onslaught as she ducked. Glass tinkled around them as he turned around.

'Are you okay?' he demanded, grabbing her face between his hands, his eyes scanning for injury. She could barely speak, Isra's hands still locked on hers, her teeth chattering painfully.

'Y-your face, it's bleeding,' she stammered.

Enzo brushed a fingertip to a cut below his eye, batting her concern away. His anger turned on Isra.

'Isra!' Enzo bellowed, slamming the table with barely restrained strength. Flames rushed off him in waves, clashing with the ice storm raging through the room. As it cut through Elara, the silver light she'd seen – whatever it was – died. The wind settled instantly. Isra's eyes shifted back to clear hazel, and she blinked, sucking in deep breaths like a drowning woman finding land. Elara was shaking as Isra disentangled their hands. The oracle surveyed the chaos warily, the ice shrouding them all, the shattered windows and the blood dripping down Enzo's face. Finally, her attention rested on Elara. But the easy glimmer in her eyes was replaced with something else now.

It was fear.

Elara brushed trembling hands over her face, pushing her hair back. Enzo stood behind her, gripping the back of her chair so hard the wood groaned.

'What the fuck was that, Iz? What did you see?' he asked through gritted teeth. She could feel the heat radiating off him, warming the room as Isra fought for control of her powers. Isra stared at the table for a long time, taking in great heaving breaths, before answering.

'I saw why Elara's shadows are blocked.'

'Why?' he demanded.

'I think she should tell you,' Isra said quietly.

Enzo rounded on Elara. 'You knew this whole time?'

Elara stared him down.

He swore, pacing the room. 'What else? You saw something else, I know it.'

'When I – when I was trying to leave, something sank its teeth into my magick. A power I've never encountered before.'

'From me?' Elara asked.

Isra nodded. 'At first, I saw darkness past your shadows. So much of it that it began to drown me. Darker than black. It wasn't a colour. It was the absence of it. Then light pounced upon me. Silver. But cold. So cold that it burned. I've only felt that type of power in one thing before. But it's impossible.'

'Damn it, Isra, what?' Enzo growled.

Isra looked at the ground as she took a shaky breath.

'The only cold I've felt like that before has come from the dead.'

The room started to spin as Elara sagged back into her chair. Enzo pulled up another chair silently next to her.

'What is that supposed to mean?' Elara demanded.

Isra shook her head. 'I don't know. My visions are *always* correct, but they don't always make sense at first.' She bit her lip, looking at Enzo. 'There was one more thing. A golden light joined Elara's magick. It was as fiery as Elara's was chill. Together, the flames turned black. And then, I saw a Star die.'

'Is that—'

'It's you, Enzo. Elara needs you to kill a god. When shadow and light combine, a Star will fall.'

Enzo was already out of the door, Elara about to follow, when Isra held her back.

'Elara?'

Elara turned stiffly. She didn't want to spend another minute in the room.

'You need to tell Enzo. He will help you. Trust me, if anyone will understand, it's him.'

'What's that supposed to mean?'

'Just, please trust him.'

Elara sighed. *Why does everyone keep telling me that?* she thought. 'Fine. I'll tell him. Thank you,' she added, 'for what you did in there. The ice . . .'

Isra nodded. 'Of course. And I think you know that deep down it's fear that's holding back your shadows. But the Light isn't the only thing you fear, is it?'

Elara froze.

'I saw the prophecy.'

Any semblance of calm that Elara had tried to grapple with now unravelled once more. 'You know.'

Isra tilted her head. ' "You will fall in love with the King of Stars, and it will kill you both." That's why Ariete is hunting you. Not just because you cannot be killed by a Star. But because—'

'The prophecy is about him,' Elara whispered. 'And he will do anything to stop it coming true.'

CHAPTER TWELVE

When Elara stepped back out into the light-drenched street, Enzo was adjusting the saddle on a glossy palomino horse, another one waiting patiently beside it as Rico stroked its muzzle.

'I'll have the horses back tonight,' Enzo was saying to the little boy, and tossed him a bag of coins.

'I love it when you come to visit,' Rico breathed, and Enzo chuckled, tousling his hair.

The boy ran off towards the stables, as Elara cleared her throat.

Enzo's eyes darkened as he turned. 'You lied to me,' he said, his voice low, dangerously soft.

Elara folded her arms. 'About what?' she asked sweetly.

'I swear to the fucking Stars,' he muttered. 'This whole time, you knew what was stopping your shadows. Tell me why.'

'Or what?' she seethed, placing her foot in a stirrup. In a deft move, muscle memory kicking in, she was mounted on the horse. 'Are you going to force it out of me the way you forced me to go to Isra's? The way you forced *Isra* to pry my most vulnerable memory from me against both of our wills?'

She clicked her tongue, and her horse began to walk.

'Where are you going?' Enzo called.

'*I'm* going back to the palace. You can go wherever you please. Perhaps to one of those delightful pleasure houses we just passed. Or maybe that bridge up ahead so you can jump off it.' She continued onwards as Enzo cursed.

'So help me gods, Elara, do not test me,' he shouted as she trotted further down the street, away from him.

'What was that? Sorry, I can't hear you!' she called back, finally losing him around the corner.

Footsteps thundered behind her and she let out a frustrated sound as he reached her. He yanked her horse's reins, bringing it to a halt. 'Let go of my horse,' she said, her tone deathly low.

'Actually, it's my horse. I paid for it.' He gave a sarcastic smile as he grabbed on to the saddle behind Elara, and swung himself on.

'What are you doing?' she spluttered.

'Something I should have done the first time I met you. Putting you in your place.'

The horse trotted through Sol until the paths began to widen, the hustle and bustle quietening. Rather than taking a right in the direction of the palace, Enzo continued on straight ahead.

'Where are you taking me?' Elara demanded.

When Enzo replied with only a dark laugh, she lashed out for the third time, struggling to get off the horse as she cursed foully.

Enzo swore in turn, the arm he'd looped around her

tightening. 'You're a *brat*,' he hissed. 'The most ungrateful creature I have ever met.'

'*Ungrateful*? What in the skies do I have to thank *you* for?'

'I'm trying to *help* you. If you won't tell me what happened to your shadows, then I *will* force you to.'

He kicked the horse's shanks, and it set off into a faster trot as the ground beneath Elara began to tilt upwards. The buildings became sparser as Enzo urged the horse up the hill. The milled stones made way for grass as the buildings disappeared entirely. His arm around Elara still clenched her in a vice-like grip that she couldn't shake, as much as she squirmed against it. She cursed again.

'You have a filthy mouth for a princess.'

'Oh, wouldn't you like to know?' she snapped, looking for any way to get under his skin.

He pulled her, so that her back was entirely flush to his front. Elara had never been so close to him, amber enveloping her senses as he leaned in. She felt his warm breath on her neck.

'Is that an invitation?' he murmured.

Well, damn it all. If he didn't meet her every taunt with one better. Her mind emptied as every jolt of the horse brought their bodies sliding together. She opened her mouth to retort, but came up short, and instead shifted in the saddle.

'Stop squirming,' he commanded. She stopped resisting him, allowing her body to relax. 'Good girl. You *can* take orders.'

She glared ahead, and Enzo made a smug sound as she gripped the front of the saddle.

'Can you *please* tell me where we're going now?' she asked, as the hill steepened, and the horse began to slow its pace.

'Someplace where you'll have no choice but to speak the truth.'

She could feel every vibration in his chest as he spoke, his deep voice humming against her skin.

'Sounds ominous.'

He laughed then, which didn't help. Elara held her posture rigid, trying to brush against him as little as possible. She could taste salt in the air, the path now starting to flatten out.

'Decided to trust me yet?'

'This is hardly giving me cause to—'

Enzo clicked his teeth again and the horse began to gallop.

'Ready to tell me?' he shouted over the winds. On either side, Elara could only see dense shrubbery. She didn't respond, jaw welded shut, though her stomach lurched at the speed that the horse was racing along.

The only thing keeping her on the saddle was Enzo's arm around her waist. One more click of his teeth, and impossibly, the horse went even faster.

It was then, to Elara's absolute horror, that she saw exactly what they were racing towards as the shrubbery thinned out. The edge of a cliff.

'Enzo, this isn't funny!' she screamed, as she understood now why she tasted salt in the air. Waves crashed far below on either side off the cliff. The end of the path waited.

'Do you see me laughing?'

She craned her neck for a split second, seeing a glimpse of his expression – brow furrowed and eyes flashing. 'Stop right now.'

'Tell me why you can't use your shadows.'

She screamed as the horse careened, the edge approaching. The unforgiving ocean glinted as it reflected the afternoon Light. They were so high that the impact would be fatal.

'One last chance, Elara, or I swear to the Stars I'm taking us all off this cliff.'

'Fine!' she screamed, right as the lip of the cliff came up. The next words garbled out of her. 'I'm scared of the Light because of what happened to me as a child!'

Enzo twitched his hands, and the horse drove to a stop, neighing. Small pebbles kicked off its hoof, bouncing over the cliff edge, as Elara tried not to vomit. He clicked once more, and the horse paced backwards.

'You fucking *lunatic!*' she seethed. 'You would have killed us all!'

Enzo dismounted, and did a terrible job at hiding his amusement. 'You're alive, aren't you?'

She dropped off the horse, bounded towards him and tried to shove him. It had absolutely no effect. 'You *cunt!*' she seethed.

One hand flew out to grapple her wrists together as she raised them to push him again. His other gripped her jaw tightly. 'Keep using that filthy mouth and I'll wash it out with soap.'

She stayed still in his grip, chest heaving. His eyes flicked to her lips, squished between his hold, then back to her eyes.

'What happened to make you scared of the Light?' he asked more quietly.

She ripped herself from his grasp, and sat on the warm grass, her legs wobbling. She took a deep breath of the salt-laden ocean air. Being near the water was calming her, now that she wasn't about to plunge into it.

'I was seven,' she said. 'And one of your father's precious Helion soldiers broke into my room. Killed three guards and climbed up my balcony. He—' A knot worked in her throat. But Isra's ice must have worked, because the usual panic wasn't quite so all-encompassing as she continued. 'He was a lightwielder. My shadows tried to protect me. But I was a child.' She hated how her voice broke. 'They were no match for him. He pinned me down and told me to repent. To repent my worship of the Dark. When I couldn't speak he shoved his light down my throat. Told me he'd cleanse me from the inside out. It scorched all the way to my lungs. I couldn't even scream. If it wasn't for Sofia, I'd have died. She fought him. Tried to pull him off with her shadows, until my father arrived and killed him on the spot.'

She pulled some blades of grass between her fingers.

'It took months for the healers to repair the damage. Took a year for me to speak again. And even then I didn't recognize my own voice.' She cleared her throat.

'That man was a fucking fanatic. Thanks to *your* father. Thanks to the propaganda he spread about our kingdom.'

Enzo had gone pale, but she couldn't stand to look at him for a moment longer.

'So there,' she said, staring out at the ocean. 'There's your truth. My shadows sealed themselves inside me that night. Whenever I try to call them again, I remember the Light. How it felt. What it did. Are you happy now?'

'I'm sorry,' the prince said quietly. 'I had no idea.'

'I don't need your pity,' she spat, as she stood up. 'And I'm done here. If you don't take me back to the palace, I'll walk.'

Enzo said nothing as she mounted the horse, then climbed carefully on to it behind her, leaving Elara as much space as he could, and guided them silently back to the palace.

CHAPTER THIRTEEN

The next few weeks weren't better than her first days in Helios, but they weren't worse either. Enzo's cruelty was replaced with brooding silence. In fact, if they weren't talking about training, they didn't talk about anything at all. Which suited Elara just fine.

He didn't bring up the Light again. Nor did he wield it in front of her. Instead, they focused on drills, hand-to-hand combat and honing Elara's illusions.

Enzo showed her how to seamlessly combine her magick with her weapon-fighting. He encouraged her to be imaginative with her illusions, to make the opponent see a ravine, or a mountain; to make them feel like they were falling, or flying.

Her dreamwalking was advancing too. Most nights, she would do it wherever she could. Usually into the dreams of unsuspecting palace staff, occasionally Leonardo's, and once, even Merissa's. The glamourer had been delighted with that one, and they'd fed swans upon a rose-tinted Aphrodean lake before Elara had awoken.

She reluctantly fell into a peaceful routine. Merissa would pass by to glamour her for the day, followed by

Leonardo – who now insisted she call him Leo, as Enzo did. The general would deliver her fruit from his mother, and then escort her to her training with Enzo. He had even begun to talk to her more often, telling her about parts of the palace that they passed, or commenting on the art and paintings and what they symbolized. After training with Enzo, she'd soak her pains away in the baths, nibble on sweet treats and catch up on the palace gossip with Merissa in the kitchen, and then head to bed, preparing to dreamwalk through the night once more.

But something inside her knew that this peace couldn't last.

She was back in her throne room. It was her birthday. Her parents were weeping as she trembled.

'Everything we did was to protect you, Elara,' they said.

'How could you keep this from me?'

Sofia paced nervously behind her as the shadows upon the walls grew darker.

'We thought if we could keep you here, sheltered from Ariete, then he would never find out.'

The dream morphed, and she was dancing with Lukas, only a few hours later, around and around the ballroom as her prophecy chimed in her head. A bloodied card fluttered to the ground, the skies flashed red, screams rang, and Elara knew who had descended from the Heavens.

The King of Stars, so achingly handsome when he appeared that Elara's eyes watered to look at him. And that perfect, cold face transformed into rage as he conjured two blades in a flash of starlight, and plunged them through both her parents within a breath.

Elara screamed, kneeling over them as their blood soaked her powder blue birthday dress.

'I heard your little prophecy,' Ariete said, his voice as lilting and smooth as honey, yet so cruel. 'Don't worry that lovely little head about it. I'll make sure it never comes to pass.'

Red starlight flared from him, and bodies in the ballroom began to drop. She screamed, eyes searching for Sofia and Lukas, before the light blinded her. But while she saw the bodies of her parents and the other fallen guests disintegrate, the starlight only washed over her.

He stood, eyes flashing. 'Impossible,' he breathed.

And then she ran.

Elara woke from the nightmare, pushed herself out of sweat-drenched sheets, blindly staggered to the balcony doors and flung them open.

The mild night air swept over her, and she took in deep gulps of it, hands pressed to the smooth, cool marble of the balcony. The sky above her was a deep red, which, she now knew, meant it was the middle of the night in Helios. As she stood there, the pain of the memories from the nightmare slowly faded, but her palms itched with the desire to get rid of the roiling energy that had built up. With nothing else to do, her mind now wide awake, she practised her illusions.

Between her hands, she began to create a miniature winged lion. To calm her mind she focused on copying exactly the illustration in her book, open from where she'd left off the night before, making sure that its mane was streaked with gold and scarlet, that its wings were plumed with lustrous white feathers. When she was done, she even added the illusion of fire to it, the little lion pacing along the balcony's edge as it breathed flames.

She looked around. Enzo had been teaching her to throw her illusions the last few days. To be able to reach her magick over great distances. She looked to a balcony across the garden from her, and picked up her illusion.

'Perfect,' she murmured.

If she could get her lion to reach all the way to the opposite side of the palace and back, without breaking, she would allow herself to go back to sleep.

With a little lurch, it stretched out its wings and soared across the garden, as straight as an arrow, perching on the balcony across the way. Excitement thrilled through Elara. She was about to guide it back to her when the doors opened, and a figure stalked out on to the balcony she was aiming at, breathing heavily. She stilled, arms out in front of her. The figure braced themselves on the curve of the balcony, one side of their face hidden as they looked up to the sky. She squinted, the distance and darkness making them hard to identify. But then they reached a hand up, pushing their hair back, and she would have known that gesture anywhere.

'Stars' sake, why me?' She cast a poisonous look to the sky. If she remained extremely still, maybe Enzo wouldn't notice her. He looked preoccupied, his head still tilted up to the stars, his expression bleak. But he was so far away she might have imagined it. Elara took one tentative step back, then another. She could do this.

Then the lion lit up with the flames she'd blessed it with.

It was imaginary, of course – it wasn't like he would feel the heat – but Enzo wasn't *blind*. She forced every muscle in her body to freeze as she cringed. Enzo looked at the creature, frowning. Then he glanced around. His eyes caught her figure, and he stilled.

May as well lean into it, she thought to herself, wincing as she raised a hand in a half-hearted wave. She heard a soft chuckle echoing on the night breeze as he raised a hand back.

He looked at the lion again, pointing to it as if to ask, 'Was this you?'

Since she couldn't shout across the garden, she simply raised her hands to move the mini mythas. As it flew back to her, she saw a mocking clap from him and narrowed her eyes.

Her lion disappeared in a shimmer, and she stayed, looking at him across the garden as he looked at her.

Without taking his eyes off her, he crooked a finger out, and Elara gasped as a thin stream of light reached across the pavilion and through the bars of her balcony. It formed letters, projected on to the tiles and Elara read them.

Well done.

She snorted, looking back at him.

His hand swirled again, and the letters changed.

What are you doing out here? Except for gawping at my muscles again.

She looked in abject horror back to him. 'I am not,' she hissed, and the night air was quiet enough that her response must have echoed through the night to him. He kissed a bicep, grinning.

Then his hand moved again. *I've been thinking a lot these few weeks about what Isra said.*

Elara's breath hitched. The letters changed again. *I think we should try with your shadows again.*

Her eyes flew to Enzo's.

He put his hands up in supplication, before swirling them through the air once more. The next sentence read: *Fear is just a monster, Elara. And monsters can be slain.*

CHAPTER FOURTEEN

'I want to do it. I want to slay the monsters.'

Elara clenched and unclenched her fists as she peered up at Enzo, who was waiting for her in his usual position at the bottom of the grand staircase, ready for training. Only hours had passed – after their silent conversation across the garden, she'd stayed up the rest of the night, turning over what he had said.

And he was right. She could no longer let fear control her life.

Leo, who had escorted her as usual, began to slow clap beside her. 'I knew his inspirational speeches would get to you eventually.'

Elara rolled her eyes as Enzo observed her.

'You're sure?'

She nodded resolutely.

'Well, princess. Looks like there's mettle in you after all.'

It was the first time Elara had ever properly seen the royal gardens, which lay on the far side of the palace from her room. She accompanied Enzo through an arch, past neatly trimmed hedgerows.

'I wanted to show you how the Light is worshipped in my kingdom. How it's used for things other than violence.'

Elara tried to relax her shoulders as she looked to the neat flowerbeds stretching in rows.

Different palace workers were kneeling in the dirt, some digging, or planting seeds, others with their hands held out as light shone from their palms.

Enzo walked towards an older woman, her hair shimmering in tight black curls threaded with gold. She turned as she heard Enzo approach and beamed.

'My little cub,' she said, standing. Her warm brown eyes were familiar.

'Aunty,' Enzo said warmly, kissing her head. When the woman looked at Elara expectantly, Enzo turned.

'Oh, this is Nova,' he lied. 'She's a guest of my father's. I'm just giving her a tour of the palace gardens. Nova, this is Leo's mother, Kalinda.'

Elara smiled, shaking her hand. 'So it's you who grows the best peaches I've ever tasted?'

Enzo frowned down at her, but Kalinda threw back her head and laughed, clapping her hands. 'I wondered why my son was stealing so many from me. For that, you can have this one here.' She reached to a tree laden with the fruit. 'Freshly plucked.'

She passed one to Elara, the light still warm upon its skin.

'Thank you,' Elara said earnestly.

'What's your magick, sweetheart? If you'd ever like to help, you know where I am now.'

'She's a seer,' Enzo lied quickly. 'Like Iz.'

Elara narrowed her eyes at Enzo as Kalinda chuckled.

'Ah, darling Isra. That girl killed nearly all my vegetables with her frost. She didn't have a green little finger, let alone a green thumb.'

'I'll tell her to come up to the palace to see you soon,' Enzo said, squeezing her hand. 'We'd best carry on with the tour.'

Kalinda kissed his cheek, giving a little bow to Elara. 'A pleasure to meet you, Nova.'

'It was all mine,' Elara beamed.

'Peaches?' Enzo asked, when they were out of earshot.

'Leo brings me one every morning.'

'Does he now?' Enzo said tightly. 'And when did you two become so close?'

'He wanted to as thanks for—' Elara paused and looked around, making sure nobody else was in earshot, '—something I did for him.'

Enzo looked bewildered at her. 'And what did you do for him?'

'I dreamwalked to him. Accidentally. And the dream he was having was . . . of when he first arrived at the palace.'

Enzo's eyes darkened. 'So you know what he did?'

She nodded.

'And you didn't tell anyone?'

Elara shrugged. 'It's not my business to tell.'

Enzo looked at her for a long time before they continued to the orchards, where more lightwielders were using their magick to help the plants and flowers grow.

'We have one of the best bounties in Celestia thanks to our light,' Enzo explained. 'Verdans, of course, are the masters when it comes to the earth. But we're the next best place; we can grow just about anything in Helios.'

He halted before a flowerbed. 'Ready for your first test?'

She took a deep breath, nodding.

Enzo crouched down. It was bizarre. Here was this arrogant prince, kneeling in the dirt, his courtiers and workers not blinking an eye at the sight.

She gingerly settled beside him, as Enzo raised his hands. Light shone from them over a patch of what looked like empty soil. She tensed at the sight of it, but didn't flinch.

And then, to her wonder, small green shoots pushed up from the soil. Enzo flared the light a little brighter, and flowers began to grow upon the stems, tiny periwinkle stars.

Forget-me-nots.

Just like that, they'd bloomed. She looked to him as he plucked them. He handed the small bunch to her. 'Feel them,' he ordered. 'They can't hurt you, can they?'

She took it, felt the velvet softness of the petals, the warmth from his magick.

'There,' he said, as she tucked the bunch behind her ear. 'You just touched something created by the Light.'

Elara kept the forget-me-nots pressed in her copy of *The Mythas of Celestia*. Every day that followed, Enzo gradually helped Elara to get more comfortable around the element she had feared her whole life. He took her to the Lantern District, where some of the most talented crafters she'd ever seen created the lights that floated around the palace, twinkling in various hues of apricot, bronze and gold. They visited the Dial Quarter, where dials were hewn from bronze, a kernel of light infused in each one, which mirrored the Light above to track the time.

They visited a museum, where Enzo pointed out how the

incredible sculptures that littered the city were carved from the same kind of light that he wielded. Wherever they went, Enzo was adored and revered. He was warm, charming, flirtatious. But no citizen feared him. Not like the people of Asteria had.

In between the Helion tours, they trained. It was as physically demanding as it had always been, but without Enzo spewing his usual verbal vitriol, Elara was able to focus more on her technique, her stamina, disarming Enzo increasingly.

He still hadn't touched her again with his light. She still hadn't asked him to.

And then, there was another nightmare, another unwelcome memory.

'Just try, Lara. I don't understand why you can't do it. It's been years since the incident.'

Lukas had been getting terrible headaches, and growing more cruel and irritable by the week. All his patience had been slowly worn away. And Elara understood why. She was useless. Eighteen years had passed, and there wasn't a wisp of shadow in sight.

'How can you expect to become queen, if you can't wield one of your most important powers?'

Tears rolled down Elara's cheeks, and Lukas threw his hands up in exasperation. 'You're too sensitive, Lara.' When she continued to cry, his eyes softened. 'I'm sorry,' he murmured, kissing her cheek. 'It's these headaches. Maester Divinet thinks it's something to do with my shadows. But I just . . . Elara, I love you. I only want what's best for you. You know that, don't you? When you ascend the throne, many Asterians will see it as an opportunity to challenge you unless you show no weakness. And these emotions . . . they're just that. Weaknesses.'

'For once I agree,' Sofia said from the door. Lukas sighed and left, making himself scarce as he always did around Sofia.

'He's too jealous, Lara. Too possessive of you,' Sofia said, approaching.

Elara wiped her tears. She didn't want to fight with Sofia too, so she remained silent. 'But these emotions of yours,' Sofia said gently. 'I can see the way they hurt you. You need to learn to put them in a box. Lock it, and throw away the key. You'll drown in your feelings if you're not careful.'

Elara sniffed. 'I know.'

Sofia smoothed Elara's hair. 'Just try it. See if it helps.'

Elara woke up with a jolt. Her heart still beating fast, she clambered out of bed and hurried to the balcony, as was becoming her habit, breathing in the thick perfume of night-jasmine on the air.

Her emotions were spilling out of that damned box; in fact, the last few weeks it had become harder and harder to keep the lid on at all.

Squeezing her eyes shut, she took a deep breath in and out, as she tidily folded her feelings away, just like Sofia had taught her.

She was sick of these nightmares. Sick of her fear following her every step. She'd made progress, yes, but it wasn't enough.

When she opened her eyes, she saw Enzo standing on the balcony outside his own room, staring at her across the way. Like he knew. Like he'd been waiting.

She nodded at him.

He nodded back.

Tonight, her shadows would be free once more.

CHAPTER FIFTEEN

It was the middle of the night, and Elara was on the same cliff that Enzo had nearly careened them off weeks before.

The sky glowed burgundy, bathing the cliff in streaks of red. Enzo had slipped out just one palace horse, much to Elara's chagrin at having to share with him after last time.

'Are you sure?' he asked, clenching and unclenching his fist. Light splayed and dimmed from it, and Elara nodded.

'I want you to attack me with your light.'

'And if the shadows don't come?'

'I've been turning it over in my head. That night, why my shadows became trapped. When my magick truly thought I was going to die, it fought. My shadows tried to protect me from that zealot's light. After that night, I wasn't able to summon them, but I'd never been placed in a position where I believed I was going to die. Even with Ariete – my prophecy had just been told. I knew I wouldn't die, so my shadows never came.'

Enzo raked a hand through his curls as he drew his sword, tossing it between his hands.

'So I have to try and kill you?'

Elara smirked. 'It shouldn't be hard. I'm sure you think about it every day.'

Enzo stuck his tongue in his cheek, a resolve settling over him. 'Fine. But we need a safe word, if it gets too much, or you change your mind—'

'No,' Elara replied. 'No safe word, no way out. You have to try and kill me. And mean it.'

She raised her own sword easily, and pointed it to the cliff. 'Even if I beg, even if I plead, drive me to the cliff. Make me think you're going to throw me over it. You forced me to tell the truth before. Tonight, I want you to force me to use my shadows.'

Enzo cricked his neck, and a veil fell over him. Flames ignited in his eyes, and fear began to pound in her heart.

'This had better work,' she muttered to herself, and then Enzo struck.

Light poured from his blade, bathing the entire cliff as it battled the deep scarlet night. Elara grunted as she parried his strike. Enzo had been going easy with her in training. Here, she was no match against the brute force of Prince Lorenzo, all-powerful son of Light. Her arm was wrenched down, no defence as her sword fell. Her survival instincts set in as she threw a swarm of illusory bats at Enzo. She lunged for her sword as Enzo blasted the bats into nothing, advancing again. Elara dropped to the ground, hands splayed as she forced her illusions over it. Enzo staggered as he saw a roiling, shifting sea of grass, just as she had willed it.

But he jumped deftly towards her, and struck her to the ground, making her lose the thread of her illusion.

She flung her sword up to block his blow, but he wrenched her wrist, and she cried out as he forced her to drop it.

The point of his blade pressed against her drumming heart, as Elara heaved. And then light burst from its point.

She screamed as it enveloped her. She shook, muscle memory taking over as it put her right back in the place she'd been eighteen years before. She wailed, but Enzo only gritted his teeth as more light poured through her.

But there was no heat in his light. No pain.

'Why aren't you hurting me?' she shouted.

'I shouldn't need to burn you from the fucking inside out,' Enzo hissed. 'Why isn't it working?'

She rolled on to her side as his light dimmed. 'I suppose I just don't believe you're really going to kill me.'

Enzo's jaw clenched as he paced away.

Elara stood. 'Stop. Holding. Back.' She raised her sword again. 'What? Has the Lion gone soft?'

Enzo gave a warning sound as he raised his weapon. She danced around him, jabbing and feinting as he defended her strikes with ease.

'I know what you're trying to do,' he said, as they got closer and closer to the cliff's edge. 'I swear, Elara. If you fall off that cliff, I won't follow you.'

'And why would you? I thought you hated Asterians.' She spat at his feet, and Enzo snarled, the blow against her sword harder this time, the light that burst from it blinding her momentarily.

'I thought you hated *me*,' she said, and lunged again, as she launched the illusion of a nightwolf at him.

He grunted in frustration, stumbling as she tiptoed backwards towards the cliff's edge. The fear was well and truly within her now. But she had to face it. She couldn't carry on being haunted. By her parents. By Lukas. Most of all, by Sofia.

'My parents killed your mother,' she said. 'Isn't that what you claim?'

She laughed coldly, as she reached the edge. Enzo rushed

closer in and grabbed her by the back of her neck, his other hand gripping the fabric at her hip, fire rippling off him in waves. It seared through her, and Elara welcomed it.

He heaved, his full lips so close that if she so much as shifted, they'd graze hers.

She swallowed, as she fixed her hate-filled gaze upon Enzo's, raising her chin. His grip tightened in her hair. She had never seen a hatred like it, what burned within his eyes for her. And she understood. Because she hated herself too for what she was about to say. But she didn't let it stop her.

'I'm sure the Light-loving bitch deserved it.'

There was a flash of light so powerful that it knocked Elara back, and suddenly, there was no ground beneath her.

There wasn't a sound around Elara as she fell. Almost as though time had slowed, she saw Enzo at the precipice, clenching and unclenching his fists, a look of shock mixed with rage upon his beautiful face.

She reached for her shadows, felt them twisting and writhing within her. But they couldn't push past the memories.

The waves crashed below.

Oh gods. She was going to die. She was really going to die.

She jabbed her hands out, again and again, but the shadows wouldn't come.

And she finally began to scream.

Time sped up, her hair whipped around her, her skirt tearing in the unforgiving riffs of the howling wind. She jerked her neck, seeing the crash of the waves growing nearer and nearer. Her body would shatter on the rocks, if it didn't break upon the sea's impact.

She looked back up, and to her horror, saw Enzo jump.

He flew through the skies, body plummeting towards hers.

'No,' she tried to shriek, but the wind stole it from her. Enzo's body collided with hers, and she sucked in a breath as he clutched her tightly. The two stared at each other, stricken, as they continued to fall, fall, fall, spinning in each other's arms.

'This is how I die,' he shouted over the wind, in a matter-of-fact tone.

No, that just wouldn't do. Enzo had followed her off a cliff. The man who hated her most in the world. The least she could do was try to save his life.

Elara tried to move her lips, but she was paralysed as they plummeted to their deaths.

'You told me you were a dragun, Elara,' Enzo said through clenched teeth, his grip unyielding around her.

Her eyes, flooded with terror, found his. Oh skies, she could see the fury writhing in them. But his warrior's tone was steady. The ocean drew closer.

'Spread. Your. Fucking. Wings.'

Elara closed her eyes, flaring her arms wide.

'Please,' she begged her shadows. 'For him, if not for me.'

Light shone around her as Enzo let go of any semblance of control, and when her shadows writhed forth, this time they seemed to career desperately towards his light – the light that flowers had bloomed from, that hadn't hurt her even when she'd begged it to.

Something within her shifted, a deep weight on her chest.

It cracked open, that lump of obsidian, shadows spewing from it. Streams of blackness poured in torrents from Elara's flailing fingers, and suddenly both she and Enzo rocketed back upwards, soaring into the crimson sky.

Elara let out a roar of delight, and Enzo looked around, startled to discover they were both still very much alive, and riding on the back of a creature made of shadow. A *lion*. A winged lion. Elara could have laughed if she hadn't left her stomach miles below.

The lion swooped, and they spun and soared through the air as Elara continued to whoop and holler.

'I did it!' she shouted above the roar of the wind as Enzo clutched her desperately from behind.

'I think I left my balls back there,' he shouted over the clamour to her. Elara simply smiled, arms raised in the air as the wind whipped her hair.

With another cheer, she guided the lion in an arc, marvelling at how solid the shadows felt. Even Lukas hadn't been able to give this kind of substance to his.

Enzo let out a disbelieving laugh as he looked below to the crashing sea.

'You're as insane as Sagitton.'

'I know!' Elara turned around to him then, and he stilled, his smile slackening. Her hair billowed around her, and she could almost feel herself glowing.

'You came for me,' she said. Enzo shrugged, a lazy smile creeping on to his face. With a burst of power, he fed his fire into the shadow lion's maw so that it billowed out of its mouth.

'Show-off.' She winked at him. Her hair drifted past his face, and she felt his hands digging deeper into her waist as they soared.

With a press of her palms, her shadows dived in a huge drop towards the ocean as she screamed in delight, Enzo shouting in alarm. At the last moment, she pulled the shadow lion up and leaned forwards to skim the lapping cobalt waves.

'Wow,' she breathed, looking back again to Enzo.

'Wow indeed,' he said raggedly, his breath still lost on the wind. She slowed the shadows so the lion could fly smoothly across the ocean, the sea spray cooling their faces. Elara swung herself round to face Enzo.

'Now who's the show-off?' He smiled. 'A little bit of power, and you're a renegade.'

She sighed as she draped her back across the lion's mane.

'You have no idea how good it feels,' she moaned, her arms still trailing the water as they flew. 'I feel invincible.'

'Power looks good on you, princess,' he said, his voice deep.

Elara regarded him. 'What I said . . . I'm so sorry. You know I didn't mean it. I just had to make you—'

'I know,' he replied. 'And I didn't mean to push you off a cliff.'

Elara made an amused sound as she eased back a little, craning her neck to look at the skies. The deep red had begun to lighten as the morning crept in. Gold mingled with crimson and burnt orange; pure bronze seemed to glitter through the tapestry.

Her lips slightly parted, she looked back to Enzo, who had been looking at the sky with a yearning in his eyes. She willed the lion to climb higher, until they broke through a mist. She stopped it, the lion's beating shadow wings the only sound.

A floor of fluffy clouds surrounded them, the light enveloping them, completely unfiltered. It bled out in a rainbow, a kaleidoscope containing every colour conceivable. She saw violet rays reach out to the South, to Asteria. The gold washed over them. Rose stretched further north to Aphrodea. She reached a hand out, marvelling at how the Light splashed her skin. There was no tension. No fear, as she let it touch her.

For the first time, she marvelled at it.

'Do you ever . . .' She shook her head. 'Do you ever wonder how the Stars created this?'

She turned to Enzo. 'I mean . . . the sheer vastness of it, the sheer beauty. How can beings so cruel have made it so?'

Enzo shook his head, looking to the Light as it made his every feature shine. 'Perhaps there is something greater out there,' he said hoarsely. 'Perhaps there is something more divine.'

CHAPTER SIXTEEN

They arrived back at the palace just as it had begun to wake. There was the sound of clinking china and hushed orders between the chief of staff and servants. Gardeners were trimming the hedges, the quiet snip of cutters in the dew-dropped air.

Elara reached for her shadows, but they'd disappeared deep inside her. She looked to Enzo, her breath hitching.

'They just need to recharge,' he said. 'They've been stuck inside you for eighteen years and were forced out all at once.'

Soothed and suddenly exhausted, Elara yawned as she dismounted.

'I'll take the horse back to the stables. Then I need to see my father. He'll be happy to hear that we unlocked your shadows.'

There was something hopeful in his gaze, but Elara's stomach plummeted.

Because of course. How could she have forgotten? She was a weapon to Idris and his son. A means to an end.

'You should go and rest,' he added.

She stretched her arms out, smiling as she nodded. 'Thank

you. For this morning. I—' She made herself look at him. For one last time. 'I truly mean it. Thank you for helping me slay my monster.'

Something softened in Enzo's eyes. Elara looked away, feigning another yawn. 'I'm going back to bed.'

'Take the day off.' He gave a tentative smile, leading the horse away. Elara watched him until he'd disappeared around a corner.

And then she weaved a cloak of illusions over herself, turned right back around and darted through the palace gates.

She tore the illusions off herself once she'd reached the foot of the palace walk – she didn't want to drain her magick too fast. But in doing so, she encountered another issue. Elara didn't know exactly how long Merissa's glamour would last. A day and a night is what the glamourer had said, and though Merissa's magick still seemed intact around Elara, she knew it would wane, and fast. The thought of the glamourer caused a slight pang of sadness in her chest. But these people weren't her friends. Enzo had reminded her of that. She was an enemy. An enemy that was only valuable while they thought they could use her. So she prayed that the disguise would hold up, at least until she was out of Helios.

She sped down the warm streets as discreetly as she could. All she needed was a horse – one that didn't belong to the palace. If she could remember her way to the stables near Isra's, she could steal one.

She turned into an ornate square that she remembered,

the one with a giant iridescent statue of Leyon wearing the lion's pelt in the centre of it.

She was close to the stables, keeping her head down, and so focused on not being recognized that she crashed right into someone.

'I'm so sorry,' she said, looking up and smiling with false cheer. 'I wasn't—' Elara's smile dropped.

The Star before her grinned a smile full of white teeth as he righted his robes. Every breath inside her became a wheeze. Blonde hair rippled down past the god's shoulders, his lean muscles tanned and shining. A circlet rested on his head, spikes of gold reaching out like rays of light. Leyon, Patron Star of Helios, god of the Light, arts and prophecy.

'I have that effect on people,' he winked. The Star was both elegant and dazzling, looking as if he'd been cut from the very marble that rendered his figure as statuary through-out Helios.

'Thank you, my revered Lord Light.' Elara kept her eyes averted, bowing before going to leave. She prayed with all her might that he'd let her, but felt a strong hand grab hers, pulling her closer.

'Who *are* you?' She froze. Leyon smiled, but though it was an easy, relaxed smile, she sensed the danger behind it. 'You don't think I can see through the glamour you're wearing?'

'Glamour? I'm not sure what you're talking about, Your Grace.' She laughed uneasily. Leyon's hazel eyes narrowed and she could feel the power emanating from him – his charm, that godly force that coated the very air, eye-watering to look at for too long. She glanced around nervously to see whether anyone else had noticed a *god* casually walking amongst them. Indeed, passers-by were bowing their head, touching their third and fourth finger to their temple as a sign of respect.

'You're not from my kingdom,' Leyon spoke softly.

Adrenaline coursed through Elara's veins. The Star's grip on her was firm and unyielding. She ran through options in her head, wondering if her shadows had regained enough strength to be cast, or if her best bet was to run. Fast.

'Raven hair. Silver eyes. An Asterian. And by your posture, I'd wager royalty.' He chuckled, the sound warm as his eyes shone with interest. 'If I were a gambling man, I'd bet that I may have just bumped into the lost princess that Ariete is so fixated on finding.'

She bristled against the title, and gave a hard laugh, trying to tug free of his grasp. 'You're certainly mistaken.'

His fingers dug in further.

'You're a smart girl. Sheltering within my domain.' He tilted his head. 'Ariete knows he cannot enter Helios without my invitation.'

The Stars' Invite. Elara remembered it from her history lessons. Stars could be invited into one another's kingdoms. But unless they were, any other visit would be a challenge of outright war. Unless that Star was Eli – the messenger god, who seemed to be welcome everywhere.

'You won't deliver me to Ariete?'

Leyon tipped back his head and laughed, the sound a rich melody. 'And see my brother get what he wants? Come now, Elara Bellereve, surely your history tutors taught you about our feud better than that.'

Elara blinked. She had forgotten in her blind panic that Leyon was the King of Stars' brother. 'Ariete is growing too brash. First, he descends – uninvited – into Piscea's territory. And only her slumber meant that this did not cause an outright celestial war. Then, he acts upon this prophecy. And cannot even kill the object of it, a mere mortal girl.' He looked at Elara. 'No offence.'

Elara raised a brow. 'None taken.'

'And now? Now he has made us look weak. Now he hunts you, disregarding his every duty. The Stars are not happy.'

He took a step back to observe her, really observe her. His gaze trailed from her feet up to her hips, lingering on her breasts before roaming her face as he sucked a tooth.

'"You will fall in love with the King of Stars, and it will kill you both." Now, I don't think I'd mind one bit if the prophecy was for me.'

'You'd be the first,' she muttered as his magick washed over her. She took an involuntary step closer to him. Save for Ariete, she had never been in the vicinity of a Star before. His charm was warm, full of light and music. Intoxicating. She could almost hear it sounding from him, achingly gorgeous compositions, could see colours she'd never even dared to imagine before, so rich and vibrant.

'I think you're too modest,' he murmured. 'Many men would be happy to die for you. Perhaps gods, too.'

'There you are!' a loud, familiar voice interrupted. Its owner's face was plastered with an arrogant smile as he swaggered over, the people in the square halting to gawp at the spectacle.

'Prince Lorenzo.' Leyon nodded his head. 'What interesting company you keep.' His eyes ran over Elara again.

A tiny muscle in Enzo's jaw ticked, barely noticeable before he bowed deeply to the Star. 'I see you've met my esteemed guest.'

'No need to skirt around it, prince. I know who she is.'

Flames leapt in Enzo's eyes, his usual gold burnished to warm orange. 'Is that so?'

Leyon's smile tightened. 'The only thing I can't quite puzzle out is why a Helion prince would be hosting his mortal enemy in his kingdom.'

Elara blanched.

'When Ariete killed her parents, my father took pity on Elara. His vendetta lay with them, not their innocent daughter. So, when she crossed the border, she became our problem. Better to know thy enemy, and all that.'

Leyon gave a shallow, tinkering laugh. 'Then your secret is safe with me. For now. Tell your father he hasn't visited my temple recently. I highly advise he does.' Threat was laced in his honeyed words.

Enzo bowed, grabbing Elara's arm. 'We'd best be going,' he said smoothly, and bowed again. 'My revered Lord Light.'

'Farewell. And, Elara? If you ever tire of playing with mortals, you know where my temple is.' Leyon winked before sauntering off, his golden hair glimmering as he strolled through the piazza, a ripple of citizens bowing in his wake.

Enzo yanked Elara along quiet side streets, pulling her along at a pace that left her panting.

'Will you just stop for a moment?' she finally got out.

'You know, you've done a lot of stupid things in the short time I've known you, Elara, but this trumps them all.' He was seething; she could almost imagine flames bursting from him at any moment. 'You *ran*.'

Elara raised her chin. 'What did you expect? That I would stay like a good little prisoner?'

'I thought—'

'What? That things had changed after last night? You are Helion, Enzo. And I am Asterian. Our very magicks abhor each other. Like night and day. We'll always be on opposite sides.'

He blinked, and the fire within him had gone. 'You're right,' he said, and he released her arm. She saw that they had reached Isra's, the eye carved into her door staring at Elara. 'I don't know why I expected any more from an Asterian. You're born to betray. You got what you wanted, and now you run.'

Indignation rose. 'And you're so noble, are you? Kidnapping your enemy and forcing her to do your bidding. I am your weapon, and nothing more. Why should I have thought you anything other than the monster you are, *Lion*?'

'Oh, I'm a monster, am I?' he said, bracing both hands on the door behind her. She was trapped, his tall frame blocking out the pale streams of the afternoon Light.

She could feel the heat that radiated from his skin, see the bronze that glowed from it.

'Of course you are. I know of the Borderland Fires.' If she had been calmer, perhaps she'd have felt scared.

'Go on,' he hissed, his voice so low it skated over her nerves, his eyes dimmed to the deepest coal.

'Women, children,' she near whispered. 'Innocents burned to ash. You obliterated a whole village in minutes. Started a fire that raged for two weeks, cutting off our trade, our food supplies.' Her eyes brimmed with tears, and she gritted her teeth against them, her face still inches from his.

'What else?' His black gaze bore into her, his expression closed and drawn.

'So you don't deny it.' She shook her head. 'Your father may think he had a reason to lay siege to Asteria. But the only people he hurt were innocents, those who played no part in the decision my parents made – *if* what you say about my mother and father is even true.' Enzo tensed. 'Your father executed his own damn people if they tried to speak out against the D'Oro's treatment of my kingdom. He's a tyrant, and you're no *lion*. Just the mutt who does his bidding.'

'Careful, princess.' Enzo's voice was low and deadly as he dipped his head, his eyes fixed on hers. 'You're very close to committing treason. People have burned for less.'

She gave a brittle laugh. 'You sound just like Idris.'

Luminous flames erupted over Enzo's body. She started, still captured between his arms. But the flames did not sear her skin. They were bitingly icy, and he drew a smile to match. His lips were now centimetres from hers.

'Then run.'

'Wh-what?'

Enzo shot her a look of disdain, as he pushed off the door. 'I won't stop you. This is what you wanted, isn't it? You got your shadows. Now you want to go home – to your throne, to your kingdom. So, go. I won't stop you.'

He turned, knocking sharply on Isra's door.

Elara looked to the stables. 'What about your father?'

'I'll deal with my father. And you'll get your wish. When you're back on your throne, we will be enemies once more.'

'Once more?'

Enzo's jaw clenched. 'Farewell, Elara.'

The door swung open, and Isra stood there, a warm smile on her face. 'Enzo. Elara.'

'She was just going, Iz,' he said tightly, walking through the door. 'I won't be the one to keep her here against her will any longer.'

Elara looked at the woman who had blanketed her pain. Who had seen it, and kept it secret. The oracle looked between them both. 'But what about King Idris's plans? What about Ariete?'

'Elara can face him on her own now. Isn't that right?'

Elara couldn't understand why tears were beginning to prickle at the backs of her eyes, but she forced the unwelcome emotions down into the box that was beginning to overflow.

Isra's eyes filled with sorrow. 'So this is the path you choose. I only wish you luck, Your Majesty.'

Elara's hands danced at her sides as she nodded. 'Thank you for . . . Thank you, Isra.'

And Enzo slammed the door shut.

Elara stood outside the door for a long time, trying to control her breathing. Here it was. Enzo had given her freedom. She tried to force her feet to move towards the stables, to continue on with her plan.

'So this is the path you choose.'

Isra's expression as she'd uttered those words had made her pause, but Enzo's had made her stop entirely. The fury, followed by emptiness. He had jumped off a cliff after her, had helped her kill the fear that had paralysed her for nearly two decades.

As she wrung her hands, wisps of shadows drifted off them, and she stilled.

And it seemed . . . whether thanks to Piscea, goddess of fate, or something else, that this was the path she was supposed to be on. Isra had said as much. Monster or not, Elara needed Enzo. She could not face Ariete alone.

CHAPTER SEVENTEEN

Merissa was tasting pasta sauce in the kitchens when Elara found her.

'Try this,' she said, pushing a spoon into Elara's mouth.

It was delicious – lemon and fresh basil dancing on her tongue. She smiled at the taste, but then leaned closer in to Merissa.

'I ran,' she whispered. 'I tried to get away. And Enzo . . . let me go.'

Merissa slowed the chopping of her onion minutely, before picking up the pace.

'And you're back.'

'Yes.'

Merissa passed her a kitchen knife and a bundle of rosemary and thyme. 'Then there's nothing else to say. Why don't you help me chop?'

Elara took it, something in her chest loosening. Merissa gave her a smile, before turning her attention to the simmering pot. Elara gathered her herbs. She didn't tell Merissa how growing up she'd begged Cook Daphne to teach her every dish she knew from around Celestia. She didn't tell her that the scent of rosemary made her want to weep. Or how terrible her argument with Enzo had been – how even more terrible the look in his eyes had made her feel. She didn't say that being around Merissa was the closest to home that Elara had felt in weeks.

She just chopped.

That night, Elara was too exhausted to dreamwalk. Her own dreams haunted her with memories, though the fear had ebbed. When she woke, she padded to the balcony, for the first time realizing that she had chosen to stay in Helios. That this place didn't feel quite like a prison any more.

Force of habit urged her to look across the way to Enzo's balcony and she stopped short.

He was stood there, on the balcony, watching her.

Did he ever sleep?

She didn't wave. Didn't call across. She just stood there, watching him watching her.

His eyes seemed to glow like dying coals in a fire, before he turned and retreated to his room.

When a smart rap woke her up the next morning, and it turned out to be Leo at the door bearing fruit, she could have almost believed that the day before had just been a dream.

But as they descended the grand staircase as usual, there was no Enzo pacing below. Instead, Leo turned to her. 'You're training with me today.'

She mastered her surprise. 'And why isn't His Highness gracing me with his presence?'

Leo gave a tight smile as he bit into his fruit. 'He believed you would benefit from my tutelage from now on. Since your magick is now fully awakened.'

Elara's stomach turned. As much as Leo was growing on her, she hadn't chosen to stay here to train with anyone else. It was Enzo who would help her kill a Star.

She followed Leo into a dusty training ground that splayed out of the back of the castle, empty but for the two of them. Straw dummies were lined up, various weapons hanging from stands.

'We'll be working on those shadows you unlocked yesterday,' Leo said. 'I thought it best we have a private practice.'

Elara nodded. 'I know you wield the Light too.'

Leo raised his hands to face each other. Elara heard a crackling noise. 'You could say that,' he replied.

Pure lightning writhed between his palms, bright white and lethal. Feeling the power rolling off him up close was far removed from when she'd watched him spar with Enzo. This . . . This was like no power she had ever seen.

Leo gave a quietly confident smile. 'I didn't rise from the slums of Apollo Row to the Palace of Light because of my good looks, you know.'

'I've never heard of anyone else with that kind of magick,' she whispered, as Leo expanded his hands, lazily rippling the lightning through his fingers.

He shrugged. 'It's far more draining for me to use than Enzo's rays. But it's useful. I can char an enemy to death in minutes.'

Elara gulped, willing her shadows to surface. To her relief, they tumbled out of her – though still not solid as they had been. Even they seemed to shy away from Leo's lightning, curling around her protectively. He noticed, laughing softly.

'Yes . . . you're going to need those. Otherwise, this is going to sting.'

Hours later, Elara groaned as she ascended the stairs, her muscles protesting after the gruelling training session with Leo. For all his manners and the small kindnesses he had shown her since she'd arrived in Helios, he had certainly kept them far away from the training ground. He'd been unrelenting as she attempted to wield her shadows, but try as she might they wouldn't take form, instead just evaporating in translucent strands. Leo had commanded her to do a hundred press-ups when she had complained about it and five laps of the training ground when she had tried to rest, or remarked on how hot it was.

Her leg twinged from where the general had shocked her with his lightning, the spot still pulsing. Utterly spent, she half-heartedly thrust her door open. Merissa was sitting on her bed, her eyes alight.

'Well, don't you look like you've been run through the hay?'

Elara only groaned. 'Leo is a sadist,' she muttered.

Merissa laughed. 'He's the general of our army for a reason. But don't worry, your warm bath is already drawn.'

'Did I ever tell you that I'm in love with you?' Elara replied and Merissa laughed loudly.

CHAPTER EIGHTEEN

Elara soaked in her bath until her skin was wrinkled as a prune, then she changed into a soft cotton nightgown and padded out on to the balcony. The warm evening air gently dried her damp skin. The stone of the balcony felt warm beneath her toes, and she sighed. She was, begrudgingly, beginning to like the heat. Merissa had left a plate of the lemon pasta they'd made together the day before, and Elara ate as she watched the lightdown.

One saving grace about Helios was that the stars weren't often visible in the deep scarlet of night. She let a ring of shadow fall from her finger, trying to wrap it around her glass of honeyed peach wine. But when it wouldn't latch on to it, she exhaled in defeat, and settled back on the low divan. Maybe it was the warmth, or the full stomach, or the endless drills that Leo had put her through, but her eyelids drooped, her body growing heavy.

The sounds around her were drowned out; the faint clang of pots, the distant murmur of voices and the birdsong, all of it faded as she breathed deeper and deeper. She felt for limbo, the space between worlds, and with a sigh, she anchored her tether, and dreamwalked.

She moved between the colourful dreamclouds, searching until one caught her eye. She'd seen it before, black and pulsing, flames flickering through it. She could hazard a guess as to who it belonged to. Tonight, she drifted closer. And with a deep breath, she plunged into it.

The heat was unbearable. She swore under her breath as she gathered her bearings. She'd dreamwalked through nightmares before, but none like this. The room was made of cold white marble – a marble that struck her as somehow familiar – yet still the flames pressed in. She heard a roar of pain and started to run towards it, the cavernous space seeming to double then triple in size around her. Finally, she saw Enzo kneeling on the floor in the middle of the space, naked from the waist up, hunched over, as light whipped his back, his hands tied behind him. He screamed, begged, deep red blood running in rivulets as the skin ripped open. Flames were beating down upon Elara, sweat coating her body. Above him, Elara could make out a trio of numbers, huge in size, painted in blood, red ribbons marking the bare walls of the dreamscape – *3, 3, 3.*

'This is not real,' she said evenly to herself, inhaling deeply. Streaks of light continued to thrash against Enzo's torso as his screams tore through the dreamscape.

Her surroundings shimmered and shifted, and suddenly she was in the throne room, and Idris was before her, reclining on his throne.

'I heard that the Asterian nearly escaped today,' he drawled, his tone dripping with disinterest.

Enzo – now clothed and standing – tensed in front of his father.

'You weak, pathetic excuse for a prince,' Idris snarled, and light gathered between his fingers. Enzo didn't so much as flinch. 'You are meant to be watching her. You are meant to be making her into a weapon to defy *gods*.'

'I'm sorry, Father,' came the monotonous reply.

'You will be. You know what comes next. Remove your shirt.'

Fabric was shrugged to the ground as Elara watched in dread.

'Turn around.'

The prince did, and Elara found herself looking into Enzo's empty eyes, as light flared behind him.

It whipped over Enzo's skin, and his jaw clenched. Elara gasped.

The lash of light came again, and Enzo breathed out harshly.

Again and again it came, until finally Enzo cried out, falling to the floor.

'Enzo!' she shouted, leaping towards him. He looked up then, with such a haunted, despairing look in his eyes that he was almost unrecognizable.

'Elara?' he rasped, his voice ragged.

The dream changed again. Once more they were back in the marbled room, though it had shrunk in size, the numbers glowing upon the wall. She took a step forwards, bringing a palm to the side of Enzo's face. He winced and she dropped her hand.

'It's okay,' she murmured. 'Breathe.'

He took a shuddering breath.

'Good,' she said. 'Now another.'

He obeyed her command. She went to put her palm to his face again, and this time he leaned into it, closing his eyes as he exhaled deeply.

'You're just dreaming,' she said, kneeling opposite him,

unwilling to move her hand. Light throbbed out of the darkness, readying to strike, and with a snarl, Elara struck her free hand out, shadows spewing from her. They choked the savage rays, quelled the source of that awful whip, and deadened the flames. Black smoke wreathed out around her until finally, her shadows won the battle, launching the dreamscape into darkness. Cool air swept over them as the flames abated, and Elara pulled the shadows back to her, letting out a slow breath as her darkness kissed them both.

'See?' she said, raising his head. 'Just a dream.'

Enzo opened his eyes warily, looking around them. Her shadows danced out towards him, and she smiled to see them, bringing her hand back to her lap.

'How did you do that?' he asked hoarsely.

She shrugged, smiling. 'I guess sometimes the Light needs the Dark.'

She rose, stretching out a hand to him. He took it, though the touch was feather-soft in the dreamscape, his gold gaze locked on hers as he stood up.

'The place could use some décor,' she said lightly, looking pointedly to the dripping, bloody numbers. She was trying not to show Enzo that she was still shaking at what she'd witnessed. His gaze followed hers, his expression bleak. 'What do those numbers mean?'

Enzo closed his eyes, taking a deep breath. 'Three hundred and thirty-three. The number of Asterians I've killed.'

Elara took a step back, dropping his hand.

'I remember every single one. Their names, their faces.' His eyes searched hers wildly.

Elara didn't know what to say. She had known he'd killed many, and knowing the exact number sickened her. Yet it stunned her that he remembered. That his actions haunted his dreams.

Her mouth worked. 'Thank you for telling me,' she finally replied. 'Next time this happens,' she added, 'just remember my shadows.' Her lip quirked. 'They seem to like you more than I do.'

His head jerked up. 'What did you just say?'

She frowned. 'I said my shadows seem to like you more than I do.'

He gave her a strange look, replacing that eerie darkness in his eyes.

'What you saw, in the throne room—'

'I won't tell a soul, if that's what you're worried about.'

His eyes fluttered shut, and something twisted within her, something that couldn't stand to see her brave, arrogant enemy look so defeated. 'And Enzo . . . I think you have your own monster to slay.'

His eyes flew open at that, but she had already turned, pointing to the wall.

'Did you know that you can make your dreamscape whatever you want once you're aware of it?' She waved a hand, and the bloody numbers disappeared, a clean marble wall in their place. Enzo sagged. 'Fill it with good memories.'

She took a step towards him. 'Here,' she pressed a soft kiss to his cheek, like the flutter of a butterfly's wing. 'There's one to begin with.'

Enzo's breathing hitched as his eyes bore into hers. He moved to grab her hand but, just like all the dreams she walked through, of another's skin against hers, she barely felt it. She looked at it, then back at him, seeing his form fade as he began to wake.

'Rest, Enzo. And remember, this was all just a dream.'

CHAPTER NINETEEN

Elara jolted back into her body, pressing a trembling hand to her heart. Her eyes flew straight to Enzo's room, to the glow now radiating from his windows. She jumped up, rushing from the balcony before he could see her, then snuck under her covers, making sure every torch was out as her heart continued to pound. She waited a minute, two, before peering through her open doors and at the balcony beyond. Enzo's shadowy silhouette was leaning on his balcony, looking directly at hers. She squeezed her eyes shut, feigning sleep until it finally claimed her.

When she woke, she willed the previous night's events far away from her mind. As she got dressed for the day, she pushed aside the image of Idris standing over Enzo. When Merissa glamoured her, she closed her eyes against the pain etched into Enzo's eyes as he'd looked at her. When Leo took her to the training yard again, she tried to rid herself of the dripping lurid numbers and the wild sorrow in Enzo's voice. She had called him a monster. But monsters were created, not born. What could Enzo have been without a father like Idris? Did it matter?

'Holy fucking *Stars*!' she cursed as a blade of light rapped on her knuckles, ripping her from her thoughts, the bite of it stinging.

Leo raised a brow. 'You think that Ariete will allow you to daydream?'

She swore again, summoning her shadows. She'd been able to manipulate one or two into a murder of crows. But as they nose-dived for Leo, they dissipated into smoke the moment they touched him.

'If I punished you for every filthy curse that came out of your mouth, you'd have no time to actually train,' he said sweetly.

'Here's a thought,' she replied, raising a sword in one hand as she pulled her shadows in with the other. 'How about you stop wounding me, and maybe I'll speak like a *princess*.'

She tried to attack again, but only served to nearly cut her own toe off when Leo knocked the blade from her hand.

He chuckled, relenting. 'Drop a hundred.'

She cast him a venomous look as she got to the ground, counting out her press-ups at a measured pace. Her core burned, but she noticed with pride that the press-ups got easier each day that passed.

'Have you spoken to Enzo at all?'

Leo pressed his tongue into his cheek. 'Why? Missing him?'

'The only thing I miss about that man . . .' she huffed, 'is the fact that . . . as a trainer . . . he was a cuddly animal compared to you.' She gritted her teeth, halfway through her set.

'A cuddly animal. I'll pass that on.'

'Please do. Add that he should be renamed "The Kitty of Helios".'

Leo snorted, bending down by her. 'I did. Speak to him that is.'

'And what did he have to say?'

'Oh, nothing about you. We were planning the Feast of Leyon tonight.'

'And what exactly is that?'

'Today marks the anniversary of Leyon's Descent – the first time our Star fell from the heavens and chose Helios as his patron kingdom. We celebrate here by holding a revel – usually by the palace waterfall.' He studied Elara. 'Why don't you come?'

Elara laughed. 'Ah yes, an Asterian with a Star hunting her attending a feast for a Helion god. I think I'll pass.' She stood, handing back her sword. 'But . . . thank you for asking.' She was trying to be a little more forgiving with the general.

'Suit yourself,' Leo shrugged. 'But I'm warning you – you're missing out on the night of your life.'

Elara had planned to spend her evening in bed finishing her latest read of *The Mythas of Celestia*, but she kept being disturbed by the sounds of the feast below – music playing, cheers and laughter. After a while, she closed the balcony doors resolutely, and again tried to focus on the story.

When she'd read the same page fifteen times, still unable to get the images she'd seen of Enzo the night before out of her mind, there was a knock on her bedroom door.

Elara frowned as she opened it, and was greeted by Merissa. 'Fancy having some fun for once?' she asked, giving her a half-smile.

Elara shook her head. 'If you're talking about the revel, as I told Leo earlier, I can't think of a worse idea.'

'You need to blow off a little steam. You have so much on your shoulders, and you've done nothing but train.'

Elara sighed. 'I suppose, but I . . . I don't know anyone.'

'You know me,' Merissa said firmly. 'Plus, I've already picked out your outfit.'

She produced a hanger with a glittering terracotta dress upon it, intricately stitched beading forming patterns of day-orchids across the fabric. 'So now you can't say no.'

Elara looked around, drinking in the emerald of her surroundings as Merissa guided her down a hidden path. Elara had a vague sense that they were at the rear of the sprawling palace. It seemed that every few steps, another trickling fountain poured in a secluded alcove, or an intricate arbour hid within the greenery. When she heard a drift of music and laughter she patted the two goldstone jewelled combs that Merissa had swept half of her hair up with.

'I've never seen this part of the palace,' Elara said as she peered into the waning dusk and saw what appeared to be a maze of neat hedges forming concentric spirals.

'Leo's mother helped design the whole thing.'

'Close enough to call him Leo, hm?' she asked.

Merissa blushed, offsetting her mint green dress, which made her look unfairly stunning.

'We're quite close,' she said. 'After all, I've worked with Kalinda for years.'

Elara smiled as they continued past, the scent of dusk-daisies and starflowers permeating the evening air. As she caught a whiff of the powdery-scented silver-white flower, she thought of the bouquets Lukas would pick for her from the palace grounds. How he would sprint away laughing while the gardener chased him with a trowel, before thrusting the flowers into her hands. Her stomach turned thinking about her old life, and Lukas, and how nothing had turned out as she'd hoped.

'So, you've never courted?' she asked, banishing him from her mind.

'Oh, no,' Merissa said hurriedly. 'Leo would never look at me that way. And I . . . well, I don't have a very lucky streak when it comes to love.'

'If Leo doesn't look at you that way, then Leo is blind, Merissa.'

Merissa blushed at that, and as they finally reached a sunken garden, Elara heard the rush of water before she saw it. The waterfall behind the palace cascaded in glittering gold down the length of a cliff face into a churning pool, framing the secluded space. Steam rose from its surface as it swirled, and throngs of people were swimming in the pool, or dangling their feet in the water. More were dancing around a crackling fire, others were sprawled upon the grass, and Elara stopped, mouth agape as a flame-thrower shot fire from his hands in a billowing cascade, whooping and swaying to the music of drums and strings. Elara turned wide-eyed to Merissa, who smiled.

'Welcome to Leyon's Feast.'

As they reached the grassy shore by the waterfall, Elara scanned it. Her stomach did a flip, her eyes searching warily for Enzo.

'Elara!'

Elara turned in surprise to Leo, who grinned as he kissed her hand.

'Oh my,' Elara said, 'has someone had a drink?'

He gave another lazy smile as he kissed Merissa's hand too. 'One or two.' He turned back to Elara. 'I thought you were "passing" on the feast.'

'Well, someone convinced me.' She jerked her head to Merissa.

'Merissa's a charmer. Aphrodean through and through.'

Elara laughed as Merissa gave a garbled thanks.

'We're sat over here,' Leo said, and pulled them towards the water's edge.

We? Elara didn't like the sound of that. But to her relief, she saw only a woman sat there, with long black braids, her feet in the water.

'Isra,' Elara called out.

Isra turned at her name, smiling as she beheld Elara.

'Well, well,' she said. 'It seems you chose a different path after all.'

She held her arms out, and Elara gingerly embraced her. 'I'm happy you stayed,' Isra murmured into her ear.

Elara smiled as she settled on the grass beside her.

'Fancy a drink?' Isra waved a bottle, and Elara took it eagerly. She'd need more than one to sate the worry of running into Enzo at every turn.

She swore loudly as she took a swig. Leo and Isra scoffed.

'Isra, what in the Stars' names is this?'

'Flamespirit, from Kaos.'

'Two more sips of that and I'll be drunk.'

Isra winked. 'Keep drinking then, princess. Stars know you could use it.'

A buzzing began to thrum in her veins as the liquor seeped into her. The drink made her feel warm and fuzzy, and her head was soon blissfully fuddled. She allowed the sounds of the night to wash over her – the relaxing buzz of cicadas, the light-hearted conversation and gossip between Merissa, Isra and Leo, interspersed with laughter. She heard other voices, the plucking of a tune and a raucous ballad being sung by someone who had definitely had too much wine.

The musician's song picked up, and she heard it soar as she felt an arm wrap around her. It was Leo's. 'You'd better learn this song, Elara,' he said.

'*Theeeeere once was a lass, who had a hell of an—*'

'ASS!' everyone around Elara shouted, laughing and dancing.

'*And liked a good roll in the green, green grass!*'

Elara chuckled as a burst of firelight from another flame-thrower lit up the whole scene. She saw lightcasters direct their hands to the sky in their drunken reverie, their rays spilling out in flaming patterns across the deep red sky. And not a flicker of fear ran through her.

She looked around the clearing as she thought of Enzo and *his* light, lazily scanning the revellers sprawled on the grass or dancing. Some were kissing and touching in their drunken hazes. She swallowed, avoiding them until someone arrested her attention.

Enzo was lying down in the grass, a pretty, curvy blonde lying next to him as she tried to play with his hair. It was mussed, his crown lopsided on it. He batted her hand away as she giggled. He looked . . . bored. Elara's cheeks heated, and she made to turn her head before he saw her, but it was too late. His drunken gaze flicked languidly to her, then away, and then back, steeling in recognition. Elara turned quickly away, accidentally knocking Leo's drink as she did so.

'A little too much Kaosian spirit for the lady,' he said warmly. She forced a laugh, looking back to where Enzo was. His gaze was burning into her, too dark to read. She met his stare defiantly until, with what looked like a scoff, the prince turned his attention away. She felt too hot, and was grateful when Isra passed the bottle back to her. She took a sip, knocking it back with a wince.

'Rough day?' Leo asked. She cast him a scornful look as Isra and Merissa got up to dance.

'You tell me. You're the one who was assaulting my poor muscles.' She dipped her feet into the warm water as he laughed, sipping his own cup of wine.

'This court,' she said hesitantly, glancing at the soft moans and open displays of affection around her. 'It's very . . . uninhibited, isn't it?'

Leo choked on his wine, laughing. 'What makes you say that?'

'Well . . . in Asteria, it would be considered improper, embracing so openly. And would be particularly preposterous if you were royalty.'

'Ah,' Leo said knowingly. 'Might you be referring to our esteemed prince?' he asked innocently.

She heard splashes in the distance as people jumped into the temperate waters for a midnight swim. Bringing her attention back to Leo, she nodded, cheeks flushing again.

'I thought he was courting that pretty chestnut-haired girl from the banquet?'

Leo threw back his head and laughed. 'Who? Raina? You're mistaken, Elara. Enzo doesn't court.' He laughed again as though she had suggested the funniest thing. 'He likes to . . . enjoy himself. You could say the pressures of his life need a release. And, well,' his lips quirked over his wine, 'he definitely finds release.'

Elara felt she may as well be the Light itself, the way her face was flaming. She took another swig, very aware of how her head had already begun to spin thanks to her empty stomach.

'Are you scandalized?' Leo's tone was teasing.

'I'm not a naïve maiden,' she replied sharply, feeling the cool steel of the dagger at her thigh grounding her. 'In Asteria we take lovers too,' she said pointedly. 'Just not so openly.'

She traced a finger around her goblet pensively. Her thoughts flitted to Lukas again.

'I had one. But we would never dream of displaying ourselves like that in front of my court.'

Leo's brows were raised at her honesty.

She smiled. 'And I don't see the fuss anyway. Love-making certainly wasn't anything to write home about.'

'Then maybe,' a deep voice said behind her, 'you just haven't found a man who knows how to seduce you properly.'

CHAPTER TWENTY

She felt water drip on her shoulder and turned in disbelief as Enzo sat down beside her. He was slick with water; it ran off his bare chest in rivulets. He was far too close to her, his wet trousers brushing her legs as they dangled in the water.

'Enzo,' she said, a little out of breath. 'Do you ever wear a shirt?'

He pushed wet curls back from his face and rested back on his elbows, an indolent smile on his face as he reached over and picked up a cup of wine from beside Leo. 'I don't hear any other women complaining.'

She muttered a prayer.

'How drunk *are* you?' she asked, looking at him dubiously.

'Pleasantly drunk,' he said. 'But still sober enough that I'll remember your conversation with Leo in the morning.' His grin widened.

She observed him for a moment, searching for a glimpse of the man from the night before, vulnerable and afraid. But with his curling lips and eyes sparking, she came up short. Sliding a look at Leo, then back to Enzo, she said, 'Can we talk?' She edged closer, her hand resting on his as she looked at him in earnest. She noticed how warm it felt, the droplets of water on it wetting her palm. His eyes flew to her hand, his nostrils slightly flared. Then he met Leo's gaze, some silent order passing between them before Leo stood and disappeared into the fray.

'This isn't going to be an apology,' she warned, and Enzo muttered a prayer under his breath. 'But . . . I stayed. Which means that I clearly want to be your . . . tentative ally?'

Enzo frowned.

'I mean, that *is* what we are. We have a common goal, a common enemy. So I suppose, what I'm trying to say is . . .' She sighed. Why had she drunk so much? 'I think I need you.'

A look passed over Enzo's face, and was masked too quickly for Elara to decipher it.

'You helped me face my fear. I'd like to work together again. And it will be different now – because I've chosen to stay.'

He looked at her for a long time, long enough that her skin started to prickle, before he replied. 'In an unfortunate turn of events, I need you too,' he said. 'So, tentative allies – I suppose that's what we are.'

Something eased within Elara, something she hadn't realized she'd cared about.

He leaned in closer, blocking out the rest of the revel.

'I had an interesting dream last night,' he murmured, so low that only Elara could hear.

'Did you?' She turned her head, gulping her wine to the dregs.

'Yes. You didn't happen to be dreamwalking, did you?' His breath was a lethal caress on her jaw.

'I don't know what you're talking about,' she breathed, staring straight ahead so that her eyes wouldn't betray her.

She could see him out of the corner of her eye, fixated on her.

She felt a warm hand touch her chin, moving it to face him. His eyes searched hers, and she willed cool indifference into them.

'You're a terrible liar.' He gave a playful smile, his touch light as he grew close enough for their lips to touch. 'Thank you.'

Her mouth worked, and his eyes flicked to her lips then drew back to her eyes.

She pressed her lips closed, giving a small nod. She went to turn away, but his hand held her close. 'There's something else I need to tell you,' he slurred. She frowned as Enzo looked around, seemingly making sure nobody was in earshot, before leaning in closer to her. 'The Borderland Fires . . . I didn't—' He sighed a heavy breath. 'I warned the village before it happened. My father gave the order, and I knew I had no choice. But I made sure everyone got out first. Then I incinerated it. It had to look real.' He breathed in deeply. 'The women, the children, they're all alive and safe, living in the Goldfir Forest on the Helion side of the border. Leo goes to visit them from time to time with food and supplies.' That wild earnestness was in his eyes again. 'I just— I needed you to know that.'

Elara looked at him, searching, her mouth agape. Between his nightmares and what he had just confessed – the *treason* he'd just revealed – she was speaking to an entirely different person.

'I believe you,' she said finally as relief crashed through her. 'Thank you. Thank you for saving them.'

He gave a curt nod, releasing his grip on her before knocking back what remained in his goblet in one gulp. Thankfully, Leo and Isra returned then, the latter throwing herself to the ground, out of breath.

'Wonderful for you to grace us with your presence,' Isra said, passing her own bottle to Enzo.

'Careful,' Elara warned. 'That stuff is lethal.'

Enzo raised an eyebrow, his eyes fixed on her as he took a sip. He swallowed it, grinning. 'Lightweight,' he whispered.

She swirled the water below her with her toes, absent-mindedly listening to Leo and Enzo as they exchanged stories of their childhood. Isra butted in now and then to correct them or grumble about the torture she'd endured at their hands.

'He was always luring Isra and me into trouble,' Leo was saying.

'Do you *know* how many times I had to save Enzo's arse before he learned to control his magick? The palace would have burned to the ground ten times over if it wasn't for me putting out his fires.'

'You're exaggerating. I had impeccable control.'

Isra raised a brow. 'Leo, was it *you* who *singed* the cook's eyebrows off that time, or Enzo?'

Leo furrowed his brow in mock thought. 'Enzo.'

'Point proven.'

Merissa appeared, looking a little fearful as she curtsied to the prince. He waved a hand through the air.

'None of that tonight, Merissa. Sit with us.'

Merissa did, producing a small basket.

'I raided the kitchens,' she said, a shy smile playing on her lips.

Isra applauded loudly and started chanting Merissa's name, the others quickly following suit. Merissa beamed as she offered Elara the basket.

'Chocolate-dipped gildberries,' she said, taking one for herself. Elara picked one up and sucked on it, swirling the velvety chocolate around her tongue. She dropped her head back in pleasure.

'Now these,' she said, savouring it, 'these *are* something to write home about.'

Leo roared, Isra and Merissa looked confused, and Elara turned to glance at Enzo. His eyes were black, gaze dragged to her lips as she sucked on her berry. Her surroundings faded to a distant drone as she looked at him, some dark part of her wanting to continue. She raised a thumb to her lips and nonchalantly licked the melted chocolate off. He leaned perceptibly closer, and she saw his fist clench in the grass. His eyes found hers, and she smiled a smile lent of her darkness.

Then the moment was shattered, the world coming back around her with a blast of rowdy music.

'I love this song!' Merissa yelled, hauling Elara up. Breaking eye contact with Enzo, Elara dragged her feet as Merissa hauled her over to the dancing by the fire. Elara joined in. She spun and whirled until Merissa's hands left her for another. A handsome soldier smiled down at her, his eyes the colour of topaz gems as he went to take her hand.

'I don't think so,' Enzo's voice said behind her. The soldier dropped Elara's hand, raising both of his in surrender as he turned around. Enzo gripped her hand tightly, spinning her arm.

Her eyes narrowed. 'That was rude,' she said.

'Was it?' His eyes were wide with play-acted innocence. 'Can't have anyone seeing through your glamour.' With a winning smile he raised his cup, filled with a swirling amber liquid.

'Ambrosia, a token of peace,' he added.

'Drink of the Stars? How expensive *is* that?'

Enzo shrugged, taking a sip. 'So you don't want to try it?'

'I didn't say *that*,' she scowled.

His gaze burned as he brought the cup to her lips. She hesitated, then, maintaining his stare, took a sip from it as he tilted it.

Warm, spiced sweetness slipped down her throat. It sparked in her veins, ecstasy mingling with the spirits she'd already consumed. She closed her eyes, sighing in satisfaction. She felt a shift inside herself as she raised her hands to the sky. She whirled in euphoria, shadows dancing behind her eyelids. She heard chanting, a drumbeat intensifying. She started laughing. Enzo was before her, dancing with her, light and fire pouring from him. Her shadows bent to him, curling around his light. She felt weightless. Then a flurry of images ran into one another beneath her eyelids, assaulting her senses. Two thrones – one made of pure, shimmering silver, the other of gold. Hungry red flames devouring them both. A roaring lion, and finally a blade plunged into a stone heart. Darker than any shadow, darker than any night.

CHAPTER TWENTY-ONE

Elara opened her eyes, gasping for air. Enzo was before her, concern plastered on his face. There was still laughter and dancing happening, and the flames leapt and cracked behind them, though now the shadows they cast on the grass set Elara's nerves on edge.

'Elara? Elara, are you okay?'

She looked at him, frowning.

'You've been standing there for ten minutes.'

'I was— weren't we dancing?'

He gave her a strange look. 'No,' he said slowly. 'After you drank the ambrosia, you went into this . . . trance. You haven't moved since.'

She blinked, the images in her head dissipating. 'I might have had too much wine.'

She walked precariously back to her group, bending to Merissa. 'I think I'm going to go back to the palace.' She sighed, a feeling weighing on her shoulders like a heavy shawl.

'Let me walk you back.'

'No, no, please. I'd rather go alone. I need some fresh air.'

Leo made to follow her, but she put a hand on his shoulder. 'I chose to stay,' she promised. 'You don't need to worry about me running off again.'

Leo pressed a kiss to her hand, and Isra hugged her once more. 'I hope to see you soon, Elara.'

She smiled. 'Me too.'

She searched for Enzo, but he was nowhere to be found, so with a shrug, she left.

She shuffled quietly back up the hidden path around the palace, the sound of her footsteps calming her and lifting whatever dark oppression had fallen over her. She was not ready for bed and found herself wandering the outskirts of the palace, to the maze that Kalinda had helped create. The breeze cooled her, the late evening hues dimming to a shade that reminded her of home. She felt a pang and thought of her parents, Sofia, her home – the life she had left behind.

The Light hung low, casting romantic shadows on all it touched. Statues of lovers embraced and lightlilacs stood proudly with open petals, their fragrance filling the summer-kissed wind. She heard the trickle of water, its sound soothing her. She followed it through the dense hedges of the maze. Glitterbugs and indigo crickets seemed to sigh, their thrumming agitation keeping her company. Her fingers trailed the soft waxen leaves of the hedge as she lost herself in the peace of the Helion night.

Eventually, she reached a small clearing at the centre of the maze, where she found an ornate fountain with two statues at its centre that stretched ten feet above her: a mermaid, in the arms of a pirate. His hands cradled her head as they looked at each other, lips parted, pleasure carved into the mermaid's face so the marble almost seemed alive.

Elara drifted around the fountain, taking it in, the sheets of blue and lavender water that cascaded from the shells adorning the mermaid's hair, the eyepatch across the handsome pirate's face. She dipped her hands in the base of the fountain, splashing her heated face, then settled herself on a bench that overlooked it. She sighed and looked to the sky. The stars twinkled back.

Always watching, she thought, throwing them a venomous glance. The strange vision had shaken her. That and Enzo's confession had thrown her off balance, new truths being revealed to her at every turn. The tumult of her thoughts were interrupted by a rustle. She looked around wildly. Then she laughed as Enzo stumbled through the clearing, stilling when he saw her.

'I was hoping you'd be here,' he said, his eyes still hazy with drink.

'Did you follow me?' Her heartbeat accelerated as he sat beside her on the bench, looking up at the cascading fountain.

'Yes,' he replied simply.

'I can see you found a shirt,' she said, glancing at the one slung over his shoulder, damp and clinging. 'Are you feeling quite well?'

He snorted, pushing a fallen wet lock from his face. 'This is my favourite part of the palace,' he said, gesturing to the secluded space.

'The fountain is so beautiful.' Elara admired it once more. 'What the artist captured . . . is the kind of love soulmates would have.'

Enzo made an amused sound, and Elara flicked him a wary look. 'Let me guess, you don't believe in soul-ties.'

Enzo sighed. 'No, I believe that they once existed. "The Ballad of the Mermaid and the Pirate" is one of my favourite tales. But that kind of magick doesn't exist any more.'

'I know,' Elara replied softly. 'Though sometimes, when

I looked upon my parents, I thought they might have been soulmates. It was as though they shared a soul, just like in the ballad. And I—' She swallowed. 'I'm almost relieved that they died together. I don't think one would have carried on living without the other anyway.'

Enzo was silent. 'Anyway,' she said hurriedly, 'the statue. Whoever carved it knew love. And knew it deeply, to produce such art.'

He looked at the statue briefly, then turned back to her. 'Or maybe they didn't know it at all, but craved it the way one craves air to breathe.'

She turned to him. 'I didn't pin you for a poet. The ambrosia must bring it out of you.'

He chuckled. 'Is it strange that I missed how you constantly irritate me?'

She smiled to herself. 'You must have had too much to drink if you're claiming you missed me.'

'I did miss you.'

She forced herself to look into his eyes, the warmth of the ambrosia settling over her. 'Please don't remember this in the morning, but I think I missed you too.' There was a beat of silence, too heavy in the night air. 'So,' she continued airily, 'do you have any other poetry to proclaim to me?'

Enzo turned then to study her, head propped on his hand. His gaze skimmed up her waist, her neck, the stray flowers in her hair. She saw a small smile form on his lips. Then he looked at her sincerely.

'You've caught the Light,' he said thoughtfully. 'But you're not just lightkissed . . .'

He looked down at her arm, tanned more deeply from hours training in the Light's rays, and he took it in his hands. The bare contact of skin made her breathing shallow as he held it gently. His eyes found their way back to her.

'You look like the Light has made love to you.' He scraped a rough thumb over the inside of her elbow, heat sparking, and she shivered, her lips parting. He gazed at her. 'Was that poetry enough?' He smiled wryly, and the moment was broken.

She gave an unsteady laugh. 'No wonder rumours of your rakish ways chase you.' She smiled back, noticing that his own smile didn't quite reach his eyes.

'Ah, with looks like this and the words to match, how could you not fall at my feet?' He stood, taking her hand. 'I think it's time I escorted you to bed.'

She looked at his hand disapprovingly.

'*Your* bed,' he amended.

'I'm *sure* you didn't mean to insinuate what you just did.'

His lips quirked. 'Why, of course not, Princess Elara. How could you ever think me anything but a perfect *ally*?'

She bit her lip, smiling, allowing him to pull her up and lead her into the palace.

When they reached her room, she turned to him, smoothing her skirt.

'Thank you,' she said, 'for walking me back. You didn't have to.'

He inclined his head. 'Yes, I did.'

'Why?' she asked, her voice low.

Taking her hand again, he raised it as he looked at her, and she had to tilt her head back to follow the movement.

'So that I could do this,' he said quietly, pressing her hand to his lips. A soft kiss like a feather sent shivers up her arm.

'Goodnight, Elara.' He turned.

'Goodnight, Enzo,' she replied, closing her door softly.

CHAPTER TWENTY-TWO

The next morning, pain pulsed through Elara as she lay glowering between her sheets. Merissa tutted in sympathy as she fussed around her, bringing her breakfast.

'You get them as badly as me,' she sighed. 'I'll fetch you some peppermint tea.'

'I'll be damned if I get out of this bed today,' Elara muttered. 'Not even His Highness will drag me out of it.'

Merissa chuckled, setting to work with the tea. There was a knock on the door, and it swung open, Enzo standing at the threshold.

'Dear skies, Enzo, I'm barely decent!' Elara yelled, grabbing a robe from the armchair beside her and wrapping it around her thin slip. His smile curled as he looked at her.

'As always, walking in without permission serves me well.'

'I'm not in the mood for your taunts today. Leave me be.'

His brow furrowed. 'You're late for training.'

'Oh really? Merissa, fetch him a medal for stating the obvious, will you?' She lay back on the pillows as Merissa hid her smile. Enzo took a tentative step into the room and looked around it, his eyes snagging on her open copy of *The Mythas of Celestia* and the pressed forget-me-nots that she was now using as a bookmark.

He blinked, turning his attention back to Elara. 'Are you unwell?'

'I have my monthly,' she replied, and his eyes softened. He closed the door, walking towards her, and she sat up in alarm. 'What are you doing?'

He sat on the edge of the bed. 'Is there any way I can help?'

'Why are you being so nice to me?' Her eyes narrowed as he rubbed his palms together. He avoided looking at her, his usual sarcastic smile on his face.

'We're allies now, aren't we? And the sooner I can get you feeling well again and back to training, the better.'

'So, you came, a knight in shining armour to distract me from my pain with your rambling.'

'I can think of many other ways I could distract you from the pain, princess,' he purred. She raised an eyebrow. 'What? You think a little blood scares me?' He smirked. 'Did you forget that I'm the warrior prince of Helios?'

Elara rolled her eyes, slumping back down on to her pillows as she tried to ignore the heat his words brought to her. She distracted herself in her favourite way, by insulting him. 'Trust you to find a way to praise yourself. It's a real talent, you know.'

'Here,' he said, ignoring her. 'Lift up your dress.'

'You know, for a rakish prince, I thought you'd be more well-versed in how to get a woman to drop her knickers. Merissa has spoken to me more romantically.'

Enzo threw back his head and laughed at that, the sound like bursting light. She gave a small smile and opened her robe, her thin slip underneath visible. Enzo shifted closer, the bed lurching with his weight until he was bent over her. Then with his eyes closed, there was the sound of crackling as he held his palms facing each other. With a furtive smile to her, he put his hands to her bloated stomach. She groaned against the sensation, the warmth immediately giving her some respite.

'That feels incredible.'

'Not the first time a woman has uttered those words in my presence.'

'And just like that, you ruined it.' She made to pull away, but he held her there, his strong hands pressing gently against her. She almost tried to fight it, but she was too exhausted and it felt too good.

'Does your magick increase at this time?' he asked, shaking a curl from his eyes as he looked up at her again.

'How did you know?'

'You act as though I don't know women.'

There was a tense pause as Elara felt a lurch of something in her stomach.

'Isra,' he said hurriedly, clarifying. 'Growing up with her I learned a *lot*. Her gifts become unruly around her cycle. It's a marvel to watch.'

Elara laughed. 'I can imagine.'

'Once, she froze an entire group of ambassadors from Altalune. Almost ruined an entire trade agreement between our kingdoms.' He chuckled at the memory.

'You're lucky to have each other,' Elara said quietly.

Enzo nodded. 'Isra is the closest thing I have to a sister. There is nothing we wouldn't do for each other.'

'How come Isra isn't still at court then?'

Enzo scoffed. 'Can you really imagine her here? She's far too impatient for the boredom and etiquette of palace life. The moment she was old enough, she left.'

'Hearing you talk about your childhood makes me miss Sofia.'

Enzo continued to warm her stomach, not looking at her. She gave a small smile. 'She was like a sister to me too. We grew up together in the palace. I remember once, when we were teenagers, succumbing to our *growing pains*, she caused a blackout through the entire kingdom.'

'How in the Stars' names did she do that?' Enzo asked incredulously. She laughed at the look on his face.

'I'd stolen her favourite dress to wear to the winter solstice ball. I told her she was just mad because I looked better in it than her.'

'Sounds like you,' he said.

Elara's lip quirked. 'So anyway, tempers grew. She told me that I was a spoilt little brat and let the darkness rip.' She shook her head. 'We had to host the entire ball by candlelight in the middle of the day. I think it actually made it more magickal, though.'

Enzo's eyes twinkled. 'Sofia deserves a commendation for her bravery, dealing with you all these years.'

'I still don't know what's happened to her,' Elara replied quietly. 'It's worse not knowing – whether she's alive or dead; whether she got out that day.'

Enzo squeezed her waist. 'We'll find out.'

She looked at him. 'We?'

He huffed out a laugh. 'Like it or not, we seem to be in this together now.'

A comfortable silence hung in the air as Elara smiled, revelling in the heat radiating from Enzo's hands as she closed her eyes. She was so drained, she barely noticed as she drifted and fell into limbo. But with Enzo's light upon her she seemed to stay there. She could still feel the pressure of Enzo's hands on her in the real world, though her dreamer's mind had begun to conjure another scenario. Enzo's hands were still on her stomach, but with a thought, she willed him to move them. His heated stare burned into her as he obliged, tracing teasing patterns over the thin material that stretched over her stomach.

'Like that?' he murmured, and she hummed a contented sigh. The circles his hand made grew bigger, sweeping lower. She met his gaze.

'Tell me what you want, princess,' he said softly.

She felt a shift, and her eyes flew open; the dreamscape shattered.

Enzo's gaze was fire as a slow smile curled on his lips. 'Having a nice dream?'

Her cheeks flooded with heat. 'What are you talking about?'

'The shadows within you are growing thinner the more you use them, princess. Which means I can see the emotions swirling in you more clearly. And right now they are red hot with desire.' His smile widened even more. 'I wonder who it was you were dreaming about.'

'Now why would a clever man like you want to taunt a woman at the height of her power? Perhaps a death wish is on you.'

'There are many things I wish from you.'

'If you're quite finished trying to get under my skin, you can go now. Thank you for . . . this.' She gestured to his hands, still on her. She had never wanted to slap the smirk off someone's face more.

He stood up. 'I'm glad you're feeling better.'

'More and more the further away you get.' She smiled sweetly.

'If you feel better tomorrow, I'll meet you for training as usual.'

She nodded, avoiding his eyes as she settled back under her sheets.

He turned from the door. 'Rest.' That stupid, taunting smile hadn't left his face. 'Oh, and Elara?'

She looked at him from behind her pillow.

'That little dream you just had? Only a shade of what I could do with you.'

CHAPTER TWENTY-THREE

Enzo once again assumed his position of begrudging teacher. Over the next few days, they fell into an easy routine of training, followed by lunch, which, true to Enzo's remark in the markets, always seemed to put Elara in better spirits. In the afternoon, she helped Kalinda in the gardens, or Merissa in the kitchens. Sometimes Isra would stop by to see Enzo, and she'd drop by the kitchen to gobble down a fresh cake or pastry with Elara and Merissa on her way out.

Her latest morning session was giving her a chance to display her improvements with her shadows. She could manipulate them with just a thought now, though they still lacked substance. Testing herself again, she threw one in the form of a shadow wraith at Enzo.

Light whizzed past and whipped her arm.

'*Ow!*' She shook off the smarting pain.

Enzo tutted at the red welt forming on it. 'You'll get a lot worse than that from Ariete if you don't put your shield up.'

She adjusted her shadows, packing in the darkness until it was a wicked, absorbing force.

'Now just imagine this is Ariete's starlight,' he said, and launched another ray of light at her.

At the last moment, she pulled her dagger from her thigh and channelled her shadows through it, swallowing his light.

'Good. But that's becoming a crutch. You rely on it too heavily. You need to wield your shadows on their own.'

'I do not,' she retorted. 'My technique works perfectly well. Or do you forget how I had you on your back and between my legs not so long ago?'

'Trust me, El. I've not forgotten. Although the next time you have me on my back and between your legs, I'm hoping there will be fewer clothes involved.'

'Brute!' She threw a shadow at him, her cheeks flushing as he dispersed it idly with a quick flick of his fingers. She ignored the curl of heat in her stomach at his words, focusing on the shadows playing at her fingertips.

'I don't remember saying you could call me El,' she mused.

His smile deepened. 'Precisely why I began calling you that.'

She shrugged her shoulders in exasperation. 'Must this torture never end? I prefer Leo's drills to this.'

With a broad laugh, he sat on the hard stone of the pavilion, the taut muscles of his bared stomach rippling.

'*I* don't remember,' he said, fire dancing between his hands, 'you ever explaining the fact that you have a dagger. Or how you wield it *nearly* as well as I wield a sword.'

She gave a mock bow.

'Now where would an Asterian princess learn to use a knife like that? Not that I'm complaining,' he added. 'It's one of the few things that makes you more tolerable.'

She refrained from throwing another shadow his way in a very vulgar shape, instead collapsing next to him with a sigh, feeling the soft rays of mid-afternoon beating down on her back. She wrestled with herself, before nodding with resolve.

'A secret for a secret?'

He looked at her uncertainly then finally nodded. 'Go on.'

'Sofia,' she began. 'Her mother, Juliette, was the captain of my father's guard. It's why we grew up together.' Sadness passed over Elara's face. 'She was found dead a few years ago.'

'What happened?' Enzo frowned.

Elara shrugged. 'We never found out. There were no wounds, so the healers put it down to an ailment of the heart. But I saw her before she was buried . . .' Elara shook her head against the image. 'She looked like she had died of fright. One of the most formidable warriors in Asteria, who had never shown an inch of fear. Petrified. I'll never forget the look in her eyes. It was as though she had seen pure evil.'

Elara shook her head, clearing it. 'By then, Juliette had taught me and Sofia everything she knew. We would train every day. My parents willed it so, after the . . . incident with the lightwielder. They already knew the prophecy, and without my shadows, I see now they wanted me to be able to defend myself however I could.'

She held the dagger between them. 'Sofia gifted me this one on my sixteenth birthday. See those obsidians? She said her shadows would always be with me, so long as I had the dagger.' Elara smiled. 'The silverstone, she said it reminded her of my eyes.' She stroked the hilt, and the dragun carved into it.

'So that's why the princess has a dagger and knows how to use it,' she finished. 'To defend myself when my gifts couldn't.'

She took a gulp of water, hands shaky.

'What?' she asked, taking in his stare.

'Have you ever used your gifts?' he asked quietly. 'I mean . . . to harm?'

She nodded. 'A couple of times, yes. The most recent one was here in Helios.'

Enzo slowly sat up. 'When?'

Elara froze, suddenly feeling like she shouldn't have answered. His piercing, bronze-flecked gaze burned right into her very soul.

'It was when I first arrived.' She saw Enzo's jaw clench. 'The moment we got into Sol, I tried to escape your guards. Some . . . found me.'

Enzo shifted imperceptibly, his eyes still on her. 'Who?' he asked coolly. Light, hard and frigid, caught her eye as it moved between his fingers, itching to shine.

'You think I was on a first name basis with them?'

'Description, Elara. Hair, eyes, what did they look like?'

'Does it matter?' She huffed out a nervous laugh.

'Yes,' he snapped.

'The ringleader was about forty. Sandy hair, scar across his temple?'

He thought a moment. 'Barric,' he nodded. There was a pause, and she let the sounds of the birds chirping in the branches of the jasmine trees wash over her as she pulled blades of grass through her fingers.

'Did they touch you?'

Elara stilled at the ice in his voice. This wasn't the drunken, charming prince, or the teasing ally. This was the voice of the most lethal warrior to grace Celestia. She didn't reply.

'Did they fucking touch you?' he asked again.

A shiver ran down her spine. Enzo's voice was usually lilting and warm, filled with fire. Now it was cool. Calm. Far too calm.

'Barric did,' she whispered. The memory that she'd worked to push down, to forget, rose unbidden, and panic gripped her. 'He made others hold me as he tore my gown. Kissed my neck. That's as far as he got before I brought his night-mares to life.'

She felt a rough hand raise her chin and Enzo's eyes searched hers. Some warmth had returned to his gaze, but ice still glittered underneath. He tucked a strand of hair behind her ear, his jaw tensing before he finally spoke.

'That will *never* happen to you again.'

'I know. I can handle myself.' She raised an eyebrow.

'Yes. But in my kingdom, you are under my protection.'

He stroked her cheek once, the gentle gesture turned her breathing shallow. At the last moment he stood and turned, his tall shadow cutting through the training ground to the palace. It was only once he'd left that she saw it. Scorched, blackened earth where he had sat, smoking madly in the afternoon rays.

CHAPTER TWENTY-FOUR

Elara woke the next morning to the smell of smoke. She coughed, arms reaching out blindly. Her eyes widening, she saw plumes of smoke rising, coming from the rough direction of the palace gates. She staggered to her feet in alarm, her view obstructed by the parapets and towers of the palace grounds.

Quickly pulling on her training clothes, she strapped her dagger to her thigh and ran out into the empty corridor, shouting for Merissa or Leo.

'Anybody? Help! There's smoke by the palace gates!'

The palace was as silent as the Graveyard and Elara fought to quell the rising panic inside. She flung herself around a corner, hoping that she was heading the right way. She began to hear the hum of a crowd and followed it. She spotted Merissa, who waved desperately, beckoning her over. With a lurch, she ran to her, holding her robe around her.

'What in the Stars is going on?' she cursed, straining over the heads of both palace guests and workers. Opposite where she had come from, there was another arched entrance to the yard, gated, and Elara saw beyond it even more crowds pressed against the bars, a roiling restless energy slithering through them.

'A public execution,' Merissa explained, peering over their heads herself. 'The bells tolled just before dawn. The biggest one we've had in years.'

Elara shook her head. '*Public* executions? You still have those?!'

Merissa looked at her as though *she* were insane. 'You don't in Asteria?'

'My father outlawed them decades ago.'

Merissa looked at her uneasily. 'You'd better not watch, then.' She turned to the spectacle.

Elara made to turn too, sickness waving over her. However, something ground her to the spot, a heavy pulling sensation in her stomach. She moved, peering through a parting in the crowd. Her breath stopped. A few steps led to a raised platform, a portico built upon it. And there, each tied to a pillar of the structure, were five men.

One, small and weaselly, had blood pouring from his nose. The next, short and muscled, had burns down one side of his face.

'Good gods,' Elara breathed.

The next looked around Elara's age, and wept through purple and swelling eyes. Blackened blood was encrusted on his lips and lids. The man beside him was cursing, deep lacerations all over his bare chest. The men who had held her down. The men who had watched.

Finally, at the end, moaning wordlessly, his tongue cut down to a blackened stump, visible as he wailed, she saw him. A sandy head, a scar across his temple.

Elara's breath quickened, her heart drumming such a song that it enveloped her, drowning out everything else – the sounds of the crowd, the gossip, the jeers.

'No, no, no,' she uttered, clutching the pillar next to her.

'Elara? Elara!' Merissa held her, concern plain on her features.

'He . . . He . . .' Stars, she couldn't breathe. She couldn't speak as the weight of what she saw before her crushed her. 'Where is he?' she snarled. 'Where *is* he?'

'Who?' Merissa frowned. 'Who, Elara?'

Elara sucked in mouthfuls of air, anger setting her chest aflame as the incomprehensible became clear. Then she saw him.

Prince Lorenzo, the Lion of Helios, all-powerful Son of Light, the deadliest warrior to grace the land in centuries. As he strolled slowly past the prisoners, clad head to toe in black, his eyes were stormy, his jaw set. He halted and turned to the crowd, looking down upon them.

'These men are charged with assault of the highest degree.' His voice carried across the space like the blade of a sword dealing a deadly blow. 'They have besmirched the name of the City Guard.' The prince spat at the feet of the ringleader as he moaned in pain. Elara lunged, trying to force the crowd apart to stop him, to make her way to the dais.

The morning light was dimmed in that moment by the glint in Lorenzo's eyes as he spoke, the crowd murmuring in disgust, taunting as the charges were read.

Elara tried to shout his name, but her voice was swallowed by the crowd.

'Let this be a lesson,' he shouted over them all, 'that this will be the fate that befalls anyone found guilty of the same. Of touching a woman against her will. Let this be a lesson,' he said, turning to the whimpering figures tied to the posts, one hand raised elegantly against the bright skies, 'that you will *burn*.'

A flick of his wrist and flames engulfed them all, their

screams coating the thick, heaving air. Some of the crowd cried in horror. Others cheered. Enzo scanned the crowd, tall and proud, until his eyes snagged upon Elara's. Her breath was stolen from her at the way the flames surrounding him burned within his eyes too. The sound of the crowd seemed to fade into the background, registering only as a dull roar in her ears, alongside distant, excited shouts of 'Burn, burn, burn.'

Enzo's stare did not leave her, and she couldn't withstand the fire that surrounded her any longer. Head spinning, she tore from Merissa's grip and ran at full speed through the palace gates, away from the baying crowd, and the Lion of Helios with them.

CHAPTER TWENTY-FIVE

Elara's breath was burning in her chest as she tore up the steep incline to the forest. The rough undergrowth tore at the soles of her soft shoes, her skirt snagging on branches as she passed. Ragged breaths escaped her as she continued, pushing herself into the shade. Far away from the sounds of death.

She slumped under the canopy of trees in the place where she had first trained with Enzo. The thought made her recoil.

She lay down, panting. The horror of what she had just witnessed continued to assault her – the flames, the screams, the stench of burning flesh and fire. Anger and shock mingled in a sickly waltz.

It was not Enzo's choice to make, and yet, he had made it anyway, the hot-headed fool. The betrayal was a knife in her gut and instead of pushing the emotion down, she let it fuel her, seething until shadows flooded the clearing. There wasn't even a slice of light, her magick swallowed it all whole.

She wasn't sure how long she lay there, trying to wrangle her pounding heart and terrible memories under control.

The darkness that surrounded her gave no indication of the time of day.

Suddenly, a crack of a twig had her on her feet. She stilled, sliding her dagger out of its sheath. Poised, she crouched low, a panther ready to strike. There was a shadow, and she pounced, knocking it to the ground. Moments later she straddled her victim, who had gone down far too easily for someone so large.

In the darkness, a familiar voice said, 'You love to force me into compromising positions, don't you?'

Elara pushed off Enzo, stomach lurching. 'Get the fuck away from me,' she hissed.

'El, we need to talk,' he sighed as he propped himself up.

'Don't you dare call me that. You're not my *friend.*'

Enzo flinched at her words as though they'd struck him.

'Elara,' he said, and his voice was hard now. 'I'm not leaving until we speak.'

'Then speak,' she snarled, whipping around to face him, arms folded like armour across her chest. Her eyes suddenly throbbed. She sank on to a flat rock and pushed the heels of her hands into them furiously.

'El,' he said again, and she turned to see him crouching near, his height meaning he had to sit on his heels to meet her gaze.

'I let myself forget who you were,' she said quietly. Then laughed dully. 'It's too easy when you charm – when you smile. Easy to not remember that you're a lion in lamb's clothing.' She saw his jaw clench and his eyes flash. *Good,* she thought. 'And then I saw him. That man, tied there. Who I'd told you about in confidence, who you knew I'd handled. And a part of my mind still wanted to believe it was a co-incidence. That there was no way that my *ally* would have gone searching for him. No way that it would be by his hand that the guard would burn.' She raised her eyes to the canopy above them.

'But there you were. Like Death itself, not a flicker of emotion as you burned them all.' She closed her eyes, shaking her head. 'Do you have any idea what you've done? This is on my head, my burden to bear now. What about the men with him, too? It's my fault that they're all dead. Because I told you, trusted you.'

There was only silence as she took a shuddering breath. 'Don't you have anything to say?'

He stood then, his face a mask in the gloom.

'Yes, I have something to say. Not one of them was innocent. They fucking *touched* you, Elara. I *saw* them – looked into their very souls, before I tied them to posts. They'd all done it before. To women who couldn't fight back. You weren't the first and you wouldn't be the last.'

He paced the ground like a wild cat. 'And this happened to you in *my* kingdom.' His voice broke then, ragged. 'Do you have any idea how that felt? That you were hurt under my protection, when you were *my* responsibility?'

He clamped his jaw shut. Elara opened her mouth to retort, but he silenced her.

'You sit here, angry that I was too merciless, too cruel in my punishments.' He circled back to her, crouching before her again. 'You ask me what I have to say,' he growled, his voice so low that she felt a fire ignite in the pit of her stomach. 'I say it was my choice, my burden to bear, and don't you dare for a second take it as your own. I have to say that I would fucking do it again and enjoy watching every last one of them suffer for what they tried to do to you.'

Then he let out a long breath. 'But I *am* sorry that I upset you. That's the last thing that I wanted to do, El. They just . . . they deserved it. So I won't once regret ending their lives.'

There was such an earnest look within his gaze that her anger began to sputter.

'You don't just get to decide something like that, Enzo. You could have told me your plans, at least warned me.'

'You're right,' he said softly. 'I didn't think about how it would make you feel.'

She looked at him, searching his eyes. She tracked the golden glimmers shining within them, but deeper than that, some of the chestnut warmth she had come to know.

Against her will, almost without thinking, she raised a hand, brushing a curl out of his eyes. Her hand rested then on the side of his head. Enzo closed his eyes, exhaling slowly.

Emotions warred within her – anger, betrayal, pride, understanding. She exhaled deeply, deciding on which to pick. But she was so tired of battling her own mind. And here was one person in her corner, someone who had carried out his own retribution – albeit extreme and bloodthirsty – for her.

'You owe me a secret.' She finally decided on forgiveness, a tentative smile on her face. He opened his eyes, a startled laugh escaping him.

'I do,' he said, pulling her down on the soft moss. She propped herself up by her elbows. He stared at the dense canopy above them, arms behind his head. She roamed her eyes over his broad chest and arms.

Without looking at her, he said, 'I created the fountain.'

Her eyes flew to his face. 'What?!'

He smiled at her disbelief, still staring up. 'I'm not just beauty and brawn, princess.' He laughed. 'It's my gift,' he explained as shimmering white ribbons cascaded from his fingers, glowing faintly. They reached out to the trunk of a nearby tree, and Elara watched in awe as his magick carved a letter into the bark.

'E?' she said. 'For Enzo, or Elara?'

Enzo only winked in reply, before he cast the light up towards the canopy, and Elara gasped, lying on her back beside him as they watched together. He dispersed the light so it looked like a thousand stars across the covering of leaves, dancing in slow patterns.

More splendid than stars, she thought to herself, smiling.

'Creating art calms me.'

Elara let his words sink in, still mesmerized by the gentle flashes playing above them.

'You take this big ugly lump of stone, and you chip and chip at it with the Light until this beautiful thing is revealed underneath.' He shrugged.

Elara's thoughts flew back to their conversation and what he had said about the art as they'd sat in the maze.

'So, if I'm to remember correctly,' she asked, eyes still glued to the dancing glimmers above, 'you've never been in love?'

His lip quirked. 'Ah, a secret for a secret.'

They sat in silence as he created rainbows and patterns with his powers, the colours vibrant, reflecting on their faces in the darkness. How had she ever been terrified of *this* light? How had she seen it as anything other than beautiful?

'*I've* never been in love,' she said, scrutinizing the canopy with a gulp. She felt a very small shift in his body next to her, and dared not look.

'Oh really?' Enzo's voice was teasing. 'Not even your darling lover that left you wanting in the bedroom?'

She could hear the smirk in his voice and struck out to hit his arm from where she was lying. She felt him catch her hand, stopping her, and he brought it to rest between them. She became acutely aware of the fact that he hadn't moved the hand that now covered hers.

She peeked at him from the corner of her eye and saw him still staring at the shelter of leaves above them, his head still propped on one arm.

'Not even him,' she said, hiding her own smile in her voice. 'Lukas and I were betrothed – our marriage was arranged when we were children.'

Enzo's skin sparked against her own. 'Is he your *soulmate* then?' His voice dripped with derision.

Elara shook her head. 'I've never felt passion for him. Or desire – true desire. That all-consuming need I've read about. I've never felt . . .' She paused, trying to find the word.

'Fire,' Enzo murmured, a soft laugh on his breath. Her stomach thrilled.

'Yes,' she breathed. 'Fire.'

Elara could feel the heat pouring from him. She dared not look for fear of what she might feel if she saw that same spark in his eyes.

She felt warmth skitter up her arm, licking the inside of her wrist as invisible flames flowed from Enzo's hand on to hers. The sensation sent rivulets of excitement running through her body, caressing her neck, warming her to her core. She felt such a visceral *longing* from the touch that her mouth went dry, the thrill in her stomach sinking lower as she attempted to change the subject.

'I loved Lukas, but I've realized since that I was never *in* love with him. He was sweet and kind. But . . .' She shook her head. 'He changed. A darkness began to grow in him. We were warned of it, you know, as shadowmancers. That if we don't control our shadows, then there's a risk of drowning in them. Lukas became unpredictable. Would fly into terrible tempers. But I'd always see glimpses of the boy I knew, and that made me stay – made me continue our betrothal. We had known each other since we were children. And—' she swallowed, forcing her voice not to tremble. 'And then he betrayed me. The boy I trusted with my life.'

'What did he do?' Enzo's voice scraped across her skin, and she risked a glance at him. His gaze was burning into the canopy, his shoulders locked.

'He summoned Ariete.'

And there it was. She'd never spoken the words aloud before.

'It was my birthday. Right before your men kidnapped me. Sofia snuck me out to the travelling fair in town, and convinced me to go to the seer's tent for a reading – a *love reading.*' Elara rolled her eyes. 'She never liked Lukas. I suppose she wanted me to see that there was another future for me. The oracle was one of Lias's priestesses. And . . . well, she told me a prophecy.'

Enzo nodded. 'I know that a prophecy was spoken about you. My father told me. But he didn't tell me exactly what was foreseen.' He paused, before asking solemnly, 'What did she tell you?'

Her hand trembled, but Enzo's hold over it grounded her, gave her the courage to utter the next sentence.

'She told me that I would fall in love with the King of Stars. And that it would kill us both.'

Enzo said nothing.

'I ran back to the palace in tears with Sofia, and told Lukas, before I confronted my parents. My parents wept – they told me that the same prophecy had been spoken at my naming ceremony. That they had done everything to stop it coming to fruition, to hide me. There was a small party that night at the palace to celebrate my birthday. Only for those closest to me and my family. It was late, Lukas and I were dancing and

I saw something fall to the ground. A bloodied Ram card from the Stella deck. Ariete's card.'

Enzo let out something like a hiss of anger.

Elara nodded. 'Lukas called upon his favour. I don't know what it cost him, and I still can't fathom why. Maybe he was angry – I mean, when I first told him he was furious before I managed to calm him down – I was his betrothed after all. Or maybe he thought he could try and kill the Star. I know,' she said, when Enzo snorted, 'it's not that easy. But he'd been growing more untethered the last few months. Whatever it was, Ariete appeared in a streak of light, and well . . . the rest you know.'

Enzo was quiet for a long time, and all Elara could hear was her heart pounding.

'You're destined for Ariete?' Enzo asked roughly.

She nodded. 'I just can't believe that my fate could be tied to someone so cruel. How can he be the other half to my soul? But according to the prophecy, he is.'

'You deserve to feel *true* love, El,' Enzo said finally as his thumb began to trace the inside of her palm. Her breathing shallowed, trying to focus on the light show. 'You deserve to be adored.' His thumb stroked the inside of her wrist. 'To feel pleasure.' It came to rest back on her palm. He paused. 'To be the one they look for first in every room.'

Elara turned to him then, and Enzo turned to face her. They stayed, looking at each other as his light refracted above them, kissing them with patterns and shadow.

'I don't just want love. I want reverence.' She looked away. 'Is that too much to ask?'

She felt a hand under her chin and trembled slightly as he forced her to look at him. He held her gaze for a long time as sparkles traced their eyes. Finally, a breath parted his lips.

'No.'

His eyes flickered to her lips, gazing intently. His lips parted, and she felt it, a palpable tension in the air, something that would consume her if she breathed it in.

'I think you would be very easy to worship,' he murmured, his voice so soft she almost melted into it.

'Well, I doubt a god will be doing much worshipping,' she said quietly, and pulled away.

Enzo opened his mouth to speak, his hand reaching for her hair, as a low growl pierced the air.

Enzo was up in seconds, as silent as a wraith, his hand on his short sword. He moved in front of Elara as she stood slowly, unsheathing her dagger.

There was another growl, softer but closer this time, and Elara looked around wildly. Enzo cursed, bringing light to his hands to illuminate the penetrating darkness.

She gasped. Not two metres away from her was a wolf. As black as her shadows, its eyes flint grey. She might have mistaken it for a nightwolf, but the animal before her had no tail of smoke, no stars within its eyes. The wolf edged closer, and Enzo moved subtly, still shielding her.

Her eyes brimmed with tears as she squeezed his arm, brushing past him and moving closer to the wolf.

'Elara, I already think you're insane, but this may be the worst time to prove me right,' Enzo whispered.

'It's okay, Enzo,' she breathed, taking another small step, her hand outstretched. The wolf prowled closer, its wicked fangs gleaming. And then, with a whimper, it licked Elara's hand. She shuddered out a laugh as she tentatively stroked the wolf's head. It let out a low rumble, sinking down on its hind legs as it pushed its head against Elara's hand.

'What the fuck?' Enzo breathed behind her, taking a step closer.

The wolf whipped around, snarling, and Elara bit back a laugh, dropping the dagger to the ground.

'Enzo, meet Astra.'

'Can you please explain what in the Stars' names is going on?'

'The dragun was my family's sigil. Sofia made the wolf hers.' Tears were beginning to brim in Elara's eyes as she knelt and wrapped her hands around Astra's neck, breathing in the scent of her – of home. 'Wolves are Piscea's domain. And well, Sof had always been a little fanatical about the Star of Asteria. Sofia isn't Verdan so it's not like she could talk to animals, but she seemed to understand the wolves. And they her. She'd tame any stray we came across – and the wolves in the Shadow Woods would stop baying when she was near. We found Astra one day deep in the palace forest. She'd been wounded. Our groundskeeper made to shoot her, but Sofia threw herself in the arrow's path to stop him. We nursed Astra back to health, and ever since, she stayed close. To Sof especially.'

Astra whined, and Elara scratched her ears. 'She's found me for a reason,' she whispered. 'What is it, girl? Why are you here?'

The wolf whined again, nudging at the dagger in the grass. Elara picked it up. 'This?'

Enzo was still standing, completely dumbfounded.

The wolf whined again, nudging her wet nose against the stones. Elara frowned. 'What, Astra?'

The wolf prodded harder at the glittering obsidian jewels. 'I don't understand,' she said.

Astra growled, her hackles rising as she looked at Enzo. The shadows seemed to darken in the forest, and Elara shivered. And then, with a whine, and a last doleful look to Elara, she ran.

'Astra!' Elara shouted, stumbling to her feet. But the wolf had disappeared into the darkness.

CHAPTER TWENTY-SIX

Back at the palace, Elara looked over every inch of her dagger as she sat on her bed. She ran her hand along the blade, pushing at the crystals embedded in the hilt.

'Didn't you say something about Sofia and those jewels?' Enzo was pacing her room as he watched Elara furiously try to figure out what Astra had been trying to tell her.

'Yes. She said that the silverstone reminded her of my eyes, and that the obsidian . . .'

She trailed off, eyes wide. 'That the obsidian meant a part of her was always with me,' she finished.

'Try your shadows,' Enzo said.

Elara tentatively raised a hand over the large, glittering stone – one so black it showed her own reflection.

A trail of shadows ran from her fingers into the stone, and she waited with bated breath, staring into the jewel.

At first, nothing happened. But then, shadows began to gush out of the obsidian – darker and heavier than Elara's. She had felt them before – knew instantly who they belonged to.

And finally those shadows morphed into a figure.

'Lara?' the voice came distorted.

'Sofia?' Elara rasped.

Enzo watched wide-eyed from where he stood.

'Lara? Where are you? Did Astra find you? Did she show you—'

'The dagger, yes. You genius!' Elara gave a watery smile.

'I don't have much time,' Sofia said, her shadow flickering and reforming. 'Lara, are you safe?'

Elara had never heard Sofia panicked before. She was the level-headed one of the two of them. Her high, strained voice was enough to make Elara rise to her feet.

'I am. But tell me where you are.'

'In the palace. Ariete, he— he's killed so many people.' Her voice broke as a cold, hard lump formed in Elara's chest. 'Louis, Gabriel, Jeanne, the entire King's Guard – gone.'

Elara shook. She had grown up around these people. Had been protected by them.

'And what about you, Sof?' she rasped.

There was a pause.

'Has he hurt you?' Elara demanded.

'Yes,' came a quiet reply.

'And Lukas? Where's Lukas?'

There was a pause. 'Lukas is—'

The shadows blipped. 'He's coming. Lara, we need you. The ball, you have to—'

The shadow disappeared.

Elara stared dumbfoundedly at the dagger, as Enzo shifted. 'El, are you—'

'I'm going back to Asteria.'

She stood, hastily wiping away her tears.

'Are you mad?'

Elara whirled. 'My best friend, as close to me as a *sister*, is being held there by Ariete – being tortured, just for knowing me.'

'And what would you do when you get there? You can't even bring substance to your shadows yet.'

'Then I'll use my other magick,' she shot back, pulling out a satchel from the wardrobe.

'You'll be walking right into a trap. Why do you think Ariete hasn't killed Sofia yet? He's using her as bait.'

'Then I'll walk into a trap! He can take me instead. But I cannot just *sit* here, pampered in Helios, running around with princes while Sof is there. Hurt. Imprisoned.'

'No. It's too risky.'

'I didn't ask you for permission!' she shouted. 'You are not my *damn keeper*.'

Enzo stalked closer, looming over her. 'Oh, I can be, princess. You are under my rule here. So, you'll find, my word is law should I wish it.'

'Try to make me prisoner again and see what happens to you.' Her shadows curled around Enzo's neck, her control running thin with rage.

'Are you threatening me with a good time?' His breath mingled with hers as she stood, seething, shadows pouring out of her. She ignored the deflection, and the look of total trust he gave her as her shadows continued to wrap tighter around his neck.

'What would you do if it was Isra? Or Leo?' she whispered.

Enzo's mouth opened then swiftly closed, his lips pressing together.

'She is all I have left, Enzo.' Elara's voice broke.

He paused, then released a defeated sigh. 'I would do everything I could to bring them back,' he said.

She nodded once, her shadows loosening.

'And she is not all you have left, El.'

Elara huffed out a laugh. 'Yes. I have you, a man who has just started to tolerate me.' She shook her head. 'I don't have anyone in my corner, not really.' She smiled wryly, becoming aware that she was gripping Enzo's arm, the bulge of muscle taut as her nails dug into it.

Enzo let out a harsh breath of impatience. 'I do not just *tolerate* you, Elara. You are my favourite part of the day.'

She gaped. Her mouth worked, trying to form words, but shock and confusion had rendered her mute. Enzo gently extricated himself from her grip.

'What do you—'

The door opened, Leo standing there with a sober expression on his face.

'I'm sorry,' he said, looking between them. 'One of the guards told me you'd arrived back at the palace together.' He took a deep breath. 'Your father, he's requesting you.' He looked to Elara. 'Both of you.'

As the doors to the throne room swung open, Elara felt once again dwarfed by the chamber's grandeur, and the man reclining in his throne, waiting for her.

Enzo strode beside her, which at least made her feel a little better. Leo hadn't said anything more as he'd walked them down the stairs, leaving them at the doors.

'Father,' Enzo said, dipping his head.

'King Idris,' Elara said, resolutely keeping her back straight.

'Princess.' He nodded. 'Son.' His tone grew tight.

'We were training,' Enzo said, when Idris didn't speak further. 'Leo told us you wanted to see us?'

Idris produced a large scroll of Asterian midnight-blue parchment. Elara saw flashes of silver script as he handed it to Enzo. 'I received this today.'

Enzo scanned it, his brow furrowing the further down he got.

Anxiety began to creep inside Elara as he finished, and handed it to her. His eyes were fixed on her, but she snatched it from him.

To King Idris D'Oro, and the court of Helios,
*   You are cordially invited to the coronation of King Lukas Saintsombre of Asteria.*
*   Asteria welcomes the esteemed royal families of Celestia, and their court, to celebrate the event.*
*   After the ceremony, there will be a masquerade ball in honour of the new king.*

Elara skimmed over the rest, her knuckles turning white with fury. When she saw a stamped gloambat – Lukas's family sigil – she angrily tore the paper in two.

'It seems, princess, that someone has usurped your throne.'

Enzo still hadn't uttered a word, though she felt a wave of heat caress her.

'My betrothed,' she got out. Her fury was about to spill out of her. 'All of this time, Lukas—'

'This is a clear ploy by Ariete.' Idris interrupted her thoughts. 'To open Asteria for the first time in decades, to allow all royal families and their courts in, to get to you. I would bet my kingdom on it.'

Idris's hands gripped the throne arms, his knuckles bulging. 'And he extends this invitation to me in ridicule. Knowing that my kingdom is the enemy of yours. He mocks me.'

Elara could barely listen. Who gave a fuck if Idris's pride was hurt? Lukas – *her Lukas* – hadn't summoned Ariete that day in some brave, if stupid, attempt to defend her honour.

He had seen it as the perfect opportunity to put himself upon her throne.

Lady Fate had intervened again. A masked ball. Courts from all over Celestia in attendance. Elara's mind began to turn.

'Of course, we shall not attend. Nor you,' Idris said pointedly to Elara. 'Your potential value is too great.'

She bristled. 'My best friend – the only real family I have left – is being *tortured* in that palace.'

Idris tutted. 'You don't know that.'

'I—' Elara bit her tongue. It would do no good to reveal to Idris how she *did* know, categorically, that Sofia was being hurt.

'And you are not going to run headfirst into enemy arms before you are ready,' Idris continued. 'My son has been informing me of your progress. And just how painfully slow it has been.'

Elara locked away the anger, the hurt, the worry. Smoothed her face.

Idris smiled in satisfaction. 'This serves as a reminder, Elara, if nothing else. Perhaps having your former lover on your throne will incentivize you to try harder.'

Elara nodded. 'As you will it, King Idris.'

CHAPTER TWENTY-SEVEN

'Merissa, I need your help.'

Elara had found Merissa in the kitchens, immediately led her outside, and not said a word to her until they were in the quiet east gardens, the indigo crickets' chirps filling the air. She looked at Merissa imploringly.

'Stars, Elara,' she murmured. 'Are you all right?'

'I'm leaving tomorrow. I'm returning to Asteria, and I need your help.'

Merissa's eyes widened. 'Elara, you can't—'

'Lukas has usurped my throne. *My* Lukas. And his coronation is tomorrow. He is hosting Ariete, I'm sure of it – Sofia . . .' She took a deep breath. 'This is my chance to save her.'

'And what about Ariete?' Merissa whispered. 'You're not strong enough to face him.'

'Then I'll find a way around him. Which is precisely why I need you.'

The next day, the plan was going smoothly, up until the point where Elara found herself glaring in frustration at her reflection in the mirror, wondering where Merissa had disappeared to after assuring her she'd be right back.

The makeup Merissa had painted her face with was lovely, her lips iridescent, shimmering dust sparkling around her eyes. Her hair rippled in inky waves down one shoulder. For once, Merissa hadn't glamoured her. The invitation was for a masked ball, and with a mask disguising her, she would blend right in with the court of Asteria as she was.

Time was not on her side. It would take a few hours' carriage ride to get to the city of Phantome, and although Elara's plan was to bypass the coronation altogether, arriving quietly while the ball was in full swing, she was still cutting it fine.

One of the only things that stood between Elara and her departure was the corset currently in disarray in her hands.

She had it pressed to her front with one hand and tried once again to reach behind and pull the loose lacing together with the other. It was impossible. With a grunt of exasperation, she let the strings go, the corset falling to the floor. There was a knock at the door, and Elara, attempting to quell her temper, flew to it.

'Merissa, you promised you'd be quick,' she said, flinging the door open.

She stopped short.

Enzo was leaning against the frame, one foot crossed behind the other. As she mastered her panic, she noted something else. He was dressed in the formal colours of the Asterian court. A black blouse was undone at his collar, a bowtie slung around his neck. His hair hung in damp curls from a bath, and the smell of amber oils filled her senses. He looked like sin.

'What are you doing?' she breathed.

'I had an inkling you might try and do something stupid. Like, I don't know, attend a masked ball, alone, where the god intent on killing you waits.'

He brushed a piece of lint off his indigo jacket. 'So I got myself ready and came here to escort you.'

A lump was forming in her throat. 'Why? Your father forbade it.'

'And I don't take orders well. I won't let you go alone. So if you need to go, then I'm coming with you.' His eyes dragged from her feet up to her dress, and Elara suddenly felt vulnerable in the thin material. Then, with a curved smile, his gaze landed on her face.

'Do you need some help?' he purred. She bit back a smile as she opened the door wider, crossing the room to the discarded corset.

'Merissa was dressing me, but she's disappeared to Stars know where.' She blew an errant strand of hair out of her face as she looked back to him, still leaning in the doorway. 'So unless you know how to tie a corset and get me into this damned gown, perhaps you could go and find her?' She shot him a sweet smile.

He looked at her, as he lazily pushed himself off the doorframe and entered the room. 'Well, princess, undoing corsets is more my strong suit, but I'm sure I can assist.'

He approached, and Elara felt heat crawling up her neck to her cheeks as he stood behind her. She looked at her reflection, the silk gown clinging to her delicately, outlining the shape of her curves. She pressed the corset to herself, gesturing to Enzo. 'You need to find the two loops in the middle and pull.'

Enzo studied her back. 'You know, I never saw the point in these things,' he murmured as his thumbs brushed her hips, holding the strings in each hand. He drew them towards him deftly.

'Why not?' she asked, her breath quickening. She saw his smile in the reflection as he began to pull on each string, the corset tightening with every movement.

'Just seems like an awful lot more for me to have to take off.' Enzo's voice caressed her ear, a low murmur. She felt goosebumps ripple through her body. Trying to fight down the delicious pleasure that his words brought to her, she focused on her reflection.

'Is this tight enough?' he asked, hitching her in roughly so that she was pulled against him. She exhaled a little breath of shock. A hand around her waist steadied her. She nodded silently as a smile danced on his lips.

'Is my hair getting in the way?' she asked innocently and swept it around to one side, the nape of her neck exposed. The hands tying a bow behind her went still, and she glanced in the mirror. Displayed in the looking glass was a furrowed brow and clenched jaw as Enzo's gaze bore into her exposed, silver-dusted neck. She knew he could smell the faint smoky vanilla perfume dabbed behind her ear. Her chest, spilling out of the bodice, was heaving, shallow breaths that she inwardly insisted were caused by the tightness of the corset and not the way Enzo was looking at her.

He lifted his eyes to the mirror, finding hers as he stood still, hands still wrapped in strings. His breath was warm, causing rivulets of fire to dance down her back. In that moment she thanked her shadows for hiding the feelings swirling through her. The air grew heavy, almost suffocating, before Enzo spoke.

'Don't we look quite the royal couple?'

Elara forced out a laugh, batting him away. He grinned and finished tying the bow, the movements rough and taut. When he finished, he stepped back from her.

'There.' He bowed. 'In another life perhaps I was a handmaid.'

She chuckled as he swaggered towards the door. 'I won't be long.'

'I'll arrange a carriage. Take the servants' staircase.' Then, with a final look at her, he was out of the room.

Minutes later, there was a quiet knock on the door and Merissa swept back in, just as Elara was almost drowning in the swathes of ballgown that she was trying to put on the right way.

'Thank the gods,' Elara muttered as Merissa hurried over to help.

'Sorry,' she said breezily, 'His Highness needed my assistance.'

Elara raised a brow. 'Oh, I gathered that by the attire he was wearing. But that doesn't explain where you disappeared to when he found himself in my rooms while I was wearing only my undergown and corset.'

Merissa's lips twitched as she pulled Elara's ballgown around, righting it and smoothing it down. 'I thought you may need a moment alone to discuss your plan.'

Elara's mind flicked to that moment alone, to Enzo's thumbs stroking her waist, the way he'd looked at her neck, the feeling of his hard body as he'd pulled her against it.

She clicked her tongue, admonishing herself. *Get it together, Elara, my gods. You'd think you were a tremoring virgin the way a few touches are making you act.*

Once the adjustments were finished, the glamourer stepped back and Elara admired the final result in the mirror.

Merissa had tailored the perfect dress for her return to her kingdom. It was the indigo blue of an Asterian evening. Silver constellations adorned her décolletage, the rest of her neck and chest left bare.

From there, the gown fell into a cinched waist and then

into a flowing skirt of stars. It glittered and shimmered as she moved. Her hair hung to her waist, threads of silver woven through it. Merissa handed her a delicate silver mask that she placed over her eyes. She looked every bit Asterian, every bit ready for a royal ball.

'Be safe,' the glamourer whispered, squeezing her shoulder. Elara put her hand on top of Merissa's, stroking it once. Then with a deep, shaky breath, she left the room.

CHAPTER TWENTY-EIGHT

The moment Elara saw the split in the sky, from bright orange crimson to dark periwinkle twilight, she knew she was nearly home.

As they crossed the border between Helios and Asteria, their carriage barely halted with the number of guests pouring into Asteria – for the first time in decades. And when that shroud of twilight fell over her, the familiar sounds and scents of her kingdom, the writhing worry within her eased a little.

After a few hours trundling through the lush lands of Asteria, indigo grass lining the silverspun roads, they reached the outskirts of Phantome. The carriage weaved through the cobblestone streets until they reached the grand gates of the Palace of Darkness. Elara's eyes welled to see them open for the first time in her life, a line of carriages filing through them.

They were encouraged to dismount and were guided by a footman towards the small lake that connected the grassy banks to the palace. Lanterns that glowed in varying shades of blue and purple floated through the night, and music was already drifting towards them as they descended the slight bank to where gondolas waited.

Enzo extended his hand to Elara and she took it, sparks thrumming within her at his touch, as he helped her into the boat. Moments later it began to drift towards the palace, steered by an invisible magick, and Elara peered over the side, her throat clogging with emotion at the recognizable silver dreamfish that swirled in pairs through the water. How many times had she swam with them when escaping the palace grounds with Sofia?

As she looked past the fish, she saw her reflection, and Enzo's beside her. The black mask around his eyes deepened their gold and brown, and his earring glimmered in the starlight. His jaw was freshly shaven, and her eyes caught on the set of it, clenched with tension. It was his only tell. Enzo was so at home in any room, any kingdom. And here he was, gliding into the court of his enemy, looking as though he could command it. She noticed up close that the navy blue tuxedo he wore was sewn with intricate silver stars to complement her gown. She hid a smile at the sight of him in the attire of the Asterian court. He looked back at her, his eyes unreadable as they settled on her glossed lips.

They'd barely spoken since he had helped her with her corset, and she found herself missing their sniping. As the gondola neared the mouth of the cove that provided an entrance to her palace, the familiar music of a waltz billowed from up ahead. She sighed to herself, and Enzo turned to her.

'Are you okay?' he asked quietly. She fidgeted with her silver mask, a twin to Enzo's black.

'Yes, I'm just trying to prepare myself. For whatever I may see in there.' She took a readying breath, gazing ahead. 'It's so strange. Everything looks the same, but so much has changed.'

Enzo nodded, looking forwards. 'I've never been this far

into Asteria before,' he whispered, turning back to her. 'It's beautiful.' His eyes roamed over her face as he said it, and she swallowed.

'Now can you see why I miss it so much?' she murmured back.

He paused for a moment, and thinking the conversation over, Elara turned in her seat to watch the guests in boats behind her.

'I do,' he said suddenly. 'I would never want to part with it, if this was my home.'

As they entered the cove, Elara bent closer to him. 'We should probably decide on aliases now.'

Enzo nodded, extending his hand. 'The name's Alec. Enchanted to meet you.'

Elara smiled, shaking it. 'I'm Nova, and the pleasure is all mine.'

Enzo's grip tightened, just a little. 'For the record,' he murmured, 'Elara is much prettier.'

Before she could respond, there was a jolt as the gondola came to a halt at a small dock at the side of the cove. A servant wearing a hook-nosed mask and lavender wig extended his hand as Elara rose from the gondola. Having disembarked, they produced their carefully forged invitations, which thanks to Merissa showed the names of the Argentes – a wealthy and sprawling Asterian family – and were led up hewn stone steps and through a door smattered with stars, into one of the main palace hallways. The grand ballroom doors were flung open, right ahead, music booming out from the space beyond.

Elara took a steadying breath as they approached, clutching Enzo's arm, and walked through them.

She swallowed down the anger writhing in her veins as memories flooded her of the last time she was here. The room was still grand, with arching ceilings whose colour seemed to hold the night sky. Thankfully, some things had changed. The floor had been cleaned, leaving no trace of her parents' blood. No screams rang out across the marble. In fact, there was no marble on the floor at all. Grass cloaked it, turning the room into a magickal woodland. As Elara walked tentatively through, she saw the touches that turned it into a dusk-kissed paradise. Twisted trees rose through the room, their midnight blue branches adorned with lavender-scented and coloured leaves. Candles floated through the air, and at the back of the room lay a small pond adorned with dark-roses and starflowers. Indigo swans floated in the pool, serene and graceful, and vines of fragrant night-jasmine climbed up the walls, creating a canopy of lilac upon the whole ballroom. And stars. Stars everywhere. Constellations lit up the roof as if the ceiling were the night sky itself.

Elara did a quick scan of the room, her eyes looking for any hint of red or black. Her heart calmed slightly. Wherever Ariete was, he wasn't here. But a pulsing energy made her still, the air heavy with charm. Her gaze caught on a figure, the magnetic pulsing air around him catching her attention instantly. Sat at a table, surrounded by adoring devotees, was the Star Scorpius. His charm felt like drowning, intense and roiling, with a faint waft of a salted sea breeze. Despite his intimidating presence, Scorpius looked bored, nursing a cup of what she presumed was ambrosia, his deep-sea green eyes dull, his light brown, waist-length locks glowing in the magickal starlight.

Elara whipped around to Enzo. 'The other Stars are here,' she breathed as panic seized her. 'Oh gods, oh gods. I don't think I thought this through, I—'

'Nova, *Nova*,' Enzo hushed, clamping down on her hand as he searched the room.

'Yes, *Alec*,' she retorted.

'You're going to take a deep breath. We are two excited courtiers of Asteria. We have masks on, the entire palace is packed with people and *you* have lived inside the castle walls most of your life. No one apart from Ariete and Lukas – and Leyon, I suppose – knows what you look like. You are going to pull yourself together and play your part.'

He pulled her to the large grassy clearing that acted as a dance floor in the centre of the room.

'Now, you're going to smile and look at me adoringly as we dance.' In the dim shimmering ballroom, Enzo took Elara's hands in his, an arrogant smile on his lips.

'You have to be joking.' She cast him a frown. 'We have to find Sofia.'

Enzo mastered an easy smile as he pulled her in closer. 'We have to blend in. To act like guests. If we begin sneaking around the moment we enter the ball, we'll be caught.'

A familiar tune started to pick up from the band hidden between the trees. The Celestian Waltz. Elara remembered her mother sweeping her around the room to its gentle rhythmic sway, her father then taking over and Elara watching as her parents drifted in each other's arms. She forced her rising panic down. Enzo was right.

'Stars above,' she muttered, her heart still hammering, as she held him more tightly.

'Scared?' he taunted, his hand still around hers.

She placed it hard on her waist as she determinedly pressed her other hand to his shoulder.

'Hardly.' With one more breath, her worries were locked into her box, and she flashed a winning smile as they began to spin. His grip on her waist tightened a fraction and a wave of heat overpowered her. His arrogant smile faltered, that cool composure slipping, before returning so quickly, she wondered if she'd imagined it. Before she could ponder it for too long, she was dipped towards the floor by Enzo.

Elara had always loved dancing, and she had always been good at it. But this felt . . . different.

'Now this is the part where you laugh delicately and tell me you've never danced with such a handsome, charismatic man.' He lifted her effortlessly by her waist then dropped her back down, not missing a beat as they continued to spin. They rose and fell, lost in their own world underneath the twilight and the stars.

'Then,' he said, 'you add that you can just tell by how I dance that I'm a *ravishing* lover.'

Elara scoffed. 'You're an average dancer,' she lied. 'So what does that say of your skills in the bedroom?'

A gleam came into Enzo's eyes as they both clapped twice, before joining hands again.

His mouth came to her ear. 'You lie so prettily,' he murmured, brushing her ear with his lips. 'Though I'd be more than happy to show you my talents, princess.'

Elara's eyes fluttered shut, if only for a moment.

Whatever Enzo was doing, it was working, distracting her from the thought of just how wrong her plan could go.

As the flute joined in, so came the next part of the waltz. Twirled and passed between partners, palms outstretched, Elara weaved through the masked men, her neck craning to find Enzo, smiling as she saw his eyes still locked on her even as he spun with other women. Her hand brushed a stranger's, and she stopped herself, only just, from sucking in a breath.

A Star's charm was coating her, the bare contact of a god's skin on hers, electric. The charm felt like storm clouds and solving puzzles; smelled like rain and cedar. Her stomach turned as she pretended to peer up shyly behind her mask, an abashed courtier overwhelmed by a Star's presence. The pale, dark-haired god glanced down at her, his cunning coal eyes fixed on Elara as he tilted his head, intrigued. Elara took in any detail she could. A black pinstriped suit, the shirt beneath unbuttoned low to show a row of silver necklaces. One with a key hung between his collarbones, another with a blade on it hung low by his sternum. She folded away the details, nodding her head demurely as his brow furrowed. Then before she knew it, Elara was whisked back into the dance.

She made her way back to Enzo as the music picked up pace, the orchestra a frenzy of violins, flutes and cymbals.

Enzo grabbed her with ferocity as she reached him, hunger in his movements dominating her as he pulled her flush to him, leading them to the demanding beat.

'Eli certainly seemed to like the look of you,' Enzo murmured, picking up his pace as the music became deafening.

'Holy shit, that was Eli? One of the twins?'

'The very same,' Enzo replied, his head whipping to where the Star was now dancing with a ravishing redhead, though his eyes were still pinned upon Elara.

Enzo smoothly moved her towards the edge of the ballroom and out of the Star's sightline as she shivered.

The melody followed them, rising when Enzo lifted her, speeding when he spun her. She could feel a frisson in the air like the raw power he wielded between his hands, crackling with energy. Her heart raced as the signal for the final steps of the Celestian Waltz sang to her. His fire fed into her, and she shot him a smile. Matching it with one of his own, he lifted her arm, spinning her with vigour. *One, two, three, four* . . .

Then mustering all her focus, she took three strides back and darted, leaping into his outstretched arms. He pushed her up, his muscles corded behind his jacket as he stretched her above him, holding her. Dizzy with euphoria, the world that surrounded Elara was left behind. She hung among the stars, envisioning plucking them with vengeance one by one, her body weightless. She barely noticed the other guests suspended around her. Then Enzo lowered her gently to the ground as the refrain stopped and they both snapped out of it, looking around the room.

Noise that had seemed distant was now loud and close – the crowd laughing and clapping as they dispersed, the music shifting into a new song. She blinked.

They made their way off the dance floor as Enzo led her to the shadowed wall nearby.

'Perhaps it's best we find other dancing partners now, mingle, and see what we can discover.' His eyes were pensive as they searched the room. 'Do you see Lukas anywhere?'

She shook her head, too out of breath to reply as she followed his gaze. Her eyes had been peeled for her pale-skinned, midnight-haired ex-lover, but by some mercy, she hadn't seen him yet.

Enzo nodded. 'Just don't stray too far,' he warned.

'I won't,' she said softly, turning, her skirts swirling behind her, the imprint of his hands still burning her waist.

CHAPTER TWENTY-NINE

'I need a drink,' Elara murmured to herself, feeling off-kilter. She had let her emotions control her; had acted upon them, with no kind of plan. And now here she was, surrounded by Stars, enemies lurking around every corner.

The Stars' various charms cloyed around her, and nothing steadied Elara's nerves more readily than a glass of sparkling honeywine. She made her way to the bar, past bustling guests and loud, guffawing courtiers, ignoring the dread mounting with every passing minute.

She joined the crowd at the bar, leaning her forearms on the cool marble as she tried to steady her breath.

'Well, well, well. Don't you look delicious?'

Elara would have cursed the Stars if it wasn't for the one just behind her. She turned slowly, gritting her teeth.

'Hello, Leyon.' She smiled.

The Star was resplendent. A shimmering suit, tailored meticulously, clung to him, his blonde hair like spun gold, the familiar circlet resting on his head. A mask to match his circlet graced the top half of his face, leaving his full lips the centre of attention. Elara had a suspicion it was a purposeful choice. Leyon tweaked a golden cuff ring as he propped himself beside her, his shoulder jostling with hers.

'It seems you haven't found your way to my temple after I so graciously extended my express invitation.' His voice was like silk, like a song, and his charm imbued the same emotion one felt when looking at an exquisite piece of art.

'I'm afraid I'm useless with directions,' she said breezily, trying to catch the eye of the tender behind the bar.

Leyon chuckled. 'You know, I think you're the first mortal who has declined.' He bent close to her ear. 'Which makes you all the more intriguing.'

Elara tried not to roll her eyes. Leyon waved a hand through the air. 'Though I can't decide if you're brave or stupid, to have walked in here so baldly.'

'Let's decide on the former,' Elara replied. 'You haven't seen your illustrious brother, have you?' She glanced around.

Leyon shrugged. 'The last I saw, he was disappearing with some pretty brunette, and the new king.'

Pretty brunette. Sofia? 'Where?' Elara demanded.

'I neither know nor care,' Leyon sighed. 'But let me share a gem of wisdom. My parting gift to you.' He leaned closer, and the usual bored and arrogant expression was replaced with earnestness. 'My brother is the god of war. When you think you are a step ahead of him, he is usually already three in front. Elara, beware that you do not play right into his hands.' He pulled back. 'It would be a shame for Celestia to be rid of such a beauty.'

The Star kissed her hand, leaving an imprint that felt like poetry as he disappeared through the crowd. Elara turned around to watch him leave and caught the burning gaze of Enzo staring right at the space where Leyon had been. She started towards him, but behind her the bartender suddenly asked, 'Drink, madam?'

She paused. She could really use something to relax her a little.

'One honeywine, please,' she said to him.

As she waited, Elara tried to gather her composure. Three Stars in the space of an hour. Thank the skies Leyon was, if not on her side, at least not on Ariete's. The bartender returned with a full goblet and she sighed in relief. As he passed it to her, a tanned hand extended from behind her, signalling to the man.

'I'll take one too,' a smooth voice intoned. 'A gorgeous woman can't be drinking alone.'

The stranger smiled. He had deep blue hair that fell to his shoulders, and eyes a brilliant blue-green, like the sea in Helios when the Light was at its highest point in the sky. He wore a mask fashioned around his eyes in cresting waves. His open shirt below showed a glimpse of an octopus tentacle tattooed over his tanned chest. And the hat perched upon his head was a tricorn. Even with the mask on, Elara could see that there was an openness in his eyes, a kindness. And most importantly, he was mortal. She smiled.

'And who might my drinking companion be?' She raised hers to his and took a sip. The honeywine fizzed on her mouth, tasting deliciously sweet and instantly putting her at ease.

'Oh, just a man who saw a poor woman in Leyon's grasp,' he mock-whispered. 'I meant to save you. But it appears you didn't need it after all.' He clinked her glass with his own, his eyes twinkling.

'Lord Adrian – from Neptuna, if you couldn't tell.' He winked, gesturing to his hair. Elara found herself laughing at the ease of his energy, buoyant after so many weeks of intensity in Helios. There was something familiar about him, his voice, his appearance. She racked her brains about what she knew of the Kingdom of Neptuna – her mother always spoke with fondness of the place. The two kingdoms had been close. They'd been the only one to try to stand with Asteria when the War of Darkness had begun. Idris of course had soon put a stop to that.

'My pleasure,' she beamed, extending a hand to him which he kissed. 'I'm Nova,' she said.

'Nova,' he said, savouring the name. 'At the risk of coming off as strong as that Star, may I have this dance?'

Elara nodded, swallowing the last of her bubbles down. She welcomed the fuzzy feeling for a blissful moment before responsibility crashed down upon her. Sofia. She had to find Sofia.

Adrian took her hand, and she stilled again. He looked to her quizzically.

'I'm sorry,' she laughed, allowing his hand to hold her waist as they began to dance. 'Have we met before?'

Adrian frowned as a violin played a dramatic and tense ballad. Trumpet notes cascaded in accompaniment, his hand soft in hers.

'I don't believe so. I'm sure I'd remember someone like you.'

She laughed her feeling of unease away as they moved around the room. 'So tell me, Lord Adrian,' she asked, 'was Neptuna thrilled with the news of the coronation?'

He snorted. 'You mean the crowning of the puppet king? My family loved the Bellereves. And I can't say the courtiers in Neptuna are pleased with the way the new king ascended his throne. We all know of Ariete's intervention. We all know of the lost princess who survived his *divinitas*.'

Elara bit her tongue against the wealth of emotions threatening to spill. *Down you go*, she commanded them.

'As an Asterian, the change surprised me too. As did the

news of Princess Elara. Has there been any word as to where she escaped?'

Adrian shrugged. 'Some rumours say she fled to Neptuna, though I certainly haven't seen a shadow princess around. Others think she may have crossed the Olympian Ocean and is hiding on the other continent.'

Elara nodded, her chest easing. 'Have you seen the new king tonight?' she asked.

'Only at his coronation. Of course, Ariete was in attendance, too. But since the moment the procession returned here, I haven't seen either of them. There was a woman at the coronation who was causing a fuss, and the moment the palace gates opened, they disappeared with her.'

Elara's stomach plummeted. That *had* to be Sofia. Her train of thought petered as out of the corner of her eye, Elara saw a flash of honey and rose gold spin past. Elara's attention caught on the woman who had brushed past her. She was breathtaking. Beauty, eye-watering beauty dripped off her as she danced. Her hair fell in honey brown curls to her waist, laced with pearls, dove-roses and swan feathers. Her skin was an olive brown hue which glowed, made richer by the deep mauve ballgown that accentuated curves only a goddess could be born with. Elara saw a flicker of smoky jade as the Star arrested her with her eyes, before Elara caught on who was whispering in the Star's ear, a disarming grin on his face.

Enzo.

As though feeling her stare, he raised his eyes, gaze locked on her as he continued to whisper in the goddess's ear. Though she wasn't just any Star, not as a charm so intoxicating, so heavenly, drifted through the room, stopping all who encountered it in their tracks. Not as Elara realized she had seen the Star's face rendered in statues and paintings throughout her lands.

'Is that Torra?' Adrian muttered behind her in awe.

Indeed it was. The goddess of lust and earthly pleasure herself. Elara felt a sharp lurch of jealousy as the goddess turned back to Enzo, laughing at whatever he was whispering.

Why did she even care? They were allies, nothing more. And most men thought with their cocks, didn't they? Enzo was just that, a man – one as susceptible to Torra's charm as any other. She bit her cheek, willing the anger rippling through her to calm. Casting him a dry smile, she turned back to Adrian, flicking her hair behind her as she allowed him to spin her.

'Who is she dancing with?' Adrian asked, following where her gaze had been.

She glanced over again then gave a nonchalant shrug as she placed both arms around his neck. 'Haven't the faintest.'

Adrian's hands slid to her waist as Torra's magick snaked around them. A curl of pleasure sat low in Elara's stomach.

The music slowed, as the band too were taken by the goddess's charm. Every couple around her drew closer to each other, as the lights dimmed.

'So, Ariete,' Elara continued, trying to blink away the magick overcoming her, 'and the new king. You haven't any idea where they went?' She tried to keep the desperation out of her voice as Adrian's hands trailed back up, grazing the sides of her breasts.

'The last I saw them, they were heading towards a huge set of doors inlaid with two draguns. Does that help?'

The throne room. Elara's pulse quickened as she nodded absent-mindedly.

Adrian's eyes had darkened, and he wet his lips as he gazed at hers. 'You rival Torra with your beauty,' he murmured as he leaned in to her, their dancing slowing. He smelled like the ocean – of sea salt and driftwood. But Elara only craved one scent as charm seeped into her veins, warm amber.

'Careful you don't bring the strike of *divinitas*,' Elara purred. Adrian chuckled, low and rough, and that curl of pleasure twined inside her. She let Torra's charm whisper in her ear, encouraging her to act upon her desires, to sate herself in any way she could, with anyone she could.

Adrian's mouth tipped down towards hers, and her lips parted, eyes fluttering shut. And then two hands grabbed her waist and yanked her out of his grasp. Enzo gave a saccharine smile to Adrian.

'Sorry to interrupt,' he said, 'but the lady's next dance is with me.'

Adrian's eyes narrowed. 'We were—'

'Finished,' Enzo said, pulling Elara away.

'Alec,' she gritted out.

'*Nova*,' he replied evenly.

But something dangerous glittered in his gaze, enough of a warning that she turned back to Adrian. 'It's been a pleasure,' she said.

'No, that was all mine,' he replied, kissing her hand. 'I got to dance with the most beautiful girl in the room.' He winked, then turned away, heading off into the crowd of nearby dancers.

Enzo's smile dropped, and Elara whirled on him.

'What are you doing?' she hissed.

He pulled her in tightly to him, and her breath hitched at the closeness in which he held her as they danced, much different from before.

'Smile and listen,' he said through gritted teeth as they began to waltz again, muscle memory taking over. 'I thought you wanted to find Sofia. Not flirt with Stars or gallivant with snakes.'

Elara sputtered with indignation. 'I do. And Lord Adrian was no snake. He was a gentleman. Someone *you* could learn some manners from.'

'*Pirate* Lord Adrian,' Enzo corrected with a growl. 'And even if he was a gentleman, is that what you want? A wet blanket to keep you cool at night?' Flames danced in his eyes.

'Well, whether a pirate or a wet blanket, both are certainly better choices than a man with no manners or grace, who spends his nights taking his pick of pretty girls every time I see him,' she spat.

'Pretty girl? Is that what you'd call Torra?' He snorted.

Elara shoved away from him, couldn't stand the feeling crawling over her, nor the charm fuddling her thoughts.

'You're right, she's a goddess. One who latches on to men who have no self-control, like you.'

Enzo's scowl cleared as he observed her. His hand gripped tighter on her waist. 'I was trying to read her with my power, see if she knew where Ariete was. Are you *jealous*?'

She tried to turn, to get away from him as terrible, wanting heat crawled up her throat. But a hand whipped out, wrapping around her wrist.

'Jealous?' Elara threw back her head and laughed indignantly. 'Why would I be jealous?'

He continued to smile back, and the sheer arrogance of it made her want to wipe it off his face.

'You're angry with me for flirting with a goddess, when you were stood awfully close to Leyon only a short time ago. Tell me, how many times did he try to fuck you with his eyes as you spoke? Did that *charm* you, princess?'

'What would you care if it did?' She smiled sweetly.

His face fell, and he whirled her down the side of the ballroom.

'I couldn't care less. Drop your knickers for whichever Star or lord you wish.'

He continued to spin and spin her, the two orbiting the same corner of the woodland room.

'I may not have your gift, but I'm not an idiot. I can tell when someone's lying.'

Enzo stilled, finally. 'Come here,' he growled, yanking her off the dancefloor. She stumbled after him, almost tripping on her gown.

'You know what?' she hissed into his ear as he tugged her along. 'Far be it from me to complain when a gentleman wants to dance with me or a Star tells me I look beautiful, since no one else bothered.' She cut him with her stare. 'Far be it from me to feel normal for one moment instead of being a pawn in a kingdom's games. Never a woman, just a *weapon*.'

'Will you just be quiet for one Stars-damned second?'

He pulled her down the corridor to the silver carriages lining each side of the grand hall. The carriages were adorned in glitterbugs and firelamps. Most had the silhouette of couples inside.

Enzo yanked her into an empty one, slamming the door as she tripped, tumbling on to him in the velvet-lined interior. Her legs were wrapped around him as he clutched her to break her fall. Elara looked to their position on the floor, both her and Enzo's masks having slipped. She smiled, removing hers as he pulled his off in one motion, and was ready to make an inappropriate joke about the way she was straddling him—

'Adrian's right,' he said, looking at her, his hands resting on her waist.

Her smile faltered. 'What?'

'You are the most beautiful woman here.'

They stared at each other, Elara painfully aware of his

hands gripping her body. How had she never noticed before how large his hands were against her? Her exposed neck was inches from his mouth, and she saw his eyes drag to it. Neither moved until Enzo broke the silence.

'You're the most beautiful woman anywhere. But that wasn't enough to say. To tell you that you look beautiful seemed a lazy way to describe how you look.'

His eyes searched hers then he huffed a laugh.

'So I didn't want to tell you that you looked beautiful. I wanted to tell you—' One of his hands raised to lift one of the thin straps of her gown back in place. 'That you look like a fallen Star.'

Elara blushed as heat crept up her. He pulled his hand away from her neck, glancing down in surprise at the glittering substance coating her skin.

'Sugardust,' he murmured, so low that she felt it vibrate through her. Enzo locked his gaze on her as he brought his thumb to his lips and sucked the dust from it, his eyes never once leaving her face.

Heat pooled from her stomach to her core as she saw his tongue swirl. That hunger in his eyes made her want to lean forwards, to feel the sparks that radiated in his gaze. She found herself moving closer, every cell in her body was drawing her to him. He leaned towards her, too, his hands tight on her waist, the press of his body hard against her. But he was shaking, tension bracketing his body, his jaw clenched.

'What's wrong?' she whispered.

He shook his head, holding himself abnormally still.

Elara reached forwards, tentatively tracing a finger over his full lips.

'Elara,' he said roughly, as she dipped her mouth towards his, 'if you kiss me now, I won't stop.'

Torra's wicked charm caressed her, giving her a jolt of confidence. Every worry left her head for one blissful moment as she allowed herself to drown in the charm's certainty.

'Then why fight it?' she purred.

His eyes dragged to her lips, darkening. 'Because, Elara, I may be a monster, but you make me want to be a saint.'

Something between a gasp and a sigh escaped Elara. 'I don't want you to be anything other than what you are,' she whispered, and gently brushed her lips to his. He groaned into her mouth, the last bit of fight in him melting into her.

Hands wrapped in her hair, pulling her forwards as he deepened the kiss. She moaned as his tongue parted her lips, the taste of him smoky and warm, like bonfires and sweet honey. She pulled his waist to her, and he moaned against her. Her breath was panting as he trailed kisses down her neck, setting her pulse fluttering.

'I've never been kissed like this,' she breathed. With Lukas, it had always felt like going through the motions, perfunctory. With Enzo, it felt as though pure fire was coursing through her body at his touch.

'Only a shade, remember, El,' he murmured against her, and she was called back to his promise in her bedroom as he kissed her again. He ground his hips up into her, and she moaned louder. When he ripped his mouth off hers and studied her, his eyes were so dark only a thin ring of gold remained. He moved his gaze down to her heaving breasts then up to her mouth.

'Stars, I've wanted to hear you moan for me,' he rasped.

Elara's breath was ragged as she reached for him again, drinking him in greedily. Enzo's tongue trailed fire down her body, delving into the dip of her collarbone. Elara twisted her hands through his curls, arching her back in pleasure. His hand hitched up her skirts, skimming her thighs and she tipped her head back. She could die of this heat, this want.

His tongue trailed down her neck, her collarbone.

'I know how much effort it took to get this ballgown on, princess, but I'm going to need it off, now.'

Elara nodded, making a needy, strangled sound as Enzo wet his lips, helping her turn so that he could undo the buttons and the tie at her waist.

When it slipped down, he pulled her back around to him until she was in his lap once more, and with a little ministration, freed her breasts from her corset.

'Gods damn it.' He palmed one, then the other, squeezing them, his rough thumbs brushing over the sensitive peaks. Elara swore. 'The way these almost spill out of those little training blouses you wear drives me mad,' he growled.

With a barely held back groan, he took one of her nipples into his mouth.

Elara shook, tightening her legs further around him as want and craving drowned her.

'How do you think I feel when you strut around shirtless, sweat running down those perfect *glamour* muscles?' she panted.

Enzo laughed before taking her nipple between his teeth. She cried out, feeling the small hurt replaced by a lap of his tongue.

'You like it a bit rough, princess?'

'Gods, yes,' she breathed. She had to get the damned dress fully off, had to have him right then in the carriage.

As though reading her mind, his hands ran up and down the strings of her corset. 'What did I tell you?' he asked, voice low and delicious. 'I'm so much better at undoing corsets than tying them up.'

With one hand, he began to work the stays, as the hand up her dress trailed to her hip.

His mouth drew back up to her lips, his tongue flicking hers. There was something desperate in his eyes as rough fingers brushed her underwear.

'Yes,' she breathed, pushing against him. '*Yes.*'

'Elara,' he moaned, as the other hand worked her restraints. 'Tell me this is all for me.' His finger hooked on to the band of her underwear, and he pulled at it, the friction of it against her core so unbearably delicious that her breath hitched. 'Tell me you're mine.'

Her eyes fluttered shut, and she opened her mouth to reply—

A jolt on the carriage and the yell of a drunkard made them both jump out of the reverie. Elara's gaze shot to the door in panic, Torra's charm clearing from her for a moment. She looked down to her and Enzo's position, to his swollen lips, her exposed breasts, his heaving chest, and pushed herself off him.

'I'm sorry,' she stammered, yanking her corset back up. She righted it, then pulled her ballgown over it, scrambling for the gown's buttons.

'El,' he said, pushing himself up off the floor. When he tried to help her she pulled away and fumbled with the latch of the carriage, swinging it open. Cool air greeted her, and she took a few paces away, until she had managed to put her dress back together properly and pull her mask back in place, though her corset now felt loose beneath.

When she turned, Enzo's own mask was back on as well, his expression unreadable. The heady magick she had been sipping was gone, Enzo's eyes bright again. She ignored her fluttering pulse, the want that still thrummed between her legs.

'I need to find Sofia,' she said, smoothing her skirts.

'El, what happened in there—'

'Was Torra's charm,' she replied. 'I know, you don't need to explain.'

He nodded tightly. 'Exactly,' he said, and something in Elara broke at the word, something she didn't know had been whole to begin with.

CHAPTER THIRTY

Elara traversed one of the dimly lit corridors, Enzo behind her. She pushed away thoughts of their kiss, of her desire for him, the way it had nearly consumed her.

Sofia was all she could think of now.

Her eyes caught on two figures pressed into a shadowy alcove, a man and a woman writhing passionately. Her eyes widened as she glimpsed white, feathered wings protruding from the male, twitching with life. She caught a glimpse of smudged glitter on the man's cheek and the scent of sandalwood before Enzo fell into step with her.

'So predictable,' he muttered, pulling her past the otherwise preoccupied Star.

'I thought Lias's wings were a myth,' she whispered as they rounded the corner.

'No, and neither is his penchant for fucking anything with a pulse.'

Elara chuckled. 'And I thought *Torra* was supposed to be the Star of lust.'

Enzo's returning smile didn't quite seem genuine. 'Like mother like son.'

Elara led Enzo on a sharp right, a shortcut that would take them to the throne room without having to walk through the ballroom once more.

There was only a guest or two milling through the grand corridors, everyone else still within the ballroom, but still they stuck to the shadows, prowling carefully until she reached the throne room doors.

Upon them the carved draguns' maws stretched open, spewing shadows across a starlit sky, all carved in black and silver relief. The doors would soon be gone, replaced by new doors with renderings of Lukas's gloambats.

She pressed a hand to the doors.

'El,' Enzo said.

She paused, turning. His face was halfway between pleading and an emotion she couldn't quite identify. 'Are you sure about this? What if Ariete waits beyond these doors? What if it's all a trap?'

'Then it's a trap. His starlight cannot kill me. And even if anything else he does can, I'll be damned if I leave Sofia at his mercy.' She took in his trepidation. 'You don't have to come with me,' she said. 'You should never have been a part of this, anyway. I promise I won't think less of you if you go.'

His laugh was empty. 'I'll leave you when the Deadlands freeze over.'

Elara tried not to ruminate on his words as she pressed the sapphire jewel clasped in the dragun's claws, and the doors swung violently open.

Like the ballroom, it was exactly as she remembered. Two thrones sat at the end of the room, the floor a glossy black obsidian that reflected the throne room's surroundings. A familiar shrouded mirror still leaned against the wall. The only differences now were the black banners that hung from either side of the thrones, with silver gloambats stitched into them.

And at the end of the room were two figures.

One was bound, kneeling, their hands tied.

Elara had already hitched her skirts and drawn her dagger. She started to run, a snarl on her lips.

Because the other figure was reclining on a throne, a black crown upon his head.

She heard flames crackle behind her, and felt a surge of relief at having Enzo at her back.

As she approached, she took in Sofia's wide, grey gaze, the gag at her mouth, her torn ballgown.

And then Lukas's bright black eyes, so much darker than she ever remembered, wide in delight, as the shadows on the wall around him swelled into monstrous shapes.

'Lara. You look more ravishing than ever.'

Her childhood love was unrecognizable. The purple shadows under his eyes were sunken, the black of them bright – almost maniacal. Something wicked pulsed around him, something that her own magick shrank at.

'Sof,' she said, rushing to her, ready to cut her bindings. But Lukas snarled, and a shadow wrapped around her wrist. Elara yanked at it, but it remained firm.

Enzo tutted behind her. 'I'd remove that if I were you,' he said.

Lukas's eyes flew to Enzo's, his nostrils flaring. 'And who are you?'

'I don't think we've had the pleasure of meeting.' Enzo sauntered forwards, ignoring Elara as he extended a hand to Lukas.

'King Lukas,' he replied. 'You may kiss my hand.' He held his palm out, slightly downturned.

Enzo smiled, bending forwards, before his own hand flew out and grabbed Lukas's wrist. In one swift move, the usurper was on the floor, with a dagger that Enzo had concealed beneath his suit jacket unsheathed and at his throat.

'So this is the betrothed who always left you unsatisfied?' he said to Elara in a stage whisper. She gave a tentative smile back, before focusing on Sofia once more and giving her shadow-bound wrist another tug.

'Release her,' Enzo commanded, his blade pressing in.

Lukas's hate-filled stare didn't stray from Enzo's, but he raised a hand and the tendril of shadow released its grip, immediately drifting away from Elara.

She was instantly at Sofia's side, embracing her. 'It's okay, Sof. We're getting you out of here tonight, you—'

Enzo relaxed his dagger, and Lukas's shadows lunged, wrapping around Enzo's throat. Elara should have known, should have warned him.

But Enzo only gave an amused snort as a flash of light, so bright it lit the whole throne room, blasted the shadows into tatters.

Lukas paled, a truly disgusted look coming on to his face.

'Oh, Lara. You really chose Helion scum to keep your bed warm?' His voice dripped with revulsion, and despite her new strength, her stomach coiled.

'I thought you had better taste.' He spat at her feet from where he lay sprawled. 'Lightwhore.'

Enzo lunged before Elara could blink. Lukas flung his magick out, to no avail as it met a sizzling shield of Enzo's fire.

Enzo's fist smashed into Lukas's nose, blood pouring as the Lion became a beast unleashed, his blows finding their mark again and again.

He paused, only to shove his hand in her ex-betrothed's mouth. Lukas clamped his teeth upon Enzo's fingers, but Enzo didn't so much as flinch as he gripped Lukas's tongue with a hand and pulled it taut.

'If you ever so much as utter Elara's name again, I swear

to the twelve fucking Stars that I will rip your tongue from your throat and feed it to you.'

Lukas wept, strangled noises coming from his mouth until Enzo let go.

'You are no king,' he hissed, raising his dagger once more to commit the final blow.

'*Stop*,' Elara implored. And she hated her stupid soft heart and the panic it felt in that moment. Despite how Lukas had betrayed her, what he'd done to Sofia, her kingdom, despite it all she still saw a glimpse of the boy she had once grown up with, and couldn't watch him die.

Enzo halted instantly. She pressed a hand to his arm, her other arm still around Sofia, who had watched on silently. 'He's not worth it.'

Enzo's shoulders tensed, and then a moment later, he let them slump as he released Lukas.

'No, you're not worth it. But you're marked now, shadow-mancer.' He spat at his feet as Lukas lay there, clutching his bloody nose. 'And you will let us leave safely.' He looked behind him. 'Come on, El. Let's get out of here.'

Elara heaved Sofia up, her body so weak and fragile, and the two began to move her, when Lukas started to laugh.

It was a cold, terrible laugh, and Elara stilled.

'What?' she demanded.

But he only continued to laugh, staring at something behind them.

'It worked,' he said, mouth fashioned in a bloody grin.

Elara turned slowly, as Sofia screamed, shaking against her.

And Ariete, the King of Stars, the god of wrath and war, swaggered into the throne room, red starlight trailing behind him.

He gave a wolfish grin as he laid his crimson eyes upon Elara. 'Hello, lover.'

CHAPTER THIRTY-ONE

The god before her was as beautiful and bloodcurdling as he had been the first time Elara had laid eyes upon him. His face was that of a young man, though he was centuries old. Black hair striped with red was combed off the Star's face to match upswept burgundy eyes. Tattoos crawled over his pale skin: playing cards, a circus tent, a ram, all alongside grotesque frescoes of war and death. The images wrapped around a warrior's bare torso – one honed to kill – beneath a sharply tailored jacket. Her eyes caught on the words that she had tried to forget since her birthday, a line scrawled under his left eye. *Divine Violence.*

Enzo leapt in front of Elara, dagger drawn. Fire rippled off its blade, and he lunged at Ariete.

The god side-stepped his attack easily, flicking a blow of starlight at him.

It knocked the prince off his feet and he landed on the floor, where he lay unmoving.

'No!' Elara screamed, running towards Enzo. He was still breathing, and Ariete looked down at him, at the fire still rippling off his fallen blade.

'Interesting,' he murmured.

Elara turned, and with a howl flung her dagger at Ariete. Her aim was immaculate, but Ariete was a Star. He whipped the knife from the air, clenching it blade-first with his palm. Then his grin grew ever wider, so wide that his pointed fangs were fully visible as he slowly uncurled his hand, rivulets of glittering blood running down it. He brought the knife to his tongue and ran the blade along it.

'Oh, how I love a vicious woman,' he sighed, a sing-song tone in his voice as he took another step forwards. His charm coated the room in a shriek of clanging swords and over-whelming bloodlust. Elara gazed wildly to Enzo, still unconscious, and reached blindly for her powers – a shadow, an illusion, anything. She flung her hand.

'Oh, no, you don't,' Ariete sang, and was upon her in two strides. Elara gave a cry as the Star gripped her hair, yanking her head back, her neck bare to him. In utter horror, she screamed as his fangs pierced her neck, and a lancing pain flooded through her. *It burned, oh skies, it burned.* 'Demon's venom,' he murmured, as she felt it drown her magick, weaken her until she sank against him. 'And the only cure is a Star's blood.' He chuckled as she swooned, Sofia screaming and pleading.

Ariete brushed a thumb over Elara's cheek, almost ten-derly, before whispering into her ear, 'If I cannot kill you, then I will keep you.' His gaze flicked to Enzo's prone body.

Elara tried to fight, tried to struggle, but the venom was dragging her down, down, down. 'No,' she croaked, one final time, hands outstretched to Enzo. And then there was only darkness.

CHAPTER THIRTY-TWO

Pain. Immeasurable, indescribable pain. Elara fought to wake up and thrashed her body, trying to force the magick of Ariete's venom out of her veins, to no avail.

Her eyes fluttered open, enough to see that she was in her old bedroom. The heavy indigo curtains were drawn, familiar books lining her bookshelves, the paintings of her favourite draguns upon her ceiling. She choked a sob and tried to sit up, tried to move.

But the venom rendered her immobile, as a figure slithered forwards, an aura of white starlight around her becoming visible with every step.

'The promised Starkiller,' came a breathy, high voice. Elara tried to drag lungfuls of air into her body, though fear was making that near-impossible as a goddess was illuminated before her.

Gem. Star of spite and trickery.

Elara had been brought up on frightening stories of this very Star and her twin, Eli. They were two halves, but together they were more powerful than almost any one star. They could cleave minds, could make the sanest man go mad. Could command a mortal like a puppet master.

Elara tried to squirm away from Gem's approach, but the Star only smiled faintly as she panted, unable to even lift herself off the bed. Like Ariete, Gem was stunning, the faint glow and porcelain perfection of her countenance ethereal. She flicked hair as white as snow off her shoulder, scanning Elara from head to toe with eyes so pale a blue they looked almost blank.

'Where's Sofia?' Elara rasped. Her throat was throbbing with pain – Stars, almost as much as when she'd had the Light forced down it. Was it from the venom? From screaming?

'Elsewhere,' Gem said airily. 'My king isn't so cruel, you know. If you comply, he'll allow her to stay with you, here.'

She knelt by Elara's bedside and brushed a stray hair from her face. Elara flinched, though her head barely moved.

'You could be content here, as long as you do as I say.'

From her touch, Elara felt wisps of white starlight creep like mist into her mind. The scent of godslilies was strong enough to make her gag, as Gem searched.

Elara squeezed her eyes shut, and with gritted teeth commanded her shadows to take the box – the one with all her secrets, all her true thoughts – and push it deeper into her consciousness.

Who are you?

The voice sounded inside and outside Elara, as Gem's blank gaze continued to pin her to the bed.

'I am Elara Bellereve. The rightful queen of Asteria,' she snarled.

A soft chuckle echoed through her mind. *Elara Bellereve. I did not ask you your name.*

'I don't know what the fuck you're talking about.' Elara heaved, gritting her teeth against the pain in her body.

How did an insignificant little princess survive the deathblow of a Star?

'Because of the prophecy,' she snapped.

Gem's magick paused, pulsing, waiting, as she replied. *What are you hiding, Elara Bellereve?*

And before Elara could take another breath, the tendrils of starlight attacked. Spears of it lanced through Elara's mind as she screamed – hard, cold, terrifying light. The tendrils pried and forced, scurrying and chasing the shadows as they ran, as they swirled together and hid. Blades swiped across her mind, cutting and slicing it as she bucked, determined to not cry out, to not give Gem the satisfaction. In her mind, she saw Gem standing in front of her, as her voice softly ordered: *You will show me what you're hiding.*

Elara fought, trying to claw herself off the bed, but the pain in her muscles protested, and another blow of light seared through her brain.

Gem's voice was as calm as a still pond when she spoke again. *Who is Alec?*

'Fuck you,' Elara gasped, disguising every thought of Enzo, every picture. The memories of them training, flying, dancing. She locked each one away.

But where was he? What had happened to him?

Finally something, Gem murmured, as she read the questions that Elara had just asked herself.

Gem laughed softly as an image was now fed into Elara's mind. It was hazy, showing Enzo hanging from a ceiling, blood pouring from gashes in his skin, his mask still on.

Elara frowned. Why was his mask still on? But she cried out as another vicious burst of pain cut through her mind, blurring the image. When it became sharper again, Ariete was there, red starlight lancing over Enzo's body for every time he refused to answer the Star's relentless interrogation.

She fought back a sob, gritting her teeth as her magick tried to fight past the venom. A wisp of her shadows swirled out of her, and lashed around Gem's neck, though it did little.

The goddess growled in frustration, before Elara was hit again by stabbing needles of light, piercing hot, the pain nearly making her black out. But the claws that sank into her brain wouldn't relent, wouldn't let her sink into oblivion. An inhuman sound escaped her, and she clenched her jaw, shaking.

I will sweep your mind to find everything you love, and then I'll destroy it, Gem's voice whispered.

Elara lay, panting raggedly.

She didn't know if what happened next went on for hours, or days. All she did know was that it was the most acute pain she had ever felt. Again and again, Gem's claws raked her mind, searching for information of the last months. Elara's willpower was slipping slowly, her mouth fixed in a soundless scream as Gem silenced her cries. She sat there suspended in agony.

Finally, she heard the chair drag back.

'Your mind will be mine before the end of this,' Gem snarled. Elara felt the Star grip her mind so tightly that she began to convulse. Then finally, Gem left her in the dark.

When Elara next woke, it was to warm liquid seeping down her throat. Her eyes fluttered, to Ariete perched on her bed, his wrist at her mouth, as she drank greedily. Blissful numbness swept through the pain.

The moment Elara realized who he was, she yanked away, spluttering up blood. *His blood.*

'Hush,' he said as she wretched. 'I need you lucid for this conversation.'

'Why are you doing this?' she whispered, forcing her sob down as she wiped her mouth, staining her hand scarlet. 'If our fates have been tied, then we can do nothing about it. If I'm to fall in love with you and be your death, why not just accept it?'

Ariete tipped back his head and laughed, a manic gleam shining in his eyes. 'Let me ask you, Elara. Do you accept it?'

She thought of Enzo. Of what he'd said in the forest. *You deserve to feel true love.*

'No,' she replied.

'Our fates are tied. But I am the god of war. If you are to be my death, then I will go down in battle.'

The room spun as the Star's raw, unfiltered magick from his blood worked its way into her system. Her eyelids fluttered as euphoria pumped through her. His blood was better than ambrosia. Utter bliss and divinity.

'Who is Alec?'

The bliss stuttered. 'Where is he?' she demanded.

'That's what I'd like to know,' he murmured back. Everything within Elara abated a moment. The visions from Gem, they weren't true. Ariete had lost him.

'Tell me everything, Elara, and I can stop your pain.'

But Elara had latched on to it now, that one ray of light shining in the night. Enzo was safe. So she only smiled at Ariete.

His face contorted in rage, the indifferent, immortal mask shattered. 'So be it,' he said, before he plunged his fangs back into her throat.

This time, when the pain came, blissful darkness was already there to eat it whole.

CHAPTER THIRTY-THREE

'Elara?' a voice whispered urgently. 'Elara?' it urged again, louder.

Dreamscapes swirled around Elara as she staggered, half intoxicated with Ariete's blood, half poisoned with his venom. The two fought each other, struggled to control her magick. But she dreamwalked on.

'Elara,' the voice beckoned.

She recognized the dreamcloud up ahead, had wandered to it so many times growing up. And with a sob, she fell into it.

Sofia sat on the shore of Lake Astra, the still water a deep indigo, the mist rolling in and around her as she watched Elara approach, attempting to walk. But the pain had followed her into the dream, and she fell to her knees and crawled.

'Sof,' she rasped.

She tried to grip on to Sofia, but Sofia's touch was nothing but smoke.

'What have they done to you, Lara?'

'Gem has been sweeping my mind. She keeps asking the

same incessant fucking question. How am I supposed to know why I survived Ariete? Why Fate wrote what she did?'

Sofia stared out to the water. 'The threads tie in mysterious ways,' she replied. 'As our lady Piscea once said.'

Elara refrained from sighing.

'What about you, Sof,' she replied gently, scared to break her friend who seemed so far from the spirited girl she grew up with. 'Are they hurting you?'

'Not more than usual,' Sofia replied. 'It doesn't matter how they hurt me, even if I knew why you survived him, I'd never tell.'

Guilt plunged through Elara's chest. 'I'm so sorry,' she whispered.

Sofia shrugged. 'Where are they keeping you?'

'In my old room,' Elara replied. 'You?'

Sofia gave an empty laugh. 'In the dungeons.'

'I promise I will get you out,' Elara swore. 'I don't know how, but we will not die here.'

'You won't,' Sofia said.

'And neither will you,' Elara said, trying to stroke Sofia's cheek.

Sofia's smile was sad. 'I hope so, Lara. You just need to fight Gem. To wait her out. She'll get bored. Just like she did with me.'

'How long will it take?'

'I don't know. But I promise it won't last forever. Ariete will want you out of here soon. For some new game to play.'

'Lucky me.'

Sofia snorted.

A flash of starlight lit up the dreamscape, and Elara flinched.

'That's them,' Sofia murmured. 'Get back to your body.'

'I love you, Sof. And I'm coming for you. I promise.' Elara reached for her friend's hand, forgetting for a moment, but Sofia stood up, out of reach.

'I hope so.' Sofia looked to the skies. 'Please don't fall for him, Lara.'

Elara stumbled back. 'I'd never fall for Ariete,' she declared in disgust.

Sofia only blinked, as Elara was pulled back into the waking realm.

The next day, and countless others that Elara could not keep track of, Gem visited her, aiming to break her mind.

She entered it with glee, distorting her memories and picking away every bit of information she could. She particularly enjoyed focusing on Elara's parents, turning her happy childhood memories into things of nightmares, twisting the echoes of her parents' dying screams into '*It's your fault.*' Still, Elara kept Enzo and the secret of her refuge in Helios locked tightly away, buried so deeply that Gem could never discover it. The darkness beckoned and consoled her each night, weightless and welcoming, like being held in the arms of the night sky, and it was only then, alone, that Elara allowed herself to think of Enzo. It was her only avenue of defiance. A way to make at least one memory – one thought – her own. She pictured his golden hoop glowing in the Light. The freckle below his left eye. The furrow of his brow when he was frustrated with her. Over and over she rendered the images – her proof that she hadn't lost her mind to Gem. Her one anchor to reality.

She was riding a fever from Ariete's venom, the god not

deigning to visit her again with his blood since that first night. The door to her bedroom opened, and she was staring at her father. 'No, no, no, no,' she whimpered, trying to move, though the venom rendered her useless. 'This is not real, this is not real, this is not real.'

'Darling, it's me,' the figure said, and her father's voice was so warm that she began to cry, looking into his face. 'It's me, and I just wanted you to know,' the warmth in his eyes was replaced with malice, 'that it is your fault that we died.'

Elara let out a shuddering sob. 'This isn't real. You're *Gem*. You're not my father.'

In the blink of an eye, the form changed, and her mother crouched before her. Sadness tinged her grey eyes.

'He's right, darling,' she lamented, 'you did this to us. If I hadn't given birth to you, the Star would not have appeared.'

Elara shook her head against the coldness of her mother's hand as it touched her face. Over and over, like a mantra, she told herself that this was not real, that it was the Star of trickery doing what she did best. But as the screams of her parents told her that she was worthless, better off dead, her mind started to crumble.

Who is Alec? came the question, relentlessly, the same as every other day. 'No one,' she replied.

Cold laughter followed, before she blacked out, as she always did, clinging on to an image of golden eyes.

When she next woke, her back was wet with sweat, her neck stiff with pain, where Ariete's bite wound throbbed. Her head lolled forwards as she prayed for respite. *Hoop. Freckle. Frown. Hoop. Freckle. Frown.* She repeated it again and again, until

233

Enzo's face came to her in her mind. She was still here. She was still alive.

'Elara,' a voice urged, and she jolted up, looking around wildly. She nearly fainted from the pain in her head, so much pain that she could barely open her eyes. 'Elara,' the voice said again.

Standing in front of her was the pale, dark-haired figure of Eli. Gem's twin. The Silvertongue. She swore, rolling off the bed away from him, thudding hard on the ground as she buried all thoughts of Enzo as deep as she could. She tried to crawl, but her body wouldn't obey.

'Stop, *stop*.' He took a cautious step closer. 'I'm not going to hurt you.'

Elara's chest heaved as she eyed Eli, bracing herself for the same cruelty his sister had shown. His piercing eyes were unreadable. His charcoal shirtsleeves were rolled up to show a black snake tattooed on his forearm, winding around it. His hair was slicked back, not a strand out of place.

'Have you come to finish what your sister started?' she spat, still trying to inch away from him.

'I came to give you this,' he said, producing a small knife.

'To put me out of my misery? Why do they call you the god of knowledge if you don't even know that I can't be killed by a Star?'

An amused sound escaped him as Eli drew the blade across his hand. 'He warned me you had a smart mouth.'

Elara's mouth dried, her body singing out for the divine elixir now dripping from Eli's palm.

'Wait,' she said, backtracking. 'Who said that?'

Eli crouched forwards, gingerly picking Elara up and placing her back in bed. He sat upon the edge, tentatively skimming a hand over the wound at her neck. She took a deep breath at the Star's contact again. That scent of rain reached her, along with his cunning, quicksilver power that never stilled, that couldn't be read.

'Ariete and my sister are fucking sadists,' he muttered, forming his palm into a fist above her mouth. 'Now drink.'

Elara held his gaze as she tentatively opened her mouth, allowing the blood to slip down her throat.

She jerked as her magick leapt towards him. Something within it sang to her, and her shadows followed it, right into the wound in his palm.

The contact caused an image to flare in her mind – Eli, sitting with a woman with white, long hair, a sky heavy with stars around them – before the Star whipped his hand away. 'What was that?' he hissed.

'I – I don't know,' she said. 'You tell me.'

He stared at her, something like fear in his gaze.

'What?' she asked.

'Nothing.' Whatever the look was, now it was gone. 'That's just . . . that's all your body can take right now. It will keep Ariete's venom at bay, at least for a few hours.'

'Why are you helping me?'

'Because I owe it. A certain prince bought my favour.'

Elara stilled. *No, no, no, no.* Every royal knew, warned as children, that one did not make a deal with the Stars. She thought to the bloodied Stella card that had wrought Ariete's wrath upon her. A Star could be called by a blood sacrifice upon their card. But if someone's wish was granted, it was rarely worth what the Star asked for in return.

'What did he do?' she whispered.

Eli looked faintly amused. 'That's his story to tell.'

'Is he okay?' she demanded.

Eli laughed softly then.

'Okay? He's feral.' Elara gnawed at her lip. Relief swept over her at Eli's assurance that Enzo had escaped with his life. But being indebted to this god . . . what had he given up?

Before she could ask more, Eli pressed his fingers to her temples.

She flinched, trying to pull away, but he held her firmly. 'What are you doing?' she implored.

'I promised I wouldn't hurt you,' he replied impatiently. 'Now stay still.'

Once the bargain was made, even a Star could not break it. It was that, and only that, which allowed Elara to trust the slippery god in front of her.

Eli closed his eyes, and Elara felt cool water over her mind, a balm against her ravaged thoughts. She almost sighed as it flowed over her, massaging her until she relaxed enough. She heard Eli's voice from far away.

'I'm placing a shield around your mind,' he said.

She felt it. Cool walls of metal, the same colour as her eyes.

'Surely your sister will realize what you've done?'

She heard an arrogant scoff.

'Not when it's crafted well enough. I'm not a Star of cunning for nothing.' She felt him tinker in her mind, adding embellishments and adjustments. When he was done, she breathed out a long sigh. Her mind was clear, sharp.

'When Gem looks in, all she will see is your mind and a few false memories pulled to the forefront. Enough for her to give up and not look past them to the wall.'

He straightened, adjusting his pinstriped waistcoat.

'I'd best be going. My favour has now been fulfilled. I've kept you as safe as I can.' Elara nodded, watching him go towards the door.

'Eli?'

The Star's eyes rested on her.

'What did he do? How did he buy your favour?'

The Star cocked his head. 'He had to tell me a truth. One that he cannot bear to utter aloud. One that could be wielded against him if I chose.'

Fear bloomed in her chest. To give up something so intimate, to a Star, no less.

'Thank you,' she whispered.

The Star said nothing more, simply nodding to her and heading for the door.

But then he halted on the threshold, turning back as though he had remembered something he wanted to say.

'I have only once before met a person with such purpose and vengeance as Lorenzo when he summoned me.'

'And who was that?'

Eli's answer was a faint smile as he disappeared from sight, the door closing behind him.

CHAPTER THIRTY-FOUR

When Gem entered Elara's room a few hours later, whatever Eli had painted inside her mind seemed to work. After giving one last desperate sweep, Gem departed, a mutter of 'waste of my fucking time' on her lips.

For the first time in days, Elara was cognisant enough to account for her surroundings. And her body was pain-free enough to move.

She slowly sat up, looking around her room. There on her bedside table was a glittering sapphire crystal ball, carved from the crystal caves of Verde. Her father had gifted it to her, a prized possession from before Asteria had closed their walls. In a framed painting directly opposite her was a rendering of 'The Nightwolf and the Silver', the white-haired maiden kneeling in snow with the wolf before they both met their ends. So many parts of her old life, preserved. As though she'd open the door and her mother and father would be waiting. As though nothing had happened at all.

She looked once more to her dragun-painted ceiling. There was Myth-eater, with his lilac hues and scrawls of ink that morphed constantly upon his parchment wings. The gatekeeper of stories. Dreamdancer, with a hide of swirling clouds, who would take her mortal dreamwalker companion soaring through the Dreamlands. Nightkeeper, who spewed shadows so black the Light could never penetrate with him near. And her favourite of all, Starfeared. She was absent from *The Mythas of Celestia*, but Elara had discovered her on just one nondescript slip of parchment stuck within the Mythas section of the palace library. It was Starfeared that she had inked upon her spine, the mirror image of the gleaming silver dragun above her, her maw alight with pearly fire.

Elara crept off the bed, wincing at her tense and locked muscles, her aching stomach, her weak limbs. She drew her silk curtains back and tried the window. It was unlocked. Heart pounding, she slid it open, scoffing at the arrogance of Gem and Ariete to not bother locking it. With the cool Asterian breeze kissing her cheeks, she peered into the inky lake that kissed the banks of her palace. She couldn't count the amount of times she, Sofia and Lukas had swum in it. She could swim through it, all the way to the woods on the other side. Surely it would be a better fate than what waited with Ariete. But she could never leave Sofia. She pushed the window shut.

She went to the door, placing her hand on the doorknob.

Her fingers froze. This was too easy. She had to be dreaming. But a quick check-in with her magick told her she wasn't dreamwalking at all. And so, she tentatively twisted her hand.

The door opened.

A dark, empty corridor stretched before Elara as she formed a plan. Her fingers flexed, and she could feel the well of her magick fill – Eli's blood was helping, preventing Ariete's venom from suffocating her power. Carefully, she weaved a veil over her, blending her into the shadows as she hurried down.

Only one thought was on her mind – *Sofia.*

Elara knew the palace better than anyone in Asteria. Her years trapped within its towers had their merits. She dodged and twisted through passageways and stairwells towards the dungeons, taking a specific shortcut she remembered. A look at the violet sky outside told her that the hour must be late, as she slipped out of a hidden passageway, before staggering to a stop.

Ariete was stood only a few yards away, speaking to someone shrouded in shadow. His back was to her and she held her breath, wrapping more illusions around her until she was nothing but air.

'She does not know.' Fear swept through Elara as she heard Gem's soft voice. 'I have swept the girl's mind. Made her beg and scream. There is nothing in there but shadows and an incessant worry for that captain's daughter.'

Ariete stretched his neck and made a grunt of frustration, then lifted his head up, looking to the ceiling. 'Do you feel the shadows growing darker?'

Gem shook her head. 'You're seeing things, my king. They are the same as they have been for centuries.'

Ariete made a dissatisfied sound. 'And what of her masked date?'

'Nothing yet. Only that he is a Helion.'

Elara's jaw clenched, and she made sure not to move so much as a muscle as Gem took a step closer to Ariete.

'What if you truly are destined for the Asterian?' she asked.

There was a callous laugh. 'Would you be jealous?' Elara frowned, as she saw Ariete caress Gem's cheek.

'I know you don't belong to me,' came the bitter response.

'That's right,' Ariete said coldly. 'I don't.'

He began to walk away. 'The ballet, Gem. Ensure it goes off without a hitch.'

And in a breath, the two Stars disappeared.

She waited minutes before easing from the door, delving further into the palace. Who in the Stars' names did Ariete think she was? What was the ballet?

Leaving these questions for later, she passed where the Stars had been standing and took a left, arriving at the entrance to the dungeons. One guard sat before it, snoring. She recognized him – Riccard. A guard who had once slipped her sweets at a boring meeting she'd attended with her parents. Something ached within her to see the familiar face, now serving someone with a heart as black as Lukas's. Above his head, etched upon the black stone of the dungeon's doorway, were the words that had always sent shivers down Elara's back, the last words that Asterian prisoners saw before their freedom was stolen from them: *May the Dark cast judgement upon your soul. May Piscea cast your fate. So worship her. So fear her.*

Making sure that her illusions were wrapped tightly around her, she darted towards the guard, focusing in on the belt he wore – and the set of dungeon keys upon it.

She hoped with everything she had that her shadows were strong enough to lift them. But alas, while the tendrils of darkness were awake and accessible, they were as ghostly and insubstantial as ever.

She crouched by Riccard's side, reaching a tentative hand out, hooking her fingers around the ring of keys. Gritting her teeth, she reached her other hand across and slowly, ever-so-slowly, unclipped them from his belt.

They jangled – and she held her breath as Riccard's snoring stopped. He shifted on his seat, and she forced herself to be entirely still. Finally his snoring resumed, and she carefully lifted the ring of keys up, away from his belt loop.

Letting out a long breath, she slipped past him into the dungeons beyond.

When she arrived at the cells, the dim fire in the sconces lighting her way, she wasted no time, running between the iron bars until she arrived at the last cell.

Inside, Sofia was curled upon a pallet of hay, still in her ballgown, now filthy.

'Sof,' Elara strangled out.

Sofia sat up. 'Lara?!'

'I'm here.' She was already pushing key after key into the lock, none fitting. She cursed, as Sofia scrambled up.

'How did you—'

'Later,' Elara said, shoving the next key in. To her relief it fit, and as she twisted the lock clicked.

The gate swung open, and she ran into Sofia's arms, holding her tightly. 'Now, Sof. We're leaving.'

Beads of sweat ran down Elara's forehead as she worked to hold an illusion over them both as they slipped through the palace. She followed the same shortcut, through the hidden passageway, up the back stairwell. The door of her room swam before her, and she blinked. Eli's blood must be wearing off. Only a few more metres. She yanked Sofia with her through the door.

And the figure sitting on the bed smiled as they tumbled in.

'You never were that good at escaping, were you, Lara?' said Lukas.

CHAPTER THIRTY-FIVE

'We used to play in here all the time.' Tilting his head to the ceiling, Lukas lifted himself off the bed. Elara had already moved protectively in front of Sofia. She was weaponless. Powerless, Ariete's venom sizzling through her blood, overpowering Eli's.

'Remember that game? Nightkeeper. The three of us would pretend we were the famous mythas, with our shadows.' He pointed a finger to the rendering of the draguns above him, a spew of shadows running from his fingers. 'Not that you could conjure a single one, Lara, after your little "incident" with that lightwielder.'

Elara's hands flexed by her sides.

'Shut the fuck up, Lukas,' Sofia spat.

He turned slowly then, pure, unfiltered hatred in his stare, now held on Sofia.

'You know, I never understood why you were so loyal to this bitch, Lara.'

'What do you know of loyalty?' Elara seethed, as a wave of nausea swept over her.

The shadows in Lukas's eyes eclipsed him for a second.

'About as much as you. Consorting with our enemy.' He sneered. 'Who was the Helion?' he asked softly.

Sofia's head whipped to her, and Elara gritted her teeth, fighting past Ariete's venom. 'I don't know what you're talking about,' she said, summoning up every inch of bravado and royal arrogance that she could.

'You sold us all out, Lukas,' Sofia said, and Elara could hear that familiar temper in her tone. The shadows grew on the walls, and she could not tell if they belonged to Lukas or Sofia. '*You* betrayed us to the enemy. To *Ariete*.'

'Lies,' he hissed, striding forwards. Elara looked around the room wildly.

'I saw the card, Lukas,' Elara said. She had to keep him talking. 'I know you summoned him.'

He released Sofia. 'No, I didn't.'

'You're on my fucking throne,' she shouted. 'Do you think me a fool? Of course you did. You planned this all along. All you want is power.' The room began to spin but she held on to her rage, begging it to anchor her.

Lukas's mouth worked, as though trying to grasp at a lie. She exchanged a glance with Sofia – the only person who knew her inside out. And Sofia read the plan in her gaze, following it to where it landed on the sapphire crystal ball on her nightstand.

Elara approached Lukas as Sofia's shadows drifted towards the ball. 'I wanted *you*, Lara,' he finally said.

'And when you couldn't have me, when our betrothal was in danger, you decided instead to hurt me,' she replied quietly.

'No,' he implored. 'I didn't want to hurt you, I—'

His mouth worked again, and he made a sound of frustration. Inky shadows began to pulse from him, and Elara knew he was lost to them.

The ball lifted gently up from where it lay, carried upon Sofia's magick towards Lukas.

'You, what? Love me? Didn't mean to have my parents *killed*? Didn't mean to *usurp my throne*?'

Lukas pressed a hand to her cheek, and she balked at its familiar coolness. 'Help me, Lara,' he whispered, and she blinked. For a moment, the shadows had cleared in his eyes, leaving them the dove grey she used to know. She staggered back from him. 'Please help me,' he said feverishly. 'My shadows—'

The crystal ball cracked over his head, and Lukas slumped to the floor.

Cool, night-jasmine air greeted Elara as she clung to the vines outside her bedroom window. Sofia had pushed open the window and now clutched Elara, her shadows wrapped around the two to support them as they scaled down the palace walls.

When the vines grew thinner, making way for only solid stone, Sofia's shadows formed into ropes that reached up and hooked around the windowsill, allowing both her and Elara to ease their way down the wall.

Elara's hands shook as she gripped on to the shadow ropes, cold sweat dripping down her back. 'I don't know how much longer I can fight this,' she breathed.

'You're doing so well, Lara,' Sofia said. 'We're nearly there. One step at a time. We'll be safe soon.'

Sofia's words gave her the strength she so desperately needed, and she held on to them.

They continued to descend carefully as Sofia's shadows wrapped tightly around Elara, supporting her further.

'My illusions aren't going to work,' Elara wheezed.

'Then we will stick to the shadows,' Sofia replied calmly. Some of her own drifted towards the ground as they approached it, and out into the night. 'Only a little further,' she said.

Elara took a deep breath, descending the last few metres, until she landed in the spongey lavender bank below. The lake yawned out beyond it.

'Quick now,' she murmured, and Elara looked back up to the palace wall, to her home, unsure when she might see it again.

'I know,' Sofia said beside her, understanding. 'But home is not a place, Lara.'

Elara nodded, turning even as tears filled her eyes.

'We're going to have to swim,' she continued firmly. 'Once we're across the lake, we'll head through the Shadow Woods. If we can get to those, and through, we'll be free. The wolves will protect us. Ariete won't be able to find us.'

'Helios,' Elara croaked. 'We push through the woods to the Goldfir Forest. We'll have asylum as soon as we cross the border.'

Elara stumbled and Sofia cursed. 'I've got you. Come on, I've got you.'

Black started to fill the edges of Elara's vision as they ran to the shore. She'd swum the moat before. She could do it again. She thought of Enzo as the darkness crept in, as she stumbled into the icy cold water.

The silver fish swirled frantically in pairs as Elara got up to her waist, teeth chattering.

'Come on, Lara,' Sofia urged. 'Don't think of the cold, or the water. Come on.'

'I-I can't,' Elara gritted out as the pain became unbearable. She tried to take another step, but her limbs wouldn't move.

'Okay, you need a distraction,' Sofia muttered, wrapping an arm around Elara's waist as she pulled her further in until water reached Elara's chest. 'Um . . . what about this prince?' she asked. 'Is he as dashing and charming as the ones we used to read about?'

But before Elara could respond, red light flooded behind her, making the moat look like blood.

'Oh no,' Sofia whispered, and Elara turned, as the King of Stars strode towards them, Gem close behind.

'Swim!' Sofia screamed.

But Elara's body was done. Though her mind pleaded and begged, the pain and the venom finally won the battle for control. She tried to swim, but instead fell under the water.

'Lara, come on!' Sofia's plea was muffled beneath the water. Elara reached out blindly, unable to speak, to breathe.

A hand plunged into the water, gripping Elara by the hair and dragging her above the surface.

Elara spluttered and coughed up water as, to her horror, Ariete hauled her back to the bank. She saw Gem pounce upon Sofia, holding a blade made of starlight to her neck.

Ariete finally let go, and Elara collapsed on to the grass, sodden. He slowly crouched before her as she gulped in lungfuls of air between coughs. 'I do love these cat-and-mouse games,' he crooned. 'And you've been a bad little mouse, haven't you, Elara?'

Her throat burned, poison and water crawling up it as she tried to scream, to plead. She looked behind to where Sofia was struggling against the goddess. 'Get the fuck off me,' her friend screamed. 'Lara! Lara! Leave her alone. I swear to the skies I'll kill you all. Leave her al—'

'Take her away,' Ariete said.

'So-Sofia,' Elara rasped. She tried to crawl, but starlight was already lighting around Gem and Sofia as they began to disappear. She swayed on her knees.

'It's all right.' Ariete gently gathered her in his arms. She didn't have an ounce of strength left in her to fight him as he lifted her. 'You're starting to understand that there is no hope. You will never escape me,' he murmured into her hair. 'Wherever you run, I will find you.'

When the darkness came, for the first time in Elara's life, she tried to fight it.

CHAPTER THIRTY-SIX

Elara looked at her reflection in her ornate mirror. Her gaze flicked from her sallow skin, to the shadows under her eyes, faint red with Ariete's venom. Then to the crimson eyes that watched her from behind.

Days had passed. Unending torment as Ariete's venom had ruined her, the Star drip-feeding her his blood – enough so she could talk, but not enough to use her magick.

She took in her dress, heavily embroidered with rubies and garnets, as a glamourer silently worked on her hair. She thought of Merissa. Then she felt like crying, and tried to focus again on her own reflection.

'You'll be the belle of the ballet,' Ariete said, strolling around the room, dressed in a suit that matched her gown.

'Why are we going?' she asked dully.

'Because I have a surprise for you.'

She tried to feel panic, but her box of emotions was firmly locked.

'Where's Sofia?'

Ariete, like every other time she had previously asked, didn't answer.

She watched as her hair was transformed by glamour into midnight ringlets, then placed carefully off her face with jewelled ruby pins that studded the curls like droplets of blood.

Makeup was smeared upon her face, hiding the dark rings. When the glamourer reached the bite marks upon Elara's neck, Ariete tutted. 'Leave them,' he said. 'The world should see that she's mine.'

'I will never belong to you.'

'Your heart, no. I'll make sure of that,' Ariete said. 'But your soul, your existence. They are mine.'

'And won't *Gem* be a little bothered by that? The two of you seem awfully close.'

He made an amused sound. 'Oh, she sates my appetite now and then. But not the way a mortal can.' He drew his thumb down the wound on Elara's neck. 'You sicken me, and yet I crave you. You know, I'm the closest to you humans. The god of war, of blood. I understand your fleeting lives, your desperation to make them count. And so, you fuck and kill and love and bleed. And it tastes so delicious to me, all of it.' He wet his lips, and she watched, unable to look away, as he pulled a knife from thin air, the weapon appearing in a flash of red.

'Look at how I bleed,' he said, cutting open the skin on his palm. Sparkling glitter welled up from the wound, a liquid stardust. 'Insubstantial.' A snarl curled his features. 'But a human's . . .' He beckoned the glamourer to him, who laid down the last pin she was about to secure in Elara's hair. The woman swayed to Ariete, moaning as he embraced her. She whispered fervent prayers as he chuckled. 'A human's blood is warm and red and so very alive,' he murmured as he plunged his teeth into her neck.

Elara flinched, looking away as the woman moaned anew.

He smeared her blood on his lips, his eyes gleaming as he pushed her off him.

'Yes, mortal blood tastes so much *more*.'

The glamourer slumped on to Elara's parents' bed, as utter fury writhed beneath Elara's skin.

'Are we really that expendable to you?'

Ariete chuckled. 'She's fine. Unlike with you, I didn't use my venom on her.'

As though in response, the woman moaned as she touched the wound at her neck, her eyes dazed in a state of bliss. 'I usually only drink from devotees. I do not relish killing mortals for no reason.'

'So what was the *reason* you murdered my parents?' she demanded.

'Isn't it obvious?' Ariete replied. 'They committed *starsin*. They heard this prophecy at your naming ceremony and hid it for decades from me, from the Stars.'

'They were innocent,' Elara said through gritted teeth.

'No human is truly innocent. Your parents certainly weren't. And they had been outrunning fate for a long time – had done terrible, awful things to escape it.'

A few of the ruby hairpins were still scattered upon the dressing table, and Elara's hand twitched over one.

'There is darkness within you, Elara, as there was darkness within them.'

'You know nothing about me.'

'On the contrary,' he grinned. 'I know you better than you do. I know that the line between good and evil is thinner than a blade. I know that you're teetering upon it.' He leaned forwards, his mouth at her neck. 'I could show you, you know,' he murmured. 'How to become the villain. How delicious it feels.'

'You know the most dangerous kind of villain?' she whispered. 'A woman with nothing left to lose.'

She whirled with a cry of pain, plunging the hairpin into his neck.

Ariete's shock changed in seconds to pain, a hiss escaping his lips. But as she tried to stagger for the door, he began to laugh, yanking the pin out.

Glittering blood poured from his neck, but Elara didn't wait to see if he would fall. She yanked at the door, but red starlight slammed into it, the lock clicking.

'Oh, you and I are going to have some fun,' Ariete chuckled, standing up straight. Already, the wound at his neck was healing. 'I see that divine violence was within you all along.'

The carriage, pulled by midnight horses, rumbled through the Dreamer's Quarter. Bookshops and galleries were crammed side by side, the dark grey cobbles beneath them slick with rain. In one pocket of the quarter sat a group of artists with their easels, painting beneath canopies in the drizzly night. Shops were lit up with a cosy glow, and there was one in particular that she'd snuck out to only once in her life – a café that had made the best hot cocoa she had ever tasted.

She flicked her gaze to the gods sat in the carriage with her. Ariete was looking out of the window, a distant smile on his lips as he toyed with a small knife. And beside him, studying her, was Eli. The god had helped her once before, but since Enzo's favour had been fulfilled, it seemed he had lost interest in good deeds. Whatever fate awaited her at the ballet, was hers alone.

'Where's Sofia?' she demanded again.

Ariete only laughed, and Eli switched his focus to his fingernails.

The carriage rattled over the Bridge of Tears, stopping directly outside the Asteria Opera House. The façade of the building was made out of a glittering bluestone, twirling features upon it gilded in silver. With a flourish, the footman opened the carriage door.

Ariete stepped out and raised a hand to take Elara's. She ignored it, making her own way down. But his hand instead clenched her arm, iron-strong as he propelled her through the crowds milling outside and towards the theatre. It was then, to Elara's relief, that she saw her people properly for the first time – and apparently safe. They seemed content enough, if a little on edge, but whatever atrocities Ariete had committed against the royal family's closest circle, it hadn't seemed to extend to her citizens yet.

As Elara stepped into the Opera House, she almost sighed. Deep blue and violet flowers spilled over the grand marble staircase, and a chandelier made with sapphires glimmered in the glowing candlelight. Vaguely familiar courtiers and other aristocrats – those who had clearly sworn fealty immediately to Lukas and Ariete – gathered in the lobby, peering at her with wide eyes as they whispered and gossiped.

'The lost princess,' she heard a whisper. 'With the King of Stars.'

The crowd parted for Ariete, every mortal within the vicinity lowering themselves on one knee. The Star nodded and smiled as he pulled Elara through, Eli trailing behind.

There was a fanfare behind her, more murmurs of excitement, and Elara turned.

Behind her, entering the theatre, with the Asterian crown

upon his head, was Lukas. He looked worse for wear, even paler and more ill than before, which gave Elara at least some satisfaction.

He smiled as he approached them.

'Captive life suits you, Lara,' he said softly as he embraced her.

Elara was stiff as she pulled away, though she cocked her head and gave a winning smile. 'I *do* look good in red.'

The amusement on Lukas's face slipped, though Ariete laughed. 'Your Majesty,' the Star acknowledged. 'Enjoy the show.'

'My lord,' Lukas bowed, 'I intend to.'

Elara was pulled up the grand staircase, and looked around wildly. She knew that the moment she reached the top of the stairs and entered the royal box, she would be trapped. This was her last chance.

'I need to use a bathroom,' she blurted out.

Ariete's gaze slid to her. 'Nice try.'

'I do,' she insisted, stopping midway on the stairs.

'I'll take her,' Eli sighed.

Ariete nodded. 'Do not let her leave your sight,' he said, continuing on.

Eli pushed her in front of him as he took her back down, and she wet her lips as she found the bathrooms over on the far side of the entrance.

'Be quick,' he said, stationing himself by the door. Elara nodded, hope thrilling through her as she went into the bathroom alone.

Only to stop still.

In front of her, the goddess smoothing her hair in the mirror turned, smiling.

'Hello, Elara Bellereve.'

Cancia.

Skies, the Star was ethereal. Silver hair that glowed iridescently, one blue eye the colour of lakes, the other the green of the sea, both sparkling as she approached, and Elara found herself overwhelmed with the smell of ocean flowers. It was a soft, comforting fragrance, but Elara knew better. Cancia was the goddess of pain and penance.

'What are you doing here?' she croaked. Elara could no longer bring herself to show the Stars a respect they did not deserve.

An indignancy flashed upon the goddess's face before it was smothered. 'We don't have long,' she murmured, and took a long pointed nail, the colour of pearls, to her wrist. With a swipe, sparkling blood gathered. 'Drink.'

'What?' Elara exclaimed.

'The prince of Helios bought my favour. And you need your strength, and your magick, for what is about to occur.'

Elara's head spun, though she still took Cancia's wrist.

'He's close,' Cancia said. 'Waiting by the Bridge of Tears. Use the strength my blood gives you, slip out of this theatre during the show. Run to the bridge. Lorenzo will arrange the rest.'

Tears gathered in Elara's eyes. She had thought herself alone, abandoned. And here Enzo was, making yet another bargain for her life. But one thing remained.

'I can't leave Sofia.'

'Your friend is taken care of. The prince's general is at the Asterian palace as we speak.'

Elara's legs wobbled, and Cancia pushed her against the counter. 'Drink,' she said softly.

And Elara closed her eyes, one tear rolling down her cheek, as she drank.

CHAPTER THIRTY-SEVEN

A violin was already playing as Elara took her seat in the box. She kept catching Eli's gaze, and forcibly looked away, making herself think of anything but her conversation with Cancia, lest the god decided to read her mind.

In the box beside them, Lukas was leaning over, and he gave a languid wave to Elara, eyes glittering. A shadow drifted from his hands towards her, caressing her cheek, and she pulled away in disgust.

She sat back in her seat and studied the stage.

A man and woman danced upon it, their movements like water. Fluid and graceful, they kissed as they danced, turning from the stage a moment before revealing a crying newborn in their arms.

The crowd applauded and cooed as the woman rocked the baby, happiness lighting her face. But then the stage darkened, as with a flash of light, a woman appeared, lit with a bright glow. The couple looked at each other in fear, before shadows plunged from the man's hands, and struck the glowing newcomer down.

Elara inwardly checked her magick, relieved to feel a surge

of her power as Ariete's venom was fought back by Cancia's blood.

The stage lightened again, the couple continuing to dance as the backdrop behind them transitioned to a palace. The baby was replaced by a young girl, dancing and twirling around her parents. When they disappeared, Elara saw a flash of white, and dread pooled in her stomach as she saw Gem, standing within the conductor's box, her arms dancing in the air as she faced the stage. A sad refrain sounded as a woman stepped on to the stage. She was draped in silver as she danced to the music, but something about her seemed oddly familiar to Elara.

The backdrop shifted to reveal bookcases. The woman moved gracefully to smell flowers, then her attention switched to a book. It was hard from Elara's vantage point to make out the woman's face. The scene moved on, now a backdrop of clouds and stars. The ballerina danced between them, feigning sleep and waking.

Unease spread over Elara. An ominous tune arose, a slow build-up of trumpets as the scene changed to a throne room, the man and woman from earlier sat atop thrones as a hooded figure strutted in. Other dancers came in, their movements strangely jerky as they danced around the throne room.

Elara squinted, and saw Gem now had her arms raised and was waving her hands as if she was actually conducting the dance, the dancers on stage following the movements exactly.

Cold clenched over Elara's heart as the hood of the figure was pulled back. Red-striped hair and white makeup streaked the dancer's face. His hands drifted to the sky and streams of light fell from them on to the figures as they screamed to the building crescendo, the violins and flutes in a frenzy. Elara whipped her head to Ariete, seeing that the starlight's source was from the King of Stars' own two hands, beaming and bending through the theatre, so it seemed the dancer was conjuring it himself. When she looked back to the stage, blood – real blood, bright red – painted the bodies of the dancers as all the figures fell, save for the prima ballerina and the dancer posing as Ariete. The crowd gasped, and Elara lunged forwards. She felt a hand grip the back of her neck as Ariete held her in place.

'What is this?'

His voice was soft. 'This is your story, Elara. And you will watch as it ends.'

She sat in shock as the interlude began, watching as blue velvet curtains were drawn across the horrors upon the stage, the ornate candelabra brightening as excited chatter filled the audience.

'Are you enjoying the performance?'

Elara looked at Ariete dully. 'Are they dead? The dancers.'

A cruel smile curved his lips. 'Dancers? Didn't you recognize them, princess?'

When Elara didn't respond he chuckled. 'Let's see. There was Pierre, your father's advisor. Noelle, your mother's handmaiden.' He waved his hand through the air. 'I don't remember all their names, but they were those who kept your secret. Everyone who tried to hide you. Dead.'

Bile rose in Elara's throat, and she swallowed it down, looking to the crowd. They were speaking animatedly, ignorant to the horrors that had taken place behind those curtains. 'I'm not worth this,' she whispered.

'Oh, but you are. Because there's still one more secret you're keeping from me.'

Despair rose inside her as the refrain of the second act began, the candlelight dimming once more as the curtains were drawn back.

Clad in a glittering gown, the ballerina – the one playing the role of Elara – was now wearing a mask, hand in hand with a tall dark-haired man. She watched the scene that had shown her capture – a masquerade ball, the masks grotesque as other dancers flooded the stage, all doing a quickened version of the Celestian Waltz.

Elara's heart pounded. The crowd clapped to the music, excitement in recognizing it. It was irritating her now, why the main ballerina moved in a way so familiar to her, dancing around the stage with a tall, masked man that she presumed was supposed to be Enzo.

The Star seated next to her was bobbing his head along with the melody, a grin on his face.

The music accelerated into a frenzy, Ariete leaning forwards out of his seat with excitement.

Do not move. Do not speak.

Elara swallowed a gasp, remaining still as Eli's voice slithered through her mind.

You must leave now, before more blood is spilled. Ariete will not stop. Everyone you love will die.

She risked the quickest glance at Eli, but he was sipping a firewhisky, the picture of nonchalance, his attention on the macabre spectacle unfolding on stage.

Now, Elara. Use your magick now.

She prepared herself, tensing her legs, ready to launch past Ariete as she raised a hand. A glimmer of illusions danced off her palm, her magick itching and leaping to be freed after so long. The music was getting so loud. Guessing she had around ten seconds to run to the door, Elara started counting down in her head. She looked to Eli, who nodded only once.

She rose slowly, gritting her teeth, and glanced back to the stage for a moment.

The figure supposed to be her was twirling in a frenzy with the dancing Ariete, the music deafening.

'I'd watch if I were you.' Ariete's voice drifted to her, although he hadn't moved an inch, still leaning forwards, mesmerized by the movement onstage. She froze in shock, her illusions sputtering out.

'Bad, bad little mouse. Always trying to run.' He tutted, knocking back his drink without shifting his gaze.

Elara did not move as she looked down at the stage. Nausea swept over her as two grey eyes found her throughout the whole crowd of dancers. A look of love and will in them.

At the same time, Gem's hands were waving madly as though creating her own symphony as her puppets danced.

The way the prima ballerina moved, how it had stirred something in Elara, finally made sense. For it was Sofia, firmly in the grip of Gem's control, who continued to hold her gaze as she stood centre stage, as the dancer dressed as Ariete came up behind her, cradling her as he pulled a knife and slit her throat.

Elara did not hear the scream that ripped through her as she lurched towards the balcony, her hands outstretched. She did not see the blood gush from Sofia's neck, did not hear the panic of the crowd, the chaos that ensued. She did not hear Ariete's cackles of glee. Pain engulfed her so thoroughly that time slowed. She saw herself from outside her body, saw Ariete turn, a demented gleam in his eyes at the performance he'd created. Saw Eli blink slowly, the only sign of *any* reaction to the display. She felt her power rip from her. She felt the hopelessness of it all. And the need to get to Sofia's still body. Sobbing with pain and grief that were tearing her mind apart, she climbed the balcony, and threw herself from it.

The last thing she heard was Ariete's gasp of shock as she fell. The crowd continued to shriek at the spectacle. At Elara's pale skin, ebony hair spilling around her, neck twisted at the wrong angle, and eyes glassy with death.

CHAPTER THIRTY-EIGHT

Elara was blinded by tears as she ran, the slick Asterian cobbles providing no purchase. She slipped, forcing her feet to move, the past few minutes repeating again and again in her head.

Sofia's face. The blood across her throat. The illusions that had risen to Elara, almost unbidden. The fall that she had made the audience and Ariete believe was real. She had felt the fall as it happened, as the illusion took hold, like being in two places at once, as she had rushed to the door of the royal box and out of the theatre. Nobody had been able to see her, the illusion too powerful to deny. Elara was not running down the Opera House's grand staircase. Elara was not rushing from the building's entrance, on to the cobbled streets. Elara was dead.

Even now, she panted at the exertion it took to maintain the illusion of her broken, twisted corpse back at the Opera House. She didn't have a plan, didn't know how long she could keep her magick there going, deceiving Ariete, before it sputtered out.

She just kept running.

Up ahead, she could see the two statues that marked the beginning of the Bridge of Tears – two weeping, kneeling women, facing each other and carved from grey stone. A shadow waited between them.

'Did anyone ever tell you that you look sublime in red?' a familiar voice called. Enzo stepped out of the gloom, but stopped, easy demeanour gone as he took in her shaken state.

'Get it off me,' she whispered, sinking to the wet, hard ground. She pulled at the crimson dress.

'*Get it off!*' she screamed, yanking at the chain of rubies around her neck. The chain snapped, gems scattering around her like spilt blood as her chest heaved and heaved, her breath coming in short gasps between sobs. Enzo swore before crossing the space between them in two strides. With one hand, he whipped out a knife from his belt, deftly cutting through the lace stays at her back. He ripped the dress away, leaving her in nothing but a long, thin slip.

'It's okay, Elara, it's okay.' He knelt behind her, crushing her to him as he breathed her in. 'You're safe now.'

She winced, and he instantly loosened his grip.

'El, I'm so sorry. Leo searched every room but he couldn't find Sofia.'

'Dead,' she whispered.

'What did you say?'

'She's dead. Ariete, he killed her.'

Enzo cursed, holding her as she sank to the ground. 'I'm so sorry, El. I'm so sorry. How did you get away from him?'

'I illusioned my death,' she said, the world growing further and further away. 'I'm trying to maintain it even now, but I don't know how much longer I can hold it.'

Enzo replied, but she didn't hear him. Her ears rang as she faintly registered the sound of running feet and familiar voices. Merissa, and then Isra. They were saying something, but she couldn't follow the words, as Enzo's arms tightened around her again.

Cancia's blood was beginning to fade from her body, Ariete's venom lurking and creeping back into her bones. But she didn't care. Not when her thoughts filled with her best friend, her *sister's* neck slashed red, the life fading from her clever grey eyes.

She saw Leo appear from the other side of the bridge, concern in his eyes as he ran towards them. When he approached, Enzo briefly explained what had happened, and Elara let it all wash over her.

'We have to get to the boat now. The moment we cross into Helios, we'll be safe.' Leo's voice seemed distant to her. Then, when the prince didn't respond: 'Enzo? *Enzo?*'

Still no response.

'Elara.'

Pure, animal instinct cut through her pain at that tone, her back straightening. It was the tone of a king, one that demanded an answer.

'Elara,' Enzo said again, his voice now far more gentle, as she heard him kneel behind her again. 'What happened to your neck?'

His thumb touched her, right next to the bite Ariete had inflicted on her.

'Your Highness,' Merissa warned. Enzo shot a hand out behind him with a hum of warning, a ball of fire between his fingers. She stepped back.

'El?' he asked again, so softly.

'He bit me.' Elara's voice had no inflection. She did not care about what had been done to her. Did not care about Enzo's reaction. 'Nearly every day since I was captured. His venom smothered my magick.' She looked into Enzo's eyes, hers dead.

He rose to his feet. His face still hadn't moved. 'Merissa, glamour me.'

'Enzo,' Merissa started, 'please—'

'*Glamour me!*' he snarled. 'That's a fucking order.'

Merissa pressed her lips into a thin line as she wove her magick, making Enzo up into an Asterian pedestrian – a pale, plain-looking man with dark hair and grey eyes. He knelt before Elara, who couldn't bring herself to look at him.

'El,' he said softly. 'I'll be back as quickly as possible.'

She nodded vaguely.

'Enzo, whatever you're thinking of doing, don't,' said Isra. 'The plan was to get her and get out. Ariete is a *god*. You are no match for him. Whatever vengeance you're intent on seeking, it *won't help*.'

Enzo rounded on Isra, his face centimetres from hers as he spoke: 'I couldn't give a fuck if Ariete was Death embodied. Not *only* did he take Elara from me. He hurt her. Violated her. *Bit her.*'

Enzo's voice broke noticeably as he paced away. 'You think I care that he's a Star? *Fuck immortality.* Even gods can burn.'

Isra made a disgusted sound, a look of disapproval on her face.

'Get to the boat,' he continued. 'Get ready to leave. It's already past eleven o'clock. If I'm not back by the time the clock tower chimes twelve, go.'

Leo gave him a tight nod, guiding Elara forwards, her arms wrapped around herself, not wanting to look at Enzo's glamoured features. He hesitated for a moment, and then strode to her, placing a gentle kiss on her forehead. 'I'll be back soon.' She couldn't make herself respond.

He spun on his heel, flexing his fingers before striding sharply into the night.

A thin coat of sweat glazed Elara as she tried to fight against the enormous strain of maintaining the illusion of her death. But the poison in her blood was awakening, and she let out a cry of pain.

Merissa looked at Leo with worry. They had reached the end of the bridge, the lake before them glistening in the darklight. A large rowboat bobbed upon it, tied to a small lakeside dock. Elara looked beyond, to Lake Astra, and understood Enzo's plan of escape. But Lake Astra also reminded Elara of Sofia. She swayed.

Isra ran forwards. 'Elara?'

She pushed Isra away gently. 'I'm sorry I—'

She couldn't breathe. She felt feverish. 'She's in shock,' Leo said, wrapping an arm around her to steady her.

Two bells rang out in the distance, echoing over the city. Half past eleven, Elara realized. How long had it been since he left?

'Come on, Enzo,' Leo said, his voice strained as he checked his pocket watch. He released Elara, who sank back into a haze of distant shock and constant effort. She didn't register time passing, not until there was a loud bang somewhere distant, and Leo cursed in a low voice as he stared at something behind her.

'For Stars' sake, Enzo,' Isra murmured. Merissa gasped, all their eyes drawn in the same direction. Elara turned to find out what it was, and saw streams of molten orange light soaring into the air. No, not light. Flames. And then there was a blood-curdling roar of pain, inhumanly loud. Away in the distance, the Opera House was on fire.

Sometime later – Elara couldn't keep track any more – Leo announced it was a quarter to twelve. Had it been fifteen minutes? Still Enzo hadn't appeared. Leo tried to lead Elara to the boat, but she shrugged him off, gazing unseeingly out across the still water and the sand at the lake's edge. More time passed. More effort, more pain in her body as the venom grew in strength.

'Five minutes,' she heard Leo warn. The whole sky was alight, the blaze from Enzo's flames licking the clouds.

'Two minutes.'

Finally, they heard pounding footsteps. Leo raised his sword, his light channelled through it, glowing lethally. But he relaxed his stance as he saw Enzo hurtling down the street, the burning sky rising behind him. His glamour was gone. He was carrying a large shape over his shoulder – and Elara now realized it was a body, moaning and grunting.

'Lukas,' she said quietly.

Enzo gritted his teeth as he hauled the usurper, whimpering, on to the pebbles and damp sand next to the dock. Lukas's clothes were singed, smoke billowing off him.

'Ariete's indisposed at the moment,' Enzo said lightly, stretching his arms out.

'What did you do?' Merissa breathed.

Enzo didn't respond, only went to Elara, checking her over. 'You can let go of your illusions now, El,' he said gently. 'The Opera House will be ash soon. Everyone will assume your body went up in the flames.'

Elara sighed in relief and let her magick go. She felt the illusion vanish, the exhausting strain in her mind finally easing down, and turned her gaze to Lukas. He was wailing quietly but still had the pride to muster up a weak sneer on to his face. She rose, walking slowly towards him, pure wrath overtaking her exhaustion and grief just for a few moments. He had started this. He had called upon a Star.

'You,' she snarled, crouching over him. 'You are the reason she's dead.'

'What are you talking about?' he rasped. 'I had nothing to do with this.'

'Liar,' Enzo spat.

'I hated Sofia, but I didn't know what Ariete had planned. Lara, I promise I never wanted to hurt you.'

'What did I say about uttering her name again,' Enzo growled.

'Call off your dog,' Lukas hissed, spitting blood on to the ground.

Enzo cracked his neck, a hollow laugh escaping him. 'It's "Lion", actually.'

Fear, real fear, flashed across Lukas's face – the first spark of it that Elara had seen. 'Prince Lorenzo.'

'So you've heard the stories,' Enzo replied.

Lukas scrambled back, but Elara lunged, tightly gripping his shirt.

'You began this, Lukas. You called upon Ariete at the birthday ball.'

'I didn't fucking call upon him,' he snapped.

Elara blinked, and nightmares grew around her. His eyes bulged in horror as she watched impassively.

'L-Lara, please,' he stammered. He tried once more to crawl away, but this time Enzo held him firm.

'I'm done with your lies,' she said. 'The last time I had the chance to kill you, I spared you. I won't make that mistake again.'

Her gaze flicked to Enzo, and flames ignited in his eyes.

'Elara, please, no. Remember what we had. This isn't you.'

'No, it's not. The girl I was died in that theatre. You won't find mercy here.'

Enzo pounced, light beaming from his hands as Lukas screamed. Elara turned around, sitting back upon the boat as his screams and pleading filled the air. She smelled burned flesh, and closed her eyes.

When his screams had quietened to sobs, Elara turned. Enzo was dragging Lukas by his hair to the water's edge. And she caught a flash of what Enzo had done to him.

'LIGHTWHORE' was branded in stark letters across his chest, and Enzo turned to her.

She nodded once, and he dumped the gasping Lukas into the deeper waters, before hauling himself to the boat.

'Fast and strong,' was all he ordered, settling next to Elara as he and Leo took up oars, paddling furiously across the murky mirror of the lake, leaving Lukas's prone body in the water.

CHAPTER THIRTY-NINE

With the lull of the boat's rocking, Elara fell into a sweet night's sleep. It was black and unending, her dreams leaving her in peace. She broke out of it now and then to hear the gentle lap of water or the quiet murmurs of her friends. But reality was too much, and so she sank back down into the comforting dark.

It was when swimming through this darkness that Elara felt a presence. Her instinct urged her awake, and she sat bolt upright, the night around her having reached its darkest point.

Silence. Too much of it. Though Leo still rowed, the paddles made no splash in the water, and the usual hum of cicadas in the blue-tinged night was absent.

She gripped on to Enzo's arm, and he turned, nodding. He'd noticed it too. He motioned to the others, and they all scanned the lake furtively as Leo continued to row, but at a slower pace.

'Something's here,' Elara slurred.

As though it had been waiting for her to speak, a clear, enchanting voice on the air began to sing a haunting melody.

The lilting tune caused the hairs on her arms to raise and foreboding to prickle down her neck, before everything she felt was overpowered by delight. She leaned forwards, enraptured as she listened. Leo dropped his oars, slack-jawed. The boat drifted to a standstill as the voice continued its lament.

It sang of times long past, of magick that flowed through the skies, and a long-lost love, a love that could never be, filled with pain and separation. Elara only realized her face was wet when Enzo brushed a tear off her face, his own eyes lined with silver.

The spell nearly took over. But a movement out of the corner of Elara's eyes broke its hold. Leo was leaning over the side of the boat, a look of yearning on his face as he reached into the water.

'*Leo!*' Elara screamed, adrenaline overpowering her grief at the song as she scrambled across the boat to him in a blur. The boat rocked precariously. Merissa was gazing stricken into the distance, Isra stretching towards the surface of the lake. Enzo swore, charging forwards to restrain the seer, as a head emerged from the water on Leo's side, a stunning creature. A siren.

Elara had heard the tales – in fact, one of her favourite stories in *The Mythas of Celestia* was of the sirens of Altalune. It was whispered that some swam in the Still Sea – nothing more than a sailor's superstition, Elara had thought – but she had swum in Lake Astra more than once, and never had she seen even a glimpse of the creature before her.

The siren's skin was as pale as snow, her hair like deep blue ink pooling in the water around her, covering her naked torso. She reached out to touch Leo's face, still singing her song. He grasped at her hand, but she drew it away whenever he came close. The face flickered for an instant, turning towards Elara – and then, suddenly, it was Enzo floating there in the water, reaching out to her with longing.

'Enzo?' Elara cried, her voice high.

'I'm here!' he shouted behind her. She risked turning for a split second and saw him hauling Isra back from the edge of the boat before lunging for Merissa, who was also clawing desperately over the side. Elara gave a cry of panic as the boat rocked violently, and only when it had slowed did she whip her head back towards the water, seeing the siren once again. She swore under her breath, closing her eyes and trying to muster up a semblance of her power.

'Your light, Enzo,' she pleaded. He grunted and cast a sweeping arc of radiance deep down into the water at his side. When Elara looked out across the lake, she tried not to scream. Within the luminous arc lay scores of sirens, their heads bobbing in the water, patiently waiting to drag them under. Another siren broke the surface next to the first, and joined in the song's harmony. Enzo swore loudly as he tried to reach for rope to tie Isra and Merissa together. Elara could barely grasp on to her magick, and so instead she grasped on to her fury. She conjured pure threat into her eyes and turned her gaze to the creature closest to her.

'Get off him,' she snarled. The creature stopped her singing, glancing in shock at Elara. The siren quickly recovered, however, a slow smile formed on her face, revealing razor-sharp teeth.

'You can't be controlled by our song,' she sighed. 'Do you know what that means, little human?'

Elara's head pounded, darkness threatening to envelop her again. Her energy was spent, and she swayed. Enzo ran to her side, having secured Leo, Isra and Merissa tightly together with the rope, his hands ready to wield.

'What a pretty pair,' the siren hummed. 'You know, I can hardly decide who I'd like first.'

'I'll char the scales off your withered fucking tail if you so much as touch her,' Enzo promised.

The siren's lovely face shifted before them, her smile turning into a sneer, what was once beautiful turning ugly with venom and spite.

'A human does not survive a siren. If you won't come willingly, you will come by force.' On her last word, the entire crowd hummed in harmony behind her, rippling as the sirens lunged forwards. Elara heard Merissa scream behind her as the boat lurched violently.

'I want him,' she heard a siren screech beneath them.

There was a chuckle as the boat lurched again, and Enzo stumbled this time, nearly falling overboard. With a shriek, the first siren lunged, her arms reaching up over the side as she dug taloned nails into Enzo's forearms.

'Kiss your sweetheart goodbye,' the siren said, as Enzo struggled to fight back, bright flames and light rippling off his hands and body. But they were to no avail, sputtering out on the siren's damp body. 'You're mine now.' And with a sharp grin to Elara, the siren pulled Enzo off the boat and under the water.

For a moment, there was nothing in Elara's vision but the light that surrounded Enzo, growing dimmer the further he descended into the lake's depths. And something took over her. It wasn't the horror and disbelief at seeing Sofia die only hours before, or the sheer desperation when seeing her parents murdered. It was a killing calm. She knew then that she would part the lake in two before she let that creature keep Enzo.

With a guttural cry, Elara dived.

The lake's ice-cold water felt like a blow to the gut and every instinct told her to take a breath at the shock. She ignored those instincts as she forced her eyes open to the murky waters around her. What she saw nearly stopped her heart.

Below the surface, illuminated only slightly by Enzo's waning light as it sank deeper, were skeletal bodies and tails, rotten flesh hanging off in scraps. She bit back a gag reflex, saving her precious air as she whirled around in search of him. Finally, she saw his light, further off now, drifting towards the middle of the lake.

Gritting her teeth, Elara kicked out, swimming furiously lower and lower, the pressure of the surrounding black waters making her ears pop. She reached the lake bed a moment after she saw the siren land with Enzo, clouds of sand kicking up around her. Elara squeezed her eyes shut against the grit in the water as she continued to swim towards the siren. And it was then that she remembered that she was powerless. No shadows to cause any damage, her illusions and dreams useless when faced with life or death.

She stilled as the siren turned, a look of feral glee on the creature's face. Enzo was unmoving, the light around him fading fast, his hand limp in the siren's.

The last glow of his light flickered and extinguished, leaving Elara in the pitch-black waters.

That was all it took – his warmth, his light, gone – for something deep within to erupt from her as all hell broke loose.

CHAPTER FORTY

A thundering boom exploded outwards. Silver light seemed to fill everything around her, along with a pulsing roar that she felt in her entire body, resounding throughout the water. The light was so bright it was almost blinding, but a shape in the glare drifted near to her. *Enzo*. The siren had let him go. She had a second to grab his hand before the silver light burned even brighter, and both she and Enzo were propelled upwards at a dizzying speed.

They broke the surface, Elara gasping for air, desperately hanging on to Enzo. The entire lake around her was flooded with the silver light, shining up from below her. The sirens had stopped their singing, and there was only silence until she saw Leo, Isra and Merissa on the boat, blinking as they shook off their stupor. She turned to Enzo but he wasn't moving. She couldn't even tell if he was breathing.

'Help!' she screamed.

With the siren's spell broken, Leo made quick work of releasing the rope knots tying him to Isra and Merissa, and rushed to the edge of the boat as Elara swam the still unconscious Enzo within reach.

Leo hauled the prince up, Isra and Merissa reached to pull Elara on to the boat after him. She collapsed on the floor still gasping and coughing, next to Enzo.

Leo was already pressing his hands over Enzo's chest when Elara pushed herself up.

'What the fuck was that?' Isra whispered in awe as the light surrounding Elara flickered then died.

Elara could only shake her head as she took Enzo's hand in hers. She didn't know what it was – only that the magick itself was not unknown to her. It was the same power that had manifested in front of Enzo as a monster, had sunk its fangs into Isra.

Leo kept pumping, and still Enzo didn't breathe.

'You can't leave,' she whispered to him, a sob making her breath shudder. 'Not you too.'

She crawled around to Enzo's head. 'Please,' she begged, her lips finding his as she breathed air into his body when Leo commanded. Isra and Merissa looked on in worry. There were tears in Isra's eyes as Elara pushed a wet strand of hair off Enzo's forehead, his face blank and lifeless.

'*Please*,' Elara half-screamed as she gave one last push of air into him.

As though it was a command that reached him all the way to the point between life and death, Enzo sucked in a breath, his eyes flying open as he coughed and retched. It took him a few moments to speak, as he struggled to get his breath back.

'You know, princess . . .' he said weakly, drawing in deep lungfuls of air, 'if you wanted . . . to kiss me again . . . you didn't have to wait until I was near death to do it.'

Elara sobbed in relief, her hands around Enzo's neck as he wrapped his arms around her immediately, pulling her on to his lap as she sobbed and sobbed, his hands stroking calming patterns down her back.

'Thank the heavens,' Merissa murmured, squeezing Enzo's hand. Leo let out a long breath, rubbing his head as he slapped Enzo's back, Isra squeezing Enzo tightly around Elara, before she glanced out at the lake and started in surprise.

'Um . . . not to ruin Enzo's near-death experience,' she said, 'but I think you're going to want to see this.' Her voice cut through Elara's exhausted relief, bringing her back to the present moment.

Enzo pushed himself up weakly, but Elara put a hand lightly on his shoulder. Still soaked, her hair plastered down her back, she rose to her feet and looked where Isra was pointing out over the water. As she stared, the rest of the group around her stilled, all of them looking out in shock.

In their desperation to save Enzo, they hadn't even spared a glance to the sirens. But now, the crowd of creatures was still. All that could be seen above the surface of the lake was a sea of heads, silently bowed to the boat.

'What is this?' Merissa breathed.

The first siren who had attacked them looked up, and swam slowly near to the boat again. She looked to Elara, and then to Enzo as he clutched her.

'It can't be, and yet it is.' The siren's eyes filled with tears as she pressed three fingers to her forehead. An ancient sign of respect.

As Elara's thoughts and exhaustion crashed into her, the siren threw her head back and a new song resounded. The clear voice was not laced with seduction but with something else. Elara listened, and recognized the feeling in the song that made her heart soar. It was *hope* that the sirens sang of. She looked nervously to Enzo again, who was watching her in awe. The other sirens had joined in, the harmonies soaring in unison, a song this time of healing and remembrance, of a light in the darkness.

Finally, each siren gradually halted their song, one by one, until the first siren finished the tune, her voice the last to carry the note. She bowed her head again to Elara.

'We will guide your way back to safety,' the siren whispered. They were the last words Elara heard before the world around her vanished, her consciousness with it.

CHAPTER FORTY-ONE

The jolt of a carriage. Footsteps. Urgent voices. The sounds drifted to her as she floated, sightless and nameless.

'It's bad. Very bad. Gem was involved, as well as Ariete.'

Gem. The name registered. She tried to grasp hold of the memory, but it floated away from her.

'Wounds from Ariete's magick ... think the bite is infected ...'

She frowned, her eyes still screwed tight. She knew she was supposed to feel an emotion. But again, the thought floated away. The darkness shrouding her hushed her, soothing her.

'Medical attention immediately ... I'm not leaving her ...'

Another voice whispered something, then came a roar.

'*I'm not leaving her.*'

She suddenly noticed that she was in someone's arms, and felt them tighten. She smelled amber, and a drifting thought told her she was home. But the word *home* felt strange, and so she frowned and forgot it.

'Take someone with you ... food ... water ... rest ... assess her when the wound has been cleaned.' The cool and stern voice drifted in and out. It was confident, feminine, mature. She liked the sound of that voice.

'I can do it myself,' the other voice snapped. 'No one touches her.'

She lurched in the warm grip around her. A passing thought found it funny, the movement. Then she almost wanted to cry. The darkness hushed her as if she was a child, easing her mind into blankness again. All she knew was that she had to keep her eyes shut so that the darkness would stay with her. The darkness was her friend. The darkness would protect her.

A soft click, and a door was closed. A familiar scent wafted to her, vanilla and something clean.

Safe, the darkness said.

'Elara.' A softer, gentler feminine voice made her wince, as did the feel of soft hands taking her own.

She flinched from the touch. Elara. Her name. She was Elara.

'I managed to get it,' she heard the softer voice say. The voice was familiar. She wasn't sure why.

'How—'

'I know someone,' came the quick reply.

Elara shifted as the arms carrying her took something from the woman.

'Thank you,' said the voice – the man – carrying her. 'Leave us now, Merissa.'

Merissa. A friend. Her friend.

Her friend, Sofia.

Blood.

Blood.

She began to hyperventilate as the darkness worked to coax her, her friend's voice too close.

'Enzo, I need to make sure—'

'*Leave.*'

She heard a small sigh and the sound of a door closing firmly.

'Elara,' she heard the gentle voice whisper. She murmured at its sound. She liked this voice. She trusted it. This voice made her feel warm.

Safe, the darkness whispered again.

'Elara, I'm going to need you to wake up so I can get you clean.'

She clutched his neck and kept her eyes squeezed shut. She didn't want to break the spell just yet. The darkness was so soft, and the world beyond the darkness just seemed so . . .

'Shit,' he muttered, and she felt herself being carried somewhere else. The darkness changed, faint colours and patterns intruding from somewhere. Light behind her eyelids. She was somewhere bright. She squeezed her eyelids tighter. 'I'm going to put you here as we run a bath, okay?'

She felt softness underneath her – a chair – and the sound of water.

When hands touched her again, she flinched.

'It's me, El. It's Enzo.'

Enzo. That name. She liked that name. She liked him. A lot. The darkness smiled. *Safe. Home.*

'It's just you and me and the warm water.'

Her eyes still closed, she nodded once, her lips trembling, tears threatening to spill from behind her lids.

When arms took her gently again, she melted into them.

'I'm going to put you in the bath now,' he said, and she nodded again. Those sure hands lifted her, cradling her, and placed her in the warm water.

Calloused hands, sure and steady, loosened dirty, pitted clips from her hair. She could feel the weight of her undergown against her in the water – clothing that still bore the memories of her friend's death.

'I want it off,' she croaked, the first words she'd uttered, though they crackled, her throat dry from disuse. She yanked at the strap on her shoulder.

Enzo's hands paused in her hair. 'Okay,' he said softly. She felt the horrid fabric slip off her, and sank further beneath the water as she let it cleanse her.

He seemed to disappear momentarily, before returning, and she heard a bottle clinking against the tiles.

'I need you to drink this now, El.' She tried to pull away. 'It's a Star's blood. It's going to hurt – because Ariete only gave you small amounts. This is a lot of it. You need a large amount to cure his venom entirely.'

She began to shake her head, and Enzo stilled her gently. 'Please, El. I need you to get better.'

Something about the desperation in his voice made her relax, and she parted her lips. A bottle was pressed to them, and she slowly drank.

After a few gulps, she gagged, but Enzo kept the bottle firm. 'All of it, princess. You can do it.' She sputtered, but continued to drink. The blood was rich, decadent and sweet – too sweet – and she gagged briefly. But Enzo didn't let up until she swallowed the last mouthful, as pain lanced through her.

She cried out, bending over in the water as she felt the blood working inside her, felt it fighting against the venom lodged within her body.

The pain was all-encompassing, and she couldn't stand it, couldn't grit her teeth through it any more. As she writhed, she felt Enzo step into the bath, his bare skin touching her back as he held her. She convulsed as he stroked her, and she pleaded to the darkness, asking it to stop her feeling. It took her hand and whisked her away from the agony so that she was merely observing.

Finally, the darkness nudged her back towards the world. The pain was beginning to subside. And Enzo was there. And Enzo was home. And she was safe.

She felt warm light sweeping through her, cocooning her and keeping her warm as he hummed a string of soothing notes. She recognized the tune faintly but couldn't grasp it. His light felt beautiful and warm, like him.

She was back in her body now, Enzo's voice murmuring to her. She caught words. 'So brave . . . you're doing so well, princess.'

She was panting heavily, her eyelids fluttering as the last shocks of pain left her. She heard the water swirl noisily down a drain, leaving her cold. But then the tap ran again, and her mind eased as warm water filled the small pool back up again. She felt Enzo's body move behind her, and his hands started to wash her, the scent of eucalyptus soap around them.

'Now this hair,' he said, and she could hear the smile in his voice.

Whatever it was about that smile became her undoing, and the darkness gave her another nudge. *Safe to see*, it whispered. And so, as water ran down her hair, wiping away the horrors, the poison and the dirt, she took another breath and opened her eyes, turning around.

Enzo stilled.

She searched his face, seeing every feature she'd held on to when Gem had torn her mind apart. Hoop. Freckle. Frown. Finally, she looked into his eyes, the flecked gold warmth that she'd locked eyes with first in the throne room, what seemed like a lifetime ago. He was kneeling in front of her in the small pool, shirtless. He brought his wet hand to her face, behind her ear, stroked his thumb over her temple.

'I've missed those eyes,' he murmured. She closed them again as tears ran freely.

'El,' he said. 'Please don't cry. You're safe. I promise.'

She opened them again, and he was still there. His hands in her wet hair, stroking and soothing.

'You're real?' she whispered, the tears still streaming.

'I'm real,' he whispered back and took her face in his other hand.

He leaned forwards and kissed one of her tears. She cried more at that, and he bent to kiss the other tear gently off her cheek. And the next. There was just the sound of his soft kisses soaking her pain and the drip of water. He moved her away once her sobs had quieted, running oils through her hair, humming that same gentle melody.

'I loved him more than the Dark loves the night,' he sang, 'and he loved me more than the day loves the Light—'

'Lions may fly, and lovers will die, but my love – that will live on,' she sang along quietly, her voice cracking as she finished the verse.

His hands stilled in her hair. 'How do you know that song?'

She frowned. 'It's an Asterian lullaby.'

A look passed over his face. 'Strange,' he said quietly. 'I thought I'd dreamed it a long time ago.'

She wasn't sure what to say, so she said nothing at all.

He reached for some oils as she drank in his details. His forearms, the way they looked when the muscles and veins were taut. The slant of his strong brows. The impatient flick he gave when his curls fell over his eyes. She studied him silently, pliable in his hands, tipping her head back as he ran oil through the ends, as he lifted her arms to rinse off the suds, as he scrubbed the awful memories off her.

Then he lifted himself out, trousers sodden as he grabbed a warm fluffy towel and bundled her in it, picking her up and carrying her back to the bedroom. She felt herself land on pillows, a soft cotton nightgown shrugged over her, before sheets smelling like vanilla were pulled into place. Enzo disappeared into the bathroom for a moment, returning in dry loose trousers, his chest bare. He walked towards the door, and she saw a glimpse of Leo standing guard as Enzo murmured something to him, before he closed the door and settled into a chair beside her.

Elara reached out blindly for his hand, emotions chattering at the outskirts of her mind. She focused on his thumb stroking the back of her hand, and it seemed to quiet them for a moment.

A soft click, and a healer entered. She recognized the cool, stern voice she'd liked and looked up. A woman stood before her, hair hanging in straight copper sheets down her sides. Her eyes were clear blue, her face open.

'It's good to see you're more aware of yourself, Your Majesty.' The healer nodded and sank down on to the bed. She pressed tentative hands to Elara's neck. 'This wound's looking much better. Looks like His Highness did a good job.'

Elara looked again at Enzo and saw his face completely blank. She squinted and saw the tick of his jaw. His eyes were ablaze as he stared at her wound.

'I'll make them both beg for death.' The words were ice. Then reining himself in, he plastered a smile on for Elara and squeezed her hand.

Cool magick washed over her like a salve, as the healer scanned her body. 'The venom has gone,' she said, then opened her eyes. 'And the wound at her neck will heal.' She looked at Enzo. 'It's her mind that we need to worry about.'

'You need not talk as if I am not here,' Elara muttered.

Enzo hid a smile. 'I think perhaps we need not worry as much as we thought.'

The healer gave a small smile as she opened a bag, pulling out two jars of liquid. As she tinkered with them, Elara saw that the contents of one were pale blue, the other darker in the falling Light streaming through the balcony doors. 'This will help you sleep.' Having finished mixing the vials, she gently prised Elara's jaw open. Elara flinched at the direct contact, and she saw Enzo shift closer.

But the healer had already dispensed two drops of the potion on to her tongue, before packing up her kit. 'Plenty of rest, plenty of food and fluids. I entrust her into your care.' She looked sharply to Enzo.

'I will be the finest nursemaid she's ever had.' He gave a tight smile, stretching in his chair. Elara's lips twitched as the healer nodded and the door clicked softly closed behind her.

'I'm scared to fall asleep.' Her voice was barely a whisper. Enzo frowned, leaning down next to her. 'I can feel the pain at bay. My thoughts crowding against the darkness. I'm worried I'll dream.'

His face softened. 'I can't keep what you've endured at bay, but I promise you I will be here for you when you wake. I'm not leaving you.'

Elara grasped his hand once more and held on to it tightly – her anchor in tempestuous seas as she fell beneath the waves.

CHAPTER FORTY-TWO

Days passed, and Elara floated in and out of consciousness. Mostly her mind was devoid of anything, but just before waking, a memory would resurface and slice her mental wounds open again, leaving her screaming. Each time she would feel warm hands encompass her, along with the sound of soft murmurs, a healer's sweet voice, then more treacly elixir.

The days became weeks – how many, she could not tell – and when she was lucid, she barely felt anything. Instead, shadows embraced her as she was fed soup and had water brought to her parched lips. There was a gentle caress, then darkness again.

One night, she woke as always in distress, drenched in sweat, eyes darting wildly around the room. Her gaze flew to Enzo who had awoken, his white shirt loose, his hair mussed from leaning on his hand in the chair next to her bed. As the healer entered the room, Enzo reached for Elara the way he had every night prior on the healer's arrival. But there was something different in his eyes, she noticed. After a moment, he left Elara and stalked towards the healer, a hushed but heated conversation ensuing. She heard the urgent words of the healer, drifting to her through the web of fear and nightmares.

'Has to . . . keep her subdued.'

Enzo's voice was a snarl. 'Enough . . . drugging her . . .'

'I serve the king.'

A tense silence.

'Then at least give it to me.'

Elara felt gentle hands take her mouth, stroking her lip.

'Open, Elara.'

She did, feeling only one drop on her tongue, rather than two, as the door clicked shut.

Enzo then eased her out of bed and led her up and across the room as he opened the large doors to the balcony. Out in the cool night air, he settled on the divan with her, wrapping them both in a blanket as he sat, Elara curled on his lap.

'You need fresh air,' he said tightly.

The rest of his words drifted away from her and she looked at him silently, the fog still over her. Everything sounded and felt so far, so distant. The medicine was swimming through her system, pleasant and warm as she tried to focus on what he was saying. Giving up, she rested against his chest, listening to the steady thrum of his heartbeat. She heard a knock at the balcony door and jumped. A head peeked around the door, sleepy-eyed and worried.

'Is she okay?' Merissa whispered, stepping out on to the balcony. If she noticed the intimacy she had walked in on, she didn't comment.

'Just a nightmare,' Enzo mumbled to her. 'Could you fix us some chamomile tea, Merissa?'

She nodded. 'Of course.'

Elara ignored her, her mind desperately trying to push the box shut on the horrors that wanted to claw and shriek their way out. Some nights she swore she heard it rattling, but there was always enough potion to silence it.

She blinked, shifting so that she was looking up at Enzo. He stroked her hair, lulling her. 'You need to wake,' he said. 'To feel. Not be trapped in this,' he gestured around her, 'fog.'

'Nightmares,' she said quietly, the first words she'd spoken properly in skies knew how long. 'There's just darkness, and then I always wake to the nightmares.'

'Do you want to talk about it?'

She shook her head, frowning, the thoughts soon dissipating, like storm clouds on a breeze. She couldn't quite hold on to the memories.

'Naming them helps,' he said, clearing his throat. 'When I have nightmares, I go outside and speak them aloud.' He laughed quietly. 'I sound like a madman, I know. But I always feel as though there is someone out there listening to me. It's like praying, but to something other than the Stars. The first time I did it, I dreamed that an angel had visited me. Though different to how *The Mythas of Celestia* depicts them. I don't remember what it said, but when I awoke, for the first time in my life, I felt safe. Strong.'

'I forgot you had nightmares too,' she said quietly.

He gave her a wry smile. 'Yes, you witnessed one of the less pleasant ones.' He paused. 'You know, my father wasn't so cruel until my mother died. Or perhaps she was just such a powerful light that it obscured his darkness.'

'I'm sorry,' she whispered. 'That my parents—' She gulped. 'I'm so sorry, Enzo.'

He squeezed her. 'It is not your apology to make.'

There was a long comfortable silence as Enzo stroked her hair. She ran her hand up and down his back as he held her, feeling the smoothness of it. Something dawned upon her, and she stilled. 'Why don't you have any scars?' she whispered.

Enzo was quiet for a long time before he spoke.

'My father had a Verdan on hand, a healer. When my back was split so badly by his light that it was just a mess of blood and flesh, the healer would patch and smooth over every part of my skin, just so Idris could inflict the same pain again. So that no one would know. The moment I became strong enough, I sought the healer out.'

He took a controlled breath, and she noticed that he was shaking.

'There was nothing left of the healer once I'd finished with him.' He let out his breath in a long stream. 'Since the moment I was able to fight back, my father hasn't dared to try and strike me with his light. But it still haunts me. I still dream about it.'

She squeezed his hand. As she looked at him, she understood. He did not want her pity. He simply wanted someone to listen.

She brushed a thumb over his hand. 'One day, he will feel every inch of pain he inflicted on you.'

'I know. I'll be the one to do it.'

If Elara was her usual self, she might have raised an eyebrow at the open treason. Instead, she settled back down against Enzo, his shoulders untensing as his body moulded to hers.

'So now you know what calms me after the nightmares. What calms you?'

Elara ran her hair through her fingers, chewing her cheek. 'Fresh air.' She gave a small smile, and gestured to the pile of books on the low table. 'Reading.' *You*, she wanted to say, the word on the tip of her tongue. She swallowed it whole.

'Reading,' he said, picking up *The Mythas of Celestia*.

'That's my favourite book.'

He raised a brow. 'Mine too.'

Her lips twitched. 'We're more alike than you think.'

With a sigh she nuzzled into his neck. It smelled so comforting, bergamot soap cut with his heady amber scent. He stilled. Finally, his arm resumed stroking circles across her back carefully, as though scared that if he moved, he would break the spell. Merissa came back in quietly, placing a pot of tea on the small table. With another wavering look between them, she gave a small smile and left again.

After a while, Elara voiced the question that had plagued her. 'That night I was taken . . . how did you escape?'

Enzo squeezed his arms tighter around her. 'I have fate to thank for that. The room was empty when I awoke, the doors locked, but I burned through the boards of the sealed windows and jumped into the moat. I wasn't running away, El,' he said quietly. 'I knew I'd have been no use to you dead or captured. I just . . . I need you to know that I didn't stop trying to get you back, not for one waking moment.'

'I know,' she murmured.

Elara's eyes closed as Enzo cleared his throat.

'Now, how about this story? "The Night Wraiths of Asteria",' he read. '"Once, long ago, in the lands now known as Asteria, the Dark was born. It was that from which everything came, and everything returned to. One such creature born of it was the Night Wraith. Merely a wisp of shadow darkening your own, or the pattern on a child's bedroom wall . . ."' He trailed off as he looked at Elara smiling against his chest. 'You like wraiths?'

'Wraiths are friendly,' she said quietly. 'We would leave food and treats out for them every Hallow's Eve. My favourite time of year. They protect the home.'

'Hmm.' He nodded. 'Tell me more.'

She chewed her cheek. '"The Nevercrow of Castor" was another favourite of mine. I loved his riddles.'

Enzo made an amused sound. 'Me too.'

'And "The Nightwolf and the Silver". That tale always made me cry.'

'When I was little, I'd always cry at "The Winged Lion's Heart".'

'But the lion fell in love at the end,' Elara said.

'He did. But it was with the Light, which he could never reach.'

Elara nodded. '"The Serpents of the Still Sea" – I always wanted to ride them. That bit in the story where they took the little girl underwater to the mermaid kingdom . . .' She trailed off.

'Have you ever swum in the Still Sea?'

'Once.' She gave a wan smile. 'With . . .' Her vision began to swim. 'With my best friend.' She frowned in confusion. She couldn't place the name; it was at the edge of her grasp.

'Sofia?' Enzo asked, gently.

Red flashed across her vision; a blade, a throat being cut, a gaping wound, a velvet-clad stage. She winced as though she had been struck.

'I'm sorry, I'm sorry . . .' The whisper of his voice was distant, but she grabbed hold of it, taking in deep lungfuls of air. When she came back to herself, Enzo was gripping her tightly, worry in his eyes.

'No, I need to.' She gritted her teeth against the pain in her mind. 'I need to feel. Need to remember. You're right. I can't keep swimming in this.'

He held her tightly as he opened the book. 'Then let's read. And tomorrow I promise to help you out of it.'

She nodded once, and Enzo pulled her back against him.

'Thank you,' she murmured to him, the medicine lulling her under.

'For what?' he asked quietly.

'For giving me a piece of you.'

She was already between worlds and fading back into darkness when he replied softly, 'You have more of me than I care to admit.'

CHAPTER FORTY-THREE

When Elara awoke again, she didn't scream. She tested the boundaries of her mind. The darkness was in place, the memories at bay, but there was something else.

Light.

She glanced up at Enzo, still asleep, his muscled arms wrapped around her. She saw the book laid on the table. Under the quiet morning Light, she studied him, closer than she'd ever dared when he was awake. Her heart pounded as she slowly released one emotion to observe him. Guilt.

There were shadows under his eyes, and she felt that foreign pang again as she allowed herself to experience the feeling. He must have stayed by her bed every night in that chair, waking when she had. She gazed at the charcoal dusting of his lashes, the softness of his forehead as he slept. With the lightest touch, she traced the freckle under his eye to another below it, running her finger to one by his other eye. Mapping out her own constellation. She let her finger run under his jaw then, tracing the smooth cut of it. It stopped then, hovering over his full lips. She saw his eye open and twitch in surprise.

'Good morning,' he mumbled, his eyes on hers.

'Morning,' she replied, swiftly removing her trailing finger.

'You didn't dream?'

'Not at all.'

His face relaxed as he lifted her.

'I can walk, you know.' She batted his arm, and he lowered her gently to the floor.

'How are you feeling?'

'Lucid.'

He squeezed her hand as they walked back into her room. The small action almost wiped the energy from her, leaving her legs trembling, and she sank on to the bed, breathing hard.

'There's something happening with my mind. Every time I grasp for something, it leaves me.'

'Why don't you rest—'

'No, Enzo,' she pleaded. 'I don't want to rest any longer. I'm tired of being weak, and drugged. Of barely feeling anything.'

Enzo nodded. 'Right, then,' he said, and strode to Elara's wardrobe, picking out the kind of two-piece she was used to training in. 'We're going to the gardens.'

He helped Elara shrug out of her gown and into the clothes, keeping his eyes on hers.

'Don't give me any more of that potion,' she said, as black spots began to dance in her vision.

He nodded, taking her arm.

'Wait – what about my glamour?'

'Merissa has been visiting each night. She's been making sure it's intact for any servant or other who may come in.'

Elara fought to quell the lump in her throat at the mention of her friend's name.

He took her arm and led her outside, his brisk demeanour

the first hint of warrior he'd shown since before the masquerade.

She followed him, her breath coming in gasps. Navigating through the palace, she let him lead her past an atrium trickling with water. Birds chirped outside. Elara hadn't heard the sound in weeks, between imprisonment and unconsciousness. Enzo continued to guide her until they passed Kalinda's garden patch. A golden-headed figure was bent in the flowerbeds with a trowel, and Elara's breath quickened as Merissa turned around.

'Elara?' she said hopefully, sticking the trowel in the mud and pulling off her gardening gloves.

The black spots that had been dancing in Elara's vision grew worse, as her heart pounded.

'No,' she said hoarsely, taking a step back. Enzo looked at her in alarm, Merissa's brow creased with worry.

'El?'

'I can't do this,' Elara whispered as images of Sofia's blank, grey stare danced around and around her mind.

She broke away from Enzo, and began to stumble down the path.

'Elara!' he shouted after her.

She couldn't do it – couldn't be around Merissa, couldn't call another a friend when her closest had been brutally murdered. The gardens swam before her as she staggered on, the path twisting, trees beginning to crop up. They all passed in a blur, the sound of rushing water growing nearer. Colour and sound flitted by her until sure footsteps caught up with her.

'El—'

'Give me more medicine,' she demanded. 'I don't want to feel this, I've changed my mind. Let me forget it all, please let me forget it.'

Enzo's worry smoothed away as he led her down the stone steps before them. 'No.'

She halted, realizing that they were in the sunken garden where the revel to celebrate the Descent of Leyon had taken place. It was empty of people now.

'No?' Perhaps she'd misheard him over the roar of the waterfall.

Enzo tilted his head. 'That's what I said.'

She looked to the skies as she tried to process what she had just heard. The sky looked bruised and oppressive, deep burgundy with heavy orange clouds, a tang of metal in the air.

'Storm's coming,' he remarked.

'Why won't you give me my potion, Enzo?' A strange emotion was swirling within her, one she hadn't felt in a while.

'Because I can't see you like this any more. I've tried to be patient and slow, but I can't stand it. This drugged shade of who you are . . . Running from your pain. It's not you.'

She frowned, confusion stirring in her. He paced agitatedly.

'I have had to sit and watch you each night for weeks. Watch you scream and cry from the nightmares that plague you, then have medicine forced down your throat as you're held down.'

She gazed at him coolly. Words were forming on her lips before she could process them. 'I'm sorry that my pain bothers you.'

His jaw clenched as he stopped, his gaze flying to her. 'That's not what I meant,' he said, his voice low.

Another emotion flickered in her. It went out before she had time to understand it.

'The Elara I know is a fighter. A queen.' Elara blinked. 'She would face her pain. *She* is not a coward.'

Thunder clapped above them, a booming sound that shook the skies, the clouds roiling.

'What did you just call me?' Elara asked quietly. There was a weight building in her. She could feel the darkness that had been protecting her was now writhing and hungry.

There was another clap of thunder, and the heavens opened. Rain poured, fat drops of it pounding down, warm in the humid Helion air. The rain began to soak him, his arms crossed in that ever-arrogant stance, drenching his loose white shirt. It triggered an irritation in her, and a stronger emotion was hiding somewhere deeper. Her palms itched.

'*Coward.*'

Black wreathed out of her, her shadows itching and leaping to be released after weeks trapped within her nerves. They twisted and formed from her palms as she held them out, eyes flashing. Monstrous shapes streamed, not animals, but something *other*.

The rain beat down, soaking her to her skin, but all she could feel was the furious darkness within her. The twisting shapes lunged at Enzo. He gave a vacant laugh, light blasting from his hands and turning her shadows to ash as he sprang up.

'Now that's more like it.' He whistled. Lightning forked the sky up above. She stiffened, flexing her fingers, wet hair sticking to her skin in sheets.

'Have I gotten under your skin, princess?'

She bared her teeth, twisting her hands. The landscape changed, the rain still pouring, but her illusioning had brought them both to a place devoid of stars, of light. Instead, this was a place so black and so overwhelming that it weighed on them.

'Nice spot,' he said in a dry voice, casting his gaze around before he sent a wave of fire to her. She threw up a shield of shadow which ate the fire whole. He sent another and another, and she wiped them out one by one, her magick craving them. Craving more.

The illusion finally shattered with a burst of his light, and she found herself panting on the lawn, water running down her.

'Is that all you've got?' he called over, and she roared, rage flying over her as she launched herself at him, and they tumbled to the sodden grass. She had no blade, nothing but her hands, which bunched his shirt between her fists.

'What about that silver magick you summoned at the bottom of the lake?' he gasped, breathing heavily. 'You have any of that to throw at me?'

Elara stilled as scrambled memories surfaced of Enzo drowning while skeletal tails and dark waters surrounded him.

'No,' she snapped. 'I don't know what that was.'

He pushed himself forwards. 'Then what other weapons do you have at your disposal?' He tilted his head. 'Tell me, princess, do you still carry that dagger on your pretty little thigh?'

His burning hot hand skimmed up her leg, her sodden skirt riding up. His fingers brushed her outer thigh.

'Ariete took it,' she replied raggedly.

She stopped breathing as her focus narrowed on his rough thumb resting lightly on her naked thigh. She could see the raindrops forming on his lashes, dripping off his lips. Enzo tilted their balance so she had to lean back on her elbows as he prowled further forward between her legs.

'What do you feel, Elara?' His voice was low and soft. Her chest heaved.

'Anger,' she hissed. 'So much anger.'

'Is that all?' A slow grin spread across his face as he tilted his head, studying her. His hand didn't leave her thigh, his mouth now sharing her breath.

'Hatred.'

'Mmm,' he rumbled. He leaned into her neck, his smell filling her senses. There was a tickle of breath, and then his nose ran up the sensitive column of her neck. She drew in a ragged breath. Desire, another foreign emotion, swirled through her. He breathed out a laugh, and in the same instant flicked his tongue on the sensitive spot behind her ear. She exhaled an unsteady breath, eyes closing.

'Are you sure that's all you feel?'

Her eyes flew open. 'Yes,' she snarled.

His half-smile remained on his face as the soft rasp of drawn steel filled the space between them. Her dagger appeared before them, and he held it up to her as he whispered on to her lips, 'Then why don't you show me how much you loathe me?'

Her eyes widened as she saw the weapon. 'How do you have that?'

'I took it from Ariete at the Opera House.'

'And you waited until now to give it to me?' Elara was shaking with rage, with exhaustion, with desire, with relief. All emotions so foreign to her after numbly wading through nothingness for so long.

She grabbed the dagger, though her eyes remained on him – his wet curls, his soaked, near-translucent shirt clinging to his muscles. Her emotions poured molten hot, and she had half a mind to fling the blade back down at him.

But instead she pushed off him, casting one last look filled with loathing. But behind it, there was want, and they both knew it.

Then she stalked back to her rooms without a word.

CHAPTER FORTY-FOUR

Elara left her dress pooling by her bedroom's entrance as she stalked into her bathing chamber. Anger steamed off her as she ran the bath, though the cold of the rain still lingered upon her skin. How *dare* Enzo call her a coward after everything she had been through?

She slammed the dagger on the countertop, its hilt clattering on the marble. Elara gritted her teeth to stop them from chattering as the water slowed. Finally sinking herself into the bath, the first she'd had by herself in Stars knew how long, she let her anger roil over her.

Suddenly, a clear thought broke through, and she sat up.

Anger. She was feeling anger. And in doing so, she hadn't thought about her pain or Sofia. She winced at the name, but as something inside her pounced and tried to shut the memory down, she flung it away with a snarl.

Enzo had forced her to feel. Outrage, hatred, desire, relief. She shivered at the memory of his tongue trailing up her neck. He had baited her on purpose.

She gave a small smile to herself as she bathed.

Wrapping a towel around herself, she stepped out of the water.

With her magick siphoned off, her mind was clearer than it had been in a long time.

When she returned to her room, she cursed. 'Enzo!'

He was sprawled on the chair by her bed, as he took her in from head to toe.

'Nursemaid, remember?' He grinned, stretching his arms behind his head. She cast him a withering look before snatching a nightgown from her chair and making her way back into the bath chamber to dress. When she reappeared, she was somewhat more decent, an emerald lace nightgown grazing her thighs. His gaze flicked to her, then away, but she didn't miss the way it darkened, igniting once more the lust she'd felt in the garden. She ignored it as she sat in front of the mirror and started to comb her wet locks.

'Do you need me to get Merissa?'

Her hands shook imperceptibly as she combed. She wasn't ready to see her yet – her or Isra. 'No, thank you.'

He stood and walked over to where she sat. 'Then I'll dry your hair, or you'll catch a cold.'

The air around her grew hot as Enzo raised his hands, before skimming them through her hair, suffusing heat through it.

Her brow rose. 'Do your subjects know you're such a good handmaid?'

His eyes crinkled as he continued to comb her hair. 'There's that vicious tongue.'

She tried to stop a smile.

But as she realized that she was feeling a sliver of happiness, Elara's lip quivered, a clagging tightness rising at the back of her throat. She tried to swallow it. Once. Twice. Her eyes began to ache as the tightness wouldn't go, even as she willed it away.

Her lip trembled again as Enzo looked over her with worry. Then the floodgates opened.

Elara let out one gulping sob, and another, before she gave in and wept. She covered her face with her hands as Enzo got to his knees, taking one of her hands. Her shoulders shook as she tried to drag in a breath, tears flooding her. She buried her face in Enzo's neck.

'It's okay, it's okay,' he murmured.

'I feel so much guilt,' she sobbed, 'for even smiling. Sofia is dead, and I'm here. It's my fault.'

'Listen to me.' Enzo pulled her away so he could look at her. 'It is *not* your fault. Do you really believe that Sofia would think that?'

Elara wiped a tear, looking to the ceiling. 'Ariete did it to punish *me*. It is my fault.'

'You know, in Helion culture, we believe that death is not an ending. It is the beginning of something. When you lose a loved one, you don't ever lose them really. They stay living on with you, their memories and their warmth. That energy passes through as each person keeps them alive by remembering them. Sofia is not gone. It's just the beginning of a different relationship with her.'

Elara's face crumpled as she squeezed Enzo's hands.

'What would she tell you right now if she was here?'

Elara laughed then through her tears. 'She would tell me . . . to get a hold of myself and stop the pity party. She'd tell me to *live*. Sofia savoured every moment of her life. She taught me to be brave, to defy the rules. She was fearless and colourful, and she wanted me to experience every wonder that life had to offer.'

Enzo pushed her drying hair from her face. 'Then *live*, Elara. For her.'

CHAPTER FORTY-FIVE

King Idris paced the throne room as Elara watched him, her hands clasped behind her back. Enzo stood beside her, his own back perfectly straight. Elara had just finished recounting the last weeks to him, the king grilling her on every minute detail.

'You directly disobeyed my orders,' Idris seethed at her. 'And you,' he turned to his son, 'nearly cost me my weapon.'

'I have a name,' Elara said coolly.

Idris dismissed her with a glance. 'Time wasted. Time that should have been spent preparing to kill Ariete, not being his *prisoner*.'

Enzo shifted beside her.

'As opposed to being yours?' she asked.

'You're a foolish girl. A spoilt one at that. Have I not given you everything? A safe haven. A palace bedroom. All the food and freedom you want?'

'A gilded cage is still a cage,' she replied.

Idris gave her a withering look, turning to Enzo. 'I have already seen to your punishment, as you well know. The only reason that *she* avoids it, is because I need her as strong as possible for our plan.'

A quiet anger began to settle in Elara's bones as she realized what Idris meant. He had already hurt Enzo. Enzo rolled his shoulders, and she thought of the perfectly smooth skin beneath his shirt.

'Punish him again,' she said, making sure threat laced every syllable, 'and I will never conjure so much as a wisp of shadow for you.'

Idris turned slowly, regarding her closely. 'What's this? The shadow princess has a heart?'

'Of course not,' Enzo snapped. 'She's just weak, and emotional. Forgive us, Father. This week will be dedicated to getting her training back in shape. We're close with her shadows. In a few weeks, she'll be ready.'

This assuaged Idris, who nodded tightly, lounging back in his throne.

'You had better be, Elara,' he said. 'You're lucky that your little trick at the theatre has helped our cause temporarily. So long as Ariete believes you are dead, we can catch him by surprise.'

Elara nodded stiffly. 'You'll be glad to know that our values finally align. I will kill Ariete if it's the last thing I do,' she replied.

The streets of Sol were quieter than Elara remembered. She followed Enzo through an unfamiliar quarter, where the alleys were wider, the squares clean and studded with carved fountains.

As they passed through the Light-washed buildings, she saw the hazy spires of Leyon's temple.

'Do you ever go in there?' she murmured, nodding her head to the extravagant columns that disappeared into the distance.

Enzo snorted. 'You know by now that I'm not the religious type, certainly not for that slick-haired, pompous fool.'

She considered that for a moment. 'No, but you're the prince. Surely you must do your duties and make a show of worshipping your great god? We had to hold a private ceremony in Piscea's temple every Hallow's Eve. It was one of the only times I was allowed out of the palace.'

'On the largest holidays, I drag myself there for the ceremony, yes. The upcoming summer solstice will be the next time I set foot in that "place of worship".'

They stopped in a small, empty square. Washing lines were strung up between the alleys that veered off the square, the smell of clean linen floating on the gentle breeze. The heat was dry and pleasant, and as she walked further on, a delicious scent of cooking drifted by.

'I wanted to show you something special to me.' Enzo leaned into her. 'I come here when things become too much for me. I'm hoping it will maybe help you too.'

He led her to the wooden door of the nearest marble building, and they stepped inside. Cool shadows greeted her and seemed to run up her arms in welcome. A small roofless atrium held a turquoise pool in its centre, with soft lightshine dappling the shade.

'Now be gentle,' he said as a warning. 'I've never brought anyone in here before.'

Something glowed within her, and she tucked it away. A feeling to treasure after so long wading through nothingness.

He took her hand and pulled her through the shade of the entrance, their footsteps clacking on stone underneath, echoing. He veered to a door on the right, and with a flash of his light, he unlocked it. Grinning, he turned to her as he opened it.

Light bathed the room. Drowned it. The space was so open that she felt weightless. White stuccoed walls graced the chamber, while a small enclosed garden was displayed beyond the great floor-to-ceiling windows. But it was what filled the room that had her enraptured.

Sculptures and statues of all sizes lined the walls, some works-in-progress, others finished and polished. Miniatures of mythical beasts lay on a workbench in the centre of the room, while life-size statues were dotted around the workbench in various poses. She took a timid step towards the one closest to her – a woman cradled by her lover, their lips almost touching. She traced a finger over the form.

'Do you like it?' Enzo asked behind her, still in the doorway. She whirled to him.

'Enzo, you created all of this?' She spun around in a full circle, admiring the art.

He gave a sideways smile as he walked into the room, shutting the door. He came beside her, close enough for her to smell the amber on him.

'I did. This is what I do to heal.' He reached for the workbench and pulled a lump of stone closer across it.

'Show me,' she breathed. He gave her a small smile. Readying his hands, he concentrated as brilliant white beams began to shine from them. He expanded the beams until a pure, almost crystalline ray was projecting from his hands. He then manoeuvred it so it started to cut away at the lump of stone. Elara watched smooth curves form before her very eyes, the rough lines carved and polished away. And watching him pour his love into his art, she felt her own jagged edges begin to soften.

The weeks that followed were some of the most peaceful of Elara's life. Enzo lied consistently to Idris, promising that he had her under a gruelling training regimen, when in fact, each day, he brought her to his studio as he worked. Elara would bring piles of books with her and lounge on a chaise longue as he worked, the steady and rhythmic tapping of his light against the stone a soft music to her as she read.

During breaks, they would sit, basking in their little world as they sipped fresh mint tea. They talked about art and music and their lives as he worked. It became increasingly easier for Elara to talk of Sofia, to keep her spirit alive. She would recount stories of their adventures as children, their dramas as teenagers and the trouble they had both landed in countless times, Enzo peppering her with questions.

Some days Enzo worked on a project that he would not let her see, a towering block of pure white stone that glimmered whenever the day's rays hit it. He kept it hidden behind a screen and she was only met with a small smile whenever she asked about it. Some days he asked her to be his muse, to sit draped on a couch as he looked to her and carved a delicate hand, or the wisps of hair covering a face.

Elara's skin was beginning to glow again, the days walking through Sol tanning her face and the quiet peace she found in company with the prince helping her shine from the inside. Her frame began to fill out too thanks to the pastries Enzo force-fed her from Bruno's, the little bakery next to his studio. The larger-than-life proprietor had taken one look at her when she'd walked in on the first day and given her a dozen pastries to take away. She became familiar with the other artists in the building too, the other establishments in the square, learning their names and trades with a smile as she found the confidence to walk amongst them, borrowing tools and running errands for Enzo.

From time to time, she would see Leo around the palace, always offering a smile as he hurried to the army barracks or training grounds, working overtime so Enzo could spend his time with her.

And Merissa . . . Elara had not dared seek her out. There was still a nonsensical guilt attached to the glamourer in her mind, as though it was an insult to Sofia's memory.

But Elara had finally summoned the courage to visit Isra.

She'd still been afraid up until the moment Isra had opened her door, but the seer's eyes had lit up the second she saw her, followed by an unrestrained hug. Isra had then bustled her inside, offering her tea and slamming the door promptly in Enzo's face.

Since then, a few afternoons a week, Elara had kept an appointment with Isra to practise her dreamwalking. The seer was well-versed in realms outside of the living, and Elara found the escape another place for her to heal.

It was on one of her afternoons with Enzo, as they lay sprawled on the lawn of the small terraced garden, eating lunch, that Elara snapped her book shut with a sigh of frustration.

'What's wrong?' Enzo asked, breaking off a piece of bread.

'I'm annoyed,' she replied, hurling the book across the lawn.

'And what did that book ever do to you?'

'The heroine of the story just lost all of her magick. Why do they always *do* that? She was so strong and powerful, and then at the end, she just gave it all up!'

Enzo chuckled, taking a grape from the platter between them. 'So you'd never give up your powers?'

'*Never*,' she swore vehemently, curling a small shadow around her little finger. 'In fact, all I want to do is learn more and more about them.' She bit her lip, a question she'd longed to ask for a while on the tip of her tongue. 'Do you think you could teach me?'

Enzo looked up at her from his food, his mouth full. 'Teach you what?'

'To sculpt. I know I don't possess the Light, but I've been thinking about my powers, my shadows . . . I wonder if it would work?'

He got to his feet, excitement radiating from him as he pulled her up with him. 'Let's try.'

They hurried back into the room, and he pulled forth a small chunk of pure white stone, clearing the workbench in front of them. He eyed it, checking something, then came around behind her. His scent wrapped around her, and her senses focused on his closeness, how his breath was warm on the nape of her neck, smelling of mint and honey.

He cleared his throat as he lifted his arms around her, raising her own so they were held out in front of her. The callouses of his palms lay against the soft backs of her hands.

'Relax,' he whispered by her ear, chuckling, and she did as he commanded. 'Now,' he said, 'I'm going to guide the Light and show you how to carve. Then you can try the same with the Dark.'

She nodded, smiling up at him. She felt his arms tighten and turned back as he began to create the power between his hands again. He barely breathed as he concentrated on infusing it through Elara's own palms without harming her until bright white enveloped both. He took her hands with his as he widened them and elongated the solid shape forming.

Then, ever so gently, he moved their hands in a dance as a curve started to take shape on the stone.

Elara gasped in awe. 'I can feel your light through me.' Euphoria seemed to take over, thrums of pleasure beginning to stir as his warmth infused her. 'Is this how you feel all the time?' she asked, her voice filled with wonder.

He huffed out a laugh as he focused on their hands again. 'No. I used to only feel this when I created art.'

'You're happy,' she whispered.

He squeezed her fingertips.

'Now,' he said. 'Why don't you try and infuse some of your shadows into this – feed them in?'

Elara nodded, setting her face in determination. She stilled her mind, calling to her shadows, her breath quickening as she felt her power rise.

'Relax,' Enzo murmured again as her body became strained. She melted into him, and exhaled as shadows began to stream from her palms. They danced along Enzo's light, caressing it in spiralling tendrils. She thought she heard him moan gently behind her, but it was such a soft sound that she wondered if she had imagined it.

Dizzy ecstasy drummed through her as his powers danced with hers, the meeting of his radiance with her shadow like a delicious finger running down her spine. Her eyes fluttered shut and her head dropped back against his chest as he moaned quietly again – she was sure, this time. She could feel her entire being throbbing with power, his light a warmth that she never wanted to leave. The sounds drowned out around them, and all she could hear was the steady thrum of his heartbeat and his ragged breath. Sighs were escaping her too as she chased the high, feeling Enzo's grip tighten as his power flared. A gasp left her. She pressed into him, and with a last burst of exertion, she directed her shadows in the same way Enzo had, allowing him to help guide the smooth curves again through their shaking, entwined hands.

Her shadows bled into his light, drowning the stone in it. She shuddered again; the pleasure so intense, it was painful. It felt like she was standing in the midst of him, her soul bare to him and his to her. She could feel a release brewing between her thighs, and the revelation was so striking that she staggered forwards, gasping. Enzo reached to stop her, breaking whatever hold he had on her. She looked up at him wildly, flustered and out of breath. His own wide eyes returned the look, his cheeks flushed.

She went to speak, to ask what in the Deadlands had just happened between them. But something caught her eye, left behind on the worktop as their combined energies waned. Elara let out a gasp at what lay before them. Seconds ticked by in silence. Finally, Enzo picked the object up with shaking hands, the carved slice sharp to the touch.

'When shadow and light combine, a Star will fall,' he whispered, mirroring Isra's words from a few months ago. 'A weapon to kill a god.'

CHAPTER FORTY-SIX

The glass was so black that Elara and Enzo could see themselves in its reflection. It was cold to the touch, a thrumming power emanating from it. Elara did not possess the sight, but she could feel the otherworldly energy that pulsed from it.

'It can't be,' Elara breathed, peering over his shoulder.

Enzo turned the shard that they had created, holding it up to the Light. 'We need to find Isra,' he muttered.

They hurried through the piazza, hope snapping at their heels as Enzo guided Elara through the maze of back alleys until they reached Isra's place. He looked around furtively before squaring up to the large eye on the door and uttering, 'Five of Cups.'

The new password worked, the door swinging open, and Enzo pulled Elara into the cool, incense-filled corridor. They burst into Isra's reading room, panting.

'Aren't you both meant to be royalty?' Isra asked sweetly,

splayed on her couch as she held a purple crystal sphere to the firelamp above her. 'Little Rico has better manners than you two. Hi, my love,' she added, blowing Elara a kiss. Elara smiled back at her.

Enzo pushed forwards. 'Iz,' he breathed, putting out a shaking hand. Isra looked disinterestedly to the black shard lying in his palm, then noticing it, she straightened.

'What is this?' she said sharply.

Elara came closer. 'We made it today, Isra. From just a chunk of stone.'

'We?' Her nostrils flared as she looked at Enzo, who clenched his jaw, avoiding her gaze. 'You melded powers? Have you told her what that means?'

'That's enough, Isra,' he snarled.

'No, he didn't. What does it mean?' Elara demanded. Isra's gaze bore into Enzo's, and Elara saw her frown faintly, before her expression cleared.

'Never mind,' the seer bit out. 'I'm overreacting.'

Elara's eyes narrowed as Isra plucked the glass from Enzo's palm and sucked in a breath. Magick began to creep through the room, Isra's frost crawling up the table as her eyes turned white. She muttered over it, before placing it down and blinking, her eyes returning to hazel.

'Is it what we thought?' Elara whispered.

'Duskglass,' Isra breathed.

'Dusk-what?' Enzo asked.

Isra blinked, wonder in her gaze. 'I had a vision of this blade, when I was just a little girl. A spell-breaker, but also something more. Something to stop a god's magick. I saw . . .' She shook her head. 'I saw you, Elara, plunge the blade into a Star's heart, and they died.'

'But . . . but you didn't know me then,' Elara said.

'Fate did.'

'What else did you see, Iz?' Enzo urged.

Isra's eyes lit up. 'The voices are whispering that it's perhaps time to lure Ariete to your own fighting ground. To Helios.'

Enzo raised a brow at Isra's words.

'My shadows are nowhere near ready,' said Elara.

'But you don't need them now you have this. You needed Enzo, and with his light you have what you seek.' The oracle thought a moment. 'I think it's high time we let the King of Stars know you're alive, don't you think?' She grinned. 'What better timing than the summer solstice in the court of Aphrodea?'

'Aphrodea?' Elara frowned. 'Why not just stay in Helios?'

'Because of all the kingdoms in Celestia, the greatest diversity flock to Aphrodea. If you want a rumour to spread, to reach Ariete where he licks his wounds from our dear prince's passions, Aphrodea would be the place to start.'

Enzo had flames dancing between his fingers as he reclined on a chair, shaking his head. 'I'd need to notify Father of any plans,' he said tightly. Elara's eyes darkened at the thought of Idris. 'Particularly if it involves letting a Star walk right into our home. Leyon would have to invite him.'

'Isra's right,' Elara said. 'So far, we have allowed fate to weave our paths. I have allowed Ariete to control everything that has happened to me. For once, *I* want to be in control. *I* want to be ready.'

'Plus,' Isra called from her couch as she idly shuffled her cards, 'it would be cruel to leave Elara here as you go alone into *Aphrodea* of all places on the summer solstice.'

'Isra,' Enzo warned.

'Why?' Elara demanded.

'You're clever, Your Majesty. Put it together. The most heightened magickal night of the year, in the kingdom of lust and earthly pleasure.'

315

'Why would you – why should that matter? Why would I care?' Elara blustered out. Enzo looked at her, his tongue in his cheek as he tried to hide a smile.

Isra chuckled. 'You two are about as subtle as Leyon's life-sized statue out there,' she said, pointing to the door.

'We're just friends,' Elara said lightly. 'He can do as he pleases.'

Enzo's eyes locked on hers, a spark of amusement in them.

'Yes, and I'm *not* about to draw the Empress card from this deck,' Isra retorted.

Isra shuffled the cards she'd been playing with and flipped the top card on the table. The Empress stared back. Isra threw her head back as she cackled drily. 'Oh, look who it is.'

Enzo rolled his eyes. 'Thank you, Iz.' He kissed the top of her head. 'Give me a few days to think things over and let my father know of the latest revelations.'

He and Elara left, traipsing through the dusty streets, a palpable silence between them.

'So . . .' Elara ventured, turning the slice of glass over in her pocket. 'What does *melding* powers mean?'

Enzo halted abruptly, turning slowly to her. 'I was hoping you forgot about that.'

Elara raised an eyebrow. 'We don't keep secrets, Enzo.'

He sighed, passing a hand over his face before looking away from her. He focused studiously on the white stuccoed wall of a house before them.

'To meld powers with someone is an . . . intimate act.'

'Oh,' Elara replied, her face warming.

'It's usually an act reserved for betrothed couples or lovers.' He cleared his throat, unable to meet her eyes.

'Well,' she said, clearing her throat as her cheeks flushed.

'It produced the duskglass for us, so I would hardly complain.'

Enzo's lip quirked then. 'Yes, I'd hardly say you were complaining at all.'

She hit his arm. 'About Aphrodea . . .'

'El, you really don't have to go. You've been through enough,' he said behind her.

Elara rolled her eyes. 'Who's going to believe a rumour without living proof? Any courtier with sense would see it as nothing more than baseless hearsay unless I'm there.'

Enzo looked amused as he caught up to her, veering them the opposite way to the studio.

'What are you smirking at?'

'Nothing.' He shrugged. 'This wouldn't have anything to do with what Isra said, would it?'

Elara stopped short, and Enzo bumped into her. 'And pray tell, what *is* it about what Isra said that would motivate me?'

Enzo's smile deepened as he pulled her to a food cart, motioning to the man behind it.

'Let's not make a fool of either of us by spelling it out, princess.'

He tossed a few coins to the seller, clutching the paper-bound goods in his hand.

'Where are we going?' Elara demanded as he steered her by the small of her back down a line of brightly coloured houses, the hill declining sharply.

'To cool off. It's sweltering today.'

Elara frowned, peering down the long hill.

'And anyway,' he added, 'don't change the subject.'

'I'm not,' she scowled, and became lost in her thoughts as they walked down the hill. It wasn't that she was in denial. She was simply *wary*. As much as things had changed between her and Enzo, as much as she cared for him . . . that ugly

317

prophecy rang through her head. She could not let herself fall in love. Not when she knew she was destined for a Star. But she couldn't deny the feelings that had been growing, nor the physical need that had started to consume her whenever she was in his presence.

They reached the bottom of the hill, and she was jolted out of her thoughts.

'So . . .' Enzo said, plucking a peach from the paper bag. 'You'd be completely fine with me surrounded by Aphrodean women, all possessed by Torra's charm at its absolute peak on the summer solstice?'

Elara's eyes narrowed.

'Or are you forgetting what only a fraction of her charm did to you in Asteria?'

'And what it did to you too,' she fired back. Images of them both in the carriage filtered through, the ones that kept her awake at night, hot and wanting. 'I don't understand why I wouldn't be fine. Do as you please.'

Enzo took a bite of his peach, shit-eating grin still upon his face as they came to a halt.

The conversation was flung from her thoughts once she realized where he had taken her. She stumbled down the verge, ripping her sandals off, spongy sea grass making way for powdered white sand. She flexed her toes in it, sighing, her white cotton dress ruffling in the gentle breeze. They'd reached a secluded cove, just a small stretch of sand and crystal-clear water, brighter than any she had ever seen. She turned to him.

'I know the ocean calms you,' he said.

Elara lay down in the sand with a contented sigh. Enzo sank next to her, propping himself up on his elbows.

'Going back to what we were discussing . . .'

'*Enzo*,' Elara groaned.

318

'I want to hear you say it.'

'Say what?' she snapped.

'That the thought of me with another woman truly doesn't bother you.'

He shifted on his side to look at her, and she couldn't tear her gaze from his. The Light beating down on him illuminated every feature. His eyes were so molten that every shade of his magick seemed to flicker and shift around his irises. His skin glowed. He ran a hand through his black hair, pushing it back off his face. She swallowed the lump in her throat as her eyes followed the motion.

'It wouldn't faze you –' his hand caught hers as he dragged a thumb down her palm '– for me to hold her hand like this.'

Her breathing shallowed as her entire focus went to that one gesture.

'To kiss her neck.'

His fingers trailed over her collarbones, scraping the sensitive point by her jaw. He shifted closer.

'Her lips.'

His thumb brushed her parted mouth as his fingers weaved through her hair.

'To pull her hair the way I like.' He tugged for emphasis and a ragged breath escaped Elara. Enzo rolled so he was over her but not touching, his arms bracing on either side of her. His hair fell between them as he dipped his head to her lips.

'To not just make love to her, but to worship her.' His lips were a hair's breadth away. If she breathed deeply, her lips would touch his.

'Wasn't that what you wanted, princess? Reverence?'

He smiled slowly at his prey as she stifled a moan. His body blocked out the Light so they were cocooned in their own darkness.

'Would it really not bother you, Elara?' he murmured.

'Yes,' she breathed. 'Yes, I would care.'

'*Finally.*' He sprang off her, leaving her blindsided and shutting her eyes against what she had admitted. Realizing what she had done, Elara rose. Without a word, her cheeks flushing red, she stomped to the water's edge. She refused to meet his eyes as she stripped down to her undergarments, making sure the duskglass was safely still in her skirt pocket, and waded in.

The cerulean waters lapped against her like a soul called back to their beloved. The Light's rays hung low in the sky as she waded out, up to her waist, then her chest, until finally she was weightless, floating. She dived under the gentle waves, opening her eyes as she flipped on her back. The clear water cooled her racing thoughts, snapping her out of her lust.

Bronzed skin dipped and rose, and she saw Enzo's powerful body cutting through the waves, droplets like diamonds spraying through the air. She scowled as he reached her with a smile, shaking salt from his damp curls. She lay on her back as he trod water.

'Ignoring me now?' He flicked water at her. She shot him her most scathing look before pushing herself further away.

'For the record, princess, I feel the same.'

Her arms stopped gliding in the water, and she tipped herself forwards.

'Is that so?' she asked primly, still not making eye contact. Enzo swam closer.

'Elara, if you were in Aphrodea without me during the solstice,' he raised his hands in exasperation, 'I would burn the kingdom to the ground.'

Her eyes flew to him. 'What?'

'You heard what I said.'

Her heart raced, the words coming before she could stop

them. 'If you really feel that way, then why haven't you kissed me again?'

Enzo looked at her incredulously. She searched his face for a moment, poison on her tongue. 'Or do you need Torra's charm to do that?'

His eyes widened, and she shook her head, stretching her arms to swim away. His hand grabbed her wrist, yanking her back to him. Her body slammed against his in the water.

'You wonder why I haven't kissed you again?' he murmured. 'It's all I've fucking thought about. You plague me, Elara. And that damned charm . . . I didn't know if that was the only reason *you* kissed *me*.'

'Enzo, I wanted to. I – I still want to,' she admitted.

He stared at her, a realization shining in his eyes so brightly that she almost tore away. In one movement, he pulled her flush to him. Her legs curled around his waist instinctively as she gasped, and her arms wrapped around his bare neck. She inhaled his scent, salt and amber. His thumbs grazed her waist, her soaked undergown thin against it. She suppressed a shiver.

'Gods, I want to show you right now what I've been planning to do to you,' he said against her as his hand came up to trace the curve of her neck. She tipped her head back, desperate for more than a graze. He chuckled against it, his thumb reaching behind her ear as he cradled her head.

'But let me tell you something,' he continued, his breath tickling her ear. 'I'm not going to kiss you right now. Our first kiss was stolen by Torra, so the next one is going to be only ours. The next time you moan for me, you'll have no charm to blame it upon. So be patient, Elara, and be ready.'

Delicious shivers ran up her spine. He was right; she didn't want to rush this. The feelings rising inside her were not just a distraction from pain on a lust-drunk afternoon. She was teetering on the edge of a precipice. She knew the moment she jumped, everything would change.

And so, she only nodded silently as he pressed a chaste kiss to her forehead.

'For that,' she said, 'you're going to pay.' And without a second thought, she dunked him under the water with glee.

Elara's heart was aglow at Enzo's confession. For the first time in weeks, she felt happiness. True happiness. There was still an aching place in her where Sofia resided, but it was buoyed by Enzo, by hope.

'Thank you,' she said to him as they arrived outside her room. Enzo had stopped at his own room as they had passed, and now he faced her in a fresh shirt and loose linen pants. 'I don't know if I've even said that to you yet. For the last few weeks; you poured your light into me.'

He took her hand, and the tension between them rose and shimmered, her lungs constricting at his burning touch. 'You already are a light, Elara. It's why the shadows flock to you.'

She smiled so brightly that it ached as he pushed her into the room. When he sank into the same chair that served as his bed every night, Elara bit her lip. 'Enzo?'

'Yes, princess?'

'I have a request.'

'Go on.'

'Will you stop sleeping in that chair? I feel awful, and it can't be good for your back. If you don't get enough—'

'It's okay.' His lip curled, interrupting her. 'You don't have to *beg* me to come to your bed.'

'Heavenly Stars and all that is holy,' she muttered, looking to the ceiling.

His grin widened further. 'I'll stay.' He eased himself off the chair, pulling his shirt over his head. Elara flushed, drinking her fill of his bare torso, and wondered just how much she'd be able to sleep with *that* next to her. He lifted the sheets, settling in behind her.

'I must say,' he muttered, 'this doesn't live up to *any* of my fantasies about us sharing a bed.' She slapped his arm behind her as he made an amused sound.

'But I meant what I said in the ocean,' he continued. 'I want to court you properly. That means some clothes *will* remain on, despite how much you may try to seduce me with those sinfully short nightgowns.'

She smiled to herself. 'I suppose I can allow that.' A heavy arm wrapped around her as Enzo settled down. But as she heard his breathing deepen, Elara couldn't help but think of Idris's earlier threats, and the words of the prophecy, as she was held by the man she certainly wasn't fated for.

CHAPTER FORTY-SEVEN

The next morning, Elara stood before the doors to the royal kitchens, clenching and unclenching her fists.

After a sleep where her nightmares hadn't chased her for the first time in weeks, she had woken up clear-headed and ready. It was time to be brave.

She took one deep breath before she pushed the door open and walked in.

Merissa was piping a cake with pistachio cream, icing sugar dusted on her nose. She looked up as the door opened, her mouth falling open. 'Elara,' she breathed.

There was a tense silence as they stared at each other.

'Can . . . can we talk?' Elara cursed herself at her stuttering. Acting like a timid fool was not something she was used to.

'Of course,' Merissa said. 'I just need to finish frosting these.'

Elara moved wordlessly toward her, picking up another piping nozzle as she began to help.

She didn't look at the glamourer as she said, 'I wanted to apologize.'

Merissa put her piping bag down. 'What?'

'I've been avoiding you and ignoring you . . . I'm sorry. I . . .'

Gods, this was difficult. Why was everything so difficult to communicate now? She swallowed hard, willing down the lump forming in her throat.

'After Sofia,' she forced out, 'I couldn't bear to be around you. It's just that . . .' She swallowed again. 'You are the closest friend I have here. From the moment I set foot in the palace, you made me feel welcome. And whenever I saw your face, I saw hers. It felt like I was replacing her.'

The tears were falling now, and she sighed, raising her hands up the air in exasperation.

Merissa took a tea towel and wiped her face gently. 'Elara,' she said sternly. 'You have nothing to be sorry for. Nothing, do you hear me?'

Elara nodded. 'I just feel like I shouldn't be able to have other friends or enjoy myself when Sofia—' She had to take a gulp of air as her sobs poured out. 'When Sofia went through what she did.'

Merissa drew her into a tight hug.

'You're allowed to feel what you're feeling. But you're also allowed to move forward. It's what Sofia would have wanted.'

Elara gave a small smile. 'Someone very wise said something similar.' She embraced Merissa again, holding her tightly. 'I've missed you,' she said into her hair, the sweet smell of rosewater enveloping her.

'And I you. I'm glad you visited. Isra dropped by yesterday and told me the news.'

'About the glass?' Elara said, lowering her voice.

Merissa nodded. 'She has a plan. For Aphrodea?'

Elara nodded. 'If Enzo can get Idris on board, we may finally have the upper hand with Ariete.'

Merissa had a knowing smile on her lips.

'What?' Elara said.

'Oh, nothing,' Merissa replied innocently. 'She just also may have mentioned how exactly you made it.'

'Dear Stars,' Elara muttered, sucking the icing off her fingers.

'All I'll say, is, if that's how close you and the prince are, you'll have a lot of fun in my kingdom. You know, I had an idea that I floated past Isra.'

'And what was that?' Elara groaned.

'You want to announce your presence to the world. And in the land of lust, let's just say it's . . . customary to greet guests with a warm welcome.'

'Go on . . .'

'When Enzo arrives, the queens of Aphrodea will no doubt kick up a huge fuss and demand he partake in the custom Aphrodean dance. It's a little less inhibited than the ones you're used to in Asteria.'

Elara sighed. 'I already know what you're going to say.'

'You're going to be the star of the show – pardon the pun. All eyes will be on you as we let the world know that *Queen Elara of Asteria is alive*.'

Elara's heart fluttered at the title. She released a deep breath.

'Well, that doesn't sound daunting at all. An easy task to captivate hundreds of people at a foreign court with a dance I don't know the first step of.'

Merissa's smile only widened. 'That's what I'm here for.'

CHAPTER FORTY-EIGHT

The solstice approached, and still Elara waited for further instructions as to what to do with the duskglass.

Enzo had taken the object they had created to the only blacksmith in Sol that he trusted, and the man had fused the slice to a hilt, fashioning the magickal glass into a knife. Since Elara had received it, it had stayed strapped securely next to Sofia's dagger, the two weapons never leaving her thigh. She barely saw Leo and Enzo, who were tied up in the war room, strategizing with Idris. Leyon had refused to invite Ariete to Helios, and so they were back to the drawing board.

Isra was frequenting the palace more and more, trying to help Elara bring substance back to her shadows.

'There's still a block within you,' she said, during their latest practice session on Elara's balcony. 'You loosened it on the cliff by pushing through your fear, but there's no . . .' She paused, trying to find the word. 'It's like your soul is twilight rather than the deep dark of the night. So your shadows have nothing to feed off.'

'Isn't that a good thing?' Elara asked, lowering her hands as the shadows around her retreated.

Isra passed her a glass of peach juice. 'No. A shadow-mancer's well of magick should be pitch black. Trust me, I dated one once.'

'You dated an Asterian?' Elara asked.

Isra nodded, lip twitching. 'Cassandra.' She sighed. 'Forbidden love and all that. It was *very* thrilling.'

Elara laughed in disbelief, right as Enzo walked on to the balcony.

'Still no luck,' he said. 'Prissy Leyon is still throwing a fit. And my father can't very well tell him the exact reason that we want to invite Ariete. So we're still nowhere closer.'

Elara twirled a strand of hair around her finger as she pondered. 'What if we didn't need Leyon's permission?'

'What do you mean?' Enzo asked. 'Ariete can't enter our kingdom without it.'

'Not without starting a war,' Elara said. 'But do you really think the *god* of war would care? If the object of his every hatred was being hidden in his own brother's kingdom? You don't think he would come, whether there were consequences or not?'

Isra's head flew to Enzo. 'She's right.'

'Outcome, Iz?' Enzo asked, and Isra's eyes flicked white for a few minutes before returning to hazel.

'Unclear,' she replied. 'Many paths have been laid out, and the way forward is too dark for me to see. But the plan is not impossible.'

Enzo nodded. 'I'll tell Idris.'

On the morning of the solstice, Elara hadn't even fully awoken when she became aware of the clamour of rumbling carts, servants shouting orders and streams of boisterous music. With a small smile, she opened her eyes and leapt out of bed, opening the doors to her balcony. She peered out, the magick of the longest day of the year hot and fizzing in the air. It was celebrated throughout every kingdom, yet Helios, with their worship of the Light, had to be the most spectacular. She lamented the fact she wouldn't be able to witness the lavish celebrations, for Idris had agreed to her plan. She and Enzo would proceed to Aphrodea and tell the world that she was alive. Then they would return to Helios and wait for Ariete – Leyon be damned.

She gazed down at the grounds, catching sight of a band practising in the shade of a copse of trees. Her eyes wandered to a whirl of servants, who carried cloths in all shades of gold, bronze and red into the palace. She wondered how Aphrodea would be celebrating, and then considered what in the Stars' names she was going to wear.

As though on cue, Merissa bustled in, her pretty green eyes even more sparkling and bright than usual. 'Happy solstice!' she squealed, kissing Elara square on the lips.

Elara's eyebrows raised. 'And that's about the most affection I'll get this week.'

'Tradition,' Merissa replied breezily. 'It's bad luck in Helios not to kiss the ones you love on the solstice.'

Elara smiled as Merissa planted her in front of the vanity table.

'Now, we have to attend worship before we leave for Aphrodea this afternoon. I know, I know,' she added at Elara's raised eyebrow in the mirror. 'But it's all for show. Enzo and the king must, at least for the sake of appearance, show that they are devoted to the Stars – Leyon particularly. It's his day more than anyone's.'

She combed through Elara's hair with her fingers, using

her magick to help style it, though Elara didn't see a glamour settle over her this time.

'Surely *I* can't step right into Leyon's temple for worship?'

'Many Helion women on the solstice wear a veil to the temple. Those devout enough believe that they shouldn't cast eyes directly at a god.'

'Stars help me,' Elara muttered.

'You, Isra and I will *all* wear them. You'll be in Helion attire, of course.' She finished with Elara's hair, casting a few sweeps of her hand over Elara's face before heading to the wardrobe.

'This dress has to make a statement. Appearance is as powerful a weapon as any sword. Asterian royalty in a Helion dress will cause quite the commotion in Aphrodea.'

She handed two flimsy bits of fabric to Elara.

'Who knows? The golden lingerie might come in handy later,' Merissa grinned. She hauled out reams of gold cloth as Elara pulled the skimpy undergarments on. Merissa wolf-whistled as she brought the dress over, and Elara pushed her teasingly as she laughed. The glamourer began to fasten her into the swarms of golden material. When Merissa was done, she whirled Elara to the mirror, leaving her there to admire her appearance as she returned to the wardrobe.

The dress was exquisite. It was a celebration of the Light. Two wisps of lace fell from her shoulders, leaving her neck exposed, the neckline grazing low. A body of gold was stitched with tiny mirrors, so small they blended into a multi-faceted bodice, the Light refracting off her as she walked. The dress glided down her curves, cinching at her waist and sweeping down to a full skirt of gilded feathers that pooled at her feet. A subtle slit carved up her left side. From behind, her back was bare, save for chains of gold that dripped down her, only her silver dragun tattoo peeking through.

Spun sugar grazed her décolletage and eyes, her raven-black waves were loose down her back, and she stared at herself open-mouthed as Merissa fixed a thin, matching gold circlet to the crown of her head.

'You look like a goddess,' Merissa whispered, coming back up behind her.

Elara turned to her, radiant. 'Says the one who could give Torra a run for her money.'

It was true. Merissa looked otherworldly. Before attending to Elara, she had already smoothed her curls, her long honeyed hair falling in a sheet across one shoulder. But now, a golden gown to match Elara's, made of silk roses all along the bust, dripped over her curves, tight to her legs as it fell to her feet. The metallic shine accentuated her bronzed skin, and a darker gold was painted around her eyes, leaving the green of them smoky. Merissa only smiled at Elara's remark as she reached back into the wardrobe, extracting two veils. She raised Elara's over her head and settled it on her so that it covered her. The veil fell down her back, covering it and the conspicuous tattoo. Then Merissa placed her own over her head, adjusting both before standing to look over her work.

They both stood in front of the mirror and held one another tightly.

'I've never seen such good-looking sinners about to step into a church,' Merissa beamed.

'I wouldn't be surprised if I burst into flames the moment I cross the threshold.'

Merissa chuckled, taking one last look at them both before leading Elara out of the room.

Anticipation thrummed in Elara's veins as they walked arm-in-arm down the grand staircase. She saw Idris by the main doors in deep discussion with Enzo and Leo. The king was dressed in cream with golden brocade, a long cape grazing the floor, a crown studded with topaz and citrine resting on his thinning hair. Elara felt her shadows writhe beneath her, desperate to wrap around Idris's throat. But she clenched her fists, focusing on the pain of her nails digging into her palms until her shadows settled.

She took in more of Enzo's appearance as she descended. His crown glinted upon freshly washed curls. He wore a white silk shirt and an embroidered jacket of a cream shade, embellished with intricate gold stitching. As she squinted, she realized what the pattern was.

Draguns.

Tiny detailed draguns, an exact rendering of the one down her back.

'His jacket,' she breathed to Merissa.

She felt Merissa squeeze her arm as she murmured, 'He requested it specifically.'

When Enzo's eyes found hers, seeming to pierce right through the veil, her heart hammered. The conversation between the men died out as Elara approached, still staring back at Enzo, ignoring Idris and Leo. When she reached the waiting group, Enzo nodded, maintaining the aloof pretence.

'The lost princess, risen from the dead,' Idris said, eyes glittering. Elara noticed Enzo stiffen beside her, and she gave more of a grimace than a smile to the king.

'I trust that everyone is prepared?' she asked.

The king placed a hand on the small of her back and Elara tensed, as he guided her down the corridor to the palace's exit. She gave only one quick glance back to Enzo as she reached the doors.

'Soldiers are already deployed to the border, and I have sent scouts further ahead into Asteria. If there is any news of Ariete making movements towards Helios, we shall hear it,' Idris replied, pulling her to one side as they crossed the threshold.

'And Leyon?' She looked distractedly to Enzo and Leo, who were walking towards the carriages.

'As far as Leyon is concerned, we accepted his refusal to invite his brother into the kingdom. Going to temple today will appease him enough for now.'

Elara nodded. 'What about when we get to Aphrodea?'

'In Aphrodea, you make sure your reveal counts. You make sure that everyone knows that Princess Elara is alive. That a Star could not kill her. And you ensure that there is no doubt, that you are Helios's weapon.'

Elara's lip curled beneath her veil as Idris looked to where his son waited. Three carriages stood ready behind him. 'You and my son may not get along, but you will put on an act. At least for a night. To show our alliance.'

Elara didn't think it wise to tell him that she and his son were currently sharing a bed every night. So, she only nodded curtly.

'Nice jacket,' Elara murmured to Enzo as he helped her into the carriage.

His lip twitched as he settled beside her.

'I'm becoming increasingly fond of draguns. What did my father want?'

'He wants to make sure my appearance counts. And told me to make sure that tonight, I show the world that I am allied to *you*.'

Enzo sat back in his seat, face unreadable. 'Then I suppose we'll have to pretend, won't we, princess?'

Elara smiled.

They waited for Idris's carriage to set off, followed by another with the King's Guard. When their own carriage began to move, Leo leaned forwards, extruding a small flask from his jacket. 'Who'd like a little *revera* wine before the service?' he said, shaking it.

Merissa's eyes widened. '*Leo*, could you be more blasphemous if you tried?'

'Oh, you have no idea, Merissa.' He winked, and Merissa's face grew pink.

'It seems the general has already had a swig or two,' Elara said.

He laughed in reply, passing the hip flask to Elara, who took two large gulps beneath her veil, before passing it to Enzo.

'We need something to get us through this hell,' Enzo muttered, taking a large swig himself. He passed it to Merissa, who debated a second before she knocked the flask back.

'What?' she asked sheepishly as everyone looked at her in amusement.

Before they knew it, the carriage had come to a halt down a narrow backstreet that led to the grand piazza where Leyon's temple stood. Emerging from the carriage, they could hear the roar of a crowd already, music and shouts drifting towards them. Elara fiddled with her veil, checking over Merissa's too before they descended into the busy streets. Members of the King's Guard, who had followed in a carriage behind, immediately formed a circle around the party as they began to meet the crowd.

It was bedlam. Crowds snaked through the alleys leading into the square, pressing in together in the sweltering heat. Enzo gripped Elara's hand, pulling her through the crowd as the people around them screamed and cried to the prince, paying homage to his light. They begged for his blessing, for a touch, and Enzo played his part well. He nodded and smiled, grasping the hands of all who reached out to him through the shield of the Guard, as he continued to drag a bewildered Elara into the main square.

The square was even worse, the masses cramming the space to enter the temple, desperate for a glimpse of Leyon, heads peering over each other, jostling and shoving. Enzo kept looking straight ahead as their group ploughed onwards, Leo charging ahead of the King's Guard. As he moved, it was like a sea parting as bodies moved aside, clearing the way for the prince. The four walked to the entrance as shouts and blessings followed them.

'May the Light bless you!' an old woman near the entrance cried out to Enzo.

'And you.' He smiled, raising the three-fingered symbol of worship out to her. The crowd went wild, clapping and swooning as they reached the steps of the temple, passing through a barrier of armed city guards.

'Enzo!' a voice shouted, and they spun to see Isra waiting on the steps, a golden veil over her.

'I nearly got trampled amongst those fanatics,' she seethed, coming towards them as she cast a withering look at the crowd. 'Whatever compels them to worship a Star that does nothing but look at his own reflection is beyond me.'

'Isra,' Merissa admonished. 'Keep your voice down. We're literally outside his temple.'

'What's he going to do? Smite me in front of all his devotees?'

Enzo snickered as he led them all into the cool entryway, the clamour of the crowd dulling behind them. 'Is my father already here?' he asked Isra.

'Yes, he's just taken his seat.'

Enzo nodded grimly, releasing Elara's hand. 'This won't take long,' he said to her. 'Stay with Isra and Merissa. After the service, we will be heading straight to Aphrodea.'

He nodded once before making his way to the inner temple doors, Leo behind him. Elara saw Enzo reach out to a small dish filled with light, adding his own wisp to the offerings, and then he was gone.

'Come,' Merissa said, ushering them in after. The service had already started, organ music resounding through the cavernous temple. There were benches lined with nobles and aristocrats – the more important they were, the nearer to Leyon's altar they sat. Elara sidled into a corner pew at the back of the temple, by a large window made of stained glass, while Merissa and Isra shuffled in beside her. The temple was stifling, the stone building doing nothing to keep out the heat. Her eyes scanned the crowd, falling on where Enzo had taken his seat beside the king. In front of them was the altar and Leo, who was leading the King's Guard close by.

There, sat on the raised dais, facing the adoring crowd, was Leyon. He lounged on a throne, the back of which splayed out into light rays that stretched out from all sides. He wore only a robe, spun from pure gold, shirtless underneath. Elara saw a peek of leanly muscled stomach as he adjusted himself, looking out smugly to the crowd.

The service commenced, the music trailing off as a priest started to drone, reciting the many wonderful things that Leyon had done for Helios and the sacred nature of the Light. Elara stifled a yawn, tuning out the blatant lies and hypocrisy.

Skies, it was hot. Her veil was stifling, she felt like she could barely breathe beneath it.

The service continued, *revera* about to be taken as a show of respect to Leyon. She watched idly as devotees queued for a sip from Leyon's ambrosia-filled chalice, as the priest blessed them with his light. It was no good, she could not stand the veil any longer. Noticing how preoccupied everyone was, she looked around quickly, before folding it back. She subtly drew a thin illusion around herself to remain unnoticeable as she took a deep breath.

Merissa looked at her sharply. 'You had better put that back on this instant.'

Elara shot her a look, sighing. She closed her eyes for a second, revelling in the rays that played across her face. A small smile came to her lips as she felt the warmth of the light, then she raised her arms to pull her veil back down. She looked back to the altar, where Enzo was staring at her, the cup of ambrosia to his lips.

She hurriedly pulled the veil back over her face before anyone turned to see what he was looking at.

'Drink,' the priest was saying in a monotone, 'and be blessed.' Enzo's eyes, which looked so warm and honeyed, did not leave her as he took a deep drink.

'Do you hold the Light close to you?'

'Yes,' Enzo breathed, still not looking away from her. Elara felt her cheeks heat and was suddenly glad for the disguise.

'Do you promise to honour beauty and art, the things that Leyon holds dear, every day?'

She *felt* the fire held within his eyes upon her skin. 'Yes.'

'Do you renounce the Dark?'

Enzo grinned, still looking across the crowd to her. She bit her lip, smiling. There was a silence as they held each other's gaze.

'Your Highness, I asked, do you renounce the Dark?'

There were murmurs through the crowd as Enzo took his time. His lip quirked.

'Yes,' he finally responded, not taking his eyes off Elara.

'Then be blessed, the Light washes away your sins.'

The priest held his fingers to Enzo's temple before Enzo bowed his head, heading back to his seat.

Isra leaned over to Elara. 'He *definitely* does not renounce "the Dark".' Merissa chuckled next to her.

Finally, Leyon stood, his palms raised in supplication. Though nothing spun from them – no fire or light. Elara frowned, leaning in to Merissa.

'Does Leyon ever show his light?'

Merissa tensed, before leaning in. 'Not that we've ever seen.'

Elara went to ask why, but the organ began again as the temple doors opened. The attendees began to stand and file out of the place of worship back into the blaring crowd who screamed, 'Hail Leyon!'

They waited for the temple-goers to dissipate until finally, Enzo appeared with the king and guard in tow.

'The carriages await,' Enzo said, and Idris nodded.

'To Aphrodea we go.'

CHAPTER FORTY-NINE

When they reached the palace once more, and she was hurried out of the carriage, Elara leaned towards Enzo. 'How are we getting to Aphrodea?'

Idris had promised he was taking care of the details, but it dawned on her that the journey would likely take days by carriage, days they did not have.

Enzo winked. 'You'll see.'

Idris led the procession, flanked by Leo and a guard that Elara vaguely recognized from her capture – an older man who had appeared with Leo after her altercation with Barric. They turned down a corridor and arrived at a nondescript door. When it opened, Elara's mouth slackened.

Light danced through the entire space, rainbows cast and refracting off mirrors that lined the walls. Tables were set up in rows, each littered with maps of constellations and stars. And in the centre of the room was a wheel. Upon it were the sigils of all the stars, along with small symbols and writings etched in gold.

'What is this place?' Elara murmured.

'I call it my *lucirium*. And it is where I Stargaze,' Idris said.

'For years I have been learning what I can of the Stars to get to this moment – to make them fall.'

As Elara walked past the wheel, she brushed Ariete's symbol with a finger. Lines upon lines of text appeared within a burst of red light. Idris glared at her as he passed his own hand over the sigil, and the light and text vanished.

'Don't touch anything,' he snapped, as they reached a mirror at the end of the room, shimmering more brightly than others, almost emanating its own light.

Idris walked right over to it and held out his hand to Leo, who took a knife and made a small cut across the King's palm.

Elara raised her brows.

Idris held up his hand and smeared it upon the relief of the roaring lion upon the mirror's frame. 'Aphrodea,' he said clearly. There was a ripple of light, and to Elara's disbelief, their reflection transformed, the mirror becoming like a window that displayed a crystal-clear picture of a garden painted in hues of rose and honey. Aphrodea.

'They're called *soverins*,' Enzo explained, looking at her surprise. 'Royal blood allows you through.'

'It's a way for royals to convene and travel between neighbouring kingdoms quickly,' Isra added. 'Gatherings, meetings, treaties – it's far easier to use this than to travel by horse if you're a monarch.'

'Of course, you wouldn't know anything about them,' Idris said, looking over at Elara. 'Your father blocked off the *soverin* from here to Asteria decades ago.' He gave a nasty smile, before walking right through the mirror, Leo and the other guard with him. There was a shimmer as they disappeared for a moment, before reappearing in the Aphrodean garden.

Elara thought back to the shrouded mirror in her parents'

throne room. Sofia had teased her once that it had been covered because it was a portal to the Deadlands, and that if she ever took a peek, ghosts and ghouls would pour from it and snatch her back with them. Had that been her parents' *soverin*? How much more about her own kingdom was there left to discover?

Elara pushed the uneasy thoughts away as Enzo led her, Merissa and Isra through the mirror.

She felt like she was falling, then flying, then somersaulting for less than a minute, before she landed firmly on two feet in what appeared to be a rose garden.

The perfume from the flowers was intoxicating, blush-coloured butterflies flitting through the air. Lively music flooded Elara's senses, making her feet twitch to the rhythm and her nerves dance. The *soverin* behind them shimmered before the image of Idris's *lucirium* disappeared. It was replaced with their reflection and a frame of roses, a carved rose-gold swan stamped at the top of it. The small garden was empty.

Isra and Merissa craned their necks as Elara stared up at the palace before her, on higher ground than where they stood, the sprawling capital of Venusa below it. The palace was stunning, looking like it was sitting on clouds. The candy-floss wisps of the Aphrodean sky wrapped around the base of the palace as white and dusky pink columns stretched higher into the sky. Roses climbed up and around the building, every shade of blush imaginable. She staggered a little as Enzo leaned in.

'Decadent is the word you're looking for,' he said.

'Overkill more like,' Isra muttered.

'Excuse me!' Merissa protested. 'This is my kingdom you're talking about.'

'Sorry,' Enzo and Isra chimed in unison.

They walked down a path and out of the rose garden, hanging back from Idris a little, who was already a short distance ahead with his guard in tow. Enzo filled her in. 'We're guests of the palace today. The queens know we're arriving for their solstice, they invite us every year. But they don't know anything about *you* other than the fact that you're a guest.' He glanced at Elara. 'That means you have to *show* them who you are.'

'Don't worry, Enzo.' Isra walked up to him, patting him on the shoulder. 'We've got it *all* figured out.'

'That does not put me at ease,' Enzo muttered.

The moment they left the gardens, they were greeted by a parade of people. They blended in with the celebrators singing jovially. Elara had never seen anything like it – the music, the food, the pure joy in celebrating the longest day of the year. Asterians didn't celebrate the summer solstice, focusing their festivities on the winter solstice and Hallow's Eve. This was so vibrant, so *alive*. She saw couples everywhere, dancing to the beat of a drum as pink washed their world, the sky lit up like sherbet. A handsome Aphrodean man danced up to her, his bronzed skin making his green eyes seem even greener.

He took her hand. 'My, why haven't I seen you before?'

'Because she's with me,' Enzo snapped, stepping between them. The man took one look at his crown and tumbled on forwards as Enzo firmly planted his hands at her waist and pushed her ahead.

Excitement thrilled through her at his touch, settling deeper as he murmured into her ear, 'Remember, princess. I'm perfectly comfortable with burning this kingdom to the ground.'

She let out a low laugh as they moved and swayed through the palace grounds to where the main building waited. She spotted Isra moving with a carefree ease; her hands twined in the sky, and a laugh lit up her face as she stomped her feet to the music, entangling with strangers. Merissa blew a kiss to Elara as she passed them. She wound her hips sensually, so casual with the way she moved her body. Elara smiled to herself. Yes, Merissa was Aphrodean through and through.

She readied herself as they reached the palace doors, the parade dancing through the open grand hallway to the ballroom.

'Elara,' Enzo said, and she stilled at the hesitant note in his voice. 'I'm a prince here, and well . . .' He ran a hand through his curls, adjusting his crown. 'They may expect me to . . . receive guests.'

Elara raised a brow. He led her to one of the walls and away from the crowd, beside a painting of Torra in a chariot upon a lake, pulled by two swans.

'It's just a stupid solstice tradition, but the queens will probably expect me to greet members of their court. And let's just say the tradition isn't exactly as *proper* as it may be in Asteria.'

'Don't worry about it,' she said breezily and marched off into the cavernous hall as he followed, confusion on his face.

The drumbeat increased, trumpets blaring as the hip-swaying rhythm of the music propelled her through the enormous ballroom, which had been fashioned to be a receiving hall as much as a room for dancing. She spotted two female figures lounging in chairs upon a dais at the opposite end of the room, viewing the spectacle. The queens of Aphrodea were as stunning as the rumours whispered. Queen Calliope, Elara remembered from her history lessons, was the woman with rose-gold hair and possessed one of the strongest seducing magicks in the land. Her consort, Queen Ariadne, had golden brown hair and clever jade green eyes, and had been a tailor before her ascension to the throne. Both of their complexions glowed a golden shade of olive.

As Elara took note of the rest of the room, she saw that people from all over Celestia were dancing; Elara had already spied a few Svetans, Kaosians and Concordians, all dressed to impress. They each knew the steps flawlessly to dances Elara didn't even recognize. She realized in that moment, her heart squeezing, just how cut off from the rest of the world and their cultures she had been. Idris was waiting, however, and Enzo squeezed Elara's waist before letting it go. 'I'd better greet the queens,' he said, leaving her with Merissa and Isra.

She watched him leave, nerves finally taking over.

Isra looked at her. 'Ready?'

She gave a nod, seeing Leo murmur something to Enzo and Idris, the two of them nodding before he disappeared into the crowd. 'Ready.'

CHAPTER FIFTY

'Ladies and gentlemen,' a man cried out, and Elara turned to see a jester prancing around a balcony above them, his voice enchanted to carry through the room. 'King Idris of Helios and his son, the *Lion* himself, have arrived. Let's give them a warm welcome!'

The crowd cheered and clapped as the music became deafening.

'And don't they both look dashing? I wouldn't mind if that lion took a bite out of me.'

Elara looked in abject disbelief to Merissa and Isra. The seer sniggered while Merissa hid a smile behind her hands. 'His name's Alfonso,' Merissa said. 'And he's arguably the best jester in Celestia.'

Elara squinted, trying to see Enzo's face, and thought she saw some faint amusement upon it, and Idris had plastered on a brilliant smile, though Elara saw right through it.

A few plucking strings picked up, and Alfonso raised a hand exaggeratedly to his ear. 'Oh? What's that? Do we hear . . . an Aphrodean welcome commencing?'

There were screams and wolf-whistles from the crowd.

'You know by now what that entails, Prince Lorenzo,' Alfonso shouted, and Isra snorted. 'And you too, King Idris, should you want it.'

Idris waved a hand through the air, and the crowd laughed as he pushed his son forwards.

'Well, it's always worth asking,' Alfonso continued. 'You know I like a silver fox as much as I like a virile lion.'

Elara scoffed.

Idris settled into an ornate chair by the queens upon their dais, as Enzo was led into the centre of the crowd, who parted and created a circle around him. Elara shifted, pushing so that she was near the front.

'Now, ladies and gentlemen,' Alfonso continued, 'today is a special day. The summer solstice strengthens our magick, the Light in the sky blessing us all. And to commemorate it, we like to have a little fun.'

There were hoots and hollers in the crowd.

'Now let's see, which of our fine ladies is going to try and seduce our handsome Helion?!'

Enzo feigned embarrassment as he briefly put his head in his hands, before settling back in the chair. Elara looked on in amusement. She knew he couldn't resist attention. The tune struck up fully, a heavy beat of drums and the trumpets, setting up a fast, carnal rhythm.

There were more shouts from the crowd, the jester riling them up.

Finally, a woman stepped out of the crowd.

'And here we go!' Alfonso shouted. 'Rosa Signo, trained under the infamous Lady Salome. Let's see if she can charm our esteemed guest.' Rosa slinked forwards, brunette hair swishing, her barely-there dress grazing glowing skin. She swished her hips as she made her way to Enzo.

Elara narrowed her eyes. Perhaps this wasn't going to be as amusing as she had first thought.

When she turned, it was to see Isra smirking, Merissa peering over the seer's shoulder with barely controlled glee.

Elara rolled her eyes. 'I don't know if I can do this.' She flicked her eyes back to the girl, whose hands were trailing down Enzo's chest as she tried to seduce him.

'Have some self-belief,' Isra scolded. 'I didn't waste my time helping you prepare all week for you to balk now.'

'You?' Merissa asked incredulously. 'All you did was sit and critique.'

'Yes, and a fine chunk of my precious time it cost me,' Isra replied primly.

'And it's a no from the prince!' Alfonso bellowed as Enzo stuck a thumbs down in the air. Rosa huffed, storming back into the crowd as another enticing woman with wine-red hair took her place. The newcomer waved out to the crowd. 'Emerald Adonis, ladies and gents!' yelled Alfonso. 'The firecracker herself. But will sparks fly between her and a flame-wielder?' Emerald wound her waist, stepping between Enzo's spread legs before spinning and lightly sitting in his lap, then bending forwards.

'Well, subtlety certainly doesn't seem to be Emerald's strong suit, but Helions aren't exactly known for it either,' continued Alfonso. 'You've seen how big Prince Lorenzo's crown is, haven't you?' The crowd laughed. 'And from a long line of seductresses, Emerald clearly knows what she's doing.' Emerald jumped up, facing Enzo as she undid a button of his shirt before sinking low. Elara's hand twitched.

'Easy,' Isra warned. 'Please don't go all lady-of-darkness on her ass.'

Elara clenched her jaw as Enzo smiled down at the

charmer, leaning towards Emerald's face, before shaking his head. 'And the Lion still isn't satisfied. Next!'

Emerald only winked, before lightly pushing off him and blowing kisses to the crowd.

When the next woman stepped out, Elara felt like cold water had been poured over her. She recognized the golden-blonde hair of the woman from the night of Leyon's Descent. She'd been playing with Enzo's hair in the grove, and seemed determined to remind him as she smirked, reaching on tip-toes to rake her hand through his curls, then draping herself over him.

'And what's this, a reunion? For those who weren't here last year, Melodi stole the prince on the last summer's solstice. Will she seduce the prince for the second year in a row?'

She saw Enzo search the crowd, his eyes finally settling on Elara.

'Enough of this,' she snapped.

Melodi tried to pull him up to dance, but he pulled his arms away, still looking at Elara. The charmer's brow furrowed, as she twisted around him. 'Ooh! It's not looking good for Melodi!'

Jealousy, hot and cold at the same time, curdled in Elara's stomach. She squared her shoulders, looking at Merissa.

Merissa nodded. 'It's now or never, Elara. All eyes on you.'

CHAPTER FIFTY-ONE

Elara took a deep breath as she weaved through the crowd, pushing herself into clear view of Alfonso. She looked over at Leo, standing behind Idris, nodded to him, and got a single nod in reply. Then she glanced up at the pink lightdown streaming through the glass palace roof. One, two, three . . .

A spotlight struck her, Leo's powers spilling towards her as she stepped out, the mirrors shining rays off her as though she was the Light itself. The music ceased, as an acapella voice sang for three beats. She waited as the crowd admired the source of the brightness, gasping in wonder as they saw her shine.

'And who is this?' Alfonso said. 'A new entrant? Who is this mysterious beauty?' Then, with a smile to Leo, who winked back, she waited a few seconds as the band began playing again, and on the next beat of the drums she released her shadows and plunged the hall into darkness.

To their credit, the band continued, using the excitement to fuel their music as screams and gasps filled the cavernous chamber. The shadows hid her while she slinked through the crowd, Alfonso continuing to commentate in excitement.

When she spotted Enzo, looking around in anticipation from his chair, she smiled. Counted down. Then, on the next drum beat, she pulled her shadows in.

Light exploded back into the room to reveal her straddling the Prince of Helios. Enzo's eyes flew to hers in shock.

There were more gasps, murmurs and whispers through the crowd.

'An Asterian?! Ladies and gentlemen, this is history being made!' the jester screeched. 'What could this mean should she charm the prince? Peace between the kingdoms of Light and Dark?!' There were hollers and cheers of encouragement as the onlookers overcame their shock. Elara was taken aback. She thought that the other kingdoms despised Asterians, and yet here was this elated mass of people from every reach of Celestia, cheering her.

'Surprise, prince,' she whispered to him as she pressed herself into him. He swore, too low for anyone to hear, clenching her waist with his hands. Her skirts hitched around her as she rolled her hips again for good measure in time to the music as the crowd cheered again.

'What the fuck are you doing?' he whispered.

She smirked. 'You needed all eyes on me, didn't you?'

Enzo let out a disbelieving laugh as his gaze trailed down to where her hips moved like water.

'Were you tempted by any of those other girls?'

'Not a single one,' he purred, bringing his eyes back up to her with earnest sincerity. In one swift move, she spun so that her back was to him, her hair cascading behind her. She felt one hand tighten as the other pushed her hair to one side.

'I didn't get to appreciate this dress from the back before,' he added.

'Take a good look then.' She arched her back, widening

her legs and dipping forwards so that her full back was on display, the delicate chains slipping across it.

She felt him lean forwards, trailing his nose up the tail of her dragun. 'I need to personally thank whoever made it.'

'Well, the prince is definitely interested!' Alfonso shouted. 'It's the most attention he's shown a charmer all night!'

She rolled her hips from where she sat. 'If you like that, you should see the golden lingerie I have on to match.'

His strong hands grasped her middle, pulling her back to him. She felt a hand snake up around her front, holding her neck as he brought her ear to his mouth.

'I never knew you were such a sadist, princess,' he murmured into it, his nose skimming her neck. 'Now you're just being cruel.'

She gave a wicked smile as she pressed back into him, arching her spine. 'What's pleasure without a little pain?'

She stood, Enzo rising from the chair behind her as she turned to him, lacing her hands with his. His eyes burned into her as he twirled her.

'Don't expect me to have a coherent thought right now, Elara.'

He pulled her in hard, his hands still gripping her waist so that there wasn't an inch of space between their bodies as they continued to grind to the music.

'Dear Stars! Maybe the D'Oro's sigil should change to a snake, the way those hips are winding!' Alfonso shrieked, and Elara laughed.

'I knew you were an exhibitionist, but this may be a new level,' she teased. She turned her neck to look up at Enzo and saw his pupils dilate, pure intent colouring his eyes.

'When you look like that, who could blame me?' He murmured the last words, his gaze flicking to her lips.

She didn't answer and instead reached a hand behind his

neck. His calloused hands tightened, and the roughness of them through the material of her dress sent spikes of apprehension through her body. Almost lazily, he ground against her, one hand now trailing down her side to the slit in her dress.

'So we're going to give them a show?' he murmured into her ear, tongue loose from the lust-filled energy now throbbing around the room. The solstice was reaching its peak, and true to Isra's word, the energy was palpable as the magick of the kingdom took over.

'Yes,' she breathed as his hand started grazing the outside of her naked thigh, his hips still grinding slowly to the music. She jolted at the sudden contact of bare skin.

'You sure you want to play with fire?' he carried on, that delicious hand creeping higher and higher, bunching the sheer fabric around her hip as cool air began to play on her skin. He grazed his thumb over her hipbone, and she moaned quietly, leaning into him. She was no longer aware of what anyone else was doing, whether or not they were watching.

'We both know my shadows are a match to your flames,' she replied breathlessly, drunk on the Aphrodean air, her every sense constricting to the feel of his devilish hand.

'Mmm . . .' he rumbled into her neck. 'You don't know what you're doing to me.'

He trailed the back of a knuckle down her thigh for emphasis, and she arched into him even more.

'Then show me,' she hummed.

His grip on her tightened, bringing slight coherence to her addled thoughts. He pushed into her more roughly, and she could feel him, hard against her.

He laughed softly. That damn breath on her neck was going to be her undoing. That and the hand that she was trying to ignore creeping higher and higher towards the ache between her legs, now slick with want.

'Enzo,' she breathed, a plea. He hissed through his teeth.

'Elara,' he bit out.

'And ladies and gentlemen, I think we have a winner!' Alfonso exclaimed. 'The prince has well and truly been seduced!' More cheers followed.

Elara blinked, registering her surroundings once more, as Enzo's grip loosened on her.

Alfonso had descended from the balcony, and the crowd was parting around him as he rushed forwards in delight, coming to a halt before them both.

'Now who is this mysterious Asterian?! Pray tell us your name, darling, as you make history right here in Aphrodea. An Asterian seducing the Prince of Helios – we've never heard such a thing. Do you think this represents a truce, King Idris?'

Elara turned to the king, still sitting upon the dais as he smiled in response, lips closed. He shrugged, something hard dancing in his eyes.

The noise from the crowd was almost deafening, cheers ringing out as she laced her fingers with Enzo's, and looked straight at Alfonso. She waited for the crowd to quiet.

'Who are you?' Alfonso demanded again with glee.

Elara raised her chin.

'My name is Elara Bellereve, the rightful queen of Asteria and survivor of the *divinitas* of the King of Stars.'

CHAPTER FIFTY-TWO

Silence. Utter silence.

She saw Alfonso look around in confusion, saw the queens stand. Her eyes flicked to Idris, who was watching with a cold amusement, as he nodded to her.

She took a deep breath, anchoring herself in Enzo's grip.

'The Stars could not kill me,' she continued, her voice carrying clearly. 'I am here tonight to show my alliance to Helios. And to tell you that the Stars are not who we think they are. They are not benevolent gods.'

Uneasy murmurs, shouts and some jeers began in the crowd.

'Ariete descended to kill my parents for hiding my truth – that I was destined to fall for him, and that it would kill us both.'

Gasps, and boos of disbelief. Elara pressed on. 'He killed my best friend, anyone I loved and touched. For something that was thrust upon me.'

She turned. 'King Idris and Prince Lorenzo took me into their home and sheltered me.' She recited the words Idris had told her to say. 'And I now stand with them – as their weapon.' She forced herself to say the words. 'Tonight, we declare it. We declare war upon Ariete.'

The crowd erupted. More gasps, louder booing, a shout of 'Lies!' and calls for Elara's head all reached her. But among it all, murmurs of concern, the smallest smattering of applause.

Idris stood. The queens were shouting animatedly to him, but he only nodded, extracting himself from them.

'I think it's high time we leave,' he drawled as he approached, and Leo led them through the crowd, unsheathing his sword as the crowd pressed closer. Elara craned her neck, seeing Merissa and Isra ahead of them, hurrying out of the room.

Still the crowd bayed, Alfonso completely silent now, the queens trying to barge through the swarm of people towards them.

They hurried down the grand hallway, following Merissa and Isra, who slipped through a pair of ornate doors up ahead.

When Elara ran through them, she found herself in a room with a grand rose-gold statue of a bull in its centre – another animal associated with the Star Torra. It looked like a library, the walls lined with shelves that stretched from floor to ceiling, all filled with foiled spines in different hues of pink.

'Merissa,' Idris called.

Merissa waited up ahead, turning as the king called for her. 'Now,' he said.

Merissa understood immediately, rosy magick flowing from her fingers and over Idris as she glamoured him. His clothes became less refined, his hair growing, nose and mouth shifting, eyes darkening. The glamour was heavy – heavier than the one that Merissa put over Elara daily. She couldn't see a trace of who Idris was beneath it.

'Outcomes, Isra?' Enzo asked, as he let Merissa do the same to him. She noticed that although the glamour laid over him was heavy too, if she focused hard enough, she could see the Enzo she knew beneath it.

Isra's eyes flashed white, as she forced herself into a brief trance, before returning to normal moments later. 'Fine, so long as we split up. The best path is for you head back to the *soverin* now with Leo and Paolo, Your Majesty. Merissa and I will then go through, and Enzo and Elara last.'

Idris nodded, looking to Elara as Merissa began to glamour her. Elara saw her own hair change colour, her dress transform.

'You did well, Elara,' he said. 'There is no doubt in my mind that Ariete will come.'

Elara barely acknowledged Idris, her heart racing.

Merissa glamoured the rest of the group as quickly as possible, while the sound of the crowd swelled beyond the doors.

'Now,' Isra said, and the glamoured king walked away with Leo and Paolo, sauntering out of the throne room doors.

When he was out of sight, Isra turned. 'You're welcome,' she said to Enzo, as she linked arms with Merissa. With a final smile, they both turned and left the throne room together.

'For what?' Elara asked, as he set off towards a set of doors opposite the ones they'd entered from.

Enzo only smiled.

Elara had to hand it to them – the Aphrodeans were known as a people of beauty for a reason.

Candles floated through the sugar-pink sky as Enzo pulled her down a path that snaked out from the library. Clouds surrounded them as they descended, and Elara was struck by how surreal they looked.

'I feel that if I reached over the side, I'd be able to pluck a cloud like candyfloss,' Elara mused.

'You can, you know.'

Elara halted, looking at him incredulously.

'Stars' honest truth.' He placed a hand solemnly over his heart. She looked to him again, hesitating, then reached out tentatively. Elara gasped as her hands wrapped around the pink cloud. She pulled a wisp off, marvelling at how it settled on her palm. She looked to Enzo again who nodded, grinning.

She stuck her tongue out and delicately touched the tip of the cloud. It dissolved immediately, the taste of sweet spun sugar coating her lips. She gasped, placing the whole wisp in her mouth.

'Told you,' he said, as they continued walking. 'Want to see what else Aphrodea has to offer?'

'Hadn't we better get back?' She looked uneasily behind her.

Enzo shrugged. 'Isra bought us some time.'

It dawned on Elara then why Isra had said 'you're welcome' earlier.

'I suppose we should enjoy our last night of freedom,' she sighed. The smell of popped corn floated towards her as Enzo led her out of the clouds and into the palace gardens. She hadn't realized how large they were earlier. Hedgerows grew in tall lines, forming different paths and clearings to get lost in.

They delved into the maze and, turning a corner, found a large clearing with stalls waiting. A few people milled around, others walking down the paths further into the maze. She walked with Enzo in tow past the stalls, eyeing the offers. One stall sold wishes, glass jars trapping the swirls of gold within. Another sold protection crystals and coins. Another, siren's tears – just a few drops to sway even the most cold-hearted of souls.

Elara and Enzo continued, swaying to the upbeat music in the background as they delved further into the hedges. The commotion of the crowd seemed to grow quieter and quieter, the courtiers around them none the wiser of the events that had taken place in the ballroom. Elara's tension slipped from her as she realized how well Merissa had disguised her. There was still a restlessness, yes, but the visitors who hadn't given chase seemed to be trying to enjoy the remainder of the night too.

They slowed in another clearing with some more stalls, by some candles that, when lit, snuffed out all surrounding light. 'What a cheap party trick.' She grinned as the tiniest wisp of shadow curled around his wrist.

They reached the middle of the maze, a large space where white twinkling glow-worms were suspended through the air, making them resemble a constellated sky. Couples dressed in all shades of the kingdom danced in the centre as a band played in the corner.

'Come,' Enzo said, looking over the dancing couples. 'I want to show you something.'

She hitched her gown, giddy, as she followed him down the twisting paths.

'I'm starving,' she said as she smelled fragrant food on the night breeze.

'Shocking,' he replied and tugged her into an opening in the hedgerows, the area full of food stands. Baked cakes filled with honey and nuts were piled high, sticky with sugar. There were oven-charred breads laid next to them, hot and flat, smeared with a tomato paste and melted cheeses.

'Now this looks interesting,' she said to herself, gesturing for one for each of them. The man behind the booth smiled at them and cut them each a triangle, as Enzo passed him some coins. Elara bit into the slice and moaned with enjoyment, the warm salty tang of tomato and baked dough dancing on her tastebuds.

'You take pleasure in everything, don't you?' Enzo asked, amusement dancing on his lips.

'I do now,' she replied, taking another huge bite. 'I'm trying to live every moment of my life as though it is art.'

They reached one of the maze's exits, which verged on to the beginning of a slope paved with rose quartz.

They wandered up it and Elara gasped. Ahead, cherry blossom trees bowed over the path, their petals covering the quartz in every shade of pink imaginable. Enzo gave a small smile as he pulled her on to the flower-adorned trail that twisted higher and higher around the palace.

'Go on,' he said.

She looked around in awe as they continued to walk up the incline. 'I promised myself, after that conversation on my balcony, that I would find something to give thanks for every day. The smell of a flower . . .' She stooped down to scoop a handful of petals, inhaling deeply.

'The way that the Light dapples through my window when I wake; the way words in a book can transport me to another time, another world.' She took a breath and turned to him as she said in barely more than a whisper, 'The way your eyes look like molten gold. The way they look as if they've trapped the Light within.'

Enzo's face softened as he took both of her hands in his, pulling her closer.

Dragunflies and glitterbugs flitted and flickered, glints of silver in the heavy air. She looked around and realized they'd halted on a rooftop, the winding, steep path landing them right on a palace terrace. She looked around wildly, but she could not see anything below them. They were in the clouds.

She gaped at Enzo, who only smiled. The cast of the Light laying over the clouds sprinkled them with rose and lavender, and the scent of sweetness hung in the air.

'I brought you here because it reminded me of the day you first used your powers properly. We soared into the sky, into the clouds—'

'I remember,' she said. 'Of course I remember. I turned around and thought how happy you looked. How *handsome* happiness looked on you.'

Soft music began playing from the square far below, the sound of a love song and a muffled stream of piano drifting up with the scent of roses.

An almost pained look shot across his face as he extended his hand to her. 'Dance with me, Elara. Properly?'

Enzo rested his hands on Elara's hips, hesitant. Watching her every reaction. His eyes were steady, the topaz and honey that she found herself constantly seeking. Her breath hitched, and he held his eyes on her as she wrapped her arms around his neck. Then without saying a word, they began to move.

It was not the sinful, lust-fuelled dance that they had performed below. Instead, it was a soft swaying, an excuse to touch. The music seemed to soar up to meet them, and the duskbirds ceased their singing as night fell.

A cool breeze tickled Elara's neck as Enzo spun her, holding her with her back to him. They stayed like that, swaying as his hands gripped her front. She was aware of every part of her skin that touched his. His breath caressed the bare nape of her neck, and fire shot down her spine. She stiffened, the intensity of her feelings leaving her torn.

Elara knew that if she stayed, if she let her heart give in to that moment, the present as she knew it would disappear.

Something cataclysmic would change between them, and she would be completely at fate's whim for whatever hurt came from it. But she was sick of her destiny being in the hands of the Stars. She wanted something for herself, wanted to ignore the prophecy – just for a night.

So she looked up heavenward, felt the hard, broad presence of Enzo's body behind hers, and with a sigh, she dropped her head back against his chest.

It was a small shift, a soft gesture.

Yet the world rocked.

He moaned softly behind her, somewhere between a whisper and a prayer. The emotion in that one wordless sound crumbled all resolve in her, and she turned. Enzo's eyes were soft and open, never leaving her face, his hands still on her waist. As the ballad reached its crescendo, he took a step closer and cupped her jaw with one hand, the other now caressing her hair.

They held that moment, a millisecond that could have been a lifetime.

Time stopped as they peered into each other's souls, a question on both their lips.

A breath.

Then his lips were on hers, and sparks flew off her in showers of white.

His touch was soft but insistent. Desperate, like a pilgrim searching for a Star. All she had been searching for was in that kiss. The world finally made sense. She grabbed the back of his neck, pulling him closer, wanting to devour the very essence of him. He broke away to whisper on to her lips, and she moaned, pulling him to her, falling deeper into the kiss. She was dizzy with it, the ache and want, unsure as she kissed him how she had ever gone so many days without his lips on hers.

Suddenly, there was a loud boom. An explosion of light painted the rose sky, causing Elara to break away, startled. She looked to Enzo, lust-drunk, his lips swollen. Flashes caught her eye, cascading from the sky in droplets.

'Lightworks,' she whispered, turning back to him. 'Was that *you*?'

'I told you that this kiss would be one for the ages.' He grinned, pulling her back to him as he flicked his hand. Another kaleidoscope of sparkles painted the sky.

'You took your sweet time,' she breathed.

He gave a half-smile and murmured: 'It would have been bad luck not to, today.'

Carefully, his lips trailed her cheeks, her eyelids, her jaw as she whispered his name again, savouring how it sounded on her tongue.

'Gods, I love my name on your lips,' he whispered, before crushing his mouth to hers again. She revelled in him until she had to come up for air, gasping.

'I don't know how I didn't do this the first day I met you,' he said, the words guttural as his hands squeezed her waist.

She pressed her forehead to his. 'Me neither,' she whispered back. They both smiled into each other, sharing a breath.

'My, my, what a sight to behold.'

Elara spun at the sultry voice as Enzo swore loudly, shifting himself in front of her.

Torra appeared through the clouds, every bit the Star of lust and beauty that she was. Her hair fell to her waist, and her face – no longer covered in the mask from the Asterian ball – was even more eye-wateringly stunning. Her full lips curved into a smile, revealing perfect, pearly teeth. There was a figure behind her, still partially shrouded by the clouds and difficult to make out.

'Torra,' Enzo said coldly.

'Hi, pretty.' She gave a tinkering wave.

'Aren't you going to greet *me*, Lorenzo?' said a male voice. 'I gave you my favour after all.'

Elara's eyes widened as Eli rose from the clouds into view, a wry smile on his face. She saw Enzo's jaw clench.

'With all due respect, what do you want?' Elara demanded.

Eli tutted. 'Now, is that any way to greet a Star who came to your aid?'

'The last time I saw you, you were happy to stand by and watch as Ariete killed Sofia in front of me.'

Eli's easy smile turned razor sharp. 'Do you think Cancia was in that bathroom by accident? That I didn't *let* her heal you as I waited outside?'

'Yes, and a whole lot of good your *noble* deed did for Sofia,' Elara spat.

'If it wasn't for me,' he continued, 'you wouldn't have had the strength to illusion your death. You'd still be Ariete's captive now.'

Torra glanced at Enzo. 'Lorenzo, I wonder if you could take a walk. Elara, Eli and I need a little chat.'

A bleak laugh erupted from him. 'Not fucking likely.'

'Oh, I think you will,' Eli interjected. He cocked his head. 'Unless you want her to know?'

Enzo stilled. His reaction unnerved Elara. She brushed her way from behind him and walked forwards.

'Know what?' She looked between the two.

She could see flames in Enzo's eyes as they burned into Eli. The Star only raised an eyebrow.

'All this threatening is awfully tacky, Lorenzo. I don't like to resort to it.'

'Know *what*, Eli?' she asked again.

He pinned her with his black stare. 'His secret.'

'Enough,' Enzo snarled.

'Enzo, whatever it is, I don't want to know. What you told Eli is none of my business.'

Eli let out a sharp laugh, and Torra threw him a reproachful glance.

'Prince.' She motioned to him with a dismissive wave of her hand.

With a strained look at Elara, Enzo began to walk. 'I'll be right over there,' he said tightly, pointing to the edge of the terrace and casting another venomous glance to the two Stars.

'What in the Heavens is going on?' Elara hissed, as Enzo moved further away, out of earshot. 'And why is everyone so committed to speaking in fucking *riddles* around here?'

Torra chuckled lightly as she threaded her arm through Elara's. Eli came to her other side, towering over her.

'This conversation has been a long time coming,' Torra said, her face resigned.

'It's thanks to one of your son's priestesses that I'm in this mess.' Elara's voice held a deadly, velvet edge. 'I'd survived twenty-three years before I heard it. Do you have any idea what it's made of my life?'

'It doesn't look like it hindered much if what I walked in on is anything to go by.' Torra tried to hide a smile. She flicked a lock of hair behind her shoulder with her free hand.

'That's not—'

'Not what, Elara? Are you really going to try and lie to the Star of lust in her own kingdom? You don't think I can feel it pouring from you?'

'Let alone see how it floods your mind,' Eli muttered.

'Get out of my damn head, Eli,' she snapped back.

He shrugged, lips twitching.

364

'I don't know what you're talking about, Torra,' Elara continued.

Torra sighed. 'This isn't the road I wanted to go down with you.'

'Then answer me this. Why me? Why this prophecy? I'm to fall in love with Ariete? So why do I—'

She paused, breathing through her nose for a moment. She glanced around once to confirm Enzo was too far away to hear.

'Why do I feel the way that I do if I'm destined for another?' She paused. 'Is the prophecy even real?'

'Everything that has been foreseen for you is to happen in divine timing,' Eli replied impatiently. 'If we reveal more, it could change the course of your path irreparably.'

Elara gave a cold laugh. 'Ah, yes. The Stars always writing our fate in the skies, then doing nothing to help us. We're puppets to you.'

'*No*,' Torra said vehemently. 'The prophecy rings true. But so does what sings in your heart. I can feel it.' She lay a palm over Elara's chest. 'Look deeper, Elara.'

She moved her hand to cup Elara's face. Torra smelled of honey and almond milk, and Elara's heart ached a little to look at her beauty. The Star's gaze flicked to Eli. 'I think you're right,' she said to him.

'Right about what?' asked Elara.

Torra's eyes grew sad. 'I cannot tell. But I hope you prove us correct.' She dropped her palm.

Elara heard running footsteps and whirled, Enzo doing the same from the corner where he stood.

Merissa came into view up the path, golden hair streaming, Isra behind her.

'Time's up,' she said. 'Your glamour won't last much longer, let's . . .'

365

Her voice trailed off as her gaze flicked between Eli and Torra, finally resting on the Star. Merissa grimaced.

'Hello, Daughter,' Torra said, smiling.

Merissa's lip curled as Enzo's and Elara's eyes widened. 'Hello, Mother.'

CHAPTER FIFTY-THREE

'*Mother?!*' Elara exclaimed. Her eyes flew between the two women. 'Tell me this is some kind of joke.'

She heard Eli chuckle as utter horror grew on Merissa's face. Isra was gaping at her.

'Yes,' said Enzo, stalking over to them. 'Please tell me this is a joke, Merissa. Please tell me that I haven't been hosting the daughter of a *fucking Star* under my roof for years.'

Elara looked at Merissa, then Torra, as the glamourer paced closer to the Star – gods, how had she not seen it before? The green eyes, the honey-streaked hair. Merissa had always had an otherworldly beauty to her, how had it never registered—

'How did you never see what she was, with your magick?' Elara asked Enzo.

'It must be because she's part-mortal. Whenever my magick swept over her, it just saw the human parts of her.'

'I missed it too,' Isra said faintly.

Merissa threw her mother a look of pure loathing. 'No one knows,' she said to Elara, her voice shaky.

'But it's impossible for Stars to bear children,' Elara pressed.

'That isn't true,' Merissa said quickly, 'and my mother—'

Elara gave a sharp bark of laughter at the title.

'*Torra* isn't like the other Stars. Not like Ariete,' Merissa added, in a hushed tone.

Torra raised her chin. 'We remember a time before Ariete claimed his crown as King of Stars, a time of peace and paradise when we first fell to this world. There are some of us who want those times back.' She gave Eli a pointed look. 'And I am not the only Star who seeks the same.'

Elara's eyes narrowed. 'You?'

Eli smiled. 'Clever girl.'

'Yes, Eli *likes* you.' Torra smirked. Eli's eyes twinkled.

Elara felt an arm snake around her waist, as Enzo pulled her close.

'Something to say, Eli?' Enzo called.

'Now, now, no need for such overprotective antics,' Torra interrupted as Eli made to step forwards. 'If what Eli and I believe is true, then you – both of you – are the key to unlocking the paradise and peace that was stolen from us. If you were to bring about the demise of the Stars ... then the Heavens can once more fall to the earth.'

'When light and dark combine,' Isra breathed.

'Say I believe you,' Elara said. 'Why should I trust *him*?' She looked at Eli. 'You're Ariete's right hand.'

The god grinned. 'What I am is a very convincing liar, sweetheart. Let's cast your mind back again to when I saved your ungrateful life.'

'Should I kiss your feet?' Elara retorted sweetly. 'I trust you as much as I'd trust a pit of serpents not to bite me,' she added, her voice hardening.

'Then you're wiser than most,' he crooned back.

Torra inclined her head, unbothered by the exchange. 'I believe that Ariete will come to Helios. I believe it may start a war. But I also believe that you have the power to vanquish him.' She looked to Enzo. 'Both of you.'

Enzo looked over the goddess warily. 'And how will you help?'

'I cannot interfere just yet.'

Elara shook her head. 'Of course you can't,' she muttered.

'*But*,' Torra said sharply, 'should you kill Ariete, I will serve you.'

'You, a Star, would bow to me?'

'Who else would there be more powerful to lead, if not a Starkiller?'

Elara heard the sound of voices coming up the petal-covered path. 'We should go,' she said to Enzo. He nodded tightly, and they walked to Isra and Merissa, who Elara regarded warily.

'One more thing.'

Elara didn't realize Eli had followed them until he bent in behind her so his charm enveloped her. It now felt like soft rain on a cloudy day, rather than the maelstrom she had felt at Lukas's coronation. Elara fought back a shiver.

'There is a light within your darkness,' he said. 'All you need do is find it.'

With that, he pulled away as Torra looked on. 'Good luck,' the goddess said, as starlight began to form around her, and Eli too. The god of cunning gave one last long look to Elara before they disappeared in a flash of light.

'El,' Merissa began, 'I didn't—'

'Let's get back to Helios,' Elara said quickly, unable to look the demi-Star in the eye.

CHAPTER FIFTY-FOUR

When they tumbled back through the *soverin*, Elara kept moving, walking past the mirrors, which now seemed duller in the evening light. *Keep walking*, she told herself. Away from Aphrodea, from the Stars, from everything.

Someone grabbed her hand, and she turned, expecting it to be Enzo, but it was Merissa. 'Please can we talk?' she said.

Elara deflated. 'Of course.'

She looked at Enzo, who was watching Merissa with a hawk's eye. 'Try not to miss the celebrations, princess,' he said lightly.

Isra looked amused. 'Oh yes, we've arrived at the perfect time.'

Elara didn't wait to ask what they meant, instead leading Merissa silently out of the *lucirium* and back up the stairs to her own room.

She maintained the silence until her door was firmly closed behind them, before turning.

'Who are you?' she demanded.

'I am everything that I was before,' Merissa said hoarsely. 'I swear to you, Elara.'

'So, what? It was just coincidence that you, the daughter of a Star, were assigned to aid me here?'

'My mother asked about you,' Merissa admitted. 'When you first arrived. She knew everything – your prophecy, how you survived Ariete's death blow. It was divine timing that I was already working at the palace.'

'I don't believe you,' Elara said, although her conviction was already waning. 'Why work in Idris's employ if you have the blood of a Star within you? Surely you could live in the Heavens if you wished?'

Merissa shook her head. 'No,' she said vehemently. 'I couldn't. Stars can have children. But they don't. And there is a good reason why – because of the weakness that it provides, the potential target. My identity has been kept hidden my whole life. And I would never be accepted amongst the Stars.'

Elara allowed the words to soak in. 'But surely your mother could have given you a home, riches . . .'

'There is a lot about my childhood you don't know,' Merissa said quietly. 'A lot that I do not feel ready to share. Torra is a Star. Not a terrible one, no. But it certainly didn't make her a good mother. Everything I have in life, I worked for myself.'

'Do you . . . do you have any Star magick?'

Merissa raised her palm, and a faint stream of rose starlight shone weakly. Elara's eyes widened.

'That's about it. And a little charm from my mother and brother – a magick of lust and love, that I refuse to use. And my glamour magick from an Aphrodean father that I never knew.'

'Brother,' Elara mused, then gasped. 'Holy shit. Lias is your brother.'

'Half-brother,' she replied coolly. And Elara knew not to

press further. Elara looked at Merissa, truly taking in the half-goddess – her eyes open and pleading, her hands clasped.

'Is there anything else you have to tell me?' she asked.

'It was my mother's blood that I gave Enzo for you to drink.' Merissa bit her lip. 'And that's it. There's nothing more about me that you don't already know.'

Elara sighed, and then without another thought, crushed Merissa to her. Merissa froze, before softening against her. 'I'm sorry,' Elara said into her hair.

'So am I,' Merissa replied.

When they pulled away, Merissa was wiping her eyes.

'Now what's this about tonight's celebration?' Elara said, eyes twinkling.

Merissa gave a watery smile. 'On the summer solstice, when the Light begins to dim, there's often a soiree in the throne room. Although the D'Oros always swear they loathe the Dark, they still seem taken by it on this night. For one night they give in to sin.'

There was a soft knock at the door. Elara answered it, and was greeted by Isra, a bottle of honeywine in her hand.

'Ready for a night of darkness and debauchery?' she asked.

Elara grinned. 'Always.'

Merissa was just applying the finishing touches to Elara's new outfit, as Elara wrapped up telling her and Isra about the kiss in the clouds of Aphrodea.

The glamourer sighed dreamily. 'So, do you think it's going to happen tonight?'

Isra rolled her eyes. 'I think this is Mer's very delicate way of asking, are you finally going to fuck?'

Elara snickered 'Skies, I want to. He's so—' She moaned for emphasis.

Merissa flashed her a wicked smile. 'Don't *ever* let him know that I said this, but if there is one thing about that man, it's that you can just tell he knows how to satisfy a woman. It's in his walk.'

Heat bloomed through Elara.

'Gods, Merissa,' Isra groaned, 'please don't tell him. He doesn't need the ego boost.' She rose from the bed and drifted to Elara's wardrobe to scan the dresses hanging inside it. She was already dressed in a stunning tangerine dress that left little to the imagination, and Elara knew the whole court's eyes would be glued to her.

'What's wrong?' Merissa asked as she noticed Elara remained quiet.

'It's just, I've thought a lot about Sofia today. How proud she'd be of me. How much fun she would have had with the two of you. She would have loved you.' She willed her tears away as she looked at the ceiling. 'Especially Isra,' she said, and laughed.

Isra's hazel eyes livened with amusement. 'She is with you, El. She's always with you.'

Merissa took Elara's hands, pulling her up to inspect her fully.

'Dear skies, this may be some of my best work.'

When Elara turned, Isra let out a low whistle. 'Are you sure you don't want to be my date? I'm much prettier than Enzo.'

Elara laughed, turning to the full-length mirror.

She hardly recognized herself. She'd never worn a dress like this before. Sheer panels the colour of emeralds slid down her legs and pooled like molten lava at her feet. A slit so high that you could see the curve of her hip crept up a thigh, showing the length of her tanned leg. Two thin straps graced her shoulders, the neckline plunging dramatically. Merissa had slicked her ebony hair up into a high ponytail, a golden cuff placed at the base of it, its length swinging to her waist. The look left her face severely open, showing every sharp plane of her high cheekbones, smoked kohl winging her eyes out felinely, her lips shimmering like diamonds, ripe for kissing.

Her eyes rested on the peek of golden underwear visible at the top of the dress's slit.

'Yes,' Merissa said, her eyes following Elara's. 'I think you're going to have to lose those.'

Isra howled and Elara pushed her off the bed, as she went to the bathroom and did as Merissa advised, nerves thrilling through her as to how the night may unfold.

CHAPTER FIFTY-FIVE

Elara's heart pounded with anticipation as she walked arm-in-arm with Isra and Merissa. With her chin high, she stilled at the top of the grand staircase, assessing the scene below. Women in flimsy fabric milled around, the sensuous thump of music feeding the dark spell that seemed cast below Elara. She saw a couple against a wall, kissing passionately; elsewhere, a woman had her legs wrapped around the waist of a tall, muscled soldier, her dress hitched around her hips. The shadows within Elara twirled, longing to feel the pleasure set before her.

She turned to Merissa, whose eyes were already uncharacteristically dark, then to Isra, whose cool gaze was surveying the scene below with a mixture of delight and desire. The three slowly began to sashay down the grand staircase, noticing with satisfaction the heads whipping their way.

Soldiers and courtiers alike snagged their gazes on Elara's bare leg, Isra's curves and Merissa's new suggestion of a dress – a far cry from the more demure gown she'd worn in Aphrodea. A handsome soldier, shirtless with his muscles rippling, came up to Isra and offered his hand.

'*Move*,' she scoffed, dancing away from his grasp. Elara stifled a laugh.

She could hear the music reverberating louder, so deep she could feel it pulsing through her. Its beat was different to the music in Aphrodea, a slow tempo with violins and drums that only added to the anticipation moving through her body.

As she reached the throne room doors, knowing Enzo must be waiting behind them, her pulse roared in her ears. From this point forward, the true debauchery would begin.

The guard by the door, his mouth gaping ajar, coughed. 'After you, ladies.'

The door swung open.

Enzo was sprawled on his throne, his jacket discarded and his shirt unbuttoned low. Commanding energy radiated from his fire-lit eyes, hazy with ambrosia, his crown tipped on his head of midnight-black hair. He was talking to Leo over his shoulder, who was exhaling pink-coloured smoke from his mouth, sucking a pipe indolently. A woman with olive skin, blue-black hair and deep brown eyes was talking and laughing with them.

'Now, *there's* my date,' Isra murmured, her eyes transfixed on the lovely woman.

'You didn't tell me you were courting someone,' Elara whispered.

'It's casual,' she replied, her eyes roving up and down the woman's body.

Elara's eyes narrowed as someone else slunk over to Enzo's side – Raina, the chestnut-haired girl from her first night at the palace. She started to vie for Enzo's attention but, to Elara's relief, she rapidly tired of being ignored and walked off.

Steeling her nerves, Elara began to walk, Merissa and Isra falling into step. They took their time down the long aisle of the throne room. Elara barely registered the sweet scent of the smoke that filled the air and the bodies writhing in the shadows of the room, dancing and grinding, or moving and moaning in nooks behind gauze sheets that lined the cavernous room's walls. Her eyes never left Enzo as she took her time, willing him to look at her.

She saw his body go rigid as though he sensed her before he saw her. His gaze flew to her. They locked eyes, the cup of ambrosia in his hand falling to the floor as a predatory look came over his face. His lips parted. Leo turned to see what had caused Enzo's commotion and laid eyes on Merissa. He choked on the smoke he was inhaling, spluttering a cough. Elara bit back a smile.

She didn't notice exactly when Isra and Merissa peeled off, only that she was suddenly alone, steps away from Enzo's throne, close enough to smell the intoxicating amber scent that followed him everywhere. He straightened in his chair, a muscle in his jaw ticking.

'Elara.' The words were low, said in a voice she didn't recognize, and her name uttered by that wicked mouth of his sent a coil of heat from her stomach to her core.

'Prince.' Her reply was barely a breath.

His jaw clenched, and she saw his hand curl against the arm of the chair as he leaned forwards. 'I thought that maybe you wouldn't attend tonight.'

She tilted her head. 'Did you miss me?'

His gaze trailed from the pools of her chiffon skirt, right up the slit of her gown. He moved in his throne and met her gaze, his usual charm and composure sliding on like a mask.

'Always.' He smiled that same lion's smile as he stood.

He extended a hand to her, his sleeves rolled to show his broad muscled arms, taut with tension. 'Come with me,' he commanded.

She leaned into him. 'I think I've changed my mind about taking orders from you.'

A low sound escaped him before he replied. 'You have seconds, princess,' he said quietly, 'before the very little restraint I have disappears and I decide I don't mind an audience.'

She took his hand, nerves thrilling through her, as Enzo led her to the shadows. Parting sheer gauze, anticipation threatened to engulf her at what lay in front of her. Furs lined the small compartment, one of many that had lined the walls of the throne room, just for the night. A low divan sat at the centre, food spread on platters on a table beside it. A large glass pipe was positioned near the seats. At one with the solstice, her dark side taking over, she turned to Enzo who followed in behind her, pulling the gauze closed. She pushed him down on the divan, and he laughed softly.

She joined him, straddling him, and with a moan, his lips crashed against hers. He was hot – feverish. She revelled in his heat as his fire-touched fingers ran down her bare back. His tongue claimed hers, sweeping her mouth. She revelled in him, aware that in a few moments, Enzo would be able to completely unravel her.

He wrapped his hand around the length of her ponytail. 'I like this,' he murmured against her neck, pulling it sharply for emphasis so her nape remained bare. Desire rushed through Elara instantly, longing for more. She ground against him, feeling him hard underneath her, and he rumbled in response. She remained there, her hair tight in his fist as he licked and kissed her neck, her moans filling the space. Then, slowly, as though he had all the time in the world, he let go, sitting up further on the divan as she remained straddling him.

'You look sinful.' He reached for the pipe.

She snickered. 'I never was that devout.'

Enzo wet his lips, looking at hers. 'Do you want some?' he asked, offering her the pipe, his voice low. Her mind was already hazy from the smoke and liquor, and she found herself nodding, biting her lip.

'Aphrosmoke,' he said, his eyes black. 'Some claim it's an aphrodisiac. Not that I think I will ever need that around you.' He sucked on the pipe deeply, his eyes never leaving her face, and she watched his lips.

'Open your mouth, princess,' he said through a held breath, his rough thumb brushing her lips open. Then he brought his own a hair's breadth from her and blew the sweet smoke into her mouth. She inhaled it hungrily, tasting a hint of candyfloss on the smoke, the act of intimacy setting flames to her as the sweet vapour dissipated quickly into her bloodstream. The taste reminded her of the clouds in Aphrodea.

The world fell away, the only feeling her pulse pounding from her core to her heart and back, driving pleasure through her veins. She moaned, arching her back as she let her head fall. Alive with carnality and uninhibited courage from the aphrosmoke, her eyes fell on the nearest platter of food. Enzo followed her gaze, seeing the chocolate-covered gild-berries there.

'I remembered how much you loved them,' he murmured as he reached to pluck one from the platter. 'How I watched you eat one, those beautiful lips of yours sucking and swirling around it as you looked at me.' He drew closer, voice low. 'I remember thinking to myself that I had never been so envious of a piece of fruit before.' He raised the small fruit between them.

Holding his stare, she licked the gildberry he'd extended and moaned in pleasure, desire coursing through her at the flavour and his words. He rumbled his approval, his hands roaming over her body, exploring every inch with greed. Then, steel in her silver eyes and hazed with the drug, she took the gildberry from him and sank her mouth around two of his fingers, sucking the melted chocolate off them.

He cursed under his breath. 'Elara,' he pleaded, need heavy in his voice, as his thumb stroked her hipbone. Then he stilled.

'Elara Bellereve. Please, Stars, tell me you're wearing underwear.'

She gave a knowing smile as she raised a brow. 'Why? What can you feel?'

His neck strained as he let out a long breath, looking to the ceiling. 'Your plan all those months ago is working. You're trying to fucking kill me.'

She laughed, reaching to kiss him, but he stilled her.

Gently, far more gently than she expected, he kissed her forehead. Then, to her disbelief, he lifted her off him, setting her back on the divan as he knelt before her.

With a deep breath, he reached for the golden crown atop his head.

'Elara, before anything more happens between us, I want to give you this. My crown.' He said it so quietly that she had to strain her ears. He placed the crown reverently on her head as a rush of laughter escaped her, her head swimming from the smoke. She stopped when she saw the sincerity in his gaze.

Elara's breath quickened as his fingers trailed from her ankle up to her calf, maintaining eye contact with her the whole time. She felt a lick of fire as magick rippled from him, following the same path his fingers had. She shuddered, leaning back. Her dress fell in such a way that a leg was exposed by the hip-high slit to the cool air of the compartment.

'Do you know how good you look wearing my crown, Elara?'

Her chest heaved as she watched his hand skim to her inner thigh, those lapping flames running a little higher.

'It suits me better than you, I know,' she teased, smirking even as her stomach flipped, every sense heightened.

He brushed his knuckles down a nerve on the soft part of her inner thigh. She sucked in a breath, tensing. The corner of his mouth twitched upward.

'It does. Keep it on. I've always wanted to know what a queen tastes like.'

He pressed a soft kiss to her knee, and she let her head fall back, her eyes fluttering closed.

'Now, are you going to finally follow orders?'

Elara's eyes flew back open. 'That depends. Are you going to make it worth my while?'

His tongue ran along his teeth. 'I'm counting on it.'

'Then, yes.'

His lips moved further up her thigh. She held her breath, wanting no feeling more than his lips and tongue on her.

'Open your legs wider for me.'

Elara obliged, settling further into her seat.

'Now take your hand, and touch yourself for me. Just like I'm sure you did many a time after our training sessions.'

He sat back on his haunches, arrogance playing on his lips. That alone had her biting her own as she followed his order, thinking of the times she *had* touched herself beneath the cover of darkness, always his hands replacing hers in her fantasies.

Breath racking with every movement, she trailed her hand down, delving beneath the opening in her dress. With no underwear on, the contact of her finger against her sex had her stifling a moan, and Enzo's eyes darkened as he watched the shadow of movement behind the sheer material.

'That's it, princess,' he encouraged. 'Show me what I'm missing.'

The slide of her hand satiated only part of the need that raked through her, and she tried to chase it, tried to follow the pleasure. But it was no good. She wanted Enzo. She made a sound of frustration.

'Do you need a little help?' he asked, as he leaned forwards, enveloping her senses in amber as he braced each side of her chair and licked a trail from her collarbone to her ear.

'Yes,' she managed to pant.

Enzo covered her hand with his, before pressing firmly. She moaned as he dragged their hands in sync along her sensitive flesh.

'Gods, I've dreamed about tasting this pretty little cunt,' he whispered, before pulling away.

Elara gaped as he smirked, pressing a kiss to her neck before lowering himself back down her body again. He removed Elara's hand, looking up at her, his mouth now hovering over her sex. 'Now say please,' he whispered against her.

She jolted as his breath caressed her, then arched as his tongue traced the material covering her flesh. She moaned as she felt the wet heat of it through the fabric, drawing a tantalizing circle around her. He sucked, eyes locked on her, and she swore, convinced she could climax from that alone. She had never in her life felt such desire and desperation, every nerve in her body pulsing.

'I'm waiting,' he murmured, as he drew his mouth off her.

Desire burned through any pride she had. One more swirl of his tongue was all it would take. 'Pl—'

A rip through the gauze cut her sentence short.

In an instant, Elara vanished as King Idris strode into the small space. Enzo looked around in confusion, then anger as the king sneered at the compartment and at Enzo, who had swiftly stood.

'Sorry to interrupt whatever *this*,' he gestured around to

the scene before him, 'is.' He frowned. 'Lorenzo, you and I need to talk.'

'Not now, Father,' he snapped, standing and scanning the room.

'You will listen, and you will listen well,' the king replied in a low snarl. With another desperate look at the compartment walls, Enzo turned fully to his father.

'Out with it then,' Enzo said coldly, smoothing his hair and putting his hands in his pockets.

'Ariete intends to march for Helios.'

'What?' Enzo breathed.

Idris nodded. 'He cannot use his starlight to simply descend, because of Leyon's wards around our borders. But he can physically enter. Word from our spies reached me now – he is calling a Star's Summit. And knowing the King of Stars, whether they agree with the breach in their patron kingdom agreement or not, he will come. I'd say we have no more than two days before he sets out.'

Elara measured her breath as she remained caught in her seam of reality.

'Although, there is something you should know.'

Enzo waited.

'In his rage, when he discovered he had been duped by Elara, Ariete destroyed the Asterian palace. There is nothing left of it. And no ruler. Apparently King Lukas disappeared weeks ago. The kingdom is now without a monarch. In utter turmoil. There is no one to succeed the throne, since most with ties to the crown were killed when Elara escaped.' The King gave a small smile as Elara's vision blurred with tears. 'So Asteria is in chaos. And ripe for the taking. Our troops have already culled scores of their measly army stationed at the border, without a ruler.'

Tears began falling from Elara's eyes as she shook silently.

She knew her army. Had seen many of the soldiers each day within the palace's grounds.

'Why?'

'Why?' Idris laughed. 'Because Asterians are vermin, Lorenzo. You know, once you shared the same sentiment. Don't tell me you've fallen for the princess's darkcraft?'

'Of course not,' Enzo snapped.

'Because I noticed how you looked at her in Aphrodea.'

She saw Enzo's face morph into disgust, even as her heart pounded. 'You told us to put on an act. We did. I still can't stand the Asterian.'

'I hope so, Lorenzo,' Idris replied. 'Because she is your enemy. I hope you never forget it.'

He left, Enzo's stance tense as he turned slowly.

'Elara?' he called.

But she remained silent, cloaked in her magick.

She heard a sigh and soft footsteps as he left the compartment. The moment he did, she collapsed, her illusion and hopes shattered around her.

CHAPTER FIFTY-SIX

Elara ran, sobbing, through the darkened corridors, illusions wrapped back around her, Enzo's crown clutched against her gown.

The sound of sensual music sickened her now as she tried to shake the drowsy feeling from her mind. Her people. Her kingdom.

While she had been soaking up the Light and running around with princes, they were being killed. Left to fend for themselves. Not just her court, but her citizens too. No ruler, no protector. They had been abandoned. By her.

She clutched her stomach as she reached her room, fumbling with the doorknob as she slammed it shut behind her. Collapsing on to the bed, she thought of everyone she had left behind – everyone who had trusted her. She should have stayed. Stayed in Asteria, even if that meant being Ariete's pet, rather than allow this fate to befall her subjects.

There was a knock on the door, and she froze. Held her breath, trying to quieten her sobs. But it came again.

She knew who it was before she even opened the door.

Wiping her eyes, still clutching his crown, she opened it.

The sight nearly ripped her heart in two. Enzo was standing before her, leaning against the door, anguish on his face. His shirt was rumpled, his curls in disarray.

'El,' he said, making to come in.

'Enzo,' she bit out firmly, blocking his path. He looked where her arm barred the door then stared at her, confused.

'Enzo, what happened back there, it can't happen again.'

'El—'

'No. Listen. Please,' she added more softly, the walls around her heart caving in on themselves. 'What happened in there,' she began again, 'should never have happened in the first place.' She drew herself up, squaring her shoulders. 'I've been selfish. Unforgivably selfish. To everyone around me. To my people, my country. Even to you.'

She swallowed down the lump in her throat.

'El, if you heard me and my father – you know I didn't mean any of what I said, and Asteria—'

'I know,' she said. 'But the truth is still the truth. We *are* enemies, Enzo. Your father has just admitted to killing members of my army. He wants to take Asteria for himself, and you would be powerless to stop him.'

Enzo went to argue, but she ploughed on. 'I have allowed my heart to lead me rather than my head. And people have died because of that. I am a queen first and I should have accepted my fate, rather than drag innocent people in by trying to change its course.'

'Elara, fuck the—'

'Stop.' She stilled his lips with a shaking hand. He studied her silently, a dark look in his gaze as she felt the burn of his stare. 'I'm sorry. I'm sorry for making out that this was anything other than a temporary alliance.'

'Elara, what are you doing?' The words were black, creeping

into her heart. She swallowed, seeing his fist clench against the wall, his jaw twitch.

'I'm sorry for involving you, when we both know I'm destined for a Star.' She held his crown in front of him. 'I think you should take this.'

Enzo looked at it, then at her, eyes glowing like embers. He pushed himself off the wall, smelling of bonfires and amber. He took the crown from her grasp. For a moment, Elara saw the urge to say something flit across his face. He brought his fist to his mouth, halting himself.

'As you wish, princess,' he replied at last, his voice quiet, his smile strained. He left then, leaving her sagging against her doorframe. He didn't spare her a second glance as he walked off down the corridor.

The moment she saw him disappear around the corner, she sank to the floor, her whole body racked with grief. She didn't know how long she stayed there, just that eventually Merissa was standing before her.

Her friend didn't say anything, only picked Elara off the floor, shut the door and helped her change. She gently tucked her into bed, sliding in beside her. She didn't ask why Elara was crying, didn't assume. Just stroked Elara's hair, before eventually falling asleep next to her.

Elara stayed awake though, watching the empty chair that Enzo had slept in every night as she had healed, knowing that nothing would be the same.

CHAPTER FIFTY-SEVEN

The next morning, it was Leo who appeared at her door, and said that he'd be taking over her training rigorously until Ariete arrived in Helios. It felt like she had been taken back months, to the last time she and Enzo had stopped speaking. Elara hated that she was relieved to be with the general, and hated that she was also disappointed. She had no right to be.

She blinked at the brightness of Sol as she rode beside Leo in silence. Enzo's absence was a cold and empty vacuum, and she had to bite her cheek to quell her welling tears. Leo looked to her as they reached the familiar path that led into the forest, where she had first trained with Enzo.

'Come,' he said gently, slowing their horses to a patch of shade among the trees. 'Elara, Enzo told me what happened last night.'

'Did you give the order?' she asked. 'To kill my border's army?'

'No,' Leo said. 'I swear I didn't. Idris gave the order directly to the troops stationed there.'

Elara nodded.

Leo wet his lips. 'Maybe you'll think I'm speaking out of

turn, but I don't care – why are you doing this?' he asked. 'Pushing Enzo away? A blind man could see that you don't want this.'

'It doesn't matter what I want. It matters what will happen if I ignore sense.'

'I know for a fact that Enzo does not care about the prophecy,' Leo said. 'Nor does he see you as the enemy any more. I see him with you. I know him.'

'What does it matter? Even without the prophecy, I have a kingdom to try and salvage, people who are dying because of me. Because I ran away.'

'Well, you *were* technically kidnapped,' Leo responded lightly.

Elara made a derisive noise. 'But I had the chance to return to my people. To run back. Stay. And fight. And I didn't. Because I'm a fucking coward. And a selfish one at that. I told myself that it was because I must be trained as a weapon. Only then could I return to take back my throne. But I was lying. I wanted to stay.' She took a deep breath. 'So you know what? It's only right that I'm destined for someone else. Enzo's heart is too good for me anyway.'

Leo let out a slow breath and leaned back to look at her against the Light.

'Elara, do you know how long I have known Enzo?'

'Since you were boys,' she affirmed.

'Exactly. Since we were boys. I have seen him grow up. I've seen him with women. I have seen him get bored week after week with whichever new girl has been on his arm. I've also seen the emptiness in his eyes. How no one seemed to possess whatever it is he was looking for.' He paused then, growing pensive. 'I've heard him speak of love and witnessed him carving it into marble. I've seen the need in his eyes for something deeper.' Leo huffed out a laugh. 'And then, you whirled in. A storm of smoke and shadows. And I don't think I'll ever forget it.'

'Forget what?' Elara breathed.

'The way his eyes lit up that first time you spoke to him, the barb so ready on your tongue.' He chuckled at the memory. 'The way he admitted to me not long after that he had never encountered someone that he felt like he knew instantly, deeply. Someone who could see right through him, when usually it was him doing the seeing. Elara, just answer me this. When the world is stripped bare, what is it you seek? Because I know what Enzo seeks. Who Enzo seeks.'

He turned his face to Elara then, his warm brown eyes leaving her soul bare. 'He looks for you in every room.'

Elara's stomach plummeted as her mind flew back to when she was lying next to Enzo in the woodlands. She fought to crush the rising in her heart, both panic and elation, the magnanimity of what she had fallen into threatening to overcome her. There was a long silence until she raised her eyes, filled with tears, to look at Leo.

'I look for him too.'

Elara managed to keep avoiding Enzo. She focused on the impending threat of Ariete, allowing Leo to work her through merciless drills, wielding the duskglass blade like the lethal weapon it was. And still, Leo's words weighed heavier and heavier on her heart. So Elara did what she did best; she pushed it all down, cramming that box within her shut, feeding her darkness.

When she wasn't with Leo, Elara pestered Merissa while they worked together in the kitchens, imploring her to show her how she glamoured. Elara wanted to understand every tip and trick Merissa knew for her own illusions.

It was on one of those days that Leo barrelled into the kitchen, eyes wild. Elara's hands froze in the dough she was kneading as Merissa sifted flour over it.

'It's Ariete, isn't it?' she breathed, her hands going slack.

Leo nodded. 'He held the Star's Summit. The Stars refused to bend their rule – Leyon staunchly. So Ariete told them that he would enter Helios, whether it started a celestial war or not. He marches for Helios tomorrow.'

'And where is Leyon now?'

'Screaming bloody murder in the Heavens. He's demanding the Stars commit a coup against their king. He wouldn't dare try to fight his brother alone.'

'Training, *now*,' Elara said, brushing her hands on her apron as she stalked out of the kitchens. 'Merissa, I need you there too.'

Merissa frowned as she hurried after Leo and Elara.

They walked down a quiet corridor. 'Does Enzo know?' Elara asked Leo.

'Yes, and he's hunting for you. I saw him storming down the great hallway moments before I found you.'

'Then we need to train outside of the palace.'

'Elara, we have just received word that Ariete will be here tomorrow. Enzo is going to be incensed if we leave and he can't find you.'

Elara let out a long breath. 'I know. I know this isn't fair to him. Or you. Or anyone. But if I see him, I am going to be distracted, and I *can't* be when I meet my fate with Ariete. Please tell me you understand?'

Leo rubbed a hand over his face. 'Fine. But if I see him before we leave, I won't lie to him, Elara.'

They made their way swiftly through the palace, Elara

taking routes now familiar to her as they finally reached the path that would lead to the forest.

'Merissa, I want you to watch,' she said as they climbed. 'Keep an eye out for any spots I leave open, any places that Ariete could strike.'

And then, as they reached flat ground, she drew her dagger from its familiar place by her thigh, struck out at Leo, and they began to dance.

Once they'd finished, Elara traipsed straight to her rooms, welcoming the ache of her muscles and the pounding of her head. The hour was late upon her return, the palace quiet with sleep. As she made to turn the corner of the corridor, she halted. Enzo was slumped against her door, a weary look on his face. She bit her lip, retreating as quietly as she could.

She couldn't do this.

His face alone set her heart thundering, the pure despair that was engraved on it – the worry. *Coward*, a voice in her head whispered. It was right; she was.

Tiptoeing away, she circled back around to a corridor that led to the palace gardens, crimson-tinted by the Helion night sky.

She eased herself up the rose trellis that crawled up her side of the palace – thinking of the times she would sneak back to her room in Asteria. She scaled the wall with ease, landing softly on her balcony.

But as she crossed her bedroom floor she hesitated. Elara knew that Enzo was still on the other side, the usual candle-light that seeped through the small gap at the foot of her door obscured by a shadow. She knew she shouldn't. That any thought of him was bound to open the floodgates that she had worked very hard to force shut over the last few days. And yet, her heart sighed as she made her way to the door. She sank against it, sliding to the floor, closing her eyes as her back pressed against the wood. Perhaps, just this once, she would allow herself this weakness. A tear rolled from her closed eyes of its own volition. Perhaps just this once, she would allow herself to be close to him, only a door between them.

As sleep gently embraced Elara, she fell into her own dreams. She was in Enzo's studio. Yet in the usual, peacefully white calm of the space, there lay a gaping hole in the floor. She walked towards the yawning chasm, a storm raging in the dark depths below it, an abyss that seemed endless.

A ball of fire, hotter and brighter than even the Light, burned from across the chasm, and she felt with an icy certainty that there was another, shining silver, behind her. Then she heard screaming – ragged and desperate cries, shouted across the void. And there, hanging from the lip of the abyss, trying to claw his way out of it, was Enzo, his fingers slipping inch by inch.

Elara woke up dripping in cold sweat, her back and neck stiff against the door. She took a few deep breaths, reminding herself that her dream had been one of her own creation. She rose shakily, squinting over at the open balcony doors. The deep red gloom filtering through confirmed that it was the darkest part of the night. She looked over at the door, but strong yellow candlelight was again seeping unhindered through the gap. Enzo was gone.

Pacing the room and peeling her sticking gown from her clammy body, she decided to head to the palace baths, craving the calm of the peace, the water and the darkness.

CHAPTER FIFTY-EIGHT

In the middle of the night, Elara had the bath house to herself, the quiet sound of indigo crickets humming outside and the dusky walls reminding her of the twilight of her homeland. She breathed a sigh, releasing one shuddering breath after another as she sank into the water until her heart rate returned to normal. She could think here, the sound of running water soothing her frayed nerves. However, her thoughts immediately flew back to Enzo. She tried to quash them, but without any distraction, she finally had to face them.

She was in love with him. And not only that, when he had kissed her in the clouds, she had felt a lightning bolt of power that she could not deny. It had felt familiar. A quiet recognition. As though after all this searching, her soul had said, '*Oh, there you are.*'

It was the words of her prophecy, now uttered by two separate seers, that fell so heavy on her. And the responsibilities that awaited her. The fact that her struggles hadn't even really begun. War was looming. Ariete was near. And she was no closer to reclaiming her throne, helping her people. As she found herself caught up in her own tangled thoughts, she heard the distant sound of the door to the bath house opening.

'Shit,' she whispered, looking around wildly for a place to hide herself. *There*. A sheet of a waterfall hiding an alcove behind it beckoned to her. She swam to it as quietly as possible, ducking under the flow and sinking down to the heated bench. She strained her ears, unable to hear much over the rushing sound of water.

She peered into the shadows and saw a tall figure undressing, distorted in the stream of water. Her cheeks heated with embarrassment at the prospect of a man being here with her. Losing sight of the figure, her breath quickened as she tried to quietly swim further back into the hidden nook. A few moments of silence passed. Then suddenly, the curtain of water parted, and her heart stopped.

'Well, princess, isn't this a pleasant surprise?'

Enzo.

A slow grin spread over his face as he stepped out of the waterfall and slicked his curls back. His muscles rippled as droplets of water cascaded down him. He took in her wet hair and shoulders exposed to the air with a hungry smile. She sank further into the water, anxiety pumping through her body. She composed her face into a scowl.

'Well, this is inappropriate,' she muttered. 'But I'd expect nothing less. I mean, why *wouldn't* you be here in a bath house in the middle of the night while I'm completely naked?'

He chuckled. 'You say that as though you're not also here . . . in the middle of the night . . . when *I'm* completely naked.'

Elara tried extremely hard not to concentrate on his broad bare chest but failed. She'd hardly heard what he'd said, so focused was she on the rivulets of water making their way down his bronze torso and disappearing into the surface that only reached his hips. With visible effort, she refrained from looking further down, and glared at him instead.

'What did you say?'

'I said,' his grin widened even more, 'why are you in here at this time?'

She shifted along the bench as she sighed, drawing circles in the water, and finally decided to at least unburden some truth.

'I had a nightmare.'

He looked at her with concern as she tilted her head back, looking up at the paintings of clouds and constellations that lined the ceiling.

'So I came here, where it feels like home.' She looked at him for a second too long. 'You?'

'I often come here to clear my head when I can't sleep,' he offered quietly. 'So every night this week.' She raised her eyebrows. 'Although I wasn't expecting a wet, naked woman to be waiting for me, one who just so happened to have her legs wrapped around me a few nights ago.' He smirked, but there was a faint strain to it. Elara rolled her eyes and splashed water at him. 'Are we just going to completely gloss over that, by the way?'

'Over what?' Elara quipped back. 'The fact that I'm wet and naked or what happened at the solstice?'

He dragged his gaze down, and although she knew he couldn't see anything below the water in the dim light, she crossed her arms and legs anyway, feeling far too exposed.

'I meant what happened at the solstice,' he said, coming closer. 'But now that you mention it, I'm far more occupied with what's beneath the water.'

'Pig.' She splashed him again, and he laughed. She held on to it, wondering how long it would be before he stopped laughing at her jokes. 'What do we need to speak about? I've already told you how I feel. We should never have gotten tangled up in this. It's already painful enough. It will only get worse.'

Her mind flicked to the words she had overheard the king saying, and they boiled through her veins. She swam further away from him even as the words twisted in her stomach. She bit her lip to stop herself from caving, from wanting to kiss him again.

'So you're saying,' he said, standing tall again in the water, 'that this is over?'

She nodded tightly. 'We need to stop. I was wrong to ignore the prophecy, to think we could be anything more than friends.'

'I've been looking for you all day,' he said, his voice low. 'You've been avoiding me. Is that what a *friend* does?'

'I've been training so I'm as prepared as possible for when Ariete arrives.'

He moved closer towards her, and she saw his eyes flash as she made out his face more clearly in the gloom. 'Don't lie to me, Elara,' he bit out. 'And more importantly, stop lying to yourself.'

Indignation rose in her. 'I'm not,' she hissed. 'We agreed to be allies. The last few weeks were a mistake – just us getting carried away from being around each other all the time.' *Coward, coward, coward*, the voice in her head screamed.

Enzo let out a cold laugh, shaking his head. He turned, making his way back to the waterfall. Then he halted, swearing under his breath as she held hers, sadness rearing its slow head at seeing him leave. He spun, droplets of water flying through the air.

'It was *more than that*,' he snarled. 'And I know you felt it too.'

He waded back to her, standing centimetres from her, the

water swirling around him, making him look like the ocean Star Scorpius himself as anger sparked in his eyes.

'Have the last few months meant *nothing* to you?' His chest was heaving, fury lacing every word. 'I stayed with you every night. I showed you my art. I gave you my *crown*. Doesn't that tell you everything? Gods, Elara.' He shook his head, looking up to the heavens. He tilted his head down. 'Do you really not feel it?' His breath was a warm caress on her lips.

'What?' she whispered.

His voice was guttural, almost broken as he replied: 'This endless *need*.'

And with a moan, his mouth was on hers.

It was nothing like their other kisses. This was Enzo in his full glory. His tongue forced her mouth open, and she yielded to him, sighing as his hands wrapped in her wet, silky hair. Every part of her body was on fire, and she gripped the back of his neck as he kissed her with a force that sent lightning shocks through her. He yanked her head back roughly, and she gasped as he trailed kisses up to her ear, his hand claiming her throat.

'Enzo,' she moaned, her chest pressed to his, both wet and slick.

'Yes, princess,' he breathed, licking his way up the column of her neck. 'Say my name. It's yours.'

She could feel him below the water, hard against her navel, and it took every ounce of strength in her not to wrap her legs around him.

His mouth flew off her as his chest heaved. His hands were still in her hair as he breathed on her neck.

'Tell me now,' he murmured. 'I dare you. Tell me now that you just want to be friends. *Allies*. Tell me that this is nothing.'

She panted against him, wanting the feel of his tongue on her again.

'Just. Friends,' she breathed. He pushed her back down on the bench submerged in water and sank down, leaning over her.

'Lie to me again,' he purred as his hand trailed up her thigh in the warm water, sending a shiver through her. He sucked on her lower lip, and she moaned again as his thumb started tracing circles on her soft inner flesh, closer and closer to where she now throbbed with an ache that had never left her.

'I hate you,' she strangled out.

He bit her earlobe gently, then pulled back, watching her writhe in the water. Then, his eyes dark with lust, he bent over her, his hand desperately close to where she needed it to be. His breath was warm as he licked the hollow of her throat and whispered—

'*We're not friends.*'

At that, his thumb stroked over her sex, and she threw her head back, shuddering. The circles became more and more concentrated as he embraced her, his thumb still working. He blew out a breath, his jaw clenching.

She devoured him with her mouth, wanting every part of him within her, forgetting all the pressure, the rules, the impending doom. She moaned louder as Enzo worked a finger inside of her, fire rippling through her. She began to circle her hips against him, and he cursed under his breath as he lifted her, her legs wrapping around his waist as he pressured the soft spot inside her that longed for release with languid strokes. She tried to reach for him under the water, but he grabbed her hand.

'Not tonight,' he said roughly. 'I want to watch as you come for me.'

She looked at him. His words brought her so close to climax, she thought she would scream over the water. Sensing her arousal, he pushed a second finger into her. She bit into his shoulder to stop herself from crying out, and that only made him groan in approval. He pressed harder and deeper as his thumb stroked her sensitive bud. She felt the build like a tidal wave roaring and cresting. It rose within her, too fast to take hold of. Pleading, she continued to grind against his fingers, his strong arms holding her.

'Enzo,' she moaned, frantic.

'Lie to me now,' he hissed. 'Tell me as you ride my fingers that we're *just friends*. Tell me as I feel you that *you* feel nothing.' There was rage in his voice, desperation.

Elara slowed, her heart hammering as pleasure invaded her. She was so close.

'You want me to let you finish, hm?' he breathed, biting her neck.

'Yes,' she pleaded, seconds away.

His fingers stilled, and she reeled back, her high ripped from her.

'What are you—?'

'Then admit it, just to me,' he breathed, his other hand grasping her jaw as he shared her exhale as though it was his life force. Her breaths came unevenly as his hand began to work slowly, the pressure building again.

'I'm a liar,' she sighed.

'I know you are,' he murmured back. 'Now come for me, Elara.'

It was the final straw. The wave crashed, and she shattered around him, clenching as he continued to work his fingers. Her climax ebbed and flowed, gold glittering around her until she finally fell back to reality. She gripped his shoulders, her chest against his as she breathed heavily. He slowly eased his fingers out of her and sat her back down, kissing her brow.

'I've wanted to make you come since the moment you

ignored me at our first meal,' he said, staring at her intently. His eyes were every bit that of the Lion from the stories, terrifying and magnetic. As though realizing it himself, his face softened, his eyes growing lighter. The last shivers of bliss seeped out of her, the daze clearing enough for her to collect her thoughts – truths that she had wanted to speak aloud since she'd turned him away at her door.

'Enzo . . .' She looked to the ceiling. 'What I feel for you . . . I've never felt for anyone before. But we both know the prophecy. You know what's happening to my kingdom. I can't fall into this with you. The only ending I see is one filled with pain for us.'

He pressed his lips together, resigned. 'If that's truly what you want.'

'It's not what I want. But it's what we both need.' Elara tried to steel her will.

Enzo was quiet for a long time. 'Fine,' he finally sighed. 'Let's get you to bed. You need to rest for what's to come.' He turned, his back rippling as he called over his shoulder, 'I have a feeling you'll sleep better now.'

They walked in silence, Elara so lost in her thoughts, she could barely string a sentence together. When they arrived before her door, Enzo leaned against the wall as he looked at her.

'Elara, tomorrow the god of war will come. We will fight together. Just as we've trained. And I just . . . I want you to remember that you're a fucking dragun. That you will beat Ariete, even without my help. I know it.'

Elara felt her heart beginning to crack.

'Anyway, that's . . . that's all I wanted to say,' Enzo sighed. 'Until tomorrow.'

'Until tomorrow,' Elara whispered, watching him walk away.

And it was as she saw him turn the corner and vanish from her sight that fear began to engulf her. A terror that perhaps, despite her conviction, she might die tomorrow, with so much in her heart left unsaid.

It was that thought, and Enzo's last words, that forced Elara to slip out of her room and out of the palace gates, to the only person she thought might have the answers she sought.

CHAPTER FIFTY-NINE

'I didn't know where else to go,' she said quietly, sinking into the comforting warmth of Isra's doorway.

Isra softened, embracing Elara. 'What's happened?'

Elara bit her cheek to stop herself from crying as Isra led her into her house, rubbing her eyes.

'This prophecy . . . I have tried to run from it, tried to find a loophole in it. But I can't deny my feelings, my truth.'

Isra sat her down, before disappearing into the kitchen with a stifled yawn. Elara heard clinks in the small kitchen as Isra set about making tea. She came in a few moments later, handing Elara a cup of hot mint and honey. She wrapped a towel carefully around Elara's shoulders, drying her hair that was still damp from the baths.

'When I'm around Enzo, I feel . . . I feel as though I am drawn to him.' She touched her heart. 'Here. I crave him even when he's right in front of me. I've tried to push him away but he won't listen.' She let out a shuddering breath. 'How can I give him my heart when the prophecy says it belongs to another?'

'You never told me what happened the night of the summer solstice,' Isra said softly.

'We were in one of the compartments on the solstice. Enzo gave me his crown, and then—'

'He gave you his *crown*?!' Isra interrupted, disbelief widening her eyes. Elara stilled.

'Yes . . . He rested it on my head. But it was just a silly game.' She paused, dread forming.

'Elara, tell me exactly what he said and did.'

'He . . .' She frowned, trying to recollect the hazy smoke-filled memories. 'He knelt before me and took the crown off. He said, "I give you my crown, Elara," and placed it on my head.'

Isra paused for a long moment, studying Elara. 'He knelt before you,' she whispered. 'Enzo has never knelt before anyone. Not even his father, the *King of Helios*, Elara.' Isra let out a long breath. 'In the Helion court, there is a tradition. It dates back centuries. To give you his crown – it means that when he ascends to power, he would choose you as his queen, or forfeit his kingdom for you.'

Elara's heart pounded. She must have misheard.

'That can't be true.'

'It is custom to give one's crown, then show them to the court as yours once they have decided that you are the future they choose. No doubt if you weren't interrupted, he would have walked out with you, letting everyone see you wearing it.'

Memories rushed to Elara, tripping over each other as she understood the magnitude of what Enzo would do for her, what he had already done.

'The sirens.' Her words were barely more than an exhale of breath. 'One looked at me and told me, *told me* that her song didn't affect me. And asked me if I knew what that meant.'

Isra nodded. 'The siren's song doesn't work on those already in love. That's the truth, Elara. Enzo is in love with you.'

Elara's hands were shaking. She couldn't stop them.

'When we first met, and you read me . . . you told me you'd seen Enzo and me combining our powers,' she said. 'You saw something else, didn't you?'

Isra sighed. 'Yes, but that's for him to tell you. Though I promise you, Elara, the fear you feel for the pain the prophecy may lead you and Enzo to . . . it's worth it.' Her eyes softened. 'Isn't it better to let your heart feel every peak and valley of life, than to close it and feel nothing at all? Isn't the pleasure of love worth the pain?'

She looked at the clock hanging above Elara's head. 'Speak to him, Elara. He stopped in here, a little while ago, on the way to his studio. Just . . . go to him. There's still time before tomorrow. For the love of Stars just tell him, will you? Tell him that you're in love with him too.'

Her footsteps thumped on the cobblestones as she ran, following the familiar route through the darkened streets of Sol to Enzo's studio.

The door from the street was locked. She didn't let that stop her, heading around the back of the building, clambering over the wall to the terraced garden and breathing a sigh of relief when she found a window had been left open.

Hesitating for a moment, drawing a shaky breath, she eased herself through the gap and into the studio.

Enzo wasn't there.

The space was as they had left it when they had created the duskglass those weeks ago, her novels strewn across the soft divan, Enzo's tools cluttered on a workbench. A carafe of water lay on the small table in the terraced garden. She entered quietly, yet more tears threatening to spill. Every blissful moment, every good, pure memory had happened in that space. She trailed to the workbench, her hand skimming the tools, a sad smile on her face as she remembered Enzo force-feeding her vanilla pastries in that very spot.

She let out a shuddering sob. He wasn't here, and Ariete was as good as upon them.

Elara turned, her eyes catching on the screen that Enzo had worked behind, marked with paint and chalk, a fine dust settled over it. His secret project. She smiled again as she ran her fingers over the material of the screen and moved it aside.

A harsh breath left her.

A woman was carved into the gigantic slab of stone that stood as tall as Elara. She was exquisitely detailed, her arms thrown out in untamed abandon, hair spread around her, and a gleam of courage in her eyes. The woman's lips were carved into a smile of half elation, and flowers – forget-me-nots, Elara realized – were impressed into the wild locks of her hair. She traced the curves of the figure beneath a dress that looked like it was being tugged by the air around them. And Elara knew, as she took a step back and drank the art in, that she was looking at herself.

With a shaking and tearful smile, she traced her eyes, mirrored in the stone, alive with triumph. The shapes had been rendered with such care, a moment captured in time.

She thought back to when she had fallen off the cliff. The fear, followed by the hope. Enzo had captured it all. Had captured her in the moment she had killed a monster.

'Elara,' a voice breathed behind her.

She spun around, heart thundering.

'Enzo,' she choked out. 'I thought you'd left.'

He stood in the studio's doorway, clutching a cup of water. 'I'm here,' he rasped.

She took a step towards him. 'It's me. This sculpture. The day we jumped off the cliff.'

'I—' He gritted his teeth, swallowing. His jaw worked, as though debating whether to speak. He closed his eyes, resolution on his face. 'I knew then.'

'Knew what?' Her voice was a breath, a whisper.

'That you were my soulmate.'

Something within her chest leapt. 'What did you just say?'

'My mother told me, not long before she left to travel to Asteria, that half of my soul was missing. She said she could see it, my perfect counterpart, waiting for me.'

'That can't be me.' Elara's voice was a rasp. 'My prophecy would not allow that.'

'It doesn't make sense, I know. But I can only tell you my truth. A truth I think you feel too.'

'But you hated me.' Her hands were tremoring, and so she pressed them to her sides.

'When I pushed you off that cliff, and realized that there was a chance you could die, something tugged in my chest. A physical pull. I had no choice in it, no sway. I jumped off after you because my heart bade me to.'

A lump had begun to form in Elara's throat. 'You were so angry with me the next day, when I'd tried to leave.'

'I didn't want to admit what I'd felt. And then, when I visited Isra after I told you to go . . . She admitted what else she had seen when she read you. She saw it too, El. We *are* soultied. The moment she confirmed what I suspected, I was in denial. I tried to do everything to stop it being true. Tried to keep hating you, to push you away. Because of who you were, the prophecy, my father . . .'

He sighed.

But now, nothing seems to matter. Other than that you know that I am in love with you, Elara. And that you are who

I have been searching for all my life. That was my secret, my payment to Eli. That my soulmate was a girl who could never truly love me back.'

'Enzo—'

'No, El.' A dam seemed to break as the words poured out of him. 'I need you to understand. You said we couldn't be anything more than friends, and I would have done it. After I walked you back from the baths, I knew.' His voice was ragged as he sagged against the door frame. 'That I would have taken the crumbs you fed me. Taken you in sips, even when I wanted to drown, if it meant I could be near you.'

Elara was trembling as each word caressed her. A silence stretched between them as Enzo fidgeted with his hands, the nerve in his jaw ticking. She looked at him, words warring on her lips, until finally she spoke.

'*Drown in me.*'

His head snapped up, every muscle standing to attention. Their gaze locked. A ragged breath escaped him. Then in five strides, he was on her. His hands gathered in her hair.

'I love you too,' she whispered against his lips. 'I think I've been falling since I met you. It was so easy to love you, Enzo. Your strength, your passion, your courageous lion's heart.' She placed a palm over his raggedly beating chest. 'I've waited all my life for you.'

The smile he gave at her words was the most beautiful thing she had ever seen, more beautiful than any marble treasure he could carve. Light glowed from him as he met her lips with his own. She arched into him, a whimper escaping her as her shadows curled around him. He held her tightly, so close that the pain was exquisite. She wrapped her hands in his curls and tugged, angling his neck so that she could kiss it. A moan left him as his hands roamed her body, unsure where to begin now that she was all his. He tore his lips from hers for a second as he wiped workings and papers from the bench's surface. Then he pulled her up, and she draped her legs around him as he lifted her on to the workbench. Lust swept her as she took him in, how undone he was – just for her.

His rough fingers hitched up her dress, and she found herself wet already as he pushed her head to the side, kissing and licking the arch of her neck.

'I've imagined you, spread on this worktable for me since the moment you entered the studio,' he murmured. 'My muse.'

She moaned against his words as he pushed back to look at her. His hand moved higher with urgency as his other began to unbuckle his belt, and he gathered her to him again.

'I went to see Isra,' she breathed as his head dipped, his hands yanking at her dress. Her breasts spilled from it and he swore, his tongue sucking and lapping until his lips wrapped around her nipple.

'Stars,' Elara strangled out. He groaned, his teeth grazing the sensitive flesh, sending arrows of fire through her.

'*Did* you, princess?' he murmured, pausing his exploration with his mouth for only a moment before trailing it to her other breast.

Elara gently leaned back to look at him. 'She told me everything. About giving one's crown. What it meant.'

Enzo paused, and pulled away. Panic raced through her as she wondered whether she should have mentioned it. Then, his eyes not leaving hers once, Enzo sank slowly before her, his tall frame sinking level with her hips. He braced the workbench with his arms on either side of her.

'I was rudely interrupted the night I gave you it. And it's a shame, since I expressed a certain desire for wanting to taste you as you wore it. But no matter. I'm sure you'll taste just as divine without one.' His smile curled as he pushed her skirt up, before hooking his arms under her thighs, his hands gripping their soft flesh. He looked up at her again.

'Something tells me you enjoy me on my knees.'

'I've never seen such a pretty sight,' Elara crooned.

'Instead of a queen, I'll make you a goddess. Then I can worship you the way I'm supposed to.' His smile turned positively feline as he hitched her dress up to her waist. She felt herself exposed to the cool air, and shivered.

'Yes,' he breathed. 'I think I'll pray to you with my tongue.'

Her foot landed lightly on his chest, pushing him back. He looked at it in confusion, then desire, as he observed her, challenge sparking in his eyes.

'Beg,' she said.

He let out a soft laugh, biting his lip as Elara smiled. 'Oh, you are wicked.'

She lifted a shoulder. 'I followed your orders, it's only right you follow mine.'

Enzo groaned, his eyes flicking to her sex. 'Please,' he breathed.

'Please *what*?' she purred.

'Please, Elara, let me taste you.' His eyes burned as they fixed on her. She bit her lip, lifting her hips and grasping her dress with two hands as she pulled it up over her, discarding it on the floor. He hooked his fingers around her underwear and pulled them off, leaving her bare. Enzo drank in her naked form, his eyes roaming every inch of her, soaking in every curve and dip. She felt his gaze as though it were a tangible thing, trailing flames down her.

She made herself look into his eyes as she opened her legs.

'Take what is yours,' she breathed, and Enzo did not hesitate.

His tongue sank on to her, pressing hard. She gasped, gripping the edge of the workbench as rivers of pleasure danced through her. Her hands tangled through his thick curls, digging in as she rocked at the sheer ecstasy of him on her. A sound she didn't know she could make escaped her as he slowly swirled his tongue.

'Gods, the fucking taste of you, Elara.' He said it as though he was angry with her. He delved between her thighs once more, finishing the sentiment with a slow, tantalizing kiss. 'Like light-warmed cherries. So. Fucking. Sweet.' He moaned into her as his arms locked around her thighs again, pressing for more, deeper and deeper. She had never felt pleasure like it. She was a deity in his arms, his lips a feverish prayer over her body, reverent, adoring. Elara arched her back, her head dropping in ecstasy as a whimper escaped her.

'I know, princess,' he murmured, pausing briefly. 'I know.'

His tongue danced, teasing and flicking before taking her all in, then dancing away again, sending waves of gold crashing and peaking through her. She felt like she was drowning; she felt like she was flying. All that existed was that moment and him, kneeling before her, worshipping her. And just when she thought she couldn't fly any higher, she felt Enzo slowly press a finger into her.

'Skies, Enzo,' she breathed as it filled her.

'My name on your lips may be my favourite sound in all of Celestia,' he said, the deep sound reverberating through her. She shivered, shifting as she tried to create some friction, anything to satiate the ache building inside her. But Enzo kept his finger still, his eyes locked on hers.

'Say it again,' he said roughly.

'*Lorenzo*,' she moaned.

With a sigh he pushed a second finger into her, and he curled them, pumping them maddeningly slowly as he swirled his tongue again. The combination sent her over the edge, and she felt herself unravel at his strong insistent strokes.

'What was it you said you'd never felt before?' He sucked slowly, and she jerked against her will. 'Ah yes,' he smirked. 'Fire.'

To Elara's utter disbelief, she began to feel warm flames lick her as Enzo pressed his tongue flat to her. A rivulet of fire danced off his tongue, and she felt embers pulsing and drawing circles around her. The heat was delicious, warm enough that she started to tingle.

A roar pounded in her ears as Enzo's tongue and flames caressed her, the heat vibrating and rippling. 'Enzo, I'm going to—'

Enzo pulled back. 'Not yet, you're not.' He pulled his fingers out of her, and she gasped at the emptiness, the shock of being so close to the edge knocking the breath from her.

'What the fuck are you doing?' she panted. Enzo ran his tongue over his lips, glossed with her, but didn't reply. He stroked a thumb lazily over her centre, causing her to jolt again.

Enzo's eyes were heavy with lust as they stared at each other, Enzo still on his knees.

'Tell me you're mine, Elara,' he said softly, and memories of their tryst at the Asterian ball echoed through her as she saw something that looked like a plea in his eyes.

'I'm yours,' she whispered. He closed his eyes and inhaled deeply. When he opened them, there was only a thin ring of gold around his pupil. And without a word, he stood up, lifting her so that her legs wrapped around his middle. He kissed her deeply, and the taste of herself on his lips made Elara shiver with pleasure anew.

He sank her to the floor, to the white sheets laid all over the studio to catch the fall of marble and plaster dust. The first rays of dawn were beginning to shine through the wide windows, refracting off the sculptures and busts that surrounded them. She turned, running her fingers over a large bust standing on the floor next to her, her thumb tracing the figure's lips. Enzo took a moment as she arched her back and stretched her arms behind her, closing her eyes as she revelled in the light and shadow playing over her.

'I'm going to carve the way you look right now into stone,' he breathed, pulling his shirt over his head. His muscles rippled, taut with tension as he bore over Elara, leaning on his forearms on either side of her.

He pulled a strand of her hair between his fingers. She smiled up at him. The Light danced over him, the golden rays of early morning bouncing off the bronze of his skin. 'Nothing will be the same after this, you know that, don't you?'

'It hasn't been for a long time,' Elara whispered. 'And I still choose you.'

'Elara,' he breathed. 'You've made me a better man, you know that? I was blinded for so long by the Light, that I never saw the beauty in the shadows. You opened my eyes. You made me see.'

Elara melted, delicate shadows swirling from her fingertips as they caressed him.

His eyes fluttered shut against them as he slowly unbuttoned his trousers, letting them fall and kicking them off as his hard length was freed. Elara stopped breathing, a dull, pounding roar drumming inside of her.

When she looked up, he was gazing at her, transfixed. 'Open your legs for me, princess.'

She sat up, leaning on her arms, her eyes on him, knowing exactly what she wanted, exactly what she was going to do no matter the consequences. And with steel in her eyes and a raise of her chin, she did as he had asked. She saw him twitch and she bit her lip, incredulous that she could elicit such a response from him without touching him. He clicked his tongue, slowly dragging his eyes to her lips, her breasts, taking his time to drink in what he'd been denied for too long, all the way down.

'Lie back,' he murmured.

She let herself fall back on the sheet as he pinned her arms over her head with one hand, the other tracing patterns up and down her thighs, so close to where she ached.

'Please,' she half-begged.

His lip quirked. '*Now* the princess has learned some royal manners.'

He pushed a finger inside of her as he licked and bit her neck, trailing kisses down to her breasts. He swirled a tongue around her nipple, and she arched into him.

'You're soaked,' he moaned in her ear as he worked her, threading his other hand with her own above her head.

Elara could say nothing at that point. Not a single coherent thought came to mind, only the want of more, more, more. She tried to urge him with her hips.

'Patience is a virtue, Elara,' he whispered against her skin.

'And teasing should be a sin, *Lorenzo*,' she retorted breathlessly. He laughed softly, slowly drawing his fingers out of her. He settled above her, his muscle-corded arms on either side of her.

His eyes were fixed on hers, his skin glowing. He looked so handsome that her eyes watered. She could feel his hardness grazing her entrance and ground her hips over it. He stilled, caressing her temple, her cheek, parting her lips. After a moment of searching her eyes, he slowly pushed himself into her.

Elara cried out, and he captured the sound with his tongue,

wanting to taste her pleasure as it danced between them. She was so full with him, she couldn't think.

'Gods,' Enzo breathed as he kept pushing. 'How do we fit so perfectly?'

Elara had thought the same, and pleasure flooded through her anew at his words. He settled all the way to the hilt, joining fully with her as she gasped.

She had never felt anything like it, certainly not with Lukas – the feeling of such fullness, such belonging, such raw desire and pleasure.

'I didn't know it could feel this good,' she gasped. She ground against him, impatient for friction, writhing her hips as he watched.

'Fucking Stars,' he hissed, letting his head fall back as he breathed in deeply. He began to move with her in rhythm, slowly at first so that she could adjust to him. He leaned back as he palmed her breast, tweaking her hardened nipple. She moaned against the sensation, pleasure rippling through her whole body at the feeling of him inside her and out. She ground harder, wanting more. He cursed again, stilling.

Elara stopped, looking at him. 'Are you okay? Is this okay?'

Enzo huffed out a soft laugh. 'You feel like fucking heaven, and if you keep doing that, I'm going to finish before you do. Which is not how *any* of my fantasies played out.'

A small thrill raced through her. 'Fantasies, hm? Tell me more.'

He gave a dark chuckle as he pulled out of her. She made a sound of protest, but he held himself over her, panting.

'Which one do you want to hear?' His head dropped to her neck. 'The one where I peeled those skimpy, sweaty training clothes off and fucked the brat out of you?'

Elara tried to regain some composure, though her body

was acting of its own accord, clawing at his back, her hips canting.

'Or when I made you sit on the throne while I knelt and tasted every sweet drop of you? I could go on and on, princess.' He licked her pulse point as he finally slid back into her. Elara moaned as something began to coil tighter and tighter in her stomach.

'Seems like you couldn't get me off your mind,' she breathed.

He made an amused sound as he twisted her hair around his hand, pulling it as he trailed kisses down her throat. 'You consumed me, Elara,' he said, quickening his pace. 'Every waking moment I wanted you near me, even if it was just to fight.'

He pushed deeper, faster, and Elara's head dropped back.

'You wanted me that much?' she asked, even as the pleasure became too much, threatened to engulf her.

'You have no idea. You have every part of me, El.'

She stilled them both for a moment, cupping his face in her hands.

'There are few things that I'm sure of in this world, Enzo. But the one thing I know is that you *are* half of my soul.' She brought his face to hers, kissing him fiercely. 'I love you,' she breathed. 'Until my last breath and beyond.'

Enzo gathered her up against him as they moved in time, as he kissed her neck, her lips, her tongue, tasting the words she gave him.

'I love you, I love you, I love you.'

She lost all resolve, the ache rising to a crashing of waves as she came, closing around him. Seeing her lose control, he came with her, over and over, their bodies slamming and shuddering in throes of ecstasy, and just her name spoken repeatedly on his lips, 'Elara, Elara, Elara.'

CHAPTER SIXTY

'I wish we could stay here forever,' Elara sighed as she lay on the light-warmed sheets. Enzo's head lay on her stomach, his body between her legs as she played with his curls, absent-mindedly twisting them with her fingers. They'd drifted in and out of sleep, but the light streamed in brighter now as the day began.

'Me too,' he whispered.

He didn't need to say more, the unspoken weight between them. It would not be long before they would have to face Ariete.

Elara watched as Enzo traced the back of his knuckle over her stretch marks, silver and rippled on her hips.

'I love these,' he murmured. 'They remind me of ocean waves.'

Elara preened under his gaze, capturing the softness of him, the stillness, while she could.

'And these,' he moaned, sinking his hands into the soft curves of her hips, padded out over the last months. 'I could just sink my teeth into them.'

'Enzo,' she laughed, batting his head away as he grinned.

'I like these, too,' he murmured, stretching up and pushing the shirt she'd shrugged on earlier aside to kiss her full breasts. 'Yes, I love these.' She rolled her eyes, her cheeks turning pink.

'What else do I love?' he pondered, his hand skittering down between her legs.

'*Enzo*,' she said again, turning on to her stomach. 'You know what I love?' She kissed the freckle under his left eye. 'This.' She ran her finger over his coal black lashes, long against his cheek. 'These,' she said. Her thumb rubbed the silk of his ear, brushing over the golden ring there. 'This.' She smiled as he stroked her hair. 'You know, when I was locked in that room with Gem,' she said quietly, playing with a stray thread on the sheet as she felt him stiffen, 'those were the details that anchored me. I kept them in a locked box in my mind when Gem tried to tear it apart. Silly, I know.'

Enzo's face was painted with emotion as he pulled her to him, so she was cradled to his chest, his heart hammering faster than before. 'I can hardly think of that without erupting into flames,' he said. 'When you were taken from me, I—' He stopped, shaking his head. 'I was ready to set Celestia ablaze.'

Elara believed it, the savage promise his eyes held as he said it. 'Come now,' she teased. 'You wouldn't have really done that. Think of all the poor innocents who would have been caught in the crossfire.'

Enzo gave a dark laugh. 'You overestimate my compassion, Elara, and underestimate how deeply *mine* you are. I would let the whole world burn if it kept you warm.'

A selfish warmth coursed through her as she nuzzled in closer to him. 'So you'd set the world on fire for me,' she mused. 'Well, *I* would turn the world to darkness for you. If you were taken from me, not a single light would shine until you were back home,' she added quietly, needing him to understand. He held her tightly in response.

The temple bells chimed the eighth hour, and Elara raised her head. 'We should get back,' she said, shrugging off the shirt and handing it back to him.

'I wish you could keep this on,' he said, taking it from her. 'I think I prefer you in it than any ballgown I've ever seen.' He stamped a kiss against her neck for emphasis.

'Territorial animal,' she laughed, pulling on her discarded dress. 'Don't let Merissa catch you saying that.'

Once Enzo had also dressed, and slung his sword around his waist, he took her in his arms and they both looked around the space for one last time. Elara drank in the sculptures, the tools and sheets, the books strewn upon the table. She never wished upon Stars. But she wished to something else then, that she might be able to come back here, with Enzo, after all this.

'Before we go back, there's somewhere I want to take you,' he said, resting his chin on her head.

The air in the Angel's Graveyard was just as she'd remembered it – thin, dry and hot. She sucked in a deep lungful of it, coughing lightly at the grit she could feel coating the back of her throat, the red sands around her shifting.

'I remember telling you that this wasn't a very cheerful place,' she said, casting her eyes warily around the circular dais they were standing on. 'I stand by that.'

Enzo chuckled, pacing the circumference of it. 'It's so strange to me that the last time we were both here, we couldn't stand each other.'

'I blame the sexual tension.' Elara smirked.

'I swear you get more arrogant by the day,' Enzo replied, walking towards her.

'I have a great teacher.' She smiled, kissing him deeply as he wrapped his arms around her. 'So why here?' she asked, extricating herself from him. She squinted against the Light and the glare of the buttercup-golden skies above.

'I have this little ritual,' he began. 'You'll probably call it superstitious nonsense. But before a battle, I always come here. I feel this kind of ancient magick, maybe a remnant of those mighty mythas who fought centuries ago.' Enzo looked up at one of the giant angel statues, its carved gold stone towering above them. Elara followed his gaze, looking out to the roiling sea of sands ahead. The red, shifting desert stretched out for miles, as far as the eye could see, eventually bleeding into what she knew would be the Sinner's Sands, the domain of the Star Capri.

'It sounds stupid,' he broke the silence, 'but walking where the fabled winged lions of Helios once did, where they fought and conquered . . . It gives me strength. To face anything set before us.'

Elara squeezed his hand. 'It doesn't sound stupid. Why wouldn't the Lion of Helios want to be around his kin?' He kissed her brow. 'Do you believe all the mythas existed? Walked this world before us?' she asked.

'I do,' he replied. 'And maybe other beings too.' Enzo sat down on the circular dais, beckoning Elara to join him.

'See these?'

His hand swept over the disc, pushing aside the red sand that coated it. He ran a finger over the stone, showing up designs and symbols that Elara had noticed before from afar. She squinted at the etchings, wind-weathered and light-faded.

'These are the Stars,' he pointed. It was a wheel, each Star's symbol spaced along the circumference of it. She saw Ariete's crossed swords at the top, Torra's rose, Scorpius's trident. A few other familiar Stars' tokens. 'But these . . .' Enzo murmured. 'I've always wondered as to what these were.' His hand arced outwards, to symbols that hovered above in their own circle, enclosing the Stars. Elara frowned as she looked to them. All the symbols were foreign – circles and rings surrounding them, some crescents, some that looked like light rays shining.

'My mother would bring me here,' Enzo said, and Elara rubbed the back of his hand with her thumb. His eyes were troubled, held in the past.

'She said it was so I would remember that I was a lion, as worthy of standing here as any of the winged creatures that fought before me. She was always cryptic – I suppose a curse of an oracle. But she promised me that she had seen my fate, and that I was more powerful than I believed. My father, as you know, was never religious. And nor was my mother. She . . . she told me that my power came from something greater than the Stars.'

He raised his hands, and light sparked from them. Elara watched as it flooded the dais, spreading out across the sands and up to the angel statues, covering them.

'But Enzo,' she whispered. 'Nothing is more powerful than a Star.'

'You are.'

She shook her head. 'I survived death, that's all.'

'No, Elara. There is something within you. I can feel it.' His eyes roamed her face. 'The same way I feel a tide turning, as though a huge chess game has begun, with players we haven't even guessed at yet, all shifting their pieces. I felt the same feeling when I first laid eyes on you. That we are part of something bigger.'

The words felt so familiar, so *true*, that Elara almost stopped breathing.

'You said, that day when we flew on a shadow lion, that you wondered if there was something out there greater than the Stars,' Elara said. 'What if it's every mortal that stands against them? What if the only thing keeping them in power is our belief in them?'

'*Finally.*' A thundering boom resounded around them.

'Fucking skies!' Elara exclaimed at the top of her voice, scrambling to her feet as she spun around for the source of it. Enzo was in front of her in seconds, his fire already blazing in one hand, a knife in the other.

'You have a filthy mouth for royalty,' the voice boomed again, and Elara's eyes widened in shock. She stumbled two steps back as Enzo craned his neck upwards, his skin paling.

'Holy gods,' he breathed.

There was a ground-shaking shudder as one of the gigantic angel statues, still enshrouded in Enzo's light, *moved*, taking its hands from its eyes.

'I'm dreaming,' Elara said, her voice shaking. 'This isn't real.'

The angel laughed, and the sound flew out across the sands. 'Oh, but it is. And we have been waiting a *long* time for you both.'

'We?'

A roar cleaved the air in two, and the very sound set Elara trembling. A wall of air hit them, and they both stumbled back. The roar came again, closer this time. And as Elara peered out across the sands from beneath the angel's shadow, she saw why.

She kept her eyes fixed on the shape prowling forwards, her heart hammering as the mammoth frame came properly into view. A winged lion. Another gust of wind hit them as the beast beat his wings. Elara's eyes fell on feathers as white as snow, a glorious mane to match. His golden coat gleamed in the afternoon Light as Elara saw wickedly long teeth behind a mouth that curved into a snarl.

'Mythas,' she whispered, transfixed.

Enzo was stock-still beside her, his eyes filled with disbelief and awe. 'So they aren't just legend,' he whispered back.

'Clearly,' she said drily.

The lion approached until it was only a few metres away, his eyes fixed on Elara as the prince raised his hand, ready to protect her if he needed to.

'Wait,' she commanded, holding her hand out to Enzo. He obeyed, his flame vanishing instantly.

The lion continued to stare at her, and she felt wisdom in his gaze. Then, before their disbelieving eyes, the lion bowed, his wings folding together as his huge mane rippled in the breeze.

'What is this?' she breathed.

'It's what you'd call a blessing,' a voice rumbled once more.

'Bleeding *Stars*,' Enzo exclaimed, jumping as he turned back to the angel.

'Manners, young man,' the statue snapped.

'How is this real?' Elara breathed, her eyes flicking between the lion and the angel.

'There is magick in this world, is there not?' the angel replied.

Elara nodded.

'There is much magick that has been forgotten or extinguished.' The angel's smile turned into a snarl.

'Who are you?' There was a distant part of her laughing hysterically at the fact that she was addressing a stone angel. Who was *talking* to her.

'My angel name is much too glorious for your human tongue to butcher. But you may call me Celine.'

'Wait, *the* Celine?' Enzo interjected. 'Who took the last stand against the lion Nemeus?'

The angel seemed to smirk. 'The very same. Who do you think he is?' She pointed to the winged lion, laying regally as he observed them.

'Dear heavens and all that is holy,' Enzo said faintly.

'But you're stone,' Elara blurted out.

'When the statue was erected in my honour after Nemeus killed me, my soul found its way in here. Mythas never truly die.'

Nemeus seemed to rumble in agreement, a deep purr resounding in his throat.

'Wait a minute,' Elara said. 'Nemeus killed you. So aren't the two of you mortal enemies?'

The angel looked to the lion, smiling. 'We have a common enemy now.' The lion growled in agreement. 'The Stars.'

'Is that why the mythas became a legend? Because of the Stars?'

'We hid. Waiting for someone with the power to overthrow them.' Celine looked between Enzo and Elara. 'Waiting for you.'

'No pressure, then,' Enzo muttered.

'Why not speak to us earlier?' asked Elara. 'We've been here before.'

'Ha!' Celine exclaimed. 'You think you both would have been ready to hear all this then? You were both so wounded, so angry at the world. Our words would have fallen upon deaf ears.'

'What is it you came to tell us?' Elara's voice grew hard, her patience with the angel wearing thin.

'What do you know of the world before the Stars?'

424

'What do you mean, "before the Stars"?' Elara asked. 'They created us. Each mortal is gifted with a drop of magick from their patron Star.'

'The Stars are liars,' Celine said sternly. 'They would have you believe that they are to thank for your powers. But have you ever noticed that not one of them can wield the kind of magick you mortals can?'

A dull roar began in Elara's ears as she thought to Leyon's temple. How he hadn't conjured a single ray of Light on the day that celebrated it.

'The Stars' main two powers are their charm and their starlight. With the two, they can influence masses, can control how a person feels. Can commit *divinitas*. But they never gifted you a thing.'

'Then who did?' Enzo asked.

'The Celestes.'

Elara hadn't heard a whisper of the word before.

'They were greater than the Stars, more powerful too. It is they who your world was named after.'

The roar in Elara's ears grew.

'It is they who your powers derive from. They, who have been eradicated from every history book, every story. They who once ruled.'

'If they're so powerful, how did the Stars come to rule?' Elara demanded.

'The Stars are powerful through their trickery. They used deception, rather than force, to kill the Celestes.'

'But how do we defeat a *god*, if the almighty Celestes couldn't?' Enzo said.

'You unite,' Celine replied. 'Too long, the Stars have kept your kingdoms divided, encouraging the blending of magick only with a betrothed from the same kingdom. But the two of you disobeyed that rule, didn't you?'

Elara felt the duskglass blade strapped against her leg.

'Combined, you are a weapon. Wield it.'

Enzo nodded. 'We'd better leave now,' he said, pulling Elara up. Nemeus rose, stretching out his glorious, feathered wings.

She made her way gingerly to the lion, who was shaking out his mane.

'Your Highness,' she said, bowing gracefully. She turned to see Enzo's lips quirking. 'What?' she muttered. 'He's definitely royalty.'

Nemeus inclined his head as though he understood her perfectly. His golden eyes fixed on Enzo's, a deep rumble erupted from the mythas's throat. Then he spread his wings and took flight, a spew of fire jolting through the sky as he opened his maw.

A horn resounded through the arid space, coming from far below, and Elara stilled.

It came again, and Enzo turned, looking back in the direction of the palace.

She knew that sound. It was the sound of war.

'Ariete is here,' she said hoarsely.

Celine's head turned, her wings bristling. 'May the Celestes be with you both.'

Enzo began to turn away, as Celine called, 'One last thing, Elara Bellereve.'

Elara looked back to the colossal stone figure.

'I would speak with you alone,' the statue said.

She gave a reassuring nod to Enzo to wait, before pacing back to Celine.

'I gift you with a piece of advice, one that may save your life.' The statue's voice was quieter now, gentle.

'Yes?' she whispered.

'Keep the Starkiller blade close to you. Whatever you do, do not give it to the prince.'

Elara frowned up at Celine, her tone a little cold as she replied, 'Why? I trust him with my life.'

'Do not ask me questions I cannot answer. Even now fate binds me from speaking further. Just trust the word of the mythas.'

Elara's eyes narrowed. 'The day that someone in this realm speaks plainly will be the day that I die.'

'Let us hope that day is far in your future.' Celine's hands shifted as they were brought back to her face. 'I pray we meet again,' she said.

The statue became still once again, Celine's hands now fully covering her eyes as Elara hurried back to Enzo. She brushed off his questioning look, a fluttering of intuition deep in her gut telling her the exchange was best left private. And so she followed Enzo into battle.

CHAPTER SIXTY-ONE

They arrived by the palace gates, Enzo's sword already drawn. The place was quiet, far too quiet. No servants milled around in the courtyard, no guards stood sentry, no courtiers wandered the gardens.

Elara pulled Enzo back away from the gates, hesitating.

'Enzo,' she began, 'if – if it doesn't go to plan in there, if Ariete takes me again—'

'Then I will follow you.'

'But what if the prophecy—'

'Elara,' he said gently, cupping her cheek. She drank in every detail of him against the light, so scared that she may never see him again. 'Do you think something as fragile as fate would keep me from you?' He brushed his lips against hers. 'I *defy* the Stars.'

Elara blinked back tears. 'I love you,' she whispered.

Enzo kissed her once more, before turning to the gates. 'Wait here,' he said. 'I'm going to locate Ariete.'

'I'm not staying here.'

'El,' he said. 'Please. Just until I know where Ariete is. You're the one he wants. You'll be doing no one any favours striding into the fray. I'll be back soon.'

She sighed. 'Fine,' she said. 'But please be careful.'

Fire rippled off Enzo's sword as he winked. 'Always.'

Elara tried not to panic as she watched him creep into the palace grounds. She fixed her stare on him until the back of his head vanished from sight.

She didn't know how much time passed as she paced back and forth, a sense of dread growing inside her when Enzo still didn't show. She peered through the palace gates, struck again by the silence. She knew that Ariete had to be somewhere within the palace.

Just as she was about to throw caution to the wind and charge into the palace herself, Enzo reappeared, running towards her.

'Throne room,' he panted. 'He's in the throne room.'

'Did he see you?'

Enzo shook his head. 'You ready?' he asked.

Elara nodded, reaching for her daggers as she slipped through the gates towards him. The scent of godslilies overwhelmed her as they walked past the flowerbeds that lay on either side of the main doors.

'I'll take the duskglass,' Enzo said.

Elara hesitated, as Celine's warning rang through her. Then she pulled out the knives, handing him the blade as dark as night. Her hand flexed around Sofia's dagger.

And they walked towards their fate.

The throne room doors loomed before them, just as they had the first day Elara was brought to Helios.

'One more time,' Elara said. 'I'll use my shadows to blind Ariete. We'll disorient him with my illusions. When he stumbles, you take the opportunity with the duskglass. Remember, you have to pierce his heart.'

Enzo nodded, jaw clenching and unclenching as Elara took a deep breath, and pushed the doors open.

Two figures waited by the distant thrones, though one appeared to be kneeling, and the crackling red light rippling off the other confirmed to Elara that Ariete waited.

She gathered the well of magick within her, her shadows already rushing from her fingers as they started to cover the room. A few more steps, and she would strike. She heard Enzo behind her but dared not turn to check. All focus was on the god who had taken everything from her. As she approached, she saw who the figure was beside him.

Idris.

Kneeling, bound, a gag in his mouth, beaten bloody.

Elara's eyes widened, but she gritted her teeth, willing herself with every fibre of her being not to feel an inch of fear as she raised her dagger.

'Hello, darling,' Ariete grinned, and she allowed herself only a second to master her shock as she studied his face. Half of it was marred with scars that spread in gold lines like a fork of lightning. They surrounded one of his eyes, which had changed from crimson to a bright orange, as though an ember of Enzo's flame still lay in there.

'I'll give you one chance to surrender before we kill you,' Elara said. 'Though it looks like you already aren't far from death.'

Ariete laughed, and held out his hand. 'Give me the Starkiller.'

Elara scoffed, her shadows rearing behind her as she prepared to plunge the throne room into darkness.

But then Enzo brushed past her, walking up to the dais.

'Enzo, what are you doing?' she demanded, her shadows sputtering out.

And to Elara's utter horror, Enzo placed the duskglass right into Ariete's waiting palm.

CHAPTER SIXTY-TWO

Black began to gather around the edges of Elara's mind as Enzo turned, beside Ariete, a cruel smile on his face.

'Enzo, what is this?' she asked, her voice betraying a slight tremor. Idris shouted behind his gag, his eyes filled with fury.

'Princess Elara,' Enzo mocked. 'Did you really think I would ever be your ally?'

'I don't understand.' The closed box within her, which had been quiet these last few weeks, was beginning to rattle.

Enzo exchanged a glance with Ariete, who let out a peal of glee.

'My father wanted his alliance. Wanted you as a weapon.' He threw a contemptuous look to the bound king, who tried to shout again. 'But I saw you for what you really were. A bargaining chip. So I let my father carry on with his little plan, as I plotted. A fair trade, with our esteemed King of Stars. Your life, and my father's, for the Helion throne.'

'No,' Elara said scathingly. 'It's not possible. The last few months—'

'Ah, yes.' A small smile played on the prince's lips. 'To

make you believe, to make you all believe. It was fun to toy with you, I'll admit. She's a good fuck,' he added to Ariete.

Elara lunged as Ariete cackled, but her shield wasn't raised, all her training forgotten, and the god whipped out starlight, binding her wrists and feet as she fell to the floor.

'Why?' The word broke from her lips.

'You're not the only one good at illusions, Elara,' Enzo crooned. 'It was easy to pretend, easier still to get you to trust me.' He chuckled. 'You're weak.'

As she searched his face, she found herself looking at a stranger's. A thousand memories flitted behind her eyes, each one a lie.

Ariete stood. 'You can acquaint yourself with the dungeons this time while I make preparations. I won't let you escape again, Elara. You will come to the Heavens with me. And while I may not be able to kill you, I'll make sure to lock you in a pocket of darkness, until the lost princess of Asteria is a mere memory in this world.'

He was upon her in two strides, patting over her body roughly as he checked for weapons. When he reached the tops of her thighs she hissed, and he grinned as he hitched her dress up, tutting when he found them both bare.

He hauled her up, propelling her towards the doors as she struggled. Idris tried to fight, to move, to shout.

'Silence,' Ariete roared, and Idris cowered.

Elara was hauled along the length of the throne room, and it was only when she reached the doors that she wrestled out of Ariete's grasp and turned, head held high, shoulders thrown back.

She gathered as many nightmares as she could from her broken heart, and fixed on Enzo's cold, empty gaze.

'I survived *divinitas*,' she said. 'I'll survive you too.'

CHAPTER SIXTY-THREE

Ariete dragged her down the dungeon steps, past blank-eyed guards and into a grim cell. She landed hard on the hay-strewn stone.

'Just a few hours, darling, and you'll be soaring to your new home.' He grinned as he clanged the bars of her cell gate shut. 'I've mapped out a perfect part of the sky for you, one where no one will find you.'

He cackled as he left her there, promising that he would be back by lightdown. She crumpled to the floor, forcing herself to breathe as the walls sealed her in. Grief clawed at her throat, a dull pain drumming in her skull. Her thoughts were too overwhelming, too much. The reality so inconceivable that it was all she could do not to unravel.

Sobs racked her body, her breath becoming shallow. Memories assaulted her. Enzo by the fountain, Enzo kissing her goodnight, Enzo dancing her through the clouds, gently washing her hair, piecing her back together, making love to her. They seared her one by one, lashes on her heart until she could feel an almost physical ache. Her shadows reared inside her, growing darker and darker. The locked box within her,

434

already rattling, now began to shake, its lid opening inch by inch until the shadows broke it apart. And all those emotions that she had pushed deep, deep, deep into the Dark pulled her into the blackness with them.

The sky was ink, the kind of darkness that appeared the deepest blue. There wasn't a star in the sky. Not a breeze or an echo. That's what first struck Elara as strange about the place she found herself. Yet the land that sprawled before her was wide open, and she took a deep, shuddering breath, and began to walk.

The grove grew and shifted around her, filling with ancient trees, their age shown by the gnarls and whorls on their trunk. As she looked up to the leaves, she saw images playing out on them – of memories that she had stifled.

The branches began to distort, to writhe out into spindly claws that grabbed her as she walked. She tore away from them, but more loomed to her other side, snatching at her dress, her hair. She started to run, though each step was like wading through mud. She fought, and ducked, but they were too strong, these trees, these memories. She saw the zealot with the light, saw herself being held against a tree by Enzo, her parents' deaths, Sofia's, Lukas's betrayal, Enzo handing the duskglass to Ariete. She sobbed and sobbed as she stopped fighting, sinking into the centre of the grove, the dress she'd been wearing now in tatters.

But the moment she sank into the soft grass, the trees abated, righting themselves as she curled in on herself. The silence was so complete it almost became a sound itself, until it was disturbed by a faint splash as rain began to fall.

Droplets of iridescent silver poured down, falling harder and faster, plastering her ebony locks to her forehead, removing the remnants of her dress, mixing with her tears until she didn't know which was which.

She lay back and let it in. She took a breath. Felt the pressure rise in her chest, felt a dull ache, and then let it crack her open, a wordless scream tearing from her. In this surreal place between life and death that she had landed in, where her body was in another world, and her soul was scattered here, the rain seemed to enter her. It spoke of grief. Of sorrow. Of unkept promises and lies, of what had made her a coward, what had made her a fool. The pain was sharp, the words tooth and claw, ripping her to ribbons. But it was real. And so, she welcomed it. She saw the fragments of her shadows in the lightless night. The horror, the disgust, the parts of herself that she'd been running from for so long.

Shadows poured from her, dancing around the grove until they convulsed and warped. She watched as they formed a figure. One who drew closer.

'I've been waiting for you,' the shadow said, its voice a terrifying rustle that crawled over her skin.

Finally, she was confronted by what she'd been avoiding for so long. Everything that she had locked away. And in its own twisted way, it was glorious. She didn't have to hide. The surrender became exquisite, and she bared her throat to the cut of her darkest thoughts, of the truths. Finally, she didn't have an excuse to fall on or a reason to keep running. She could simply *be*.

The rain continued to fall, pummelling her skin. Her shadow lay down beside her. She reached for its hand and interlaced their fingers.

The rain began to wash away who she was. It peeled back

Elara's skin, the tatters of her soul, the damage in her heart. Gods, did it hurt.

The shadow spoke again. 'How long have you been running from me?'

She did not reply.

It spoke again. 'You fed me. Yet, you never once looked at me.'

Elara felt pity, gritting her teeth against the onslaught of the heavy, pellet-like raindrops.

'How did you think you could wield your shadows against a Star when you cannot even face them yourself?'

Elara was still, letting the words ring in her ears.

'Where am I?' she croaked.

'In your own dreamscape,' the shadow rasped. 'Deep within it. Further than anyone should go. You are here to surrender.'

'Surrender?' She laughed emptily. 'I've surrendered enough. My heart. My kingdom. What is left of me to give?'

'Everything, Elara. Every dark, awful part of yourself.'

She did not reply, though she felt the truth of it in her bones.

'Now you begin to see,' the shadow rasped. 'The Dark cannot exist without the Light, nor the Light without the Dark. You contain both, Elara. It is no use running from the darkness within and accepting only the day. It is also no use shunning the Light and caving to shadows. Surrender.'

And with complete clarity, like the dawn breaking through the night, she understood. She was not perfect or imperfect. She was not a villain, nor a hero. Simply herself. A girl who had lost and grieved and made her way the only way she knew how. So she had fallen in love. That did not make her a fool, nor did it make her weak. It made her courageous.

'You were always told you felt too deeply. That you were

too sensitive. But you cannot change who you are, Elara. So instead, all you did was swallow those emotions. And now, here we are.'

'And now, here we are,' Elara echoed.

'What you should have been taught is how brave it is, to be vulnerable in such a cruel world. How it is better to feel every ray and shadow, than to feel nothing at all.'

And so, Elara lay back on the swirling, rolling grass, and let herself feel.

She grieved – for her parents, for Sofia, for who she had believed Enzo to be. She drowned in her fear of what the future may hold for her. And as she did, the rain continued to peel back her old self until chinks of silver shone through, the black tar that coated her soul sloughing away. Her shadow held her hand, murmuring soft words of kindness. And with one last cry, she burst open, brighter than any Star and darker than any shadow, like a storm awakened.

CHAPTER SIXTY-FOUR

Elara bolted upright on the floor with a gasp, taking in the dank cell, the flickering torchlight. She felt power surge through her skin, the same deep, ancient thing from her dreamscape.

Suddenly, she realized what was amiss.

Pain, she thought in disbelief. The ache that constantly seemed to weigh upon her heart had gone.

A bubbling laugh almost escaped her before she caught herself. Enzo's betrayal threatened to pull her under again. A small, fragile part of her was holding on to a glimmer of hope that this was all some cruel trick, an elaborate ruse. Something was nagging away at her mind, a thought that felt immensely important but wouldn't surface. She bit her lip, pulling a strand of her hair between her fingers as she went over and over every detail of her memories with Enzo.

She didn't believe that Isra could have known of Enzo's plans. Neither Merissa, nor even Leo. She *couldn't* believe it, that they would *all* betray her like this. But they had only known her a few months, whereas they'd known him their whole life. Who was she to them, really?

Elara pinched the bridge of her nose, trying to bring sense to her thoughts. She had *felt* the soul-tie between her and Enzo. That could not be a lie. Why would he have created duskglass with her only to hand it to the one they made it to kill? Why would he have maimed Ariete only to side with him?

Her eyes narrowed as she replayed Celine's warning. She had advised her not to give the duskglass to the prince. Something about the wording bothered her. Why? Why not warn Elara more plainly about Enzo? Why had the angel been civil to him at all if she had known the truth?

Elara's mind worked and reasoned as the Light passed through the chink in her cell window. Finally, as she heard sure-footed steps outside her cell, she knew she had reached a conclusion. There was only one way to test her theory. She saw a jewelled, bronzed hand reach to unlock the door.

Elara did not move as Enzo swaggered into the small cell, past the guards, who didn't so much as shift from their posts. The prince kicked the barred gate shut behind him, and locked it. She feigned disinterest as her gaze swept the cruel lines of his face, catching on the sheen of his earring, the faint scent of godslilies permeating the space.

He was twirling the sharp blade of duskglass, its black surface glistening in the candlelight.

'Careful you don't cut yourself,' she said, her tone lazy.

Enzo turned to her, a slow smile creeping on his face. 'I have to say, Elara, I'm a little wounded that you're not more distraught. I expected to find you on your knees.'

Elara snorted. 'You always rated yourself too highly.'

Enzo's smile curled venomously.

'You know, I've been wondering why you have that.' She pointed to the blade in his hand. 'Why you bothered creating it with me if you were working with Ariete,' she said, examining her fingernails.

Enzo narrowed his eyes, but no answer came.

'A blade to kill a Star,' she continued. 'What a weapon indeed.'

'I'd watch how you talk, lest you find yourself in the Deadlands tomorrow.'

Elara chuckled. 'Oh no, I don't think so. You see, Ariete cannot kill me, remember?' She stood. 'So perhaps it's you who'll meet the Deadlands soon.'

She blinked, and the first illusion she had been working – that of a weaponless, defenceless Elara – vanished, a blade now visible, holstered upon her right thigh. Quick as a flash, she pulled it forth, its wicked glass gleaming onyx black. Enzo staggered back against the wall, the exact same dagger held in his hand as he looked in confusion and fear to hers and then his. She approached him slowly.

'What was it you said to me? "You're not the only one good at illusions."' She clicked her fingers, and the blade in Enzo's hand turned into Sofia's dagger, as Elara waved the *very* real duskglass blade in her own. The blade she had kept the whole time. And with a smile, she plunged it into his chest.

CHAPTER SIXTY-FIVE

Enzo lay gasping in a pool of his own blood, his hands shaking as he tried to staunch the flow seeping from his chest. The colour of it began to shift, glittering. Elara looked over him, her face devoid of feeling.

'A little advice from an angel,' she said, crouching down before him. 'Call it woman's intuition.'

She ran her finger over the protruding knife sticking out from his chest as he panted. 'You hid the truth from us for all these years. The ways we could destroy you.' She looked in disdain to the colour leaching from Enzo's face, his eyes. 'Isn't that true, Enzo?'

She paused, raising a hand to her lips in mock apology.

'Or should I say – Gem?'

A snarl painted white lips as Enzo's image slowly transformed into the pale Star, her white hair soaked with her glittering blood, her colourless eyes filled with hatred as she convulsed.

'How did you know?' she gritted out.

'Your mind games are sloppy,' Elara sighed. 'Star of trickery, and you can't even get that right. I'll admit you had me

442

fooled at first. And after Celine warned me to keep the dusk-glass blade, I knew I had to hide it in an illusion. But there was something that nagged away at me, a feeling I couldn't shake about the wrongness of it all. You see, I couldn't for the life of me understand why I kept smelling godslilies. And then when you walked back in, it clicked.' She grinned to Gem. 'Details are important, and I'd memorized every one of Enzo's. No freckle. No frown. And your earring was silver, not gold.'

She sighed, standing up, and looked pitifully down at Gem. 'The blade didn't touch your heart, I made sure of that. I can spare your life if you tell me where he is.'

Gem laughed weakly. 'Not a chance.'

Elara's face turned solemn. 'I give you my word, Gem, that you will leave here free if you tell me where you're keeping Enzo.'

Gem's eyes narrowed as she coughed, wheezing. 'Why would you help me?' She grimaced. 'After what I did to you?'

'Because I am not like you.'

Gem observed her a moment. 'Fine,' she hissed.

Elara pulled the blade free and Gem cried in pain. 'He's being held in Idris's *lucirium*. I charmed the guards there,' she panted.

Elara smiled coldly, flexing her fingers around the Star-killer's hilt. 'You helped kill Sofia. I want you to know that I would have made your death agony for that – let alone for what you did to me.'

Her shadows lunged, billowing down Gem's throat. Gem's eyes widened as Elara plunged the blade back in, this time right through the Star's heart.

'You gave your word.'

Black tendrils snaked out of Gem's nostrils as Elara continued to choke her, a thrill drumming through her. The light in Gem's pale blue eyes began to dim, her face turning grey as she clawed at her throat.

'No. I said that I wasn't like you.' Elara drove her blade further through the god's chest. 'I'm worse.'

The moment Elara killed Gem, the Star's spell over the guards broke. She saw them both slump to the floor as they were finally released from the goddess's torment. But Elara had bigger things to worry about. She wrapped her shadows around the bars to her cell and *pulled*. It was delight she felt coursing through her veins as the bars bent and twisted under the pressure from her shadows, now utterly free.

When the guards finally awoke, she knew it would be to the corpse of the Star. But even if they sounded an alarm, it would be too late.

She side-stepped their bodies, summoning an illusion as she turned herself into nothing and strode out of the dungeons.

Mercifully, the corridors were still empty. She wondered where all those who lived in the palace had gone – hoping that they had fled the moment Ariete arrived. She sent up a prayer for Merissa, before sprinting towards the *lucirium*.

She thought it strange that there were no guards stationed outside. A rattle of the doorknob told her the door was locked, but locks couldn't stop her now. She pushed her shadows into the seam of the door until the lock clicked, and then shoved the door open.

Slumped on the floor, on the other side of the door, was Leo, unconscious.

And beyond him were Enzo and Idris, Enzo turning

towards her in shock, while Idris remained slumped in a chair. One of the king's eyes was swollen shut, his nose coated in dried blood. And the *soverin* behind them was cracked.

'What happened?' Elara breathed.

Enzo said nothing, pacing towards Elara and crushing his lips to hers. She nearly sobbed, to be held in his arms once more. But she forced herself to remain focused, as she pulled away gently.

'Well, well,' came a sneer behind them. 'It seems I was right.'

Enzo turned slowly to his father, who was looking at the two in disgust from his one good eye.

'You stupid, stupid boy.'

'Careful, Father,' he warned softly.

Idris hauled himself up. 'What did I tell you about your soft, foolish heart? All these years, wasted, trying to train you into a warrior. And the first glimpse of some Asterian *cunt*, you betray your kingdom.'

Light – a bolt of it so strong – slammed into Idris. The king flew back, crashing into one of the mirrors that lined the room, and glass shattered.

'Say one more word,' Enzo whispered.

The shock upon Idris's face was quickly mastered as he laughed weakly. Before his own light flared to life, a terrible, snaking whip, and struck Enzo across the face.

Elara cried out as Enzo grunted, clutching his face. With a growl, she summoned her shadows, but Enzo held out his hand. 'This is my fight,' he said and, reluctantly, she stepped back, though her heart hammered.

Enzo conjured his own light – a wall of it – and blasted it into Idris, whose head cracked back against the mirror. The king hissed in pain, before he sent another whip of light, which this time struck Enzo's knees.

'Enzo,' Elara pleaded.

'No, Elara,' Enzo replied sharply. He panted, eyes fixed on his father.

Idris staggered up from the wall and approached, nothing but contempt painted on his features. 'You know, you get that weakness from your mother.'

More rays struck, and Enzo stayed kneeling upright, though Elara could see his whole body wanting to buckle.

'Don't you dare fucking talk about her,' Enzo panted. Blood ran down his body, such an awful twin to the image she had seen within his dreams.

'Do you want to really know why she was killed?'

Elara stilled, and even Enzo seemed to hold his breath.

'I have searched for as long as I can remember for a way to defeat the Stars. And upon my quest to know, every seer in my employ sought the truth alongside me. Until finally it was spoken to me. The answers came from two seers, each who brought me a vision. The first was of a glass so dark it swallowed even starlight. And the seer called it *duskglass*. Can you guess who told me that? Which little Svetan girl I allowed to stay in the palace?'

'Isra,' Enzo whispered hoarsely.

Idris chuckled. 'The second vision was of a girl, just born, with a magick so dark she could survive *divinitas*. A girl who would fall for the King of Stars, and it would kill them both. Two Starkillers. And it was spoken to me. If the King of Stars was killed, so the rest of the Stars would fall.'

'What does this have to do with Mother?' Enzo growled, though Elara said nothing, her mouth dry.

'Because I have held a string of Elara's fate as much as Piscea has. The seer who brought me the second vision was my wife.'

Elara's heart turned to lead. 'What did you just say?'

'Lorenzo's mother was one of the most powerful seers in Helios. And when she uttered the prophecy, divined by the Stars or some other fate, I sent her to you. The newborn princess of Asteria. I could hardly believe my luck. I ordered her to take you, to steal you away in the night immediately after your naming ceremony.'

'No,' Elara whispered. Enzo raised his head slowly.

'Yes,' Idris replied. 'But it seems my soft-hearted wife had other ideas. To warn your parents of the prophecy, rather than adhere to her king's command. It didn't help her in the end. Your parents still killed her, just for knowing what she did.'

Nausea rippled through Elara.

The king spoke in a monotone, as though he had no attachment to the words he was saying.

'A shame, really.' He glanced over at her. 'And so I lost you, your father making Asteria impenetrable, keeping you behind walls, though my men tried to find . . . ways to reach you.'

Elara's hand twitched, a spew of shadows flying from them, though Idris only looked to them in amusement.

'You sent that guard,' she said hoarsely.

Enzo was fixed on Idris, utter fury writhing in his stare. Fire began to lick the light ropes that bound him.

Idris smiled. 'One of my most trusted soldiers, and the moment he touched you he turned into a fanatic.'

Elara had always loathed Idris – before she had even met him. But as the king spoke, revealing his hand in every miserable moment in her life, she promised herself that if Enzo didn't kill him, she would.

'You've played your hand a little too early, Idris,' she said, forcing her voice steady though barely restrained rage made her shake.

'I tell you this so that you understand. That all you have

ever been, since the day you were born, is a weapon. A weapon that I was destined to wield. You have become brash, disobeying orders, running to Asteria, seducing my son and following your silly little *heart*. I hope now that you understand your place. Your life is in my hands.'

'If Ariete couldn't kill me, then I doubt you can,' Elara drawled as she composed herself.

'Perhaps not,' he said. 'But I can hurt you, until you stop resisting your destiny.'

Rays of light flew to Elara, but Enzo roared, flames hungrily devouring the light that kept him bound. He leapt in front of her. Fire rippled into a shield against his father's magick.

'Your mother's son indeed, betraying your kingdom.'

The king's voice had ascended into a roar, and he slammed light into Enzo, knocking him to the floor. Elara's hands were already raised, but Enzo raised his own, stopping her.

'You know what I said when Elara's parents killed your precious mother?'

Idris crouched on his haunches before his son, lifting his chin. '"*Good.*" It was what she deserved.'

Elara started to smell smoke. 'Enzo,' she said hoarsely.

Enzo's eyes flicked to her – fire dancing in them, but pain, so much pain, threatening to suffocate those flames.

'I killed my monster,' she said. 'It's your turn now.'

Flames leapt from Enzo's body, and Idris hissed as he was pushed back.

Enzo stood slowly, taking step by staggering step as more fire billowed from him, racing around the room.

'You won't kill me, Lorenzo. You're a coward,' Idris spat, though Elara was satisfied to see a gleam of fear in his eyes as the flames approached.

'Am I?' Enzo gave a wry smile as he looked to his magick,

towering and dancing around them. 'Was it cowardly for me to weep as my father struck me over and *over* again? Or was it cowardly for *you* to exert your power over a little boy?'

'Lorenzo,' Idris warned as the flames began to lick his boots.

'I was a child.' Enzo's voice finally shook. 'You may have erased the scars from my body, but you couldn't erase them from my mind.'

Enzo shook his head.

'But I am not a little boy any more. Nor a prince. I am king,' the Lion of Helios finished. 'Long may I reign.'

Fire flared towards Idris, and he summoned light to try and deflect it. But Enzo's flames were too furious, too powerful, and they ate through the king's shield, wrapping around his body. The king tried to scream, his mouth opened in agony, but Enzo's lip curled as he shoved flames down the king's throat. His father's body shuddered and convulsed. The flames turned from orange, to blue, to bright white. With a final roar, Enzo pushed his hands out, his voice filled with years of pain wrought upon him. And the almighty King Idris of Helios turned to ash.

CHAPTER SIXTY-SIX

'I'm so proud of you. I'm so proud of you,' Elara whispered over and over as she clutched Enzo. He was kneeling, his flames dying as they both looked to the pile of ash on the floor. She dabbed gently at the cuts across his body with her dress.

Enzo said nothing for a moment, before blinking, his eyes returning to their normal gold. 'We should go. We can still use the element of surprise with Ariete.'

Elara nodded, standing slowly. 'But you should see a healer first.'

'There are none in the palace. The place is deserted.'

'What happened, Enzo? How did Ariete—'

'He got me as I was scouting the palace. Told me that my father, spineless worm that he is, had already confessed everything under duress. About the duskglass. His plans to make the Stars fall.' Enzo's jaw clenched. 'I was thrown in here with my father shortly after by Leo, the traitorous piece of shit.'

Elara went to reply, but as though on cue, there was a stir by the door.

'Wh-what happened?' Leo slurred, holding his head as he stood.

'I knocked you out, you fucking disloyal bastard,' Enzo swore, magick already rushing off him.

'It was Gem!' Elara shouted, rushing to stand in between Enzo and Leo. Enzo blinked as Leo raised his hands, pressing himself against the door. 'It was Gem. She used her charm upon the guards.'

Leo's face changed from confused, to wounded, to amused. 'Fucking Stars, Enzo. You really think so little of my loyalty? I've had your back since we were boys.'

Enzo breathed heavily, studying Leo, his nostrils flared.

'Enzo,' Elara said softly.

Enzo's magick extinguished, and Elara slipped out from between them, as Enzo embraced Leo.

'Sorry,' he mumbled. 'And sorry for knocking you out, as well.'

Leo let out a dry laugh as he slapped his back. 'You've done worse to me.'

'We need to find Ariete. Now. Is Merissa out of the palace?' Elara asked.

Leo nodded. 'She started helping the evacuation of the building when the war horns sounded. As far as I know, she went to Isra's until it was safe.'

'Good.' She looked at both of them. 'I've been thinking about how we can finally catch Ariete off guard. I have a plan. And I'm going to need you both to perform like all our lives depend on it.'

Elara settled back into her cell, her shadows pulling the bars straight again as she waited. With little deliberation, she felt for her tether, closed her eyes and dreamwalked.

The cell was darker when Elara sank back into her body, her trip complete. And just in time, as she saw the deep scarlet streaks across the sky.

Lightdown was here.

The gate to her cell opened with a shriek of metal on stone.

Ariete stood there, Enzo beside him. The warmth in Enzo's gaze had completely evaporated. Ariete stepped forwards.

'Ready to spend the rest of your miserable life in the Heavens?' Ariete asked.

Elara raised her head. 'I'll be happy so long as it's far enough away from you.'

Ariete laughed as he pinned her wrists behind her with a stream of starlight, and marched her out of the cell.

'We have one more stop first,' he said, and Elara sidled a glance at Enzo. His eyes were fixed ahead, but she didn't allow herself to panic. If Ariete changed the battleground, then they'd adapt.

As they ascended to the ground floor of the palace, she heard the distant, muffled noise of a crowd, as if one was gathering outside the palace. She was propelled past the *lucirium*, where Leo stood guard with a blank expression on his face.

'Bring out the king,' Enzo snapped to him, and Leo nodded sharply, eyes still vacant, before disappearing into the room.

They continued onwards, the humming growing louder until they were in the same yard where Elara had watched the execution of the guards. The gates this time had been opened, and though it was a quieter affair than Enzo's public execution, the yard was still nearly filled with members of the public. There were nervous murmurs, the citizens of Helios seeming unsure what to expect. Ariete thrust her up on the dais.

'People of Helios,' Ariete's voice rang out. 'I am here today to claim back my possession. One that has been hidden from me, by all of *you*.'

The crowd cowered at the magick that crackled off him, while Elara remained predatorily still.

'I am a forgiving god. And so I will not punish you for your transgressions. Nor my *brother*.'

The god did not appear, and Elara wondered where he was – was he truly such a preening shirker that he would hide instead of defending his patron kingdom?

'But I want to settle some rumours, while I am here. It seems that you may think us Stars not so powerful as we would lead you to believe. Because this girl escaped my *divinitas*, perhaps you think we could not destroy you all, should we so wish. Perhaps –' he let out a maniacal chuckle '– you think that any one of you might be able to escape the same fate.'

He gave a cruel smile as his charm slithered through the crowd, the cries of battle, the shriek of swords echoing from it.

'Your king thought that he might become a god. So I am here to show you all the fate that befalls you should you try the same. A remembrance of the power of your Stars. Bring out Idris, the Unfaithful.'

There was a pause, and Elara bit back a smile.

'Idris!' Ariete shouted again.

Silence, before uneasy murmurs began once more throughout the crowd.

Leo walked slowly up to the foot of the dais alone, and Ariete turned to Enzo.

'Where's the king?' Ariete hissed.

'Oh,' Enzo replied nonchalantly. 'I killed him.' Flames burst from his hands as Ariete staggered back. 'And you're next.'

There were gasps and shouts from the crowd as a wall of fire sprung up around the dais, protecting the crowd from Ariete.

On cue, Leo began to push the crowd out of the courtyard and into the shelter of the palace, with assistance from the guards that appeared from every exit – his loyal guards, no longer under Gem's spell. *No more innocent lives lost*, Elara had ordered him.

She turned to where Ariete was already summoning weapons from thin air, and let her shadows loose.

Light was extinguished instantly, a blanket of darkness encapsulating her, Ariete and Enzo, though she could see through her magick clearly. Ariete stumbled forwards as Enzo jumped from the dais. She watched him run back to the palace as she yanked tapestries of illusions to her, jumped off the dais too and finally drew back her shadows.

Standing now, where the crowd had once been, was a sea of silver eyes and raven hair, all smirking in unison.

Ariete lunged forwards with a bloodcurdling scream as Elara hid in the crowd of her clones.

'I know how you love to play, King of Stars. Come and catch me!' the voices yelled in unison as the whole crowd began to run through the courtyard, all exiting in different directions.

The Star scanned the running figures, though Elara didn't stay to find out what he did next. The last she heard was a growl of frustration and pounding footsteps heading away from her, as Ariete gave chase.

CHAPTER SIXTY-SEVEN

Elara ran around the palace until she found steps that led up to one of the building's rooftops. She launched up them, hearing the sound of running footsteps behind her. When she whirled, Isra grinned at her, keeping pace with her easily.

Isra had been the first person Elara had dreamwalked to hours before, as she'd mapped out her plan.

'Outcome?' she breathed by way of greeting.

Isra's eyes flickered white quickly, as they turned a corner. 'More than one.'

'Deaths?'

'In many of them.'

Elara blew out a breath. 'What's our best chance?'

Isra's eyes flickered once more, and she didn't answer for a while. 'You must summon your silver light,' she said at last.

Elara slowed. 'I don't know how to,' she replied, as they reached the rooftop.

'You will,' Isra said quietly. 'It's the only way.'

Elara nodded, allowing herself to feel the uneasiness then letting it go. 'Stay on there,' she said, pointing to a parallel rooftop across a small gap. 'Guide me to whichever choices are going to lead to Ariete's death.'

Isra nodded, squeezing Elara's hands before deftly hopping across the parapets and leaping across the small gap to the opposite palace rooftop.

Elara turned, wrapping illusions of invisibility around herself. She looked over at the woman who was pacing nervously near the edge of the rooftop, and scaled the distance so she had a clear view of both the woman, who was smoothing her black gown, and the top of the steps.

When Ariete's livid face came into sight above the steps, the woman smiled.

'Took you long enough,' she called across the rooftop as Ariete seethed.

'You know I've had just about enough of our games, little mouse,' he spat, marching at her.

'Really? But we've been having so much fun.' She slunk forwards, closing the gap between them, as Elara crept towards both of them.

'You know,' the woman continued, 'you still haven't revealed why you can't kill me. What about me is so powerful that I survived a Star's death blow? Who am I, Ariete?'

It distracted Ariete enough for his starlight to sputter. Elara was so close now.

Close enough to see how the black and red hairs slicked down the back of the god's neck.

Ariete lowered a hand to the figure's face, tilting her chin. This was Elara's moment. Her hand shook as she raised the duskglass blade with one hand.

Ariete crouched, bringing his lips down to the figure before whispering to them, 'Well, you certainly aren't Elara.'

Crimson light slammed into the woman, and her raven hair lightened, pale skin deepening.

Merissa's head lolled as she fell lifelessly to the ground.

'Merissa!' Elara screamed as her illusion was torn from her. With a growl, Ariete spun, his hand whipping out. It latched on to Elara's wrist. She summoned a shadow, a viper flying through the air at him.

He dodged it, as Elara summoned the next shadow, this one a crow that dived for his eyes.

'Isra?!' she called, seeing a blur of movement from the opposite rooftop out of the corner of her eye.

'Another illusion!' Isra shouted.

Elara swept one around them, the ground swirling beneath their feet as quicksand appeared.

Ariete grunted as his feet stuck in it, fending off the crow as Elara advanced.

But the god quickly fought off the illusion, a slam of starlight dispersing it, the shadow crow with it, bringing them back to the rooftop.

'You forget who you joust with, Elara. Your little mind tricks won't work on me.'

'That must be why you believed I've been dead all these months,' she retorted, and Ariete's eyes flashed with fury.

'Shadow!' Isra ordered.

Elara threw a spew of them at Ariete, who stumbled back from the force.

'Duck left!' Isra shouted, but Elara was too slow as Ariete threw a knife through the air, nicking her arm.

The blow broke her concentration, and her shadows shattered as Ariete advanced.

Again, and again, she took Isra's orders, to conjure shadows and illusions, to move right or dodge left, as Ariete tried to fend her off, and she pushed him closer and closer to the edge of the palace roof. He tried to shoot starlight out towards Isra, but the seer saw his moves before he made them, dodging them with relative ease.

He conjured another throwing knife and launched it once more at Elara, but another yell from Isra had her missing it, shifting their surroundings faster.

From fjord caps in Sveta to the ocean depths of Neptuna, Elara whipped image after image at him until he was disoriented. At last, the god of war stumbled.

'Merissa?!' she yelled over at Isra, as she sent a shadow, this one an arrow, piercing through the air. It plunged into Ariete's leg and he swore as sparkling blood flowed from the spot.

'Alive,' Isra shouted back, and Elara gave a sigh of relief as she continued, shadows swarming and blinding the god.

There was no end to her power, no bottom to the well. Whatever had happened in her dreamscape had removed any limits on her. And for the first time, she felt hope. That she could actually vanquish the god before her.

She did not tire, even as the god did, until finally he was on his knees. He was panting, luminescent blood spilling from various gashes on his body. Ray after ray of starlight tried to knock her down, but she had been drilling with Enzo's light for months. She disarmed each one with a shield of shadows that grew more wicked as it absorbed each hit.

'Time for the monster!' Isra called.

And Elara smiled.

She took a deep breath, one palm raised as the blackest shadows she had ever conjured grew and shifted behind her. Bigger and bigger they grew, until they blocked the light-down behind her, casting darkness over Ariete.

Because standing at Elara's back, wings spread, was a dragun. Born from herself.

Ariete blinked, looking to it in shock, then Elara. 'It's you,' he said softly, scrambling back so that he was almost dangling off the edge of the roof. Elara approached, and so did the dragun.

It bent its head over Elara, maw open as it clamped down upon Ariete's arm. He screamed in agony as her shadows kept him pinned, while she raised her duskglass blade.

'Elara!' Isra shouted. But it was too late. With his free hand, Ariete had conjured a sword, its hilt carved into a ram – flashing rubies glowing within its eyes. In one swift movement, he plunged it through the mouth of her dragun, and it dissipated, the shadows exploding into nothingness.

Before she could draw breath, he sprang at her with his blade. At Isra's alarmed shout, Elara twisted to avoid it, which she realized too late had played right into Ariete's hand as he used her one off-balance moment to pull her to the floor. In a leap, he was on his feet, one foot upon the wrist that held the duskglass.

His grin was one of feral delight.

And Elara realized, it had all been too easy. That Ariete had danced her around the rooftop, letting her gain confidence, before showing her what it really meant to fight a god of war.

'Outcome?' Elara wheezed, winded – one last desperate attempt to Isra.

'Winged lions,' came Isra's quiet response.

A code word. She nodded. Stall Ariete, that's all she had to do.

'You know, this was fun at first,' Ariete said as his starlight wrapped around her. She fought against him. 'But now this is all becoming rather an inconvenience.'

With a shout, she tried to lunge a shadow at him with her free hand. With a tut, Ariete stamped on the wrist beneath his boot, and she screamed as pain flared and she heard a bone snap. Then, with a kick, he sent the blade off the edge of the roof. Elara sobbed in horror as she watched it tumble away and vanish from sight.

'*No!*' she screamed.

He pointed his sword to her throat. 'Now, I may not be able to kill you, but you can still bleed.'

With a last burst of strength, she poured shadows from her hand, the wisps writhing down the building.

The sound of wings pumping the air resonated through blood-red skies. Elara felt the roof reverberate beneath her as Ariete scanned the horizon, his eyes narrowing. Elara scrambled, trying to stand, but Ariete grabbed her by her hair and pulled her tightly to him.

Two gigantic, black feathered wings appeared as her shadow lion rose.

'Get your hands off my queen,' a voice said, threat lacing every word.

Elara almost wept as she saw Enzo on its back, one hand curled in the lion's midnight mane as the other wielded the duskglass blade.

Thank skies for Isra. Isra had warned Elara that the only favourable outcome would be if Enzo waited until the last moment to play his hand. And now was the very last moment.

Ariete dropped Elara, the princess grunting in pain as she hit the ground behind him. She saw a movement, and looked over at Isra as the seer brought her hands down violently on the rooftop in front of her. White frost rushed from the area she hit, spreading a bridge from her rooftop to Elara's, where it kept going, running in a path to the Star as it crawled up his feet, freezing them in place. Elara threw out her one good hand, lancing shadows around Ariete's wrists. And with a snarl, Enzo leapt, the duskglass in hand, arcing it towards Ariete's chest.

Elara heard the wet thunk of a blade embedded in flesh and gasped in disbelief. Enzo had done it. Had pierced Ariete's heart. It was done, it was over, it was . . .

A low chuckle echoed through the air, but it was not Enzo's. She leaned forwards, trying to see past Ariete as red starlight cracked through the ice, freeing the god's feet. Both he and Enzo turned. Time slowed as Enzo's mouth opened in shock, a frown on his face as he looked down at the sword plunged into his stomach.

Elara crawled forwards. 'No.'

Enzo's shaking hand lunged with the duskglass towards Ariete's heart, but the Star laughed as he twisted the sword. Enzo cried out, his arm falling, and Ariete laughed again, louder this time as he ripped the sword from Enzo's flesh. Enzo fell to his knees, his shaking hands trying to staunch the blood.

'*No!*' Elara screamed again, a sound that tore her throat.

She lurched towards Enzo, screaming his name. Ariete stood, his bloody mouth a grin as he looked on. Enzo kept the duskglass clutched in his palm as the Star raised his sword once more.

'Enzo!' she screamed again, and with a cry, Elara summoned her shadows from her uninjured hand, and knocked the sword from Ariete's grasp. He growled, reaching for it when Isra, still on the opposite rooftop, let out a snarl and unleashed the last of her reserves, a rush of ice fully encasing the Star in a moment, before she promptly collapsed.

Elara gathered another lot of shadows and slammed them into the palace roof, obliterating a hole beneath Enzo.

Enzo fell, terror in his eyes, and Elara scrambled to the edge before diving after him.

Air rushed around her. Her wrist pulsed with pain, cradled to her, the other arm outstretched. The shallow pool of the throne room was looming beneath him. She flung out shadows with a grunt, wrapping them around Enzo just in time. He groaned, resting against the hard shroud of shadows as he was gently laid in the pool. He clutched his stomach, trying to stop the blood that flowed freely. Elara's feet touched the floor, a twin stream of shadows cushioning her landing. Scented water sprayed as she leapt into the pool and knelt before Enzo. Her shadows unconsciously morphed back into her dragun, wrapping around them both as the pool began to tint red, soaking both their clothes.

'No, no, no, no,' Elara whispered, clamping her hand over his, shaking as she tried to staunch the flow beneath the water. 'Enzo,' she gasped, 'Enzo, stay with me.'

She clenched her eyes against her pounding head as the cost of her magick finally caught up with her, along with the exhaustion from the fight.

'It wasn't meant to go this way,' he murmured.

Elara sobbed, clutching Enzo, cupping his face with one hand.

'El,' he moaned, his eyes hazy.

'*No*,' she snarled. 'You can't leave me. I've waited my whole life for you.'

Tears rolled down Enzo's cheeks as he tried to prop himself up, raising her chin weakly with one hand. 'There was never a happy ending for us. There never is for star-crossed lovers.' He smiled sadly. 'But I don't regret a second. I would do it all again, welcome every pain to feel myself falling in love with you again. You are the love of my life, El. My love of lifetimes.'

Elara sobbed.

'Take this part of me,' he whispered, conjuring a small ball of light in his palm. 'Just a glimmer of my light.'

'What? I can't—'

Enzo nodded. 'You can. They say that about soulmates, you know? That they can lend each other magick. You need to take it. Just in case. To finish Ariete.'

Elara's tears fell. 'Please, Enzo, don't do this.'

'You have to live, El. For your parents. For Sofia. For *me*.' His eyes fluttered closed, and he sighed.

'I have only one regret,' he whispered.

'What? No, Enzo,' she sobbed, gripping him to her, trying to shake him lucid.

'That I didn't tell you sooner.'

'Tell me what?'

'That you were my angel.' Enzo leaned forwards, kissing her softly as he pressed his light-filled palm to her heart. And she wasn't sure what magick was shared between them as she felt his power flood through her, but her dreamwalking gifts reared to life, pulling them into a memory.

CHAPTER SIXTY-EIGHT

A young boy with black curls lay on his front, a sob escaping him as his back pulsed with pain. Father had called him a coward, and so the boy had replied, 'I'm not a coward. I'm a winged lion.'

Father had laughed cruelly at that. And as his light had carved into the little prince's back, he'd taunted, 'You want wings, little Lion? Here are your wings.'

The prince tried to shift in his bed, but the places where his wounds had been still pulsed and flared with pain, no matter that the healer had smoothed his skin back together. He let out another sob, trying to stay as still as he could.

'Please, please, please,' he whispered, looking out of the windows to his balcony. 'If there is someone out there that can hear me, please help me?'

He grasped on to his plea as tears tracked down his face, wetting his pillow and he repeated it over and over in his head, until finally the tears stopped, and he drifted into sleep.

Sometimes, Enzo's dreams frightened him more than real life. As he opened his eyes to his nightmare, his breath came too quickly as he looked around the marble room. He could hear a whip snapping, and the sound set him shaking.

'No,' he cried. 'Please, no. I'll be good, I promise. I'll try harder.'

The whip sounded closer again, flashes of light painting the room, and the little prince screamed, knowing what was to come.

'Please,' he sobbed. 'Someone help.'

There was a popping sound in the wall as the marble parted before him. He scrambled back, his jaw agape as a girl fell through the room and landed on the floor with a yelp. This was certainly not like his other dreams. The little girl stood up, brushing her nightgown primly. Enzo took another wary step back.

The little girl finally looked at him, her eyes narrowing. 'Why are you crying?' she asked. Her eyes were silver and her voice funny.

'None of your beeswax,' Enzo replied, sniffing loudly as he crossed his arms.

The girl huffed out an impatient breath. 'You know, Lukas gets told off when he says that. It's not polite.'

'Well, that's babyish. I'm eight years old. I can say what I like.' He cast her a sideways glance. 'How old are you?'

'I'm five and a half, and you're not very nice.' He noticed that shadows were curling out of her, their tendrils touching him. He knew that darkness was evil. But these shadows felt nice. 'They seem to like you,' she said as he brushed off a tendril.

'I'm sorry.' He stepped closer. 'I've not had a very good day. My father hurt me.'

The little girl's silver eyes softened. She walked right up to Enzo before he could move.

'What did he do?'

Enzo turned to show her his back, but a fresh sob of frustration escaped him as he found it smooth.

'He hurt my back. But no one believes me.'

'I believe you.'

Enzo stared at the little girl in surprise.

'Why did he hurt you?' she asked.

'Because I told him I was a lion.'

She cocked her head. 'Well, you do have lion eyes. And you seem very brave. I think you are a lion.'

Enzo smiled. He couldn't remember the last time that he had.

'I'm sorry that you're sad,' she said. 'You know, whenever I'm sad, my papa sings me a song to make me feel better. Sofia says it's stupid, but she also says I shouldn't dreamwalk by myself, so I don't really listen to her.' The little girl grabbed Enzo's hand. He could barely feel it, but still sat down next to her. 'Lie down,' she commanded.

'You're very bossy for a five-year-old,' he grumbled.

'Five and a half. Now, close your eyes.' She lay down next to him, her black hair tickling his face. She was still holding his hand. 'Close them!' she ordered. He did, squeezing them shut.

'Now, listen carefully. I want you to remember this song. And when you sing it, it will make you feel better. It's a magick song.' She stroked his hair clumsily.

'Ready?'

Enzo nodded, his eyes still shut tight as the little girl began to sing.

'I loved him more than the dark loves the night. And he loved me more than the day loves the light—'

'Lions may fly, and lovers will die – but my love, it will live on,' Enzo finished, his voice cracked as he sang, one shaking hand in Elara's hair as tears wet his face.

Elara blinked as the surroundings of the throne room came back to them.

'I remember,' she whispered. 'I remember it all.'

'You were mine before I knew. We are destined, you and I. By something other than fate, other than Stars. We will always find our way back to each other. We have before, and we will again.' With his palm still pressed to her chest, he rubbed his thumb over her heart. 'Even in death, I will be by your side. My love will live on.'

Elara let loose a shuddering sob as the memory buried itself in her heart, alongside his power. Pain and anger pulsed through her at the joke fate had made of her life. It was a cruel irony. A divine orchestration to have met Enzo as a child and be led back to him. To search her whole life for love and have found it with her soulmate who was now dying in her arms.

Elara memorized his face, every feature that she'd spent hours replaying in her mind – his golden eyes, the scent of warm amber, his soft parted lips, the callouses on his hands. She closed her eyes as her tears continued to fall and gripped his hand with her uninjured one.

'My princess.' He smiled. And with a sigh, he brought her lips to his, pressing the duskglass blade gently into her lap. Golden power pulsed between them. It rippled through the pool, setting a glow around the throne room. Both of their cheeks were wet as she drank him in, kissing him gently, memorizing every single featherlight touch. His kernel of light finally settled in her being, fizzing in her bloodstream as it mixed with her shadows. A cry erupted from her as she clutched his face, unable to let him go. 'My soulmate,' were the last words on his lips, before his head fell back.

Elara let out a scream that tore from her soul. It was an ancient sound, something born from a part of her that she had buried her whole life.

The lack of Enzo's warmth, of his light, was such an absence that Elara swayed where she sat. She heard a slam from above, the sound of ice splintering.

In a flash of red starlight, Ariete landed a few feet from where Elara sat, something in his arms. She staggered forwards out of the pool, leaving Enzo's body, her heart screaming with every step she took away from him. Her broken wrist was limp against her chest, yet she did not care that she was going into battle one-handed. Or that her head pounded. Or that her magick was now a near-empty well.

As Elara approached, she realized what Ariete was holding. Merissa struggled weakly in the Star's arms, a knife at her throat.

'You put up a fight, Elara, I'll give you that. But it's time to come home now.'

'Let her go, Ariete,' Elara uttered, palming the duskglass. There was nothing left in her to shout. Her soul was with Enzo. The only thing possessing the husk of her body was vengeance. Vengeance and darkness.

'I killed your parents. I killed Sofia. I killed your precious lover. And if you don't come with me now, I'll kill your beautiful maid. Then I'll go back to the roof where your little ice-wielder lies unconscious and kill her too.'

Elara inhaled, spiralling into her power. Though it protested and shrieked, she yanked it to her. Then with a cry, she attacked.

Dark slammed into Merissa, tearing her from Ariete's grasp. The shadows wrapped around her friend as they pulled her to Elara, setting her on her feet.

Merissa staggered back behind her.

'Stay with Enzo's body,' Elara said to her. 'If I die . . .' She pressed the blade of duskglass into Merissa's hand. 'Finish him.'

Before the Star or Merissa had a chance to react, things from Elara's own deepest nightmares flocked around her into the form of shadows. Winged things, angry things. They flew, pouring out of her of their own volition and into the already darkened evening sky through the gaping hole above them. The shadows spread, extinguishing every bit of light that seeped into the room so that they were left in gloom. Ariete took a step back.

'Monsters are not born, they become,' she said. Her voice did not sound like her own. It was distant, so distant. As though she were underwater. 'I want you to see what you've made me. Know it was you who unleashed it.'

She brought her hands together, gritting her teeth as her broken wrist flared with pain. She closed her eyes as Enzo's light mixed with her darkness inside, the humming intensifying as her very essence turned into duskglass.

Elara opened her eyes as the throbbing blend of powers rested between her hands.

She poured it into one palm as the other conjured a rope of shadow that slammed into Ariete, knocking him to the ground. Then she threw her injured wrist out, cursing, as long, wicked shards of duskglass flew from it. The dark blades sank into Ariete, pinning him to the floor as he screamed in agony.

He tried to summon his starlight – there was a flare of red, but then it sputtered and died out. The duskglass had worked, his power stifled.

Elara approached Ariete slowly. One step after another.

'Who do you pray to, King of Stars?'

Ariete panted, gritting his teeth in pain.

She gave a smile, though she knew it was not a human smile. His red stare was filled with hatred as he lay pinned and panting. His glittering blood poured from the blades piercing his immortal skin.

'I used to pray to *you*. To all the Stars. Enzo did too. You never listened. Never once answered our pleas.'

She crouched down, yanking a slice of the duskglass out from where it pinned his thigh. He bellowed again.

'You could try and pray to me. But I don't think I'll listen either.'

With a deep breath, she raised the slice above her head, aiming it for his heart.

She hesitated.

Coughed, as she felt a blade tear through her back.

Turned to look into Merissa's green, determined eyes as the demi-Star pushed the duskglass dagger further into Elara's back.

Looked to Ariete, whose surprise quickly turned to horror.

'What have you done?' he said to Merissa as Elara sank to the ground.

Elara's trembling hands came to rest on the blade protruding from her chest.

'Why?' she whispered to Merissa.

Merissa knelt before her, the set of her mouth firm. 'Remember who you are,' she said, 'and the world will remember it too.'

A ringing began to sound in Elara's ears as a coldness swept over her. She slumped on to her front. The ringing became a word, repeated again and again.

RememberRememberRememberRemember

A deep understanding resounded through Elara as the phrase finally took hold, and she died.

CHAPTER SIXTY-NINE

'This is your story, Elara.'

Elara could hear Merissa's voice faintly as she swam through the darkness.

'You are a queen, from a place long forgotten. You ruled the very heavens long before the Stars, with your soulmate. The Sun and the Moon, they called you. The very first soulmates in the world. Beloved by all, we would worship the Sun by day, basking in his rays and thanking him for making the crops grow and the flowers bloom. He could shine his rays to the depth of someone's very soul, could heal and warm.

'Under the cover of dark, we would pray to you. You wielded light in the darkness and cast illusions – you could walk through dreams, blessing or cursing them. You watched over lovers as you flew your dragun across the sky and blessed us under your silver light, allowing those who could not be together during the day to be together at night, keeping the rest of the world dreaming.

'Yours was a tragic love story. Two lovers destined to watch each other from across the skies, never able to touch, never able to meet.'

Merissa sighed deeply. 'You ruled in companionship with other titans. The Celestes. Until the Stars fell to this world. They were jealous of your power, of your love, and on one fateful night they tricked you. Any who have heard the stories think the Stars slaughtered you all, but the Stars know the truth. Ariete could not kill you. Instead he bound you and the other Celestes to mortal bodies, so that you'd be cast from the Heavens to Celestia.'

Elara heard faint cold laughter at that, and a scoff as Merissa continued. 'But you were cunning. You cloaked yourself and your allies in an illusion so the Stars would not recognize you in human form. Ever since, you have been wandering through Celestia, reborn again and again, searching for your Sun.'

Elara was weightless. Ancient. Godly.

She felt the Stars' magick unravel around her like a thread, releasing her as the duskglass worked its magick.

'It turns out,' Merissa continued, 'that all you needed, was to find him. And finally, in this lifetime, you did. For it was always your powers together that could defeat a Star's magick, that could unbind even the most powerful of spells.'

There was a horrible, painful movement in her chest, that she *knew* was the duskglass blade being pulled out of her. And then, a blaze of light, as magick forced its way out of her, making and unmaking her, fixing her bones and healing her wounds while she screamed. Blazing silver coated the room as her eyes opened. She *saw*, for a moment, the ropes of magick that had wrapped around her for centuries – glittering red and imprinted with symbols and blood, shining as red as Ariete's furious eyes beyond.

Elara sat as the ropes withered and vanished, feeling the thick muscle of her heart stitching itself back together.

'Oh, thank the skies,' she heard Merissa breathe. 'I was right.'

'*You*,' Ariete said, livid. '*You promised.*' He tried to move, but the shards of duskglass held him in place.

'What's happening to me?' Elara whispered, wildly looking for Enzo, still behind her in the pool, still lifeless. 'Who am I?'

Ariete let his head fall back to the marble, his anger momentarily eclipsed by glee.

'You're *the Moon*,' he crooned. 'And I just killed your precious *Sun*.'

Elara began to crawl towards Enzo.

'It's no use,' Ariete called as she dragged herself back into the pool, next to his body. 'There's nothing that you can do for him. Your *special* powers may have protected you from my killing blow, Queen Moon. But Lorenzo's couldn't.'

'He can't die!' Elara shouted. 'Merissa, you told me yourself that the Stars could not kill us.'

Merissa's eyes were filled with tears. 'Yes,' she whispered. 'But unlike you, Enzo's human body can be killed by a Star. He will be reborn again, but he will not remember you. You would have to spend another lifetime searching for him.'

Elara cursed the both of them as she finally reached Enzo, and latched on to him. Gripping his wrists she felt a weak flutter there, barely a pulse at all.

'Please,' she begged. And she knew that this time, she was not praying to a Star, or the sky. She was praying to herself, to the duskglass that now swam in her veins. 'Please,' she begged, closing her eyes, 'save him.'

Enzo was in her blood, and it was their magick that could defy the Stars. She felt the power there, and dragged it to her, though her body protested, though her mind tried to give up. Yet with a will born only of an entity that shone brighter, the darker the night, she gripped on to it, teeth bared, and with a final cry she pressed her lips to Enzo, as their shared magick

473

poured back into him. Then, holding on to her tether, she dragged both herself and Enzo into her dreams.

Enzo rose, gasping for breath, his eyes bewildered as he took in their surroundings. Elara's dreamscape was made of twilight, deep violet rolling hills and an indigo sky. Still holding Enzo, her focus split between reality and the dream, she watched the red ropes, the same type that had bound her, break from his body and wither away.

'Enzo?' Elara whispered, cradling him, looking upon his face. He glanced around, terrified, before his eyes fell on her.

'El? Are we dead?'

'No,' she sobbed. 'No, we are very much alive.'

'I found you. Through all these lifetimes, I found you,' he whispered, his lips close to hers. She pulled away from him, wiping her eyes.

'You remember?'

'I had one foot in the Deadlands when I saw us in our original forms – shining across the sky from one another.' He looked around the dusk-tinted landscape. 'Where are we?'

'We're in my dreamscape,' Elara replied, steadying her voice. She choked down another sob as he frowned at her. 'Our powers . . . they saved you. They stopped a Star's magick. You aren't dying any more, only dreaming.'

'Then we must wake,' he said. 'And finish Ariete once and for all.'

She smiled, gazing at him. The Sun. So bright and golden that her eyes burned, so glorious that she could not bear to turn away.

'I defy the Stars,' she whispered.

'I defy the Stars,' he echoed.

And tumbling, Elara reached for her tether and fell back into her body.

Ariete's red gaze was fastened on Elara, fury writhing in his stare. Merissa was kneeling near him, her eyes troubled as she looked to Elara.

Elara instantly looked for Enzo. He was still, but his pulse was steady, the wound in his stomach healed. In moments, he would wake and—

'You stole another death from me,' Ariete raged, still pinned where he lay. An errant strand of hair fell in his face, blood and sweat dripping as he seethed.

'What?' she snapped, gripping on to Enzo's hand.

'You tampered with the *fucking law of nature*! He was meant to die!' he bellowed.

'Elara, you did it,' Merissa whispered, running over towards her and Enzo.

The Star growled, incensed. 'She stole from me. So now, I'm going to steal from her.'

With gritted teeth, Elara watched in horror as he pulled his arm *through* the duskglass pinning it down, tearing through muscle and sinew as he stretched his hand out, his fingers curling as he *yanked*.

Golden thread spun through the air, pouring from Enzo's chest, right above his heart as it coiled into Ariete's out-stretched palm. The Star held it above himself, spooling it into a ball.

'What have you taken from him? What have you done?' Elara screamed, lunging towards him.

'No, Ariete. *No*,' Merissa pleaded. She swiped, snatching for the glowing ball, but Ariete closed his eyes, and it disappeared.

'Good luck waking him without a *tether*, Elara. I hope he doesn't lose himself to the Dreamlands while you try.' He licked the blood from his teeth, smiling. 'Time's ticking. Until we meet again, *Your Majesty*.'

Elara watched in horror as Ariete pulled the rest of his body *through* the duskglass blades with gritted teeth, the same way he had his arm. Red starlight gathered around him. And with a triumphant, ragged cackle he snapped his fingers, soaring back on to the rooftop.

A roar of rage tore from her.

'*Coward!*' she shrieked to the opening in the ceiling, watching as his running figure disappeared from sight. Then with a shuddering breath, she ran back to Enzo's body. He was breathing evenly, his face peaceful, an ethereal glow surrounding him. She shook him, trying to wake him as she screamed his name over and over. But Enzo remained asleep, lost within Elara's dreams.

EPILOGUE

Elara sat on the golden throne, rubble around her, a gentle breeze from the jagged hole in the ceiling tickling her cheek. She cast a pale glow over the throne room, the same colour as the moon now shining in the sky outside. The din of excitement and drinking came to her, muffled. For days, citizens had crowded outdoors, gazing in wonder at the new heavenly body in the night, staying out under its cool silver rays. When it had first risen, it had been to terror. Oceans had crashed and shifted, tidal waves flooding the coasts of Celestia. Wolves had howled and her people had screamed as the gigantic luminous orb had taken its place in the skies.

Five days had passed, and the usual burgundy of the Helion night was now pitch black – only the stars, and skeletal moonlight, illuminating it. Each kingdom's light had been snuffed out by Elara's livid, monstrous shadows. She had sworn to Enzo that if he was taken from her, she would turn the world to darkness, and she was nothing if not true to her word.

Enzo's body was being guarded around the clock by Leo,

Isra or herself, as the new King of Helios's soul rested in the Dreamlands and his body remained in the land of the living.

And she? She was still Elara. But she could feel in her bones something ancient. Something that had long slumbered, and was now awakening.

Dark circles shadowed her silver eyes, which flitted to the door as she heard the clatter of footsteps. Torra's dark form sashayed down the throne room, her hair pulled back severely from her face.

'I was wondering when you would show up,' Elara said quietly. Torra made her way to the throne and bowed before her. With an impatient gesture, Elara motioned her to rise. 'So I take it you heard the news?'

Torra raised her brows. 'The whole *world* witnessed the moon rise into the sky out of nowhere. It's a little hard to miss.'

'Did you know this whole time?'

Torra cocked her head. 'The prophecy was made known to me before I knew the full truth. I could only guess at it, until I laid eyes on you at the coronation ball. That look you gave me – those eyes – that was when I knew. I confirmed to Merissa who you were. She has been helping you both all along.'

'Ah, the prophecy.' Elara leaned back in her throne. 'I will fall in love with the King of Stars and it will kill us both. It seems the wording was a little off.'

'On the contrary.' Torra gave a cunning smile. 'The Sun *is* the King of Stars. He ruled above them all. With you, his queen.'

Elara's silver gaze pierced her.

Torra spread her hands. 'Well, you *did* fall in love with a Star, and you *did* both die . . .'

'The person I once was died,' Elara breathed.

'Prophecies . . . such tricky little things. *Filled* with riddles.'

Elara sighed as Merissa appeared at the doors. She walked hurriedly down the throne room, her face glowing in the twilight. When she reached the throne, she looked between her mother and Elara.

'My Queen,' she curtsied. 'Mother,' she added coldly.

'How many times do I have to tell you, Mer? There's no need for any of that. For the love of Stars, Elara is just fine.'

'Sorry.' Merissa smiled sheepishly, giving Torra another wary glance. 'Leo's drawn up the information you requested from Asteria. And Isra has organized a list of duties that need attending to in quick succession both in Asteria and here. Your throne is vacant. Ariete is still nowhere to be seen. Then there's the matter of your official coronation.'

Elara looked at her sharply, and Merissa paled a little.

'I thought I wrote to the Asterian council and told them that a coronation won't be going forward until Enzo wakes,' she bit out.

She'd been relieved to hear that despite Ariete's destruction of the palace and murder of so many of her court, one or two of her father's advisors had survived, and were trying to gather a supporting council in her stead.

'They're worried that without someone to officially take rule of Asteria, more opportunity for rebellion will arise, for others to stake their claim.'

Elara sighed, rubbing her temples.

'I think I'll take my leave now,' Torra interrupted. 'I need to return to the Heavens, and put on a show about how horrified I am by your awakening.'

'Is Ariete not aware you've been helping us, now that he knows who Merissa is?'

Torra shook her head. 'I've led him to believe I shunned

my daughter a long time ago. That she is on the opposing side of our cause.'

Elara nodded, deep in thought. 'Thank you, Torra. If I have need, I'll call for you.'

Torra bowed, kissing Merissa on the cheek before summoning a deep pink starlight, and vanishing before them.

'As to what I was saying,' Merissa continued gently once Torra had left. 'You are next in line to the throne. With Ariete nowhere to be found, there is no better time than now to return to Asteria and take what is rightfully yours. Then there is the matter of Enzo giving you his crown . . . Helios could also be yours if you wished.'

Elara steepled her fingers as her attention drifted. The details of court seemed so trivial. A coronation, claiming her throne . . . She was apparently Queen of the Stars-damned Universe, thrown from the skies.

'I'm not returning to Asteria yet,' she murmured. 'And I'm sure as the Deadlands not ruling over Helios without Enzo.'

'You're not?'

She rose from the throne. Without glancing at Merissa, she walked out of the throne room and down the grand hallway until she emerged into the gardens.

She knew Merissa was following her, and waited as she looked upon the forget-me-nots that Enzo had made grow with his light.

When Merissa had settled beside her, she spoke. 'I will appoint a member of the Helion council that I trust to oversee court matters in our absence – they can liaise with the Asterians too. Ask Leo to gather me a list.'

'Our absence?'

Elara breathed in the scent of jasmine, heavy in the black night. She smiled gently at the silver orb in the sky, before her thoughts turned venomous, as her gaze caught on the twinkling stars surrounding it.

'I made a vow to my soulmate. We are going to awaken the Sun. We are going to find the Celestes. And then the Stars will fall.'

THE END

ACKNOWLEDGEMENTS

This book is a tapestry of all the people that I love, and it would not exist without every one of you.

To Mama and Papa, your endless love and support, as well as the many bedtime stories and fairy tales you told me as a child, are the reason I can write today. I am so lucky to have parents like you.

To my sister, Alessia. We have been creating worlds together since we were children. Without you, the very idea of *Heavenly Bodies* wouldn't exist.

To my brother, Andre, for keeping my imagination active with the myriad of games we used to play growing up.

To Nana and Grandad. Nana for always believing that one day I'd write a book, since that first 'Abandoned Island' story I read to you in Year 7; and Grandad for passing on your amazing storytelling skills – it obviously runs in the family.

To Marco, for *everything*. The dedication says it all, but *Heavenly Bodies* would not be where it is if not for you, your vision and your love.

To my girls, Abby and Amy. Soulmates come in friend form too, and our souls are definitely tied. Thank you for understanding me to my core. For encouraging me, for that task of writing a smut scene that we did last Christmas (LOL), which led to the spicy scenes in *Heavenly Bodies*, and for being the first people to EVER read my book. I love you both so, so much.

To Olivia Rose Darling, my incredible friend. Having you with me every step of this new journey has been an honour and a privilege. I have you to thank for so much, but most of all I have you to thank for being my friend. I feel lucky every day that our paths crossed, and that I have someone beside me who grounds me, pushes me and inspires me with her never-ending talent.

To my wonderful agents, Jill and Imo, for helping *Heavenly Bodies* find its new home with my dream publishing houses. Thank you for believing in this book. And a huge thank you to Andrea and Nick for helping it find some amazing international homes, too.

To my amazing editor Vikki, who has understood my characters and stories from the jump, and who has helped me make them shine – I have enjoyed every part of working with you and your passion for the series means so much. And to Lydia, thank you for being so incredibly supportive and providing me with invaluable guidance. A huge thank you to the rest of the Viking team. Thank you to Lucy, Rosie, Ellie, Saxon, Charlotte and every other person who took time to help push *Heavenly Bodies* out into the world.

To Amanda and the Penguin Random House Canada team including Natasha, Sue, Evan, Deirdre and Danya – I'm so excited to work on the future books together, and thank you so much for all your hard work and for being *Heavenly Bodies*'s North American home.

And finally, thank you to you, my dear reader – old or new. The fact that you've read this book has made my wildest dreams come true. You are so special, and I can't wait for you to stay on this journey with me through Celestia.

IMANI ERRIU is the author of the romance fantasy series Heavenly Bodies. She is a graduate from the Manchester Metropolitan University where she received a Bachelor's Degree in English Literature and Creative Writing. She spent most of her childhood in the forests of the English countryside, which definitely gifted her an overactive imagination. When she isn't crying over her own fictional characters or daydreaming up her next plot twist, she can be found eating pasta and watching "The Office" on repeat.